# BLOOD ON THE BROADCAST

For Sophie and her infinite patience

ISBN: 978-1-7384022-1-2

I'd like to take this opportunity to show gratitude to my wife and my father who served as an initial test audience and who gave me the belief that the early, oh so very rough, copy of this book had some merit.

I also want to extend my appreciation to my beta readers; Leslie Merritt, Marguerite Labbe, Bill Greenberg, and Alan McKnight, who picked the necessary holes when required.

A special mention too for my editor, Sara Massoudi, who deftly removed so much nodding, head shaking, and chair leaning and left me with a worthy final product.

And lastly, I want to save the final, most important acknowledgement for you, the reader, for taking a chance on a debut book by an independent author.

\-     Shannon

# 1

Old suspicions died hard in Belfast. It was the third time in the last hour Jacob had noticed the twitching of the curtain in the upstairs bedroom. Belfast's housing estates were still divided by ancient grudges and on a street like this, memories lingered and a stranger in a strange car stood out.

The clock on the dash read *0235*. Jacob stifled a yawn and reached for his thermos. The storm had returned in full force, a precursor to the imminent heatwave that would swelter the city and then disappear with the last days of summer. He poured his coffee and did his best to ignore the tightness creeping slowly across his lower back as the rain beat a relentless but comforting staccato across the windscreen of his old Renault Clio.

It was almost an hour later when Jacob heard them coming. The PSNI land rover was not built with stealth in mind. Rather, it was a product of its environment; four tonnes of lumbering machine, thickly armoured to protect the crew inside from high velocity rifle fire and improvised explosive devices. The remaining dissident terrorist groups still viewed the police as a legitimate target and local youths made a competitive sport out of pelting police vehicles with stones and bricks when the mood took them.

The cumbersome vehicle manoeuvred itself carefully down the narrow confines of the old street. The estate had been built back in the fifties when private cars were a luxury. Now, they were packed tightly nose to bumper on both sides of the road, leaving barely enough room for one vehicle to squeeze through at a time.

The land rover stopped and a peeler stepped down from the front passenger side, hunched against the rain as he walked towards where Jacob was parked. In his side mirror, Jacob watched a second officer lingering, at the rear of his car, his torchlight pointing into the backseat in the unlikely event something of interest was lying about.

"Evening, Sir," the officer said as Jacob wound down the window. "We've got a report of a man acting suspiciously in the area." The Constable was young, fresh faced and stumbled slightly over his words. His eyes flicked from Jacob to the Nikon camera and attached lens sitting on the passenger side. Jacob guessed he was only a few months out of training and was caught between maintaining a conversation with Jacob while considering what powers, if any, he might have to use for this situation. "Would you mind telling me what you're doing here?"

"Working, unfortunately," Jacob replied with an easy smile. He'd been sitting in the same spot for going on five hours and was bored out of his tree. The police arrival was a welcome distraction.

"Seems like you got people worried."

"Like the old biddy in number twelve?" Jacob nodded towards the house of the curtain twitcher.

The Constable hesitated. No doubt he had been told by the dispatcher who had assigned him to the call that the person who had made the report had specifically requested not to be identified and not to have police call with her. "What kind of work?" he asked, quickly changing the subject.

Jacob answered by reaching for his wallet and

passing the officer his ID.

"Jacob Kincaid. Private Investigator." The officer read aloud. He looked from the card to Jacob, back to the card, back to Jacob and then to his loitering colleague, who he then approached.

The conversation didn't carry over the beating rain but a few seconds later the second officer walked up to Jacob's window. Although he appeared to be of similar age to his colleague, his relaxed stance was enough to make it clear that he had a good deal more service. He handed Jacob his ID back and then tucked his hands between his flak jacket and green raincoat. "Horrible night," he said, already soaked through.

Unlike the nervousness of his colleague, the second peeler gave off a comfortable, almost bored air, talking to a stranger on a dark, miserable night on one of the roughest estates in Belfast. He was young, probably not quite into his late twenties but hard eyes, dispassionate and critical, belied his relatively youthful appearance. The man had seen a lot during his time on the job. Jacob knew the look well.

"One for indoors," Jacob agreed. He knew that in their brief conflab, Officer Two would have confirmed for his less experienced colleague that there was nothing illegal going on, and nothing for police to concern themselves with, unless he had some sort of suspicion that Jacob was the local pervert. He would have also advised his young colleague to run a check on Jacob and his car, to make sure there were no warning or relevant flags against his name while he kept him busy in conversation.

"An actual private detective. Never came across one of those before."

"Well, we are private."

The officer offered a smile, one of civility rather than humour as he studied Jacob, probably seeing a man who looked younger than his thirty-two years, with a mop of dark hair that was receding up his forehead faster than he cared for and a once athletic frame slowly turning stocky. A sudden flash of recognition passed over his features. "Here! Weren't you a peeler?"

Jacob hid his grimace and nodded.

"Over in Coalburn?" He named the station in West Belfast where Jacob had started his policing career.

"That's right, Coalburn response and a couple years with the Major Crime Team."

The officer nodded again before something clicked for him. "Weren't you-"

"Yes," Jacob said quickly, having no desire to rehash ancient history. "One and the same."

Officer Two paused as he clearly tried to think of something diplomatic to say. "Jobs fucked," he offered after a few seconds, repeating the familiar mantra heard in police station workrooms the length and breadth of Northern Ireland.

Jacob laughed. "Jobs fucked."

This time the officer's smile seemed genuine. "So, what are you doing up here in some shithole estate in North Belfast at three in the morning?"

There was no point lying and there was no secret to protect, so long as he kept names out of it. "Some Doctor from the Royal is doing the dirty on his missus," Jacob said as he leaned forward, eager to share with a former compatriot. ""She's the suspicious sort and hired me to find the proof. Waste of money to be honest, as her fella's anything but discrete. I tailed him here last weekend straight from work. Lovely wee thing met him at the door. Probably have enough to show the wife but holding out for a pic of a kiss or a hug or whatever. Leave no doubt for the woman."

The officer straightened up and Jacob sensed the warmth fade. They might both be caught in the rain at 0318 in a shithole estate in North Belfast, but one of them was making sure the public slept soundly in their beds while the other was a predator, living off broken marriages and other assorted misery. The man didn't need to say it, Jacob knew he wasn't exactly doing God's work.

The junior peeler returned and gave his mate a nod; Jacob's details checked out. Brusquely, the veteran wished him a good and they both left, hurrying to the cover of their truck.

"Stay safe," Jacob called after them but they either didn't hear, or chose to ignore him.

The land rover chugged out of the street, leaving Jacob alone with his coffee, his camera, and a darker mood. He wanted to call them back. He wanted to tell them that he had taken pride in being a police officer. Taken pride in working a patch in what was one of the hardest and most deprived areas in Northern Ireland. How he'd treated everyone fairly, how he gave every investigation a fair shake.

When it all came crashing down around him, he had been lost. Pride was one thing, but Jacob had no idea just how much he needed the police. The job had been his life. The long unsociable hours, the dangerous work and the small circle of friends made up almost exclusively of other peelers. He had accepted it all because he loved being a police officer. He put bad guys away and as far as he was concerned, there was no better calling. And then suddenly, it was gone and at twenty-eight years old, Jacob found himself adrift.

The segue into private investigation had been a natural move. With his uncle looking to retire it made sense for him to take over the business. A temporary move and a chance to make some good money until he found his feet again. Four years later and Jacob was still firmly on his arse.

He pushed the thoughts from his mind, did his best to block out the pain in his back and settled into his seat.

It wasn't until the dashboard clock read *0535* that he got what he was after. Dawn had appeared and dragged the sun with it, giving a respite from the torrent of rain. Doctor Neil Rourke, cardiologist, and adulterer, was a handsome man. Tanned and fit, with salt and pepper hair and a chiselled jaw, he turned at the doorstep and embraced the woman in the blue nurse's uniform.

Jacob raised his camera and snapped the required pictures. The good Doctor walked to his car while his lover, at least fifteen years his junior, watched from her front door, giving him one last wave and an air kiss. Neither glanced in Jacob's direction as they parted.

Jacob set the camera back on the passenger seat and started the engine. He moved to pull out but stopped, allowing Rourke's Volvo, coming in the opposite direction, the right of way. The man gave a smile and friendly wave of acknowledgement as he passed, happily oblivious, for now at least.

Jacob drove home through pink and orange puddles on empty streets and felt pretty empty himself.

# 2

He rolled over and blindly grabbed for his mobile to silence the piercing alarm. Reading the time through bleary eyes Jacob dropped the phone and pushed his face down into the pillow with a grumble. He had a meeting with a prospective client in an hour and business was nowhere near good enough for him to fob her off.

He let his heavy lids close for a second and woke with a start, fumbling for his phone to see it had just gone nine. Throwing back the duvet he hurried across his bedroom straight into the shower. It was a quick wash, but the hot water cleared away some of the grit behind his eyes and eased the tightness in his tired muscles.

Even freshly clean, the man looking back at Jacob in the mirror as he quickly brushed his teeth told him that he looked like hell. His short beard had grown untidy, black circles underlined both eyes and his skin was pale from a lack of sleep and proper nutrition.

Jacob knew he should have made an effort for the meeting but he was already running late, had no fresh shirts pressed and both of his suits were crumpled and in need of dry cleaning. He quickly changed into the same jeans and sweater from the night before and pretended he couldn't smell the faint telltale musk of worn clothing.

The living area of his one-bedroom apartment in the upmarket Saint Anne's Square complex was dominated by two large bookcases pressed against one wall, neatly ordered, and filled with detective fiction and true crime. A worn, but comfortable sofa and matching chair bordered a long coffee table where Jacob tended to eat most of his meals.

His apartment overlooked a piazza that housed several popular restaurants, the MAC theatre, and a gym that Jacob maintained a membership for, but rarely used. Beyond the piazza sat St Anne's Cathedral and its forty-metre stainless steel Spire of Hope. Saint Anne's had given this part of Belfast its designation as the Cathedral Quarter, one of at least seven recognised cultural quarters in the city, which even to a place as contradictory as Belfast, seemed excessive.

His office was only fifteen minutes away and he tended to walk most days, rain or shine. In Belfast, it was usually rain but the showers from the previous night had held off and the sun peered cautiously through a thick blanket of cloud.

Although his grandfather didn't know it when he originally purchased the small first floor office space back in the early seventies, the location of Kincaid Investigations was now considered prime real estate. Slap bang in the city centre, sitting on a pedestrianised street, the property was less than a stone's throw from one of the main commercial and social hubs in Belfast. Every day, thousands of people walked past the offices of Kincaid Investigations and more than likely, not one of them paid any notice to the windows with the white stencilled magnifying glass and the lettering bearing the firm's name.

The office sat above an artisan coffee shop, the type that now seemed to be on every Belfast street. A queue of customers lined out past the door. The uncomfortable wooden benches and smashed avocado on toast had replaced an ancient greasy spoon café with worn, red leather seats and a gut busting Ulster fry a couple of years before. "A metaphor for a changing Belfast," Jacob had told Helen mournfully on the day the coffee shop had opened, as he clutched a Fairtrade cup of a rich, dark roasted Guatemalan blend that really hit the spot. Helen had rolled her eyes at his faux sociology and went back to her novel.

His sole employee was already seated at her desk when Jacob dandered in. She held up her watch while Jacob hung his coat by the door. "Looks like I owe you lunch," Helen said. "Was certain you'd still be dead to the world."

Jacob smiled and took one of the two waiting coffees. "Looks like you just missed the rush." He gave a contented sigh after taking a sip, beginning to feel at least partially alive. "Columbian," he declared.

"Honduran."

"Close enough."

Jacob had met Helen on his first case after taking over Kincaid Investigations. Tall and fit with auburn hair kept short, Helen was now coming into her late forties. She was a handsome woman with a strong chin that gave her the look of a fighter. Nevertheless, she had been kind to the bumbling investigator, out on his own for the first time, and miserably hungover more often than not, mourning a lost career and a lost relationship.

The pair had struck up an unlikely friendship during the course of his investigation, based mainly in her large house in the affluent surroundings of Cherryvalley. As far as Jacob could tell, Helen didn't work and lived alone, yet she had paid his fee upfront and then gifted him a generous bonus sum after successful completion of the job.

A week later she had paid a social call to his office a week later and after seeing the shambolic state of the place and after being reassured that no, a bomb had not gone off, had declared that it wouldn't do and that she would have no other option than to come and sort it out. Four years on and Jacob still wasn't sure exactly how much he knew about Helen or why she kept working for him. She certainly didn't need the money, which was good, because he certainly didn't pay well.

"Miss Amato is coming in for nine thirty," Helen said.

"Load of balls, most likely."

"Such a way with words, Master Kincaid. Not sure I could have put it quite so succinctly."

Jacob attempted a cheeky grin. In his experience, running a private investigation business tended to attract a disproportionate amount of loonies and time wasters. While the email from one Natalie Amato didn't suggest she was a weirdo, she had said nothing about what she wanted Jacob to investigate, requesting to meet in person before disclosing anything. He had nothing else in his calendar but scheduled the appointment for the following week to give the impression that he did.

He crossed the small reception area into his office and sat himself at his desk. Once logged in to his computer he uploaded the pictures from the previous night's job, selecting the clearest and most salacious before printing them. The glossy A4 prints went into a plain envelope. Jacob scrawled *Rourke* across it in permanent marker before placing it in the desk drawer on top of a mostly full bottle of *Bushmills*.

Job done, he leaned back into his chair and contemplated his office as he sipped his coffee. The little room was sparse, just his desk, two chairs and a worn leather sofa by the window. A pin board was attached to the far wall but most of the space on it was taken up by flyers for local takeaways rather than anything concerning actual investigative work.

Hung on the wall behind him were two framed photos of Jacob in the rifle green uniform of the Police Service of Northern Ireland were on display.

The Jacob in those pictures looked a good deal fitter and fresher faced than the iteration now contemplating them. One was with Jacob and his uncle, the other with him and his parents. Harry stood beside his nephew in his old dress uniform, beaming proudly. Jacob's father, on the other hand, had turned up in a grey suit and looked back from the picture with an air of disappointment, as he did with any matter concerning his son.

Voices from the main office brought him from his reverie. Helen opened the door and ushered his potential client in. As he set eyes on Natalie Amato, Jacob immediately wished he had made an effort in making himself at least half presentable before he had left his apartment.

She had a slim, athletic figure with a honey-hued natural tan and wore minimal make-up. Dark chestnut hair fell past her shoulders and a pair of keen and intelligent hazel eyes held a natural warmth as she regarded him. She was dressed casually but the jeans, leather jacket and boots all appeared to be of high quality, as did the large, stainless steel chronograph watch clasped tightly to her left wrist.

Jacob, by contrast, felt like a bag of shite tied in the middle.

"Natalie Amato," she said as she offered a hand. Her grip was firm and her tone confident.

"Jacob Kincaid." He replied, nodding to the seat across from him. He sat down quickly, banging his knee on his desk as he did so. Natalie Amato was kind enough to pretend not to notice. Instead, she waited for him to direct the conversation.

"Your email didn't tell me much, Miss Amato," Jacob said, resisting the urge to rub the throbbing knee. "Nothing, actually."

"Natalie, please, and no it didn't," she agreed. "But that was intentional. I wanted to be discreet for one and I felt I would have a much easier time explaining this in person."

"Fair enough. What's the job?"

She rubbed her hands together slowly as if considering how to begin. "I was a journalist for a number of years, over in London but I'm from Belfast originally."

Jacob nodded along. He had been finding it difficult

to place where she might be from. Her tone lacked the brashness normally associated with what would be considered a traditional Belfast accent. Living across the water for a few years, combined with a hunch that Miss Amato had grown up in one of the more affluent suburbs at the edge of the city, perhaps with some after-school elocution lessons thrown in for good measure, had softened the edges of her accent.

"I moved back home a few years ago and continued as a journalist, writing for the Belfast Sentinel. I also released a novel which was reasonably successful. One thing led to another and I recently fell into podcasting. I produce and present a show called Miss Gumshoe. We dealt with true crime at first but we began to diverge into mysteries, the paranormal and unexplained, urban legends, disappearances." She waved a hand. "You get the drift."

"There's good money in that?"

"We get somewhere between eighty and one hundred thousand listeners per show."

"Every month?"

"Weekly."

"Jesus."

Natalie smiled, showing a perfect row of oyster-white teeth. "The real money is in subscriptions. People pay for different perks. Early access to episodes, exclusive content, things like that. We've cultivated a pretty die hard following. Add on advertising fees and yes, it's a profitable venture."

"Until?" Jacob prompted.

"I write and present the episodes but it's not a one woman show. I employ a production assistant, an editor and a sound technician. I sometimes hire other writers and I often use contributors. People who have knowledge about the story of the week. My last contributor was a journalist, Roisin Dunwoody." She paused, as if Jacob might recognise the name but he gave a single shake of his head. "We had worked together briefly at the Sentinel. She was a quiet girl, but nice. Always had an interest in the darker things. The supernatural and the occult, things like that."

"Your use of the word was doesn't sound promising."

"Have you heard of the Followers of Eden?"

Jacob frowned at the sudden change in topic. "A little," he said. "They have that mega church outside Carrickfergus, right? You can usually see them down in the city centre most days. Handing out leaflets about bettering yourself, self-improvement through membership, things like that."

"They call themselves a church but that's a lie. They are a cult and a dangerous one. Roisin, for whatever reason, had a real grievance against them. She came to me a few months ago, completely out of the blue. It'd been a number of years since we last spoke. Anyway, turns out she had done her own investigation on the Followers. At least a year of work to exposé some pretty damning stuff."

"A real scoop."

"You'd think so, but the Sentinel wouldn't touch it. Neither would any other paper or any of the local news channels. The Followers have too much clout."

Jacob thought for a moment. "Aren't they backed by some big-time property investor? Ivor something." He remembered a Follower thrusting an information pamphlet with personal testimonies into his hand a few months ago.

"Ivan Gould. He's poured millions into the Followers and he still has millions left. He's just one of a number of major financial backers."

"That's the guy."

Signs for Gould Construction could be seen over most building sites in Belfast and beyond. Usually with an image of Gould himself; an overweight, white-haired man in his sixties, always with a wide smile, an expensive suit and yellow hard hat. "So, the Followers have the funds to make life uncomfortable for the mainstream media. Roisin needed someone independent, right?"

"That's right. We went to work and what we produced was our biggest success. A three-episode arc looking into the shady dealings the Followers have been mixed up in. We're talking coercion, extortion, intimidation, money laundering. Anything you can think of."

"Makes you miss the days when a church only dealt in sex scandals."

Natalie ignored the weak attempt at humour. "We had a wrap party on the night the last episode was released. A small shindig in Roisin's apartment, just the six of us. When I woke up the next morning, the episode had already hit eighty thousand listeners. I texted Roisin but didn't hear anything back. I wasn't too worried, most of them had a fair amount to drink and I assumed she was sleeping it off. I went to work on our next episode but the day went by with nothing from Roisin. She had always been talkative on our group chat and she was buzzing to see how the finale would be received. I tried calling her but she didn't answer her phone. Then I texted around but no one had heard from her since the party."

There was a knock on the office door and Helen opened it, returning a second later with a tray holding a pitcher of water and two glasses. She set the tray down and caught Jacob's eye as she walked back to the door. He gave her a small, surreptitious nod in return. There might just be something here, if Miss Amato ever actually got around to telling him what the job was. Jacob poured a glass and passed it to Natalie.

"Thank you," she said as she took it. "I knew something was up. I drove over to her apartment. There was no answer at the door. Then I peered in through the letterbox and…" She stopped to clear her throat. "I could see her lying there. I called an ambulance and they arrived along with the police, who ended up putting the door in." Natalie paused and took a long drink.

"What happened next?" Jacob prompted.

"The paramedic confirmed she was dead. Police set up a scene. I had to give a statement as it was me who discovered the body."

"When was this?"

"Six weeks ago."

He cast his mind back but couldn't remember the story making local news. "I'm sorry you had to go through that. I've been in the same position a few times myself. It's never pleasant." Jacob tapped his finger on his desk. "Natalie, what is it you're asking me to investigate here?"

"The detectives turned up after an hour or two, then their Sergeant an hour later. They said her death was accidental. There was a broken glass and a dried-in wine stain next to her body. They believed Roisin slipped on the spilled wine, hit her head off the table and died."

"That seems pretty clear cut."

"No," Natalie said firmly, her eyes taking on a sudden harder edge. "Roisin had been getting threatening letters in the post, her car tyres had been slashed the week before."

Jacob held a placating hand. "I'm sorry. It's just...well, it's a hell of a jump from threatening messages and criminal damage to outright murder, if that's what you're getting at." He rubbed at his chin thoughtfully. "That being said, I'm surprised the police shut the investigation down so quickly."

Natalie sighed. "Well...there's more. This is where it gets complicated. The keys to Roisin's apartment were on the kitchen counter and the door had been locked. She 'd been rattled by the threats and had heavy duty bolts installed. When the police forced entry, the door hinges came off before the bolts gave way."

"Alright. But there would be multiple ways..."

"-There is only one door into the apartment. There's no attic. Roisin lived on the fourth storey and the fire escape is at the opposite end of her floor. There are no drain pipes close to her windows, which were all locked from the inside anyway." Natalie counted off each point on a finger. Evidently, she had made this argument before.

Jacob poured himself a glass of water. "I'll be honest, this is well above my normal remit. I work unfaithful spouses, benefit cheats, missing people...."

"-That's not all that you do though, is it?" Natalie asked as she reached into her handbag and produced a printed A4 sheet which she handed to Jacob. "I'm also led to believe you have at least some history in investigating strange cases. The disappearing painting at the Red Door Art Gallery?"

"I wasn't aware that even made the papers," Jacob lied, as he looked at the article outlining the mystery of the stolen painting and the solution of the looped security tape.

"I've asked around. It's not just the Red Door. There was man who faked his death by tricking everyone into thinking he had gone overboard on the Stena Line. Not to mention the disappearance of the Lord Lieutenant's daughter." Jacob looked up sharply at the mention of the latter. "I know that last one was kept out of the public domain but research is my business. I didn't contact you on a whim, Mr. Kincaid. Your background is why I came to you specifically. I need an investigator with an open mind, one who wouldn't laugh me out of their office when I'm effectively asking them to take on a real-life locked room mystery."

Jacob ran a hand through his hair. A dead girl, a locked apartment, and a cult of crazies. He could give it a basic shake. Enough to satisfy Natalie Amato's curiosity and bag himself a very easy payday. Now it was a matter of haggling an acceptable price.

"Alright. I'll take the job. Just so we're clear, I charge the same rate no matter the type of investigation."

"I'll pay eight hundred a week, plus any expenses incurred while progressing the case."

"That...could work."

"Eight hundred to guarantee I'm your sole client until the investigation is satisfactorily completed or until I terminate your services." As Natalie spoke, she leaned forward, resting her left arm on Jacob's desk. Her watch glinted in the light and Jacob caught sight of the *Breitling* lettering on its face. Natalie certainly wasn't short of a bob or two, which quelled some of the lingering worry.

"You drive a hard bargain, Miss Amato."

Natalie smiled before glancing at the watch. "I'm meeting with my production assistant this morning. Have your secretary send me an email with your banking details and I'll transfer you the first sum this afternoon," she said as she stood. Jacob hurried across the office to open the door for her. "Tomorrow, I'd like you to meet me at Roisin's apartment. You know Hilden Mill?"

Jacob nodded. "Out by Lisburn." He led her across the reception area.

"Shall we say half nine?" she asked, standing at the threshold, holding out her hand again.

"Half nine, it's a date," Jacob said as they shook.

Natalie's lip quirked and it looked as if she was about to say something before deciding against it. Jacob watched her descend the narrow staircase and disappear out onto the street.

"Smooth," Helen said. "Very smooth."

Natalie Amato's perfume lingered. "I remember Marlowe's words," Jacob replied, as he slowly closed the door, watching Helen's brow furrow. "What the hell does Marlowe know?"

Helen rolled her eyes as she realised he was quoting some obscure movie she'd never heard of. She had no appreciation for the classics.

# 3

With nothing else to occupy him, Jacob had spent the rest of the day familiarising himself with his current case and found pickings were slim. BBC Northern Ireland had a piece on their website following the initial discovery of a body at Hilden Mill but there had been no follow-up after it was determined to be an non-suspicious death. The Belfast Sentinel had published a small piece about the loss of a beloved colleague but only made reference to the incident as a tragic accident in her home.

As for Roisin herself, there was nothing of interest. A sparse Facebook account showed a pretty woman in her late twenties, with long dark hair and sad eyes. Her friend group appeared to be small, with the same few people appearing in most of the photos and commenting under her posts and birthday messages. Aside from that, Roisin's activity on the platform was sporadic at best.

It appeared her entire journalistic career had been spent at the Sentinel, with all of her work handily archived on their website. However, rather than the hard-hitting investigative journalist that he had expected, most of Roisin's work involved stories of local colour and human interest. Fluff to pad out the paper. Unless this year's Hillsborough Dog Show had turned particularly violent, there was nothing in Roisin's work outside of Natalie's podcast to suggest she was worth the bother of killing.

His enquiries at a provisional end, Jacob turned his attention towards his client. It was important to have an idea of who he was working for. At least, that's what he told Helen when she came in with his lunch to find him perusing Natalie's Facebook profile.

"Creeping. I believe that's what the kids call it these days," she said as she handed over his ham and cheese toastie.

"It's research," Jacob replied testily. "I need to see who we're working for and if she's on the level. Considering she wants me to look into a murder that isn't a murder."

Helen held her hands up defensively, clearly delighted at how easily she had got him to bite. "And what have you found exactly?"

"That Natalie Amato is quite modest about her success."

Her podcast, Miss Gumshoe, had over five thousand monthly subscribers on Patreon. Her X profile had over fifty thousand followers and it appeared she was soon planning to branch out onto YouTube. Her debut novel, *Caught Red Handed*, had made a number of best seller lists.

She was also the subject of several recent articles about her successful transition from journalist to author and podcaster. He brought up a piece from the *Ulster Bugler* to show Helen. The page had a shot of Natalie in front of an abandoned farm house, hands stuffed into a long winter coat, scarf wrapped tightly around her neck as she smiled brightly for the camera, a contrast to the foreboding house looming behind.

"She moved back to Northern Ireland eight years ago," Jacob said, reciting information he had previously read. "Went to work for the Sentinel but got bored of working in traditional news media and was looking for a new challenge. Saw how popular Podcasts were getting and managed to get on board just as they really took off. Mentions she has a son, nothing about a husband or partner."

"Vital intelligence," Helen agreed. "Have you tried stalking her on Instagram yet?"

"No," Jacob replied, concentrating on unwrapping his food.

Her Instagram was the first thing he had looked at. A few pictures were from formal gatherings and award shows, but the majority were casual nights out with friends, pictures taken on park runs and hikes, or at family events. A lot of the images featured an awkward looking teenager who Jacob assumed to be Natalie's brother. He got an impression of a woman with an active lifestyle and a close social circle. For someone who was as successful as she was, Jacob had been expecting a bit more flash and glamour on display but saw little evidence of either.

Helen sat herself on the edge of his desk and crossed one leg over the other. "I checked the account just as I was leaving to grab your food. The money from Miss Amato has already been transferred in."

"Yeah? So, what's bothering you?" Jacob asked, noting the tone in her voice.

She shrugged. "Seems like a waste of time."

"For eight hundred a week, my time can take the hit. Maybe she doesn't trust the police and wants a second opinion. I could go tomorrow, agree with the police assessment and our work for Miss Amato is done."

"Obviously you talked to her for longer than I did, but does she strike you as the type of person who just drops something? The woman with all these successful little ventures?"

Jacob took a bite out of his toastie. "No," he admitted as he wiped his mouth with a napkin. "I suppose not."

"And she's admitted to you that her and Roisin weren't particularly close. They were former colleagues who only re-connected to make the podcast."

"So?"

"So, she just throws away eight hundred pounds to get a stranger to look into a death that the police have already dismissed as an accident."

"You think there's more she's not telling me?"

"Maybe. I guess you'll find out. Anyway, you may eat the rest of that on the go. You're meant to be meeting with Patricia Rourke at two."

Jacob glanced at Helen's watch as she tapped it, managed to drop a swear word around a mouthful of scalding cheese and made for the door.

Patricia Rourke ran a large architecture firm. Her office on Lanyon Plaza occupied the top two floors of a glass-curtained monstrosity now so common in Belfast, slowly replacing some of the last remaining Edwardian and Victorian architecture that had survived the Luftwaffe Blitz of the forties and the domestic terrorists of the seventies and eighties.

Jacob rode the elevator to the top floor and met the same receptionist who had greeted him last time he was there. She informed her boss through the intercom that Jacob had arrived and then promptly ignored him as he waited.

Mrs. Rourke was a busy woman and had conducted their only previous meeting at her office as well. There was an element of discretion in the location, Jacob knew. While her husband might never be home, between his work at the hospital and vigorous philandering, the two teenage sons who adorned the pictures on her desk, almost certainly were, and might start asking the wrong sort of questions.

Tall and rigid with sharp distinguished features and dark red hair tied into a smart bun, Patricia Rourke emerged from her office after keeping Jacob waiting in the foyer for ten minutes. Her expression was cold as she beckoned Jacob forward. He couldn't quite bring himself to look into the piercing emerald green eyes and wondered if it was the same face she wore for everyone or just the man making money from her misery.

She led him into her office and didn't invite him to sit. Jacob noticed her computer was on and that she had been looking at the website for the Grand Central, a luxury hotel in the city centre. Jacob guessed that if Doctor Neil Rourke might be in the doghouse at home, he wasn't living like it, setting himself up for life as a newly single man in such swish surroundings.

"You have something for me." Patricia Rourke said, eyes turned to the envelope in Jacob's hand.

Wordlessly, he handed it over, knowing the pictures would tell their tale. Mrs. Rourke took the envelope and went to her desk. She studied each picture slowly and deliberately. Her expression didn't falter. Once she reached the final picture, she gathered them all, placed them back in the envelope and put it in the top drawer of her desk. She stared at it for a few seconds. "Thank you for your time, Mr. Kincaid." she said, her attention focused on the far wall, rather than at Jacob. The slight crack in her voice was barely audible. "Your final payment will be sent later this afternoon. Close the door on your way out."

Jacob took his cue to exit. He glanced back as he reached the door but Mrs. Rourke's gaze continued to focus on an unseen point on the wall. It wasn't until he closed the door behind him that he heard the first wracking sob, muffled but unmistakable. The receptionist looked up as he passed, her smile carefully neutral as she pretended not to hear.

"Always good to have another satisfied customer," Jacob said, nodding his head back towards Patricia Rourke's office.

The woman's expression turned into a hard glare that Jacob could feel burning into his back all the way to the elevator.

# 4

Hilden Mill sat a few miles from the outskirts of Belfast. The sprawling site had stood since the 1800's but had been derelict for years, slowly deteriorating as the demand for the linen it produced dwindled. The Mill had resisted numerous attempts by property developers to revitalise it and had survived repeated arson attacks by local vandals. It was only recently that a developer had been bull-headed enough to outlast the setbacks and make something on the site.

The results of the revitalisation were impressive. The shell of the original red-bricked mill was retained, its interior turned into a luxury apartment block. Several of the smaller surrounding buildings had been similarly converted along with the construction of a further three hundred townhouses.

The dense foliage which had once reclaimed the tumbledown site had been cleared to make way for a private park, tennis courts, a leisure centre and an artificial lake. Sitting on the serene surroundings of the Lagan towpath, Hilden Mill had been transformed into one of the most exclusive residential locations in the country. Jacob's battered Clio, which had disconcertingly started to vibrate anytime he went over sixty miles an hour, was an ugly blot amongst the gleaming range of luxury cars on show.

Natalie had beaten him there. Standing beside an Audi SUV, she was talking on her phone and offered a friendly smile as Jacob approached. She was dressed for the forecasted heatwave in a smart, blue linen shirt and white trousers. She held up a finger and he nodded, turning back towards the Clio to allow her some privacy.

Two teenage boys, each carrying a tennis racquet and dressed like they had stepped directly off the pages of a Ralph Lauren catalogue, walked past. "Nice car, mate," one said to his friend, loud enough for Jacob to hear as the second boy sniggered dutifully.

"What was that?" Jacob asked, pushing himself up from his slouched stance against the Clio's door. The two boys turned, surprised. Neither answered, instead looking at each other. Jacob took a step forward. "I asked what you said."

The boy who had spoken looked around nervously. "I was just saying I liked your car." His accent was posh, refined. The kind you would hear along the Gold Coast of North Down. Evidently Hilden Mill had lured some of the swish crowd away from the yacht clubs and fairways of Holywood and Ballyholme.

"No, you didn't. You were being a wee big-mouthed prick," Jacob said.

"Look mate, just leave us alone, alright?" The boy had a slight shrill to his voice, apparently shocked someone would have the temerity to take issue with being mocked.

"Everything ok here?" Natalie asked as she approached.

"Grand," Jacob replied gruffly.

Natalie watched as the two boys took her interruption as their chance to skedaddle. "Do you often pick fights with children?"

"Only when I want to feel like a big man."

Natalie regarded him seriously for a second before smirking. "Roisin told me some of the kids around here were proper little shits." She turned back towards what had once been the main Mill building and pointed. "That was hers," she said, indicating a set of windows halfway along the top floor. Jacob followed her finger.

Like she had told him in his office; four storeys up and without a drainpipe or fire escape nearby.

She led him towards the apartment block, producing a key card from her pocket as they neared the communal entrance and pressed it against the pad. "Roisin give you a spare?" Jacob asked, holding the door open for her.

"Uh...No. Not exactly. I saw the key card sitting in a bowl on the kitchen counter when the police were here. I swiped it."

"Ok. Why?"

She gave a simple shrug of her shoulders as they crossed the lobby. "I had a hunch I might need it," she said without elaborating further. There was a lift but Natalie walked past it, heading for the stairs.

Jacob paused. "You said it was the top floor, right?"

"That's right. C'mon, it'll do you good. Expend some of that energy you didn't get to use brawling with those kids."

She took the stairs at a pace Jacob would have considered unreasonable over flat ground. By the time they reached the third level he was doing his best to hide the fact he was puffed.

When they reached the fourth floor, they walked through a set of double doors led to a marble tiled corridor that split off in both directions. "4F." Natalie said as she turned left and stopped at the nearest apartment door, fishing in the pocket of her trousers for a key.

"Another hunch?" Jacob asked.

"I was still here when they came to replace the door. Told them I'd leave the keys to Roisin's father but figured he'd only need the one."

Natalie unlocked the door and they stepped through to an open plan living and dining area, with a cloak room without a door to their immediate left. The living space was dominated by two large windows on the far wall. Even with the sunlight of a bright summer's day streaming in, Roisin's apartment radiated a grey and lifeless feeling. Soulless, Jacob supposed, its purpose as a home lost with the death of its owner.

He scanned the room quickly, noticing an untidy bookcase in one corner, shelves on the nearest wall and in the kitchen, two small tables and a long coffee table in the living area and a cabinet holding a television and an X-Box. Not one piece of furniture had any photos on display.

"This is where we found her," Natalie said as she walked over to the coffee table in the centre of the living room, her shoes echoing on the polished wood. Jacob followed, noticing a dark stain on the floor. "Red wine," Natalie explained.

"Her family hasn't been around to clean up?" Jacob asked, looking from the stain to the thick layer of dust on the coffee table.

"Doesn't look like it. It was only her and her dad as far as I know. I got the impression they weren't close."

"Did you meet him?"

"Briefly. When I stopped by to give him the key and then at the funeral. He was....a cold man," Natalie said carefully.

"He had just lost his daughter."

"Maybe," Natalie replied.

Jacob stepped away, taking in the rest of the apartment. Dirty glasses and plates were piled in the sink, while empty wine and champagne bottles and empty boxes of beer sat beside the bin. Apart from the leftovers of the party that had never been cleaned up, the kitchen was tidy and freshly outfitted. The appliances looked as if they had barely been used. "How long did Roisin live here?"

"As far as I know she moved in when the apartments went on the market. So, three years or so?"

"A place like this wouldn't be cheap. Especially for one person on a local journalist's wage."

"Her father helped."

"Nice of him for someone who wasn't close."

"He's minted. He owns some sort of engineering

company. He probably decided once he set Roisin up with her own place that his fatherly duty was done."

"What about a partner?"

"No."

"Friends?"

Natalie held up two hands with a shrug. "We weren't particularly close when we worked at the Sentinel and the podcast was pretty intensive. It didn't leave a lot of time to really get to know each other well. I'm not saying she didn't have friends, it's just she never really talked about any."

"Who else was here the night of the party?"

"Just myself and Roisin and the rest of the podcast staff."

"I'll need to talk to them."

"Of course. Although we all left at the same time."

"All of you?"

"There were only five of us and the party had wound down."

"What about your staff? Were any of them close with Roisin?"

Natalie hesitated for a second. "Her and Luke Fisher went on a few dates."

"What's Luke's role on your show?"

"Writer. Freelance. He hasn't worked with us since Roisin's last episode."

Jacob waited, expecting Natalie to say more but she didn't elaborate. "You still have his contact details?"

"I do."

He nodded as he moved across to bin beside the kitchen counter. He stepped on the pedal and peered inside. Aside from a few strips of empty medication foil, it was empty. He reached down and lifted the strips out. They were all for the same drug: *Prepentaline.*

Jacob was familiar with the name. *Prepentaline* was used to combat the effects of anxiety and epilepsy, amongst other conditions. It was also a heavily abused, at least it was when he was still on the force. Often taken with other drugs, it produced an apparently excellent high, but had the notable setback of occasionally stopping the user breathing if they got their doses wrong.

The drug could also cause dizziness and confusion if abused. If Roisin had taken *Prepentaline* and mixed it with alcohol, it only strengthened the likelihood of an accident happening.

"Was Roisin a drug user?"

"Not that I know of." Natalie said, glancing at the foil packets.

"No box or prescription label. Did you see her taking anything the night of the party?"

"Just drink."

Jacob checked the cupboards for any other packets of the drug but couldn't find any. Police would have disposed of any medication recovered at a local pharmacy and it seemed they had been thorough in their checks.

He went into the master bedroom. The room was large but bare, holding nothing more than a king-sized bed, two bedside cabinets, a set of drawers and a walk-in wardrobe. Jacob opened the wardrobe, large enough to be a room in its own right, and ran his hand along the walls, feeling for any cracks or bumps and finding none.

"What are you thinking?" Natalie asked, watching him from the doorway.

"Just pondering the locked room problem," he replied as he walked to the window. Unlike the living area, the window here had been knocked out from the original red brick and was a good deal smaller. The sash window had to be unlocked before Jacob could slide the bottom portion upwards. It locked out, leaving a half foot of space between the bottom of the raised window and the sill. Too small for anyone to slide through even if they managed to scale the wall or somehow lower themselves from the roof.

"You were a police officer, right?"

Jacob glanced behind him. "That's right. Eight years."

"Hmm," Natalie intoned. "You look young to have done that much time."

"Well, you look young to have a podcasting empire."

Natalie laughed. "Empire is a bit of a stretch. Maybe a provincial duchy." She folded her arms and leaned against the door frame. "Why did you leave?"

"Searching for a new subject for your podcast?" he asked, kneeling beside the bed and lifting the bottom cover to reveal a space empty of anything other than dust. Natalie chuckled as he ran a hand along the wooden floor.

"It's an interesting topic, you have to admit. An ex-cop turned private investigator who moonlights by looking into mysteries and assorted strangeness."

"Yep. I'm a real enigma," Jacob said as he stood back up and brushed his knees.

"Oh, no doubt. But you didn't answer the question."

"Just fancied the change," Jacob said, stepping past Natalie and into the second bedroom without meeting her eye. The space had been converted into an office of sorts. A gaming chair sat beside a desk holding two monitors, a printer and a scanner. "No computer," Jacob noted, pointing to the space in the cabinet where wires hung loose. "Haven't seen any tablets or laptops either."

"Would the police have taken them?"

"Not for an accidental death." He went to the window and saw it had the same dimensions as the one in the master bedroom. Again, Jacob checked it, sliding the sash upwards and getting the same result. No one was getting in through these windows. "What about her phone? Did you see it on the night of the party?"

"I don't think so. But I couldn't say for sure."

Jacob nodded and returned to the living area with Natalie in tow. He looked up and pointed, only then noticing a small door on the ceiling. "I thought you said there was no attic."

"There's not, technically. I got talking to one of the other residents the last time I was here."

"Not the day you found Roisin?"

"No, maybe a couple of weeks afterwards." She noticed Jacob frowning. "I couldn't shake the feeling that something wasn't right," she explained. "And when I came back the feeling didn't go away. Anyway, I got talking to Mr. McGinn who lives down the corridor. Apparently, all the top floor apartments were meant to have attic space but the idea was scrapped. The wood is rotten and was too costly to replace."

"So, what's up there?"

"It was the old loft for the mill. But before you ask, I already checked. The door up to it is barred by a steel grille and a thick padlock."

The ceiling was high, close to fourteen feet by Jacob's guess. More than enough to badly injure anyone foolhardy enough trying to jump down.

He returned to the front door. The frame sported two gouges where the locks on the original door would have been bolted across. One was at Jacob's head height, the other by his knee. "Was the original door composite like this one?"

"Yeah. The police had a rough time putting it through. They had to take turns trying to smash it in with their battering ram."

"Enforcer," Jacob corrected. Composite style doors were a bastard to put in, even with the sixteen kilograms of hardened steel the enforcer brought. The door would have offered a sturdy form of security on its own. The added locks would have made a tough job even harder for any would-be intruder. Roisin must have been properly scared.

"What about the letterbox? Same place?"

Natalie considered it for a second. "About there, yeah."

"Do you think someone could have slid something through the letterbox?" Jacob wondered, idly lifting the flap and letting it drop. "Like a wire hanger to slide the bolts across?"

Natalie thought about it before shaking her head.

"The bolts were pretty hefty. Even if you could open them that way I don't think you'd be able to push them back across."

Jacob nodded again. It had been a shot in the dark.

"You know, this is actually a whole genre in literature," Natalie said. "The locked room mystery, I mean. There's Murder on the Orient Express, The Hollow Man...

"-Murder in the Rue Morgue, The Big Bow Mystery, In the Morning I'll Be Gone...." Jacob interrupted, annoyed at the subtle insinuation that he didn't know what she was referring to.

Natalie brightened. "You've read them?"

"Of course. What kind of Private Detective dabbling in assorted strangeness would I be if I hadn't?"

In truth, although Jacob was a rather fanatical reader, he was only dimly aware of the genre. The only one of the books he named that he had read was In The Morning I'll Be Gone and only because it was set in Northern Ireland and had a police Detective as its protagonist. He had skimmed the summaries of the others on Wikipedia the night before, seeking inspiration for possible solutions and getting enough of a gist to bluff his way through a discussion on the topic.

He stuck his head into the cloak room. Two coats, a hoodie and an umbrella hung from the pegs. An open safe sat on a shelf. "Was this unlocked last time you were here?"

"I don't know. I don't think I ever noticed it before."

The safe was electronic and still had power but was empty aside from Roisin's passport. Jacob leafed through it and then threw the passport back into the safe.

Stepping out of the cloakroom he let his eyes to wander over the apartment. Eventually they drifted back to the kitchen. "There's a vent there," he said, nodding towards it.

"I saw that. Is it too outlandish to suggest they pump something in, knock her out or kill her and then stage the scene?"

"Not impossible, but improbable. First, you'd need someone with the skill to do it who also has access to certain chemicals. Even if you succeeded, if the death was unexpected, which Roisin's was, a post mortem would have been directed. I'm not an expert but I would have thought the presence of something strong enough to knock out or kill someone would show up in the examination. He studied the vent. "I think I remember reading a Sherlock Holmes story when I was in school. The bad guy killed someone by putting a snake through the vent."

"The Adventure of the Speckled Band," Natalie answered. "The snake actually ended up killing the villain, not the victim."

"Well, it's the best I have so far." Jacob said, only half joking. He reached up and took hold of the vent's metal grille. To his surprise it came away from the wall completely. He swore and quickly fixed it back into place.

"No Indian swamp adders hiding in there?"

"Unfortunately not," Jacob replied, wiping his hands on his jeans. Reaching into his pocket, he took out his phone and did a quick walkthrough of each room, snapping pictures of everything he and Natalie had just discussed.

"Back in a minute," he said, as he exited the apartment. He went left first, walking the length of the corridor until he reached the fire exit. He pushed it open and stepped out onto the steel staircase that ran up the side of the building. The door wasn't alarmed and had no handle to open it from the outside. If anyone was looking to sneak into the building via this means, they would have needed someone else to prop the door for them.

Jacob took a picture of the door and closed the fire exit behind him. This time he walked past Roisin's apartment to the opposite end of the building. The staircase that led to the old loft was off the corridor, hidden behind a swinging wooden door. Evidently, the builders hadn't taken as much care on the areas the tenants would not be using. The small space was dark and cold with the walls cracked and peeling.

As Natalie had said, access to the staircase was blocked by a security grille and a thick padlock with only a short shackle of steel exposed. It was a clever design. Even the heaviest duty bolt cutters would have a hard time snapping the thick steel and even if they could, they wouldn't be able to get a grip in the limited space between the steel and the main body of the lock.

Jacob gave the lock a tug but it held fast. He repeated the same trick with the grille and got the same result.

Bending down, he saw that the wall next to the lock had been stained with a black blotch and the peeling paint had bubbled. An old blemish from the Mill's glory days, Jacob guessed. He snapped a picture of the lock and the grille before returning to Roisin's apartment to find Natalie patiently waiting.

Jacob took a final look around the room before sitting down on the edge of one of the sofas. "I just don't see it," he said. "You're paying me eight hundred quid a week. I could tell you what I think you want to hear but I'll be honest. The only way in was securely locked. The windows are inaccessible and much too small for anyone to fit through. There's no hidden entrance, no chimney and the attic is too high for someone to drop through, not to mention securely barred from the corridor."

Natalie bent over the sofa Jacob was sitting on, resting her elbows on the back of it. "Roisin was barefoot. The direction she was lying meant she would have had to walk over broken glass."

Jacob shrugged. "A little bit of good luck before a large dollop of bad."

"What about the way she fell?" Natalie pushed herself up and placed her heel at the edge of the dried-in stain and lowered herself backwards. The top of her back touched against the corner of the table Roisin had fallen against. "And Roisin was a tall girl, had at least three inches on me."

"Could have slipped in the wine, one foot forward while the other went out from under her." Natalie stepped aside so Jacob could provide a clumsy demonstration of what he meant. "She could have fallen awkwardly instead of straight back."

Jacob stepped away from the table with another sigh. The obvious answer was usually the right one and the glaringly obvious answer in this case was that Roisin Dunwoody, drunk and possibly high, had slipped, cracked her head and died.

"I know this is a leap," Natalie said. "One I can't explain. That's why I came to you specifically."

"Let's say, for argument's sake, you're right. In that case we now have more questions."

"Like?"

"A suspect, for one. Motive, for another."

"The Followers. They are fervent."

"Enough for them to kill?"

Natalie shot him a look. This was Northern Ireland; people had been killing other people over religion and politics longer than the place had existed.

"Ok, stupid question. Let's think about the cult then. What's their motive? You said they were trying to threaten Roisin but they had done nothing violent against her physically. The show was out so the damage was already done. If they were willing to kill over this, why not do it when it would have an effect? At this stage the horse has already bolted."

Natalie cleared her throat.

"Ah. There was more."

"A lot more," Natalie said, gently fiddling with the bezel on her Breitling. It was an uncharacteristically nervous gesture.

"With a plan to release it down the line."

"No." Natalie shook her head. "I made the decision to stop when we did. Miss Gumshoe was going to have nothing further to do with the story."

"But you said it was your most popular piece?"

"It was and Roisin got death threats and nasty phone calls and emails. Our business address got a few letters threatening legal action. I began to notice strange men lurking about my street."

Jacob frowned. "You didn't mention that yesterday."

"It was probably just me being paranoid," she said, waving the thought away, "But I have a son at home. I make a comfortable living without getting myself mixed up in anything dangerous. I didn't want to put myself front and centre."

"But?"

"But... I offered to help Roisin produce her own podcast about the Followers. I'd take a cut of the profit and in return give her some guidance on how to create and publish a workable product, help her through the process, recommend people."

"But Roisin died and now you think it might have been your fault."

Natalie looked across at him sharply. "No. This isn't me on a guilt trip. Someone needs to answer. Someone needs to make sure Roisin mattered. Someone killed her and they think they got away with it."

"And you're willing to accept the consequences of going down that path?

Her usual warm smile took a grim edge. "Yes, I am." Dark hazel eyes turned to him. "Are you?"

# 5

Jacob considered Natalie's question as he drove back towards Belfast. He knew little about the Followers of Eden other than the fools he saw down the street most Saturdays, dressed in all-white uniforms and usually gathered at City Hall, Victoria Square or some other place with a guaranteed crowd. If Natalie was right and there was a connection, was he willing to get involved?

The speed of the answer surprised him.

Yes, he was.

The Private Detective bit was supposed to be a means to an end. A way to make a living using a skill set that was useless in any other profession other than the one he had left four years ago. Outside a few select jobs, like the theft at the Red Door gallery, Jacob found little satisfaction in his work. Cheated spouses didn't get their happily ever after, swindlers didn't their comeuppance and missing people didn't want to be found. His business dealt with dishonesty and infidelity, shysters and criminals, the crazies, the addicts, and every loser in between, and Jacob knew it was taking a toll.

Which led him to his next question. Was he willing to work the case out of a sense of finding justice for the death of a young woman, or was he doing it for himself? A chance to puff-up a long-bruised ego. Or maybe he was just lonely and liked the idea of being in contact with someone who, if nothing else, at least seemed to have some appreciation for his skills as an investigator?

Jacob frowned, unhappy with the morose direction his mind was taking him. He phoned Helen to tell her he wasn't returning to the office and decided to throw himself down the rabbit hole.

Traffic had died down from the morning rush and Jacob made it from Hilden Mill to Saint Anne's Square in a little over twenty minutes. He fixed himself a whiskey and ginger ale, noted the time was barely past noon and decided it would be wasteful to throw it away after it had already been made.

The temperature had rose steadily during the morning and had stifled the apartment while he was out. He opened the double doors to the balconette and was rewarded with the gentle touch of a summer breeze. The piazza below was bustling with an early lunch crowd enjoying the sudden upturn in weather to dine alfresco.

Jacob leaned on the guard rail as he took in the view but stepped back quickly as it gave a low groan of protest. He gave the rail an experimental tug, and found it had come loose from the wall, with at least one screw having fallen away from its fitting. He performed a quick calculation of the cost versus profit of plunging to the piazza below and the injuries sustained, if he survived, versus the large sum the property management company would have to pay out in Court over their shoddy workmanship. With the rough sum totalled up, Jacob decided he would contact the management company and have someone fix the rail.

He set the whiskey and ginger on the coffee table and went over to the kitchen counter, hoking in one of the drawers until he found a pen and a notebook. The first two pages were filled with jottings from a previous case, dated two years prior. Ripping these pages out, he dropped them in the bin and seated himself on the sofa, scrawling out some initial notes about what he had observed in Roisin's apartment. Finishing with a rough sketch, aided by the pictures he had taken, he included all possible entry and exit points, even if he had already ruled them out as being usable, as well as the vent in the kitchen.

Under the drawing he wrote *ROISIN DUNWOODY,* and in the line immediately beneath, drew a question mark. He needed to know more about the dead girl, either through friends or family.

Next were those with a connection to the location and the incident. He took a new line in the notebook and wrote *INVOLVEMENTS.* Natalie had mentioned a Detective Sergeant attending the scene, perhaps he could shed some light on what he had found and whether he had any sort of suspicion the death was anything other than accidental. He wrote DS, NAME, STATION? under the Involvements heading.

He was reasonably sure he had ruled out Roisin's apartment having any hidden entrances or trap doors, other than the sealed attic, but it

wouldn't hurt to find out more about the building, just on the off-chance there was something he had missed. He jotted HILDEN MILL PROPERTY MANAGEMENT FIRM onto the next line.

He'd also need to talk to the party goers. Natalie had said they all left at the same time but as far as anyone knew, they were the last people to see Roisin alive and one of them, Luke Fisher, had shared a romantic history with her. He wrote and then underlined Fisher's name.

Setting the notebook down, he lifted his Chromebook off the coffee table and brought up the website Miss Gumshoe was hosted on. He clicked on the first episode of Natalie and Roisin's production and lay himself across his sofa.

Notes from a piano, slightly warped, played the podcast in. The tune slowly swelled to a haunting crescendo which signalled Natalie's cue to talk. "Murder and mystery, crime, and passion, the gruesome and the unexplained. You'll find it all when you sit down with Miss Gumshoe." Jacob smiled as Natalie worked her way through the show's preamble, imagining her sitting in a darkened studio, headphones on and clutching a steaming mug of coffee as she leaned forward to talk into her mic.

Her presentation was relaxed and natural. When she introduced Roisin, the dead girl was awkward, almost shy, but Natalie was expertly able to coax her along as she began setting the scene for their production.

"The subject, or subjects, I should say, for today's episode are the Followers of Eden. Now, for any of our listeners outside Northern Ireland, the name might not be familiar but I understand this church has really gained a lot of popularity locally over the last few years, isn't that right Roisin?"

"That's right. "The church was founded roughly thirty years ago but its rise in the last ten has really been-"

"Miraculous?" Natalie offered.

Roisin laughed and Jacob could feel a release of tension. "For lack of a better word, yes."

"From what I understand the church has a number of prominent members, including Ivan Gould who owns one of the biggest construction firms in Ireland but the figurehead is an American gentleman named Seymour Huber."

"Or if you prefer to give Huber his self-appointed title; Grand Emissary."

"Believe me folks, when I say we could easily dedicate several episodes to the exploits of Mr. Huber alone, I am in no way exaggerating." Natalie and Roisin both laughed. "If possible, Roisin, could you give the listeners a concise recap of the life and career of this gentleman?"

"I can certainly try. The first twenty years are the easiest because we have no record of the man existing until then. No birth certificate, social security number, nothing. It wasn't until he gained a degree of notoriety in the late seventies that we have any kind of detail, a police report naming him as a member of an occult initiatory organisation."

"I don't know what that is and I'd guess my listeners don't know either."

"Ceremonial magic meets Freemasonry," Roisin answered. "Huber rose through the ranks quickly and it was only a few years later that he moved on to form his own group of free thinkers and free lovers in the California desert."

"Dear listeners, Roisin is being very diplomatic. From what you told me earlier, they were a sex cult."

"A sex cult with a promise to improve the success of its converts in their personal and professional life," said Roisin. "The cult grew rapidly but unfortunately for Huber it all came crashing down when the US Government attempted to prosecute him for fraud and racketeering. The case was eventually thrown out after several years of legal wrangling but the cult was finished and Huber was broke. He fled to the South Coast of Ireland with his two wives and a handful of his most devoted disciples."

"A strange place to end up, from the deserts of California to the rugged coastline of South Ireland," replied Natalie. "Stone cold broke, a reputation in tatters and not one, but two unhappy wives Not to mention the coast of Southern Ireland is rural and traditional, for the most part. A polygamist cult leader could rightly have been expecting to be chased back across the pond, but somehow Huber wasn't.

Roisin murmured her agreement. "It speaks to his skills as a conman that he was able to get to where he is now."

"And if you think the story has been strange so far, wait until you hear what happens next."

"Shunned by the locals, Huber befriended a circus."

"I'm going to pause a moment so my listeners can take that in."

"A struggling circus by all accounts," Roisin continued. "Insular, isolated, uneducated. They became the first members of the second iteration of Huber's cult. Huber dubbed them the Followers of Eden and began touring Ireland under the eaves of the circus big top, before eventually settling in Northern Ireland twelve years ago."

"And eventually his following grew to the point that an old circus tent didn't cut it?"

"That's right. By this time Huber had reinvented himself as a paragon of success and proclaimed himself as the Grand Emissary. The cult had mixed archaic religious doctrine with a cult of personality surrounding Huber. He realised he needed a permanent base of operations and he settled on a sprawling piece of land a few miles outside of Carrickfergus."

"Carrickfergus is a small town about ten miles or so outside of Belfast," Natalie cut in for the benefit of her non-local listeners.

"Unfortunately for Huber, the land he was after was already owned by a local farmer."

"And how'd he take that?"

"Not well. Huber decreed the land belonged to his church."

"Convenient."

"Wasn't it?" Roisin replied, now firmly into the swing of things. "The church began a process of intimidation against the farmer and his family."

"And when you say intimidation?"

"Threatening letters, phone calls. One morning the farmer woke up to find one of his barns had been graffitied with the Follower's ideogram, a five-pointed star with a symbol at each point, signifying their most sacred virtues. Huber had also begun to conduct religious services on the farmer's land and organised placard protests at his gate."

"A difficult issue for the police to deal with," Natalie said. "If you muddy the waters enough the Followers could argue their right to religious freedom was being infringed."

"Which is exactly what they did. The farmer eventually took the church to court. At this point the followers were now financially backed by Ivan Gould and a number of other prominent businesspeople."

"And this is where this story takes a tragic turn," Natalie said, taking over once more. "Before the case got before a judge, the farmer fell into a slurry pit and sadly died. His widow, partially disabled and faced with a future without her husband but with all of his debts, sold the land after a derisory offer from the Followers."

"Huber declared the incident a victory for his true believers and with the assistance of Gould Construction, built a Tabernacle on the site, followed by a walled compound with housing for the most devout members, a school and various other buildings."

"Now we're obviously not accusing the church of any involvement in what was a tragic accident..."

By the end of the half hour episode, Jacob's drink lay untouched on the table beside him. Natalie certainly knew how to keep her listeners rooted to their sofas. He listened to the next two parts back-to-back. Together, Natalie and Roisin outlined incidents of extortion, intimidation, and shady recruitment practises. Jacob remembered what Natalie had told him in Roisin's apartment; that they had barely scratched the surface. Whatever Roisin knew must have been damning.

At the end of the final episode, Natalie thanked Roisin and asked about what lay next.

"Well, I'm rather excited to announce that I'll soon be starting work on my own series, further delving into the Followers and Seymour Huber."

"I think I can speak for everyone listening when I say that I can't wait," Natalie replied. "Can you give us a hint on where your investigation might take us?"

"Where to start. For one, Ivan Gould's wife has not been seen in public for years and she's only one of a number of people involved with the church to go missing..."

Jacob zoned out as Roisin pitched the podcast that she would never make. He lifted the Chromebook and performed a quick Google search. It yielded plenty of results for the Followers but it all appeared to be either self-publication, glowing testimonials from current members or pieces from local news sites praising their charity work. In Belfast alone they had opened a soup kitchen and taken over the ownership of three homeless shelters, fully renovating each.

Next, he searched for the Followers and Miss Gumshoe and was rewarded with a few results, including a press release by the Followers condemning the lies, slander and defamation made against them. The release ended with the promise of legal action against the podcast.

Changing tact, he typed in *Ivan Gould Wife*. The search returned plenty on Mr. Gould but little about his disappearing spouse Roisin had mentioned. He quickly scanned through a few articles and a handful of images of the woman. All of them were old, taken in the years before the Tabernacle and compound were built in Carrickfergus. He skimmed another article and finally got a name; Margaret.

But Margaret Gould didn't bring up anything of note. No social media profiles and no news articles or appeals about her supposed disappearance. If she really was missing, no one seemed to care.

Returning to the search page, he tried combinations of keywords involving Huber, and his Followers. All he got in return were the same articles as before. He dutifully scanned through each piece but it wasn't until the fourth page of results that he finally got something.

It was a blog, a rough looking one. The author identified himself as Tomas McKinstry, a freelance writer based in Belfast. His posts went into detail on several incidents that Roisin had touched on, including Margaret Gould's disappearance, but was written close to three years before the Miss Gumshoe episodes had been released.

Jacob read through the pieces quickly. McKinstry's style of writing was grating, written in the first person like he was trying to emulate a James Ellroy novel. He detailed how he had approached Huber following a service, trying to confront him about allegations made against the church and getting strong-armed for his trouble by several men in smart suits. He tried a similar stunt at the opening of one of the renovated homeless shelters where Huber was making an appearance and judging by the accompanying photograph, had been tossed out head first.

Jacob tracked the growth of McKinstry's obsession through each new post. He shaved his hair, grew a beard, and began sleeping rough. After a couple of nights on the street he got picked up by one of the outreach buses and was brought to a meeting before he was recognised and chased out.

His accusations against the church were impressive in their scope and breadth but Jacob wasn't sure how much validity they held, especially as McKinstry failed to name any sources or in the end, back up any of his claims. His final blog was a short message about a temporary hiatus from the investigation along with a vow to not to let matter drop but there had been no update in the two years since.

Jacob scanned back through the blog but nothing new jumped out. He was about to close the page down when he took a second glance at the profile picture McKinstry had been using. A vague gnawing of familiarity ate at him but it took a second for Jacob to realise where he had seen the man before.

Leaning forward, he quickly brought up Roisin Dunwoody's Facebook profile and scanned through the pictures. He was just about to give it up as a bad take when he stumbled across what he was looking for. It was an old picture of Roisin, arm-in-arm with a man of around the same age as her.

The man's blonde hair was stylishly messy, he was clean shaven and a damn sight healthier looking than the hollow-eyed picture used on his blog, but it was unmistakably Tomas McKinstry looking back at him. He scanned through the rest of Roisin's albums and saw McKinstry appear a number times.

Jacob picked up his phone and rang Natalie. "I hope you don't mind the call," he said after she answered. "I don't suppose Roisin ever revealed where she was getting the information for her investigation?"

"No. She played her cards very close to her chest. But every journalist would, when it comes to protecting a source."

He pondered that for a second before asking another question. "You ever heard of a journalist called Tomas McKinstry?"

"A little. We were introduced once, at some sort of writer's workshop. He was freelance but did a bit of work for the Sentinel when I was there. Driven, maybe a bit too much. He was really gunning to make a name for himself."

"Was? Is he dead?"

"No. At least I don't think so. He...had his issues. Last I heard he was up in Gransha."

Jacob sighed. Gransha. The loony bin outside Derry. "Did you know he was looking into the Followers? More than that, did you know he and Roisin were friends?"

"No," Natalie said, the pitch in her voice lifting slightly. No, that's news to me."

"Roisin never mentioned him?"

"No, never."

"You think you can get me his contact details?"

"I'll text my old editor at the Sentinel. She's probably got them saved somewhere."

"Let me know. Another thing, you said you left a set of keys to Roisin's apartment to her father. Do you remember his address?"

There was a hesitation before Natalie answered. "Loughbeg Road. It's a few miles outside Ballymena. Are you planning on talking to him?"

"Seems like it might be the decent thing to do," Jacob said, scribbling the address beside the question mark he had drawn in his notes. "Let him know that someone is looking into his daughter's death."

"Maybe..."

"What?"

"This is your investigation. I certainly wouldn't want to tell you how to run it but I highly doubt you'll get any help from Arthur Dunwoody. This other thing, the history between Tomas McKinstry and Roisin, to me, that seems worth following."

"Sure," Jacob agreed. "But I'd be remiss if I didn't cover every base. It's what you're paying me for."

"Ok, Jacob." Her tone hadn't sounded less than convinced.

"I don't suppose you remember the number of the house?"

"I don't but you won't need it. It's the mansion with a front lawn bigger than the pitch at Ravenhill."

"Alright, thanks. I'll be in touch tomorrow."

"OK." She paused as if she were going to ask something more but apparently decided against it. "I'll talk to you later."

Jacob stood up and stretched. The ice had melted in his drink and the ginger ale had gone flat. He dumped the whiskey in the sink and reached for his phone again, typing a brief message.

**Off tonight? Fancy a drink?**

The reply came a minute later.

**Extra shift but finish at 4. Spaniard?**

*

Jacob got to the bar early, cringed when the barman greeted him by name like they were old friends and ordered a pint. Any amount of custom tended to pack the small pub out, but as Jacob lifted his drink he spotted a couple in the back booth collecting their things. He hurried over to claim the table, ignoring the dirty looks from a couple of heavyset women at the bar who were too slow off the mark.

He leaned back into the wooden bench with a contented sigh. The Spaniard could only be described as eclectic. Almost every bit of free space on the walls was adorned with random tat. Photos of far-flung locations, sombreros, band posters, crosses, and religious memorabilia all competed for space. The clientele was older, most of the customers were over twenty-five and looking for a quiet place to enjoy a drink and have a natter. There was rarely trouble which made it an ideal spot for peelers and ex-peelers alike.

Jacob had drained half his pint before he spotted Michael, scanning the crowded pub from the front door. Six foot, blonde and muscular, he would be the perfect face for the next PSNI recruitment poster. As a peeler, he was a natural, but had never harboured any ambition to go beyond response, the same role he had occupied since he and Jacob had passed out of Garnerville together twelve years before. Jacob didn't blame him, Michael was good at his job, knew the drill and with his base wage, environmental allowance, and generous overtime rate, enjoyed a comfortable living with no stress attached once he left the tall security walls of Coalburn behind after each shift.

He waved as he saw Jacob before making his way through the cramped surroundings. "Alright, lad. How's it going?"

"Not bad. You?"

"Can't complain."

"How's Coalburn treating you?"

"Sure, you know yourself."

Jacob nodded and just like that, they were all caught up.

Michael went to the bar and returned with two pints. "How's the new business going?" he asked as he handed one to Jacob.

It had been the new business for four years now, but Michael had always felt awkward around the subject, embarrassed for Jacob at how his career had ended and angry at the bosses who, in his mind, had let a good peeler swing.

Jacob told him about the new assignment and Michael listened attentively. "What's she like?" he asked when Jacob had finished.

47

"Who? Natalie?"

"Aye."

"Determined."

"Headcase?"

"No." He answered the question quickly before pondering it for a couple of further seconds. "Or if she is, she hides it well." He retrieved his phone from his pocket and brought up Natalie's Instagram. "Pretty though, headcase or not."

"Yeah, she is," Michael agreed. "Just not enough chest hair and rough beard for my liking." He quickly scrolled through the photos and it took Jacob a few seconds to realise he was leaving a like on each one. He snatched the phone back. "Cheers, mate. Now I look like a creep."

"More of a creep."

They sank their first round and ordered a second. Whilst Jacob did his best at social media damage control, he asked Michael for his opinion on the case. His friend shrugged his broad shoulders. "Seems like the girl slipped in wine, banged her head and died. All this other stuff it's suspicious, sure, but coincidental. You checked the room, can't see any way in and it's locked securely. I'm sure the detectives who investigated did the same."

Jacob nodded. It was fine and dandy forming the conspiracy in his head but it all came back to the problem of a dead body in a securely locked room. "Indulge me, Michael. Hit me with something outlandish."

Michael drummed his fingers on the table. "Someone comes to the apartment. The girl lets them in. They argue and he shoves her down. She cracks her head. He panics. He locks the door and puts the bolt across and gets out another way."

"What way?"

"Rope ladder out the window?" Michael tutted and snapped a finger. "No, you said the windows weren't big enough for someone to fit through." He thought for a second. "Maybe they hid in the apartment after they killed her? Slipped out after police put the door in?"

Jacob shook his head. "There was nowhere to hide. If you had told me no one had lived there I wouldn't have questioned it. The only possible place was the wardrobe but from what Natalie told me, the police checked there."

"Drugged?"

"I thought about it. Everyone left the party at the same time. There is a vent in the kitchen but you'd need someone to know what they're doing to pump the gas in. Even if you did, surely it would show up in the autopsy."

"They could have missed it," Michael said, before taking a long drink. "I had a drug overdose a few weeks back. Was talking to one of the mortuary attendants while I was waiting for the coroner to finish up with the body. He was telling me the office is seriously understaffed. They're flying in people from England on the weekends to keep up."

Jacob sat back. "There were a few empty strips of pills in the bin. Prepentaline. Didn't see any boxes or a prescription label."

"You wouldn't. They took Prepentaline off the market a couple of years back. If your girl had some, it wasn't from over the pharmacy counter." Michael waved a hand as Jacob considered that. "The girl was drunk and now you're saying she's popping pills too." He shrugged, making it clear what he thought the obvious answer was before finishing his pint. "What are you going to do?"

"Work it as if it were an unexplained death. Get every bit of information I can and present it to the client."

"So, what's your next step?"

"Talk to the DS who attended the scene."

Michael snorted. "Good luck with that. He's under no obligation to talk to you and I don't think telling him you're a private eye is going to hold much sway."

"He can only say no."

"And you're certainly used to hearing that."

Jacob drained his pint. "Another?"

"Aye, go on then."

# 6

Jacob felt as though someone had taken a mallet and gone to town inside his head while a partner in crime had planted two long nails behind his eyes and was slowly forcing them forwards. With a groan, he raised his head as Helen entered his office. She held a cup of coffee in one hand and a tall glass of water in the other. He mumbled his thanks as she set both in front of him, along with a strip of paracetamol.

"Big night?"

He nodded glumly. An hour after crawling out of bed and the hangover had Jacob firmly in its embrace. His head was heavy, his mouth dry, and a dull pain had settled behind his eyes with no sign of going anywhere fast.

Helen, giving a flawless performance of a disapproving mother catching her son gallivanting on a school night, regarded him for a moment. "Well, you look awful."

"Thanks, Helen," Jacob managed to croak. "You always know how to say the right thing."

"It's a sign of age catching up with you, you know? Not being able to handle the drink like you used to."

"You're going to lecture me about getting old?"

Helen smirked. "I'm in my prime. You on the other hand..." She gestured at the sorry sight slumped in the chair.

Jacob groaned his concession. He and Michael hadn't left the pub until well after last orders had been called. It had seemed like a good idea at the time. Wearily, he unwrapped two paracetamol tablets and downed them with the water.

Helen reached for the empty glass. "How's Michael keeping?"

"Same as ever. Could still drink for Ireland if the police career doesn't work out."

"Still with his man?"

Jacob shook his head. Michael hadn't mentioned Dean and Jacob knew his friend well enough not to ask.

"Shame. They were good together." Jacob gave a noncommittal grunt, too wrecked by his hangover to even contemplate discussing Michael's love life or lack thereof. "Right, well, deep and fascinating conversation notwithstanding, I've got some work to be getting on with," Helen said as she left him in peace, closing the door behind her.

Jacob rubbed a tired hand over his face before reaching for his desk phone and calling Natalie. "Any luck on that number for McKinstry?" he asked once she had answered.

"Well, good morning to you too," she replied cheerily. "Not sure about a phone number but my friend at the Sentinel is working on getting me an address."

"Good stuff. Listen, it might be a long shot but do you remember the name of the Detective at the scene? The one in charge I mean."

"Hold on a second." Jacob waited, listening to the sound of footsteps followed by rustling paper. "O'Connor," Natalie said. "No first name but the card he gave me says he works out of Lisburn Station."

"Lovely. Talk to you in a bit." Jacob ended the call and immediately dialled 101, the non-emergency number for the police switchboard. When the operator picked up he asked to be put through to Detective Sergeant O'Connor at Lisburn PSNI.

The call was answered after a few rings. "CID Sergeants." The man on the other end had a southern lilt to his voice. Dubliner, if Jacob had to guess.

"Sergeant O'Connor?"

"Speaking."

"Sergeant O'Connor, I apologise for bothering you but I am hoping you can help me."

"Alright." His tone suggested he was already on guard.

"My name is Jacob Kincaid, I'm a private investigator. I've been hired to look into the death of Roisin Dunwoody. I understand you were the supervising officer for that incident."

"A private investigator?"

"That's right." Jacob confirmed, not wanting to say too much more. He hoped O'Connor would take the invitation to speak and therefore limit how much truth he might have to bend.

"Well, that was a police matter, Mr. Kincaid. You understand I simply can't discuss it with just anyone."

"I understand fully, Sergeant," Jacob replied, giving some reverence to the man's rank. "I'm not asking you to breach data protection or divulge anything you shouldn't. I'm just looking to get some information to take back to her family." Lie number one and Jacob hoped O'Connor wouldn't press him further.

He heard O'Connor sigh. "The poor girl died in an accident. A tragic one certainly, but an accident all the same. Those are the facts of the matter, Mr. Kincaid. I'm really not sure what else you're after...."

"If I could just get a few moments of your time," Jacob cut in quickly, sensing O'Connor was about to brush him off. "I know you're a very busy man but I'm just looking to help Roisin's family. Maybe give them some form of closure. They're desperate."

O'Connor sighed again. "It's a waste of your time. That much I can tell you."

"It's my time to waste. I can come down to the station or-"

"Alright," O'Connor interrupted. "Alright. Look, I'm in Court today. Lisburn Magistrates. There's a café on Market Square, not too far away. Loughrey's. If you want, you can meet me there at two. Although I'm warning you now to manage your expectations."

"Thank you, Sergeant," Jacob began, but the line was already dead.

With time to kill, Jacob typed Hilden Mill into his search engine. A bit of digging eventually revealed what he sought; the company who ran the site; Scanlon Property Management. Their office was on the Woodstock Road over in the East of the city.

Finishing his coffee, Jacob made the short walk from the office to the multistory carpark attached to his apartment complex. As he started the Clio's engine, he did some rough calculations of the amount of alcohol he had consumed against time elapsed and concluded that if was stopped by the police he probably had enough alcohol lingering in his system to fail a breath test twice over.

Fifteen minutes later he made it to East Belfast, mercifully unmolested by any cops and got the Clio parked on a narrow side street of closely packed terrace housing. As he walked past the gable wall of the end house, he could smell the fresh coat of paint on the mural.

Rather than a display of some great sporting event or local celebrity, the mural depicted a wide-eyed gunman, completely out of all human proportion, hidden behind a balaclava, cradling an AK-47 and apparently busting for a shite. Even by the remarkably low standard of some Belfast murals, this was something special and Jacob felt the eyes of the turtle-heading terrorist follow him all the way up the road.

The employees of Scanlon Property Management seemed to be busy as Jacob walked in. Two were sat at their desks, both talking to young couples over a stack of paperwork. It was a blisteringly hot day. Jacob wiped the sheen of sweat from his forehead and stood around awkwardly until a man popped his head around the corner of a back office. "Can I help you?" He was overweight, with thinning hair and smooth, babyface features that made him look younger than he probably was.

"I hope so. I was looking to talk to someone about a property over in Hilden Mill. I believe your company manages the development."

"That's correct, yes." His expression suggested he had already surmised Jacob was not in the financial demographic of a potential customer.

"It's about the murder of one of the residents," Jacob replied, raising his voice for the benefit of everyone in the office.

The man hurried over to him. "Why don't we talk in my office, hmm?" He said, reaching out to guide Jacob away from the main floor. "I apologise, but I didn't catch your name Mr....."

"Kincaid. Jacob."

"Peter Scanlon." He closed the door to his office and crossed to his desk, offering Jacob a seat. "Now, what's this about a murder? I did hear you correctly, didn't I?"

"I'm a private detective, Mr. Scanlon," Jacob said as he sat down. "I've been hired by the family of Roisin Dunwoody to investigate the circumstances surrounding her death. Do you recognise the name?"

"I do. I'm actually dealing with the matter myself." Scanlon paused at the sound of heels clipping quickly along the tiled floor outside. Jacob turned to find an attractive, dark-haired woman in her thirties with a face like thunder, standing in the doorway.

"What's going on?" She demanded, crossing the room to stand behind Scanlon.

"My wife, Catherine," Scanlon explained. "Catherine, this is Jacob Kincaid. He's a private detective looking into the Roisin Dunwoody matter."

Catherine waved the name away as if it were a bad smell. "That was an accident."

Peter Scanlon nodded his agreement. "We've been trying to get arrangements made so the property can be sold on. Was it Arthur who hired you?"

"Uh, no. Another family member."

"Forgive us, Mr. Kincaid." Peter Scanlon paused to scratch the bridge of his nose. "Your visit has taken us rather by surprise. As Catherine said, we were very much under the impression Miss Dunwoody's death was an accident."

"Possibly," Jacob admitted. "Probably, in fact. But the person who hired me wants to know all the details."

Scanlon stole a quick glance at his wife before turning back to Jacob with his hands held out. "How can we help?"

"Well, it's a bit of an odd question, I know, but are you aware of any passages or doors in Roisin's building? Anything that was retained from the old mill building that people could get access to?"

"No, nothing like that. Aside from the outer walls and the floors, almost everything else in the main mill building was demolished. It was little more than a shell before the apartments were built."

"What about the attic in Roisin's apartment? If someone was looking to gain access to it?"

"Oh, that wouldn't be possible. There is a staircase leading up to the attic area but access to it is blocked by a security grille, barred and secured at all times."

"Locks can be forced."

"They can," Scanlon conceded, "But we made sure to use a high-quality lock. We wanted to be certain none of our residents would go up and then come straight back through the ceiling." He smiled ingratiatingly.

"So what's the purpose of it?" Jacob asked. "The attic?"

"It was a loft when the mill was operational," Catherine replied curtly. "The initial idea was to give the top floor residents of that building access to use as an attic. Unfortunately, the wood in the loft was found to be rotting in several places and the builders decided it would be too costly to replace the whole floor. The attic doors were already installed in each apartment but after the idea was scrapped the doors were sealed to make sure no one attempted to use the space."

Jacob nodded. So far what he was being told married up with what Natalie had relayed to him. "Sealed how?"

"Just a few nails," Peter Scanlon said. "Not much, but enough to ensure you couldn't push it open from below."

"What about keys to the padlock?"

"I'm not sure we're comfortable with this line of questioning, Mr. Kincaid," his wife replied, folding her arms across her chest. "Are you trying to suggest we were somehow negligent and contributed to this woman's death?"

"I'm only trying to get the facts. I want to give a grieving family the answers they need."

A little melodramatic but it seemed to do the trick as husband and wife shared another look. "Cecil Armstrong is the site supervisor," Peter Scanlon said. "He keeps the keys in his office but I hardly think he would be, how would you say, a person of interest?"

"No?"

"Well, he's at least sixty, and without being cruel, not the lightest man on his feet."

"I see."

Scanlon's smile was sympathetic. "I'm sorry we couldn't be of more help." He rose slowly from his seat. A silent gesture for Jacob to follow suit which he ignored.

"What do you know about the Followers of Eden?"

For the first time since she had entered the room, Catherine Scanlon looked away from Jacob. A flash of surprise flashed over her husband's face. "What about them?" he asked.

"Did you know Miss Dunwoody was looking into them before her death?"

"No." It was Catherine Scanlon who answered, now turning back to look at Jacob. "We didn't."

"But you are aware of them."

"We are," she replied. "A number of people in our sector are members of the church."

"We're just regular old Presbyterian though," Peter Scanlon said with a weak smile.

Jacob scratched his chin and then slapped his thigh gently. "Well, sounds like another thing I can cross off." He stood slowly but turned as he reached the door. "One last question. The construction firm who built the village?"

"Sweeny Brothers." Peter Scanlon answered. "Based down in Newry. What about them?"

Jacob looked from Catherine and back to Peter, not seeing any type of reaction. "Nothing. Forget I asked."

Back in the Clio, he phoned Helen and asked her to look up Sweeny Brothers Construction, to see if she could dig up anything of note about the firm.

"Anything I should be looking for in particular?" she asked.

"Scandal, innuendo, employee complaints," Jacob replied, knowing he was scraping the barrel. "If they've got form for carrying out a murder in a locked room, that might be relevant."

"Leave it with me." Jacob could feel her rolling her eyes on the other end of the line.

Starting the car, he took the A55 out of the city, following the Hillhall Road into the outskirts of Lisburn. It was a little before two when he made it to Loughrey's. The small café was still doing a decent trade following the lunchtime rush. He took a table at the back and ordered a water and coffee.

O'Connor came in a few minutes later, looking around until he spied Jacob watching him. He was a heavy-set man with a ruddy complexion, greying hair cut short and a goatee beard that didn't hide his weak chin.

"Mr. Kincaid?" He asked, holding out a meaty hand. His grip was stronger than Jacob had anticipated, suggesting a once fit man now fighting a losing battle against time and sedentary office work. His clothing was smart. The dark blue pinstripe suit was tailored and did an admirable job of hiding some of his bulk while his black framed glasses sported a Prada logo.

"Private detective, eh?" O'Connor said as he sat down. "Thought that sort of stuff was for the movies. I've certainly never come across one before."

"Well, we are Private."

O'Connor didn't make any attempt to pretend he found the joke funny. "Look, I respect that Miss Dunwoody's family are grieving but they're wasting money by hiring you. Not that you care, I'm sure."

Jacob smiled politely. For a man who had never encountered a private investigator before, he had a notable hostility towards the profession. "They came to me," he said, keeping his tone pleasant. "For what it's worth, I've been to Roisin's apartment and came away with the same conclusions you did. Initially at least."

O'Connor shrugged. "So why am I here?"

"So I can tell the family I spoke to you. Let them know I've covered every base." Jacob paused as the waitress returned to take O'Connor's order. He waited until she left before continuing. "Or maybe I'll see something with a set of fresh eyes."

O'Connor bristled but kept his voice measured. "I'd be mightily impressed if you did. Between the responding officers, their sergeant, my two detectives, the crime scene photographer and myself, there were a hell of a lot of eyes in that apartment."

"What do you remember about the incident?"

"Nothing out of the ordinary. It was phoned in as a concern for safety. The local response officers had to put the door in and found Miss Dunwoody inside, clearly deceased."

"And they followed procedure? They didn't-"

"They were extremely efficient," O'Connor said, cutting him off. "Set up the scene immediately. By the time I arrived the paramedic who pronounced life extinct had already been and gone, a statement had been recorded from the last person to see Miss Dunwoody alive and they had tasked a local crew to pass on the death message to her next of kin down in

Ballymena."

It was rare for some of the specialised branches to give their uniformed colleagues any degree of praise but O'Connor had been quick to jump on any potential suggestion the first police on scene had not acted as they should. While he may have been defending fellow officers from an outsider, Jacob didn't get the sense that O'Connor was bending the truth either.

"So everyone there was in agreement? About the death being accidental?"

O'Connor nodded. "Aye. The local sergeant was a young fella. Quite new in the post. In cases like this they'll call out detectives just to make sure. I attended, agreed with him and we got the undertakers tasked to take the body to the mortuary at the Royal."

"And there was nothing suspicious found during the post mortem?"

"No," O'Connor said, his brow furrowing. "Why would there be?"

"I'm just looking at all the angles. The person who hired me suggested there might be more to this incident. That Roisin was murdered."

"Christ on a bike!" O'Connor gently slapped a hand on the table. "Murdered?"

Jacob offered a shrug in return. "So they seem to think."

"Do you know how many murders happen in Northern Ireland every year?"

"Around thirty, on average."

"In a good year, that's about right. And how many people do you think die in accidents in the same period?

"I get the point."

"Do you? Because it seems like you're leading Roisin Dunwoody's family down the garden path. The girl was three sheets to the wind, not to mention she quaffed a few tabs too."

"Prepentaline?"

"Yes. There was a couple of empty strips in the bin. Not enough to overdose on but enough to seriously dull her senses, even without the wine. We found a couple of boxes of them in a kitchen cupboard. No prescription for them."

Jacob leaned back in his chair as the waitress returned with the sergeant's coffee. He watched O'Connor stir three sachets of sugar into his drink. "What do you know about the Followers of Eden?"

O'Connor didn't look up from his coffee as he stirred. "What do they have to do with anything?"

"Roisin had been looking into them."

"I'm aware. Her friend who found her really went for that angle."

"Natalie?"

O'Connor tapped his spoon against the edge of the cup. "Left messages with the switchboard for me a few times, wanting to discuss her little theory."

"What did you tell her?"

O'Connor snorted. "Nothing! It had nothing to do with her. Once we got the next of kin details, that was our point of contact. Natalie Amato was a witness..." He stopped suddenly as the pieces fell into place. "Jesus Christ. That's who hired you, isn't it? Family member my hole!"

There was no point denying it. Jacob instead held two palms up in a *You Caught Me* gesture.

"I should have bloody known." Jacob's deception had rankled the man and the weary patience was now replaced with cold anger. O'Connor stood up, pushing against the table, spilling coffee over the rim of his mug as all eyes in the café turned towards them.

"Roisin was being targeted," Jacob said, standing up as well. "Threatening letters and phone calls. Her car was vandalised."

"And it was all reported to the local police. Every incident was investigated by the local response team."

"I'd like to speak to the IO's. If you could pass me their details-"

O'Connor's laugh was incredulous. "I can't do that as you damn well know. I didn't recognise the name at first but it just clicked. You're not a police Officer anymore, Mr. Kincaid." O'Connor jabbed a finger towards Jacob. "I'd advise you to stay out of police business." With that, he turned on his heel and stormed out of the café.

Jacob followed, dodging around the waitress and out onto the street. "At least tell me if anything was found by local response," he said, jogging to catch up.

"Nothing," O'Connor replied, quickening his step. "I checked all the logs myself. No suspect for the criminal damage and no prints left on the letters."

"What about the phone calls?"

"Pre-paid mobiles. No payment info. They had been looking into tracking the e-mails but I imagine that's been kiboshed with the victim dying in an unrelated matter." O'Connor had paused at a pedestrian crossing, waiting for the traffic to stop.

"Did police seize Roisin's phone or computer?"

"Why would we?" O'Connor asked through gritted teeth.

"Just curious."

The sergeant shook his head as the green man flashed. He took a step onto the road but paused, turning back to Jacob. "I did my job, Kincaid. I shouldn't have to explain myself to a washout like you but we checked that apartment. I didn't just write it off. We looked over every inch of it for anything suspicious and before you ask, yes, I checked the the the attic angle too. Satisfied? Because if you're not, I'm warning you now, leave well alone." He wheeled away, leaving Jacob standing at the lights.

"Is that a threat?" Jacob demanded, loud enough to turn the heads of a few people in his vicinity.

O'Connor turned too. He looked as if he was about to say something but instead shook his head in disbelief and disappeared into a throng of afternoon shoppers.

"Is that a threat?" Jacob repeated to himself, ashamed at uttering such a cliché. Maybe Helen was right, he had been watching too many movies.

# 7

The offices for Lisburn and Castlereagh City Council were only a ten-minute walk from Loughrey's café. After going back and paying for the coffees, he followed the map on his phone.

As he walked, his mind went to the missing computer in Roisin's office and the unaccounted-for phone. The police hadn't taken them, so had someone else? Possibly, but that didn't necessarily mean there was anything nefarious involved. Her father had a key for the apartment. He could have collected both devices, perhaps hoping to retrieve a final memento from his lost daughter.

Lisburn and Castlereagh City Council was situated in a modern civic building picturesquely perched on the banks of the river Lagan. If he kept walking, Jacob could have followed the flow of the river directly to Hilden Mill.

Inside, a helpful receptionist pointed him towards the planning department on the second floor, where an altogether more unhelpful employee told him he should have phoned ahead. Jacob apologised and asked to see the relevant plans and maps for the redevelopment of Hilden Mill.

Half an hour later he was invited into a side room where a stack of paperwork had been laid out. Jacob rummaged through the sheets until he found what he was looking for; a map of the finalised proposal for the main building of Hilden Mill.

It was as Peter Scanlon had said. Save for the floors, almost everything else in the building had been gutted and replaced. He was able to pick out the staircase leading up to the loft and the fire escape on the other side. Both had been part of the original mill building before construction began, but as far as he could tell, nothing else had survived. If there had been any back corridors or staircases, they were long gone.

He leafed through the rest of the maps before turning to the employee who had remained, apparently watching to make sure Jacob didn't swipe anything. "Is there a map for the Mill before any work was done?"

"All the relevant paperwork is in the file." The employee replied, clearly resentful of the time lost with this enquiry.

"That's what I'm asking," Jacob said, carefully choosing his words. "There isn't one. Would the builders not have made one before they started?"

"All the relevant paperwork is in the file."

"Thanks," Jacob said, leaving the room. "You've been very helpful."

\*

"Sweeny Brothers Construction," Helen said as he stepped back into Kincaid Investigations.

"Sweeny Brothers Construction," Jacob repeated.

"Absolutely nothing of interest. High industry rating and apparently high employee satisfaction ratings too, from what I can see online. No scandals, swindling, fraud or anything else of note."

"Any potential link to the Followers?"

Helen shook her head. "Not that I can see. Whole family appears to be devout Catholic, judging by an interview I was able to find in one of the society rags. The one brother not involved in the business is a Priest down in Louth."

Jacob mumbled his thanks and headed to his office. "I've sent you an email," Helen called after. "Another suspecting spouse."

He paused at the door. "You tell them we're tied up

at the moment?"

"I did. But I promised a call back by tomorrow with a view to penciling in an initial meeting next week."

"We're working on retainer for a sole client, Helen."

"You really think you can drag it out that long?"

Jacob shrugged as his phone vibrated in his pocket. He shut the door to his office behind him before answering.

"I have an address for you," Natalie said.

"For McKinstry?"

"Mm-hmm. Star of the Sea apartments, Maritime View, Belfast. Sounds picturesque."

Jacob laughed. "Sounds it, but isn't. It's a hostel down near the docks. It's mainly for street drinkers and addicts but they also use it as a halfway house for recent releases from Maghaberry prison. Rough place."

"Oh. I guess Tomas isn't doing so good."

"No," Jacob agreed. The residents of Star of the Sea were certainly not amongst life's winners. "I managed to get a meeting with that Sergeant earlier and the people who supervise Hilden Mill."

He quickly filled her in on what O'Connor had told him about the empty Prepentaline cartons, and the dead end turned up from the visits to Scanlon Property Management and the council offices. He waited as Natalie processed the information and wondered if she was going to say it. A locked door to a locked apartment. No way in and no way out. Pills mixed with alcohol; her senses dulled enough for her to slip in a pool of spilled wine.

"Did you turn up anything else?" she asked instead.

Jacob thought for a moment. "O'Connor says the police didn't take Roisin's phone or computer."

"You think it was stolen?"

"Not necessarily but a journalist in her twenties with a missing phone and without a computer, laptop, or tablet in her home strikes me as a bit weird. Do you know if Roisin kept a record of the reference numbers for the crimes she reported?"

"Yeah, she did. The police left a card for each time they called out. She said she almost had enough to start a collection."

Jacob clicked his tongue, annoyed at himself. It was something he should have thought of at the time. "I'd like to get a look at them."

He knew it was unlikely that he would garner anything useful. As far as crime went, the incidents were all low level and like O'Connor said, would have been investigated by local response officers. Jacob knew the drill. They would have attended, taken Roisin's details and perhaps a statement. For the damage to her car, they would have done a check for any CCTV and conducted door to door enquiries. For the phone calls, there might have been a request made to try and track down subscriber information. When nothing turned up, the case would have been filed away by their Sergeant as awaiting further evidence.

"No problem," Natalie answered. "I'd like to meet tomorrow anyway. Review how we're getting on."

"Sure," Jacob said slowly, "But I really don't have anything else to catch you up with."

"I know, but I'd like to get a feel of where we're at and discuss what our next step is."

"Alright. You, uh, fancy getting a drink or a bite to eat? I know a place..."

"I'm recording for the podcast tomorrow afternoon but I should be finished up around three or so, if you can meet me at the Wheelman Studio over in Weaver's Court. All the people who were at Roisin's should be there, save for Luke Fisher. We can drive out to Roisin's after, if that suits. Look for those cards."

When the call finished, Jacob pocketed his phone with a heavy sigh. Frustration suddenly bit at him. Although he was being paid handsomely for the effort, it was becoming apparent that this case was nothing more than a dog chasing its tail, and he was the one barking.

His mood was in no way improved by the

unrelenting hangover. Deciding to duck out early for the day, Jacob said his goodbyes to Helen and went home, stopping for a takeaway en route.

By half five his fish supper was finished and he was bored. A common feeling when he wasn't on a job. Sitting in his apartment alone with only four walls and the snatches of conversation from the piazza below for company.

A sudden urge to go to the gym faded quicker than it had arrived. Instead, he turned on the tv and blasted some Nazi's on the PlayStation. He couldn't concentrate on saving the world from fascist scum and after dying for the third time, threw the controller down on the sofa.

He paced, restless in the apartment that had boiled during the hot day when he was out and now struggled to get any sort of cooling touch from an absent evening breeze. He lifted an Elmore Leonard novel from the shelf, reread the first page four times and put it back.

Turning the console off, he checked his phone. No missed calls or messages, not that he had expected either. The time on the screen read half past six. He grabbed his car keys and headed for the door.

Ten minutes later he was on the M2 heading towards Ballymena. The Loughbeg Road was in the sticks and Jacob doubted he would have found the place without a map. The majority of dwellings, almost all of them farm houses, were situated well back from the road, down long, secluded lane ways.

Arthur Dunwoody's address, as Natalie had said, was not hard to recognise, with a perfectly cut front lawn big enough to land a jumbo jet. Two lines of pin oak trees shifted lazily in the warm evening, shielding a long driveway that wound its way through the immaculately kept garden.

The house itself was a white render, two story mansion with a glazed balcony looking out over the expansive lawn. A much smaller house, which Jacob guessed to be the renovated structure of the site's original dwelling, stood to the left of the driveway. A separate building for visiting guests, he assumed.

The door to the mansion was answered by a tanned, fit looking woman in her forties, whose features creased as she regarded the man standing on the doorstep. "Mrs. Dunwoody?"

Her expression was severe. "Mrs. Hamill," she corrected. "Mr. Dunwoody's housekeeper. Mrs. Dunwoody is no longer with us."

Good start. "My name is Jacob Kincaid. I was looking to speak to Arthur."

"Is he expecting you?" Her tone made it clear she already knew the answer.

"No, but-"

Mrs. Hamill had already begun to close the door in his face and was only stopped by Jacob placing his foot against the frame. "Shall I call the police?" she asked.

"If you could just tell Mr. Dunwoody that I'm here and I'm a private investigator. If he tells me to Foxtrot Oscar, that's fine but I'd prefer to let him make that decision, not the help."

She stared at him for a moment. "Wait here."

Jacob kept his foot in the doorway until she was out of sight. Two minutes later, Mrs. Hamill returned and beckoned him inside. He followed the woman into an open plan kitchen and dining room overlooking a body of water which Jacob assumed to be Lough Beg.

Mrs. Hamill disappeared and Jacob wandered over to the open doors. The house was on raised land and gave a commanding view over the Lough and the green country beyond. Across the shimmering blue water, the silhouette of a church spire peaked out from above the canopies of a clump of tall trees, cut off on its own private island.

"They call it Church Island," a voice said from behind him. Jacob turned and found himself facing Arthur Dunwoody. "Imaginative, I know."

Jacob was almost taken aback at the man standing in front of him. Arthur Dunwoody was ridiculously handsome. Tall, tanned and flint jawed, he had a towel draped over his broad shoulders. His thick brown hair with the slightest hint of grey at the temples was wet. He wore a simple plain t-shirt and pair of snug shorts which perfectly showed off a muscled pair of legs and developed chest.

"I wasn't expecting any visitors," Dunwoody said. "Mrs. Hamill had to interrupt my evening swim."

"You swim in the lake?"

"No, my indoor pool." His grey eyes were cool, unflinching. Jacob didn't think of himself as someone who was easily intimidated but Arthur Dunwoody had an undeniable presence about him. He wasn't a man of violence or anger, at least on initial impression, but someone who naturally commanded and expected respect.

"Mr. Dunwoody, my name is Jacob Kincaid. I'm a private investigator. I was hoping I could talk to you about your daughter."

He waited to be told to get out. The slate grey eyes held firm and Jacob matched their gaze, sensing Dunwoody was sizing him up. A few seconds that felt like an eternity passed until Dunwoody said, "Let's take a walk." Jacob followed Dunwoody as he took the steps out of the kitchen to the rear of his estate. "Who hired you?" He waited until they were a distance from the house before asking the question.

"A friend of Roisin's."

Dunwoody grunted. "I suppose it wouldn't get me anywhere asking for specifics?" Jacob shook his head. Another grunt. "What is it that you want, Mr. Kincaid?"

"Roisin's friend has a belief that your daughter's death was not accidental." He searched Dunwoody's face for any flicker that betrayed even a hint of emotion but the older man gave nothing away.

"I see," he said without breaking his stride. "What do you think?"

"I think she died inside a locked apartment. I'm not a shyster, Mr. Dunwoody. I'm genuinely investigating this incident but there's not much to go on."

"No, the police officer dealing with the matter told me as much."

"Sergeant O'Connor?"

"That's right."

"I've spoken to him already." This time Dunwoody stopped. His eyes softened slightly as he looked at Jacob again. "He wasn't overly forthcoming with any details," Jacob continued, sensing a sliver of an opening. "Is there anything you can think of that didn't sit right with you?"

"Other than the bruising on her chest?"

"Bruising?"

"A single bruise, yes. O'Connor didn't mention it to you?"

"No. But then he was under no obligation to. As far as he was concerned the matter had been explained and the line was already drawn under it. You must have heard from the coroner following..." He trailed off.

"The post mortem?" Dunwoody offered. "I did and the bruising was noted but there's plenty of reasons to explain how Roisin received it and most were not sinister enough to necessarily point to murder."

"Did he mention anything else. Defensive wounds? Scratches? DNA?"

Dunwoody shook his head before moving off again. Jacob fell in step beside him. "The Pathologist who performed the preliminary examination may have ruled it as an unexplained death if it wasn't for the issue that Roisin was apparently alone in her apartment when she died. As it was, they were happy to rule her death as accidental."

"What do you think?" Jacob asked.

"I went to the apartment, the day after the examination. Just to see for myself. There is no way in or out, apart from the front door. Seeing the place in the cold, grey light of day, I think I gained some measure of acceptance."

The two men stopped at the water's edge and stood

in silence, looking out across the lough towards Church Island. It was beautiful country.

"Do you know of anyone who would want to hurt your daughter, Mr. Dunwoody?"

He shook his head. "No. But then, I didn't really know Roisin. I'd probably tell anyone who asked that we drifted apart as she got older but the truth is we were never close. I didn't understand her. Her issues as a teenager. She outgrew them and then took a career choice I didn't agree with."

"As a Journalist? I'm led to believe she was quite talented."

Dunwoody gave a slow exhale. "School sports days and agricultural shows. Let's not kid ourselves, my daughter wasn't exactly Marie Colvin. That being said, when I heard about her work with Miss Amato, I admit, it took me by surprise."

Jacob nodded along, trying not to betray anything.

"That's why you're here, isn't it?" Dunwoody asked, shifting his body to look back at Jacob. "You think there's a link between the story she was working on and her death. Miss Amato danced around the issue at Roisin's funeral."

"How much did she tell you about the work she was doing?"

"Nothing. It was Liam who got me up to date."

"Liam?"

"Roisin's brother. They'd recently reconciled and she was keen to tell him all about her new venture. I was impressed."

"Why?"

"Do you know much about the Followers?"

Jacob shook his head, content to play dumb.

"Influential to say the least," Dunwoody continued. "A few people in my circles have been swayed by them the last couple of years. Don't see the attraction myself but you can't deny their appeal. Like I said, I was impressed. Roisin was finally showing some gumption. Following a story that mattered." Dunwoody sighed deeply and began to walk away without a word. Jacob quickened his pace to catch up. They came to a stop at a stable with a fenced paddock. Two horses peeked out from their stalls.

"You ride?" Jacob asked lamely, looking to fill the lingering silence.

"No. That was Roisin's passion." Dunwoody rested his elbows on the fence. "At least Roisin had passions, even if I didn't understand most of them. Liam on the other hand, has all the talent in the world and squanders it."

"Another career choice you didn't agree with?"

Dunwoody turned slowly and Jacob thought he had overstepped his bounds. Instead, the older man fixed his attention back on the paddock. "No, on the contrary. Liam works, or rather worked, for one of my company's. A good job with good prospects. Drugs were the ruin of him. Nowadays he is content to wait me out and collect his inheritance."

Inheritance. The word seemed to hang in the air. There were a lot of reasons to kill. More often than not, money was at the top of the list.

"What does your company do, Mr. Dunwoody, if you don't mind me asking?"

"We install fire suppression systems."

"Like sprinklers?"

"Sometimes but we specialise in gas suppression systems."

Jacob felt a flutter in his chest. "Chemicals?" His mind drifted to the vent in Roisin's kitchen.

"In its simplest terms, yes."

"How did Liam take Roisin's passing?"

"Probably as you would expect him to," Dunwoody replied. "They had a falling out a short while before Roisin died."

"I thought you said they'd just reconciled."

Dunwoody's grunt bordered on amused. "You must be an only child. Siblings fall out and make up. That's their nature." Regret flitted over his features. A brief glimpse of the man behind the mask. "Do you have any further questions?" he asked, as the façade returned.

Jacob replied with a silent shake of his head.

"Then I hope you don't mind if I ask you to see yourself out."

Jacob made it ten steps before Dunwoody called after him. "Mr. Kincaid? If you do find something untoward about my daughter's death and you find someone amenable, I'd like to know."

Jacob shifted uneasily. "Like I said, Mr. Dunwoody, there's not really a lot to go on to suggest it was anything other than an accident. But I promise I'll follow every angle."

"It'll be worth fifty thousand if you get me a name."

"You can't be serious."

"No?" Dunwoody gestured to where they stood. "Money is no object, Mr. Kincaid. It's all I have left."

"I'll do my best," Jacob replied but Dunwoody had already turned back towards the empty paddock. With all his success and riches, Arthur Dunwoody looked like the loneliest man in the world.

Jacob phoned Helen as soon as he reached the Clio. He apologised for calling her at home but he wasn't planning on coming into the office before meeting Natalie the following day and wanted to ask her to do this before he forgot.

"Alright," Helen said, drawing on her well of infinite patience. "What is it?"

"A fire suppression engineer."

"What's that?"

"Who," Jacob corrected. "Can you find me the last known address for a Liam Dunwoody? Probably in his twenties or thirties."

He was back in Belfast before nine and picked up a second dinner from McDonalds, taking it home and eating it on his sofa. As he finished the last of his burger with a final, remorseful bite, he told himself he had to make a change and he would. It just wouldn't be tonight.

Picking up the remote, he flicked through the tv channels, finally stopping on one at random. He sat with the television blaring without watching it, considering the info he had gleaned from Arthur Dunwoody. He had called on the man as a courtesy as much as anything. Now he had the makings of two half-baked theories.

The first was the possibility that Roisin was pushed rather than fell. The bruising on her chest could have easily been caused by a hard shove. However, he was still faced with the need to find a work around for the locked room problem. Could the killer have hid out in the apartment the entire time, only slipping out when the place was locked up again the next day? It was a long shot, but so was everything in this case.

The second theory was a damn sight more interesting. Liam Dunwoody would have had access to all sorts of chemicals, the means to use them and with a sizeable inheritance to double, a rather compelling motive.

There were problems of course. Access to the vent in Roisin's apartment would take at least a forty-foot ladder to reach, with the killer having to lug their equipment up, keep it there until the job was done, and all the while rely on the hope no one would happen to look out their window or walk by.

Reaching the vent via the roof would have been the easier approach but roof access was locked behind the same security grille and heavy-duty padlock that barred the way to the old loft.

Arthur had said aside from the bruising, nothing untoward had stood out in Roisin's post mortem. That meant the toxicology results had not shown any notable traces of anything foreign in her body. That was a mark against the gassed room theory but Michael had said the mortuary was under severe staff shortages. Could an overworked pathologist have taken the scene of an apparent accident in a locked room at face value and half-assed their examination?

There were a lot of if's and but's in the scenario, Jacob knew. Yet at the same time, it was possibly the strongest hypothesis he had so far, solving the mystery of how the person escaped from the locked room if they were never there in the first place.

When he finally turned off the tv, the conversations in the piazza had died away hours before. As Jacob climbed into bed, an uneasy silence had settled over the city. The tranquillity was occasionally punctuated by the wail of sirens as the police rushed to calls of domestics, street fights and joy riders. Hot days raised temper and temperature in equal measure.

It was a warm, sticky night and Jacob lay on the mattress, sheets and duvets kicked away to the foot of his bed in an attempt to get even halfway comfortable.

Time marched on but sleep wouldn't take him. He fetched his Chromebook, accessed the Miss Gumshoe site and picked an episode at random. Dylatov Pass was a well-known mystery but he enjoyed Natalie's spin on the disturbing fate of the Russian hikers lost in the Urals. The sound of her voice was comforting in his empty apartment.

The podcast ended before sleep came. Jacob hit the replay button but it was another two hours of restless tossing and turning before he finally drifted off into an uneasy slumber, a pillow pulled close to him.

He woke with a start, fumbling for his blanket, not because of the cold but for some unconscious childish desire to shield himself. A nightmare, but Jacob couldn't remember what had spooked him from his sleep.

He was breathing hard and lay with the duvet wrapped around him, listening. Slowly he sat himself up. A sheen of sweat covered his bare chest.

A chill shot through him but the night was still uncomfortably humid. The window to his bedroom was open as was the door to the balconette across the far side of his living room. He reached for his phone and read the time; *0303*.

A sense of creeping dread took hold. It was a familiar feeling, a sense that something was not right. Something he could not identify but knew was there. He'd felt it before, more times than he could count. The empty house with the burglar still hiding inside. The copse of trees where the suspicious male had disappeared into. He'd even had it a few times since he quit the force, a handful of select cases he had taken on as a private investigator, where the rational explanation was not forthcoming.

The dark apartment beyond his bedroom door lay completely still. No sound reached through the window. Beyond his walls, the streets of Belfast had fallen into their own restless sleep.

Jacob threw the blanket back and crept towards the bedroom door. Something was out there. He knew it in his bones. "Hello?" His voice was shaky and unnaturally loud in the stillness beyond. He wasn't sure what he wanted to hear, and was certain if someone answered back he wouldn't have thought twice about shitting himself.

He could feel the clamminess on the back of his palms. A bead of sweat trickled down his face to sting an eye. "Come on," Jacob whispered, trying to steady his breathing. Eyes adjusting to the darkness, he scanned his apartment, eventually resting on the wide-open doors of the balconette.

Clawing unease dug its way to the bottom of his stomach. Had he left them like that? A flicker of wind ruffled the lace curtains that framed the balconette doors and goose pricked his skin. He wasn't sure what drew him over, but he edged himself closer.

Long shadows covered most of the deserted piazza but not the figure in black who stood at its centre. Jacob swallowed. He couldn't make out
the shape of the person or the clothes they wore.

Blanketed by the night and his unlit apartment, there was no way the figure could see him from where it stood, yet its head suddenly snapped upwards, looking directly at where Jacob stood.

It was a primeval instinct that took over, sending Jacob stumbling back into the protective cloak of his dark apartment.

He wasn't sure how long he stood in the shadows, heart thumping but when he forced himself back to the balconette, the figure was gone.

# 8

The Wheelman Recording Studio was located in an enterprise park, not far from the centre of town. The security man in guard hut looked up from his paper long enough to raise a hand in greeting as Jacob walked through the pedestrian gate.

He found the Wheelman building at the far end of the lot, sandwiched between a CrossFit gym and a post-production studio, catering for the myriad of international movies and tv shows drawn to Northern Ireland by attractive tax breaks.

The door to the studio was locked. Jacob pressed the intercom and waited for someone to answer. With no one around, he allowed himself a wide yawn. He had spent the remainder of the night on the sofa, too freaked to go back to bed. He drifted off through sheer exhaustion a little after five in the morning and woke up an hour later.

"Yes?" A static tinged voice came through the intercom

"Jacob Kincaid, here to see Natalie Amato."

"Oh! I'll be out in a min."

Roughly a min later, Jacob was met by a man in his early thirties, slim with dark hair swept to the side. He was dressed casually, with an unbuttoned blue shirt over a grey t-shirt and jeans so tight they had to be cutting off circulation to all the wrong places. He sucked greedily on a vape pen and introduced himself as

Natalie's partner, Ciaran McCourt.

"I knew Natalie employed other people but I wasn't aware she had a partner."

"Well, partner is perhaps a bit of a generous description," Ciaran replied, somewhat sheepishly. "Natalie writes most of the episodes herself, picks the subject and helps with the research. I guess you can say I do a bit of quality control but my main focus is marketing. You know, getting the podcast out there and growing the brand." He took another puff on the vape and blew out popcorn scented smoke. "We'll be expanding onto YouTube in the very near future."

"Natalie also mentioned a sound editor?" Jacob asked, doing his best to recall the brief details Natalie had previous mentioned.

"That's right, and a production assistant."

"Right," Jacob said. "Natalie's told you why I'm here, I take it?"

"She told us you were coming by, yes. A real-life Private Eye. There must be a future episode in this."

"So, you were at Roisin's flat?" Jacob said quickly, before Ciaran put any real thought into the idea.

His sigh was sad and a little too practised. "I was."

"You, Natalie, and the rest of the team? The sound editor, the production assistant, and the writer?" Jacob flipped open his notebook to a blank page.

"Yep. Mairead, Arjun and Luke."

Jacob took down the names. "I understand Luke doesn't work for the podcast any longer?" Natalie hadn't been forthcoming about why the former writer had been given the boot and Jacob hadn't pressed the subject at the time.

"That's correct, yeah. He was let go after the last episode about the Followers of Eden."

"Why?"

Ciaran shifted uncomfortably. "I think that's something you should ask Natalie about. It was her decision."

"Alright. What about on the night itself? How was

he behaving?"

"A little obnoxious. Maybe a bit too much to drink. At one point I
caught him and Roisin arguing in the corridor."

"About what?"

He shrugged. "I don't know. But it seemed pretty heated."

"Was Luke being aggressive?"

"Actually, if I had to guess, I'd say Roisin started the fight."

"What makes you say that?"

"The body language, I suppose. Luke was standing there and taking it, Roisin was doing most of the finger pointing. I only remember because it was so unlike her. She was a quiet girl."

"How much did you have to drink that night?"

"Nothing. Nothing alcoholic, at any rate. I'm tee-total." He declared the fact proudly before sucking in another lungful of vapour.

"And the rest?"

"Pretty far on."

"Including Roisin?"

"Especially Roisin."

Jacob nodded and then paused, allowing Ciaran a break to suck on his vape. "What time did you leave?"

Ciaran pursed his lips. "I'd say around one or so."

"Who was still at the party?"

"No one. We all left together."

"In the same car?"

"No. I drove Arjun and Mairead home. Luke lives out in Jordanstown so Natalie offered to take him, save me some petrol money."

"When did you hear about what happened?"

"The next afternoon. Natalie had been texting into our WhatsApp Group, asking if anyone had heard from Roisin. Then she phoned me a couple of hours later to give me the news." He paused as if he wanted to say more.

Jacob decided it best to play along with. "Go on,

Ciaran."

Ciaran shut his eyes and pinched the bridge of his nose as the debate raged inside him about whether he should say anything further. Kenneth Branagh he was not. "It's just...Roisin. She was near paralytic by the time we left. What happened, it's sad but if you saw her that night, I don't think you'd be shocked."

"You think it was an accident?"

Ciaran nodded.

"Natalie seems to think differently."

"She does," he agreed before shaking his head wearily. "C'mon. I'll bring you through to Natalie." He led Jacob through the lobby into a corridor and followed it until he reached a door marked *Studio A*.

"Did you know if Roisin was a drug user? Pills specifically." Jacob asked as Ciaran reached for the handle.

"Pills?" Ciaran echoed, surprised at the question. "No, I don't think so."

Jacob thanked him. Ciaran's story matched with what Natalie had already told him, although Roisin being wrote-off drunk was new information. He had imagined the event as an intimate soiree with wine, cheese and hearty back slaps rather than a full-on session.

Studio A was divided by a thick glass partition with Jacob on the side that held the recording and sound equipment. A young man seated in a swivel chair swung around as Jacob and Ciaran entered. He was young, somewhere in his mid-twenties with dark mahogany skin, jet black hair and a matching beard cut stylishly short.

Beyond the glass, Natalie was seated alone at a round wooden table, talking into a microphone. Jacob listened and realised it was an advert for a fitness app, a pre-recorded snippet that would be added to the main show during editing.

"Jacob Kincaid, Arjun Bano." Ciaran said, diverting Jacob's attention away from Natalie. The young man in the chair reached out a hand. Ciaran flicked a switch on the equipment next to Arjun and leaned forward to speak into the mic. "Natalie, Jacob Kincaid is here."

Natalie gave a thumbs-up in acknowledgement, set her headphones on the desk and walked over to join them in the small room. "Jesus." Her friendly smile curled as she got a proper look at Jacob. "You look awful."

"Thanks," he replied flatly. "I'm getting that a lot lately."

She held a hand to her mouth, not quite able to stop an embarrassed laugh. "Sorry, I didn't mean it like that. Is everything ok?"

"Yeah. Rough night's sleep."

"With that heat, tell me about it," Ciaran said over Natalie's shoulder. "I had to peel the bed sheet off of me at one point."

"Jacob, you look like you could do with a caffeine boost." Natalie said. "You want to speak to Ciaran and Arjun while I get the coffees in?"

"I've already spoken to Ciaran but if Arjun has the time?"

"Sure," Arjun replied. His tone was friendly, the accent pure West Belfast. Jacob waited until the others had left and kept the interview short. Arjun remembered little about the night, admitting that he was very much the worse for wear, but what he did recall backed up most of Ciaran's account.

"I thought I was going well but the last drink finished me off completely. I don't even remember getting home."

"Oh yeah? What was your poison?"

"Gin. Same as Roisin."

"Was she as stocious as you?"

"Worse. At least I didn't crash until the end. The drink was barely down Roisin's throat before she was topping up. I mean, I thought I was doing well but Roisin was lapping me like she was Usain Bolt."

"Usain Bolt was a short distance runner."

"Sorry?"

"What about Luke Fisher?"

Arjun clucked his tongue. "Arsehole."

"Not sad when Natalie let him go?"

"Not at all," Arjun said, folding his arms. Jacob nodded but didn't reply, pretending to make notes. He waited, letting the conversation lull, knowing Arjun would speak to combat the awkward silence. "To be fair, I used to get on ok with him," he offered after a few seconds.

"Oh yeah?" Jacob asked, keeping his tone conversational as he looked up from his notebook doodle. "What changed?"

Arjun opened his mouth to speak but stopped. "You'll need to ask Natalie."

Jacob tapped the notebook with his pen. "I'm hearing that a lot today."

Natalie returned to the studio a few minutes later with a round of Cappuccinos accompanied by a pretty woman in her early twenties. Her dark hair was tied into a messy bun. She wore thick glasses over a lightly freckled face and her sweater and jeans hugged themselves tightly to her figure in a way Jacob found rather pleasing. She smiled shyly as Natalie introduced her as Mairead Donaghy.

"Shall we give you the room?" Natalie asked, handing Jacob his coffee.

"Yeah, thanks. We won't be long. Just a few questions, if that's ok?"

Mairead shrugged lightly. "Sure."

He waited until the door had shut and Mairead seated herself. "I understand you were at the party and everyone was pretty far gone."

"Yeah. Well, apart from Natalie and Ciaran. The joys of being teetotal, he gets to be our designated driver."

"What about Natalie? Is she teetotal too?"

"Oh, no," Mairead laughed in a way that suggested Jacob was being ridiculous. "I think she wasn't originally planning on staying as late as she did."

"Why did she?"

"Luke and Roisin. We all knew about their fling and didn't think it was a big deal but as the night wore on he was becoming a bit much."

"In what way?"

"I dunno, just chancing his arm, you know? Too much in her space. I think Natalie ended up staying to make sure everyone left at the same time and then made sure Luke went home."

"Too much to drink?"

"Luke? Oh definitely."

"Sounds like a bit of a dick but maybe a bit harsh to fire him."

"Oh, he wasn't fired over that," said Mairead.

"No?"

"Natalie drove him home and he tried it on with her too. He wouldn't take no for an answer until she basically kicked him out of her car."

Ciaran and Arjun had been reluctant to spill the details of Luke Fisher's firing but Mairead, bless her, had no such qualms.

"Where does Natalie live?" Jacob asked.

"Um, somewhere over in East Belfast. Nice big house but I don't remember exactly where."

"You've been there?"

"Just once."

"Was Luke there too?"

"No. This wasn't long after I began working with the show, so a bit before Luke started."

Luke didn't know where Natalie lived but he knew where Roisin was. His pride had been hurt. Drink in, wits out and blood up. Hilden Mill to Jordanstown and back to Hilden Mill could be done in an hour or less.

Then all he had to do was pull off an impossible murder, make it up to look like an accident and escape from a locked fourth storey apartment.

"Ciaran thinks Roisin's death was accidental. What about you?"

She shrugged. "I try not to think about it." Her deep brown eyes turned sad. Jacob caught himself starting a second longer than he should. Seeming to notice, Mairead offered another shy smile.

"Is there anything else you can think of that I might not have already been told?"

She shook her head.

"Alright," Jacob said as he reached into his wallet and handed her a business card.

"Fancy," she said, examining the plain white card. "It must be such an exciting job. Does it ever get dangerous?"

"Absolutely. Someone sicced their Jack Russel on me just last week."

She laughed at the weak joke which emboldened Jacob enough to reach across and take the card. He scribbled his personal number down and handed it back. "If anything else comes to mind, give me a call."

Mairead took the card and looked it over. "Did Ciaran and Arjun get a card too?"

"No," Jacob admitted. "That's just for you. Even if you can't think of anything relevant to the case maybe we could still grab a drink sometime." He just about managed to finish the sentence without cringing. It had been longer than he cared to remember since he had asked a woman out and about the same amount of time since he had been shot down.

Mairead turned the card over twice and then pocketed it. "Ok." Her smile held but her tone suggested Jacob shouldn't hold his breath.

He found Natalie waiting in the corridor. "Sorted?" she asked.

"Sorted."

"Good. C'mon, we'll take my car."

Jacob waited until they were on the motorway and heading towards Lisburn. "Tell me about Luke Fisher."

"What about him?"

"Him and Roisin."

"He asked Roisin out after our first writing session

together. She said yes. Luke's a good-looking guy, keeps himself fit, so no big surprise. They dated for a bit before Roisin broke it off, the whole let's stay friends thing."

"And Luke took it bad?"

"He sent her a few texts afterwards, nothing too worrying but Roisin mentioned it to me and I told him firmly that I expected him to remain professional if he wanted to continue writing for the podcast. He sulked about the telling off for a bit but got over it. Then at the party he had too much to drink."

"So you stayed and made sure he went home?"

"Took him right to his front door. I assume Mairead told you what happened next. I love the girl, but she can't hold her water."

"Luke made his move and was told no."

"No and in no uncertain terms," said Natalie. "He didn't take it well."

"What do you mean, didn't take it well?"

"Hold your horses, my white knight," Natalie said, holding up her hand. "I didn't need a hero to ride in and rescue me. He threw a tantrum, that's all. Called me all the names under the sun and then got out. I phoned him first thing the next morning and told him he was no longer employed with the podcast."

"Have you heard from him since?"

"Twice. A nice message a minute or so after the phone call to tell me I was an ugly bitch."

"Charmer."

"And then the day after, somewhat more contrite. He was asking if Roisin's death was definitely accidental."

"He asked if the death was accidental? Didn't that strike you as suspicious?"

"Not especially. I don't think it was an accident either. Myself, Roisin, and Luke wrote the episodes together. We knew more than anyone what the Followers were capable of. He was probably freaked out, same as me."

"Did you tell him your thoughts?"

"No. I only told him what the police had concluded."

"Did he seem like a man with anger issues?"

"Not until that moment in my car. He kept it hidden but the way he turned so suddenly? Yeah, I'd say he has issues."

"Angry enough to kill?"

Natalie glanced across at him. "Luke?"

"Spurned man kills woman is hardly a leap."

"No, I know but it seems so...unlikely."

Jacob laughed. "If you say so, Miss Locked Room Mystery." Natalie conceded to his point with a tut and turned her focus back to the road. "Most murders are committed by someone known to the victim," Jacob continued. "I'm not saying he's a suspect but you have to admit, if something suspect did take place, he'd be someone we'd want to talk to."

Natalie nodded but didn't offer anything further.

"There's more. I talked to Arthur Dunwoody. Did you know Roisin had a brother?"

"No. She never mentioned any of her family really."

"He's a fire suppression engineer. That means-"

"-He installs systems that use gases to fight fires," Natalie cut in as if it were common knowledge. "But I thought you said it was unlikely Roisin could have been killed that way."

"It is," Jacob admitted, leaning back into his seat. "But not impossible."

There were no mouthy teenagers hanging around the car park when they arrived at Hilden Mill. In fact, there was hardly anybody in the complex judging by the lack of cars. It was a Thursday, the end of the working week was in sight for those not already on their holidays, and the continuing heat wave had seemingly enticed the residents towards the beaches and promenades of Bangor or Portrush.

"Just need to make a quick visit," Jacob said as Natalie parked.

The site manager's office was helpfully signposted.

They followed the directions and found it in a ground floor apartment.

The door was answered almost immediately by an overweight man well into his sixties. His hair was wispy white and his complexion ruddy and his brow creased as he took in the two strangers on his doorstep. "Yes?"

"Mr. Armstrong. I'm Jacob and this is Natalie. We're cousins of Roisin Dunwoody's."

"Yes?" he repeated.

"We're beginning to clear out Roisin's apartment but we noticed a couple of her personal effects are missing."

"Now listen here..."

"-Oh, I apologise," Jacob said, jumping in quickly. "We think they're still in the apartment. Most likely up in the attic."

"No," Armstrong said flatly.

"No?"

"There is no attic. It was never floored."

Jacob looked at his faux cousin as if this was an unexpected revelation. Natalie to her credit, did a credible job of looking suitably surprised. "I was under the impression there was access to the attic via a staircase."

Armstrong exhaled slowly. "Locked and barred. Has been since before anyone moved in." He made an effort to close the door and was stopped when Jacob stuck his foot against it. He was getting rather proficient at the move.

"Maybe Roisin borrowed the key?"

"No." Armstrong appeared to be fond of the word. "We don't loan keys. All we bloody need, some silly bastard falling through the ceiling and suing us. Now move your damn foot."

"What was that about?" Natalie asked, after Armstrong slammed his door closed.

"Just crossing the I's and dotting the T's," Jacob replied. Peter Scanlon was right. Armstrong was brusque, sharp, and not a person of interest.

They used the card Natalie had swiped to get into Roisin's building and this time took the lift to the fourth floor. As Natalie turned the key to the apartment, the door across the corridor opened and a woman poked her head out. "Oh, hello," she said. "Are you friends of Roisin's?" She was in her early-fifties, tall and fit, with tanned skin weathered by the sun and the good-natured cheeriness of a person Jacob would cross the street to avoid.

"Yes, we are," Natalie answered, half in, half out the door to Roisin's apartment. "I think we met briefly. On the day..."

"Oh yes, of course!" The woman said quickly before shaking her head. Awful business." She looked at Jacob with sympathy.

"Awful," Jacob agreed rather lamely.

"So sad to think of the place lying empty."

Jacob held out his hand. "Mrs..."

"Jameison." Her grip was strong, the skin of her palm rough and calloused. "Helen Jameison."

"Jacob Kincaid. Were you and Roisin close?"

"Oh no, not really. Bit of an age gap and she kept to herself. Always said good morning or hello though. Some of the people in here wouldn't so much as look at you if you tripped down the stairs and landed at their feet...." She trailed off and Jacob was about to take his chance to wish her a good day. "I suppose I should have known something was up when she didn't appear after the fire alarm went off."

"Fire alarm?" Jacob asked.

"The night before the police found her. Half two in the morning and the bloody fire alarm goes off. Scunnered I was, even if I don't sleep the best anymore."

Jacob could feel Natalie practically vibrating beside him. "There was a fire in the building?"

"Oh no. A false alarm. Well, so the others were saying. I think it was one of the little shits who live downstairs playing a prank. They play with matches, set fires. I've heard they go and burn stuff down by the tow path."

Jacob remembered the scorch marks on the wall next to the grille that blocked the loft staircase. Evidently some of the kids in the building used the space as a hang out spot. "How long did the alarm go on for?"

"Fifteen minutes or so, I'd say. Had to wake Cecil up to reset the thing. He lives over in another building and took his sweet time dragging himself out of his pit."

"And it was loud?"

"Loud enough to wake the dead." Helen Jameison's face fell. "Or not."

It took another two minutes before they were able to extract themselves from Mrs. Jameison. Natalie waited until they stepped into Roisin's apartment before she grabbed Jacob by the arm. "You must be thinking what I'm thinking."

"That the alarm was a diversion?" Jacob replied, guessing Natalie's train of thought rather than stating his own. "Arthur Dunwoody told me last night that the post mortem examination noted bruising on Roisin's chest."

Natalie slapped his shoulder eagerly. "You kept that quiet! It makes sense, doesn't it? The killer sets the alarm off. Roisin comes to the door believing it's genuine and her killer forces his way inside."

Jacob clicked his tongue but said nothing.

"What?"

"It's not a bad theory," Jacob began.

"But?"

"But. It all comes back to the locked room problem. Same with every idea we come up with."

Natalie sighed. "The fire alarm going off is suspicious," she said, her voice taking on a hint of impatience.

"Sure," Jacob agreed. It was one more detail to add to the list of things that weren't quite right. The fire alarm going off, the open safe, the missing phone and computer. He walked to the centre of the flat and stood still, taking the place in once again.

Natalie moved beside him. "If you had to go with the theory that the killer used the fire alarm as a distraction and killed Roisin, what would be your next step in logic?"

"He could have left but chose not to. Either because leaving the bolt on the door unlocked would draw suspicion or because the fire alarm would have brought everyone else out of their apartments, so he waited, worried about being spotted. But it was late, as soon as it was declared a false alarm everyone would be straight back to their beds."

"So he had the chance to go, but didn't," said Natalie. "He wanted to stage it to look like an accident. Leaving the door unlocked would raise too many questions, especially for someone as security conscious as Roisin."

"Which meant he stayed in the apartment all night and most of the following day. What time did you arrive?"

"I don't know exactly. Maybe around three?"

"And you left when the police closed the scene?"

"Yeah. I ducked out for an hour or so to get something to eat but came back in plenty of time before the scene closed."

"So the killer, if there was a killer, would have waited until the apartment was clear and slipped out. Jacob walked back into the main bedroom and slid open the walk-in wardrobe. There was certainly enough space for a fully grown man to hide. "The police checked here?"

"Yes."

"You're sure?"

"I watched them myself. The wardrobe and under the bed."

Sergeant O'Connor had been quick to defend the first officers who responded but Natalie should not have been allowed to remain in the apartment. Instead, she had stayed long enough to not only swipe the keycard to the building but to observe the officer's search of the property. Was O'Connor lying to cover up his colleagues' mistake or was he simply unaware? Jacob guessed it was almost certainly the latter but also doubted O'Connor would have told him if it were the former.

"Alright, let's see if we can find these calling cards. Have a look over there," he said, pointing to the cabinet beside the sofa as he went into the kitchen and started on the drawers.

"Think I got them," Natalie called over to him after a quick rummage through the cabinet. She handed Jacob a small stack of cards, each with a PSNI logo on the top right corner.

He flicked through them quickly. The cards had been ordered by date, oldest to newest, and each officer who had attended had provided a reference number for each incident; the year, month and day followed by a unique six-digit number. They had also provided their name, an e-mail address or a work phone number, their home station, and the offence they were investigating.

"Twelfth of April; suspicious circumstances, Sixteenth of May, misuse of telecommunications, Twenty ninth of May; misuse of telecommunications and harassment, First of June; suspicious circumstances, Fifth of June; Intimidation, Twelfth of June; suspicious circumstances, Nineteenth of June, criminal damage."

"That was when her tires were slashed," Natalie said, as she watched Jacob.

"Escalation." Jacob leafed through the last two cards. "Two more suspicious circumstances."

"What does that mean?"

"Pretty much as it sounds. Something suspicious was reported but there was no identified criminal offence to go along with it. You said Roisin had seen men lurking about?"

"Yes. Wouldn't that go down as stalking or harassment?"

"Only if there was any evidence it was the same person, or on behalf of that person." Jacob flicked through the cards idly. "I'll see what they can tell us. At least one of the officers who attended is bound to get back to me."

Natalie nodded. "And then?"

"Speak to McKinstry, Fisher and Liam Dunwoody."

He walked over to where Natalie had found the contact cards, intending to put them back and then stopped. "Did you see this?" he asked, lifting another card out from the cabinet. It was a simple design; the top half of the card was black with the name of the business and its West Belfast address in white font. The bottom half was a green circuit board design.

"No. What is it?"

"*Compute Yourself*," he said as he read the title. "Computer repair, data backup, virus removal." He held the card out to her. "With my keen investigative mindset, I'd say I have a fair idea where the missing computer is."

Natalie took the card before fixing him with a measured look.

"What?"

She shrugged. "I don't know. You're hard to get a read on, Jacob. Sometimes I think you're on board with this and sometimes I think you're just humouring me."

"You're paying me to be on board. I'll track down and bottom out every lead as far as I can. I'm a professional. Or so I tell myself."

Natalie gave a half nod. "Fair enough." She playfully tapped his nose with the card. "You think it's worth following-up on?"

"Not like we have much else to go on."

"No," Natalie agreed, scanning her eyes over the flat. "What are we missing?" she asked, echoing Jacob's earlier question to himself.

"Beats me," Jacob said. He sauntered lazily over to the long living room windows and looked down. The idea of someone lugging canisters of chemicals or gas up all the way up a ladder seemed suddenly absurd.

He turned away with a tut. "There's no trap door, no holes in the wall. No window big enough to squeeze through and no drainpipe to shimmy down. A trained ape didn't scale the building and no one shoved a snake through the vent."

He glanced over to the kitchen. Natalie tried to follow his line of sight. "What is it?"

"Nothing. It's just..." He went over to the kitchen space and reached for the vent. As before, the grille came away with only a slight tug. Slightly higher than his head height, Jacob had to stand on tip toes to reach into the space. He felt dust and dirt and then his finger brushed something solid and smooth. Stretching, he tried to reach but his fingers couldn't get purchase on the surface of the unseen object.

As if reading his thoughts, Natalie fetched a chair from the kitchen table. He took her offered hand to help balance himself and reached his hand into the vent again and pulled out an old tablet.

He blew some of the dust off the screen. "You recognise it?"

"No," she said excitedly as Jacob handed it to her. "That was some impressive work."

"Luck," Jacob said, attempting to sound modest. "I should have checked the vent properly the first time when the grille came away so easily."

Natalie turned the tablet over, examining it. It was an older model and had no battery life left when she tried to power it on. "Good hiding place if you're trying to keep it out of the wrong hands."

Jacob brushed his palms on his jeans. "Isn't that what the safe is for?"

"The empty and unlocked safe?"

"Fair point."

They searched the apartment for a power lead without success. "I think I have one at my office," Jacob said after they had given up the hunt. "I knew keeping a collection in some random drawer would pay off eventually."

"Then let's go," Natalie said, buoyed by the discovery.

Mrs. Jameison was standing by her door, waiting for them as they stepped into the corridor. Both offered a friendly nod as they passed.

"Your friend will be glad," she called after them "He doesn't seem like the patient type."

They both stopped. "Friend?" Natalie asked, turning back to the older woman.

"The young fella waiting in the car. I caught him loitering out here. Think I scared him half to death. Said he was getting bored of waiting for you two."

Natalie glanced at Jacob who signalled for her to hang back as he jogged down the corridor. He reached the top of the staircase just in time to see a shadow cross the lobby and disappear.

# 9

"Somewhere in his twenties or thirties, I think. Clean shaven, brown hair, Um....let's see, what else?"

"How was he built, Mrs. Jameison?" Jacob prompted. He'd taken the steps back up to the fourth floor two at a time and had immediately, and breathlessly, began to ask Roisin's nosey neighbour for a description of who she had been talking to.

"Stocky?" Mrs. Jameison offered as if unsure herself. "Not too muscly but not skinny."

"Height?"

"Average."

Jacob puffed his cheeks and glanced at Natalie. They certainly weren't going to pick someone out of an ID parade with Mrs. Jameison's descriptions.

The trip back towards Belfast was made in silence, both pondering who was watching them and why. "Security maybe?" Natalie suggested, sounding in no way convinced.

Jacob shook his head. "You'd assume Mrs. Jameison would recognized him and he wouldn't have needed to have lied to her about what he was doing."

He leaned back into the seat. Half an hour ago he had thought the investigation was nothing more than him pissing in the wind. Now, a slow shiver crept up his spine. Not fear, but excitement. It had been a once familiar sensation. The anticipation that came with a sudden crack in an investigation, a previously unseen avenue opening up, even if he didn't know where it led, at least not yet.

They came off the motorway at Stockman's Lane and took Kennedy Way up to the Andersonstown Road, finding a parking space outside Compute Yourself.

The only occupant in the shop was a man in his fifties, seated behind the counter reading a newspaper. He looked at Jacob and Natalie over his glasses.

"Hi there," Jacob said. "I was looking to pick up my cousin's computer. "She left it in a couple of weeks ago."

"Alright, no worries." The man stood slowly. "What's the name?"

"Dunwoody."

He snorted. "A couple of weeks ago? Couple of months more like." He left the counter and went into the back room, returning with a high-end PC chassis that he set on the counter. "I told your cousin if she didn't collect it in time, it meant more charges for safe storage."

"That's fine," Natalie said, producing a debit card from her handbag. "How much?"

"With the storage, the security programs and the factory reset, let's call it an even two hundred."

Natalie's hand froze. "Factory reset?"

"As requested."

"Why?" Jacob asked. The man shrugged. "What was on it?"

"Not much as far as I could tell but some people don't feel comfortable wiping their PC themselves. Worried they might miss something."

"The security programs? Did she say what they were for?"

The man frowned. "Isn't that something you could ask your cousin?"

By the time they made it back to Jacob's office, Helen had already left for the evening. The coffee shop was still open for business but Helen had locked the metal security gate leading up to Kincaid Investigations.

Jacob it and the main door, before setting Roisin's

computer down on Helen's desk.

Natalie followed him across to the small kitchen and watched as he began to dig for a power lead in a cluttered drawer.

"Help yourself to a coffee or tea."

"I'm good," she replied diplomatically, spying the instant swill Jacob kept for his clients.

"Something stronger? I've a bottle of Bushmills in the top drawer of my desk."

"The Private Eye with a bottle of whiskey in the top drawer. That's a bit banal, isn't it?"

"Only if I break out a Jazz record and start pontificating about it. Bonus cliché points if I start referring to you as a Dame." By now he had managed to untangle one lead from the mess in the drawer but found it didn't fit the tablet.

"Ah, you're from the classic school of gumshoe I see. No doubt counting down the days to Autumn so you can break out the trench coat."

"Exactly. Nothing better than lighting a cigarette in a dark alley and looking world weary."

"All you need now is a femme fatale."

Jacob looked up from his search of the drawer. "That's you isn't it, Miss Amato?"

"Me? No. I'm the mysterious client leading you down a dark path of danger and deceit." She smiled, apparently enjoying the silly banter.

"Sounds awful," Jacob said, moving to a second drawer.

"It does but you'll be equipped with enough laconic quips to see you through."

Jacob laughed as he continued his rummage. "Looks like we're in business," he said, coming up with a lead that slotted into the tablet's power socket. With the lead still attached, he hurried into his office and plugged it into a free socket. He powered the device on and waited. "Hmmm...shit."

He could sense Natalie deflate beside him. There was nothing on the device beside a few basic apps. It looked like everything that hadn't come pre-installed with the tablet had been wiped. "I knew it was too good to be true." She gave Jacob's desk a light but frustrated slap.

Jacob clicked on the sole folder on the home screen to find it held only a single file. When opened, all it contained was a single line of gibberish:

**RD2403!@RD148£RD0602**.

"A code?" Natalie asked, leaning in closer.

"I guess, but for what?"

She scrunched her features. "The computer?"

"The computer was wiped and reset. Why password protect it?" He took another look at the jumbled characters. "RD for Roisin Dunwoody?"

"And the rest, Mr. Turing?"

"Beats me."

Natalie sighed. "Same. Maybe I should take it home? Work on making sense of it."

"Up to you. It might be safer here though." Jacob nodded to the safe built in to the wall behind him. "Whatever this is, Roisin wanted to keep it hidden."

Natalie nodded slowly. "Alright," she said after a few seconds of deliberation. "But let me snap a picture on my phone." She did so, before glancing at her Breitling. "I need to get going."

"Hot date?"

She scoffed. "Yeah right."

Jacob removed the power lead from the tablet. "I'll need to get Luke Fisher's address off you."

"Sure. Is he going to be your next stop?"

"Tomas McKinstry first. But depending on how it shakes out, I might try and get with Fisher as well."

"Tomorrow?"

"A good a time as any."

"I'm free. I'll go with you."

"If you like. With the amount of work you're putting in, you could have saved yourself some money and done the investigation yourself."

She winked and tapped the face of her watch. "Meet

you here tomorrow at ten?"

"Sounds good."

Natalie said goodbye and closed the door to his office behind her. Jacob waited a beat before he picked up the tablet and had only reached the safe when he heard her scream.

He bolted towards the sound, flinging the door open to find Natalie struggling with a person dressed head to toe in black. The figure had forced a rag over Natalie's face while she fought desperately to free herself.

A primal fear took hold of Jacob as the figure's attention snapped towards him. Their features were hidden by a wool balaclava. White thread, stark against the black cloth, had been clumsily stitched into the mask, pulling the loose material tight around the face, leaving only tiny windows for a mouth and a pair of dark, predatory eyes. The result was a grotesque and unnatural sight designed to elicit a particular reaction. It was effective. Jacob took an unconscious step back and before he could think, the masked man was on him. Natalie groaned as the figure shoved her bonelessly to the floor.

Jacob took a hard punch to the ribs and only just managed to get a clumsy arm up to block a follow-up shot to his jaw but was rewarded with another punch to his unprotected midsection. He stumbled as the figure forced their attack. A hard thrust kick caught him square in the chest, flinging him back into his office, crashing down against the edge of the desk. The tablet fell from his grasp and clattered next to him as sharp pain stabbed through his upper back.

The man was on him. Small and junkie thin, but freakishly fast and much stronger than his frame suggested. Jacob kicked out, catching his attacker on the shin hard enough to cause a hiss of pain and a step backward. Jacob jumped up, trying to close the distance and take the man down with his long out of practise Judo, but he too quick, breaking free of Jacob's grip on his jacket with a quick spin of his heel as he pivoted away.

Jacob persisted. Head down, he lunged forward and managed to grab a handful of jacket only to receive a stinging punch to his left eye he hadn't seen coming. He stumbled, dropping to one knee.

His vision was blurred and he could just about hear the footsteps approach over the ringing in his head. The man took hold of his sweater as Jacob fingers brushed against the dropped tablet. He fumbled for the device as his attacker reached forward with the same rag he had used on Natalie. Jacob swung a desperate shot. The masked man grunted as the tablet screen bounced off his skull and spun out of Jacob's grip, clattering on the floor.

With his adrenaline shooting straight to the moon, Jacob vaulted to his feet as the stranger took an unsteady step backwards. The decision of fight or flight had been decided for him and now Jacob wanted to finish it.

The man, maybe trying to work out what he had been hit with, or still half loopy from the shot, had his attention on the tablet. Jacob planted his right leg and swung with his left fist. At the last second the man turned and tried to dodge the blow but only succeeded in catching the punch on his temple. He lost his balance, falling to a knee and then flopping onto his backside.

Before Jacob could think about hitting him again, the man scooted backwards, rolled over his shoulder and in a display of athleticism Jacob would have appreciated at any other time, sprang to his feet and bolted for the open door.

Jacob ran after him but a moan from Natalie as he reached the staircase, snapped him out of it. He hurried next to where she was lying. She groaned again, putting one hand on her head.

The masked figure had dropped the rag next to her. Jacob picked it up and held it well away from his body. "Jesus!" He coughed, getting a faint whiff of whatever the fabric had been soaked in. "You ok?"

"I think so," she said slowly. Her voice was calm but her speech slurred. "I think I passed out."

"I'm not surprised," Jacob said, his breathing heavy as he fought to keep his voice level. "Whatever is on this is toxic."

"Who...Who was that?"

"Your guess is as good as mine."

She sat herself up, waving away Jacob's assistance. He fetched a glass of water from the kitchen. By the time he returned she was standing, using Helen's desk to steady herself.

"Maybe I should call an ambulance?"

"No, I'm fine. I think."

He held out the glass of water with a shaking hand. Natalie waved it away. "Let me take you to hospital."

She shook her head firmly. "No, I'll be alright."

"Would you have a seat at least?" Jacob pulled out the chair from Helen's desk and Natalie sat in it heavily. He set the glass of water on the desk and then moved across the office to pick up the tablet.

The screen had been obliterated by the sudden, violent contact with the masked man's cranium. Jacob tried to turn the device on without success. He tried it again with the power lead connected and got the same result. "Shit." He walked into his office and placed the tablet and rag in the safe and locked them away.

"Pounds to peanuts, that guy was the same one who was spying on us at Hilden Mill," he said, returning to Natalie.

She was resting her head in her hands but looked up as Jacob spoke and nodded weakly in agreement. "And was after the tablet," Jacob continued. "But why? For the code?" Natalie still didn't reply. "I guess the post mortem can wait." He moved next to her. "You sure you're ok?"

"I'm sure," she said with a tired smile that suggested she was anything but. "I think I just want to get home."

Images of pedestrians getting ploughed down by an out-of-control Audi SUV flashed through Jacob's mind.

"I'll drive."

Natalie didn't argue. Whatever chemical had been on the rag had sapped it out of her. She took the offered hand to aid her down the narrow staircase and leaned against the wall as she waited for Jacob to lock the security gate.

She had parked on Montgomery Street, one road over and was able to make the short walk under her own power although Jacob stayed close in case she keeled over. She handed him the keys to her car and got in the passenger side. As he turned on the ignition he considered whether he should just drive her to the hospital anyway.

"Straight home," she said, reading his thoughts.

Home for Natalie was in the East of the city. A quiet, leafy road called Cairnburn Gardens in the fashionable and affluent suburbs of Belmont. Jacob had kept a close watch on the rearview mirror throughout the drive but was satisfied no one had followed them as he pulled into the driveway of Natalie's house; a large, detached Edwardian style construction, sitting well back from the road and bordered by high hedges on either side.

"I'm in the wrong line of work," Jacob said as he parked the car in front of the impressive house.

"How will you get back?" Natalie asked as she unbuckled her seat belt.

"Call a taxi."

She nodded; her eyes heavy. "I'll pay for it."

"Don't be daft," Jacob said as he got out and hurried around to her side.

This time Natalie declined the offered hand. "I can make it."

Jacob was entirely unconvinced of that and followed close behind as she walked to her front door, laboriously taking the three stone steps leading up to it.

She reached for the handle. To Jacob's surprise, the door was already unlocked. He was pondering that as Natalie let out a deep sigh, half a second before her knees buckled from under her.

Reflexively, he jumped forward, only just catching her as she collapsed. They landed in an awkward tangle of limbs, teetering on the edge of the lip of the top step, only prevented from both going arse over head by Jacob's hand shooting out and bracing against the lower step.

With one leg pinned under his own body and the other by Natalie's inert form, Jacob grunted with the effort of manoeuvring the limp body to a more upright position. "Natalie?"

She didn't answer. Her eyes were closed tightly and her head lolled against his chest. "Natalie!" Jacob tried again, with slightly more urgency, shaking her by the shoulder. "Natalie!"

"Mum?"

Jacob turned his head to find a rather alarmed teenage boy looking down at him and the unconscious woman he was holding on his front door step.

# 10

"Uh…"

"What happened?" The boy asked, wide eyes flitting between Jacob and Natalie.

"She fainted." Jacob said, giving himself a quick mental slap. The sudden appearance of the kid had caught him by surprise.

"Bring her in here!" The boy said, pushing the front door open and hurrying into the house.

Jacob reached under Natalie's legs and placed his free hand around her back. He tried to stand and almost toppled backwards down the steps. He gritted his teeth as he tried again and this time succeeded in lifting the unconscious woman off the ground. Natalie's slender frame was considerably heavier at dead weight and he just about made it to a standing position.

Arms straining with the effort of his clumsy cradle carry, Jacob followed the boy into the hallway and then through into a large, modern living room. With his arms about to give out, he dropped Natalie as gently as he could onto a long corner sofa.

The boy crowded his shoulder as Jacob knelt beside her. "Can you grab me a damp cloth and a glass of water?" The youngster complied without question, scooting out of the room. Jacob took a cushion and placed it under Natalie's head before wiping the sweat from his brow with the back of his hand.

"What made her faint?" The boy asked as he returned, handing him the cloth.

"Well, it's a hot day," Jacob said, thinking quickly. "The heat probably got to her." And the chloroform. But he thought it better to leave that part unsaid. The kid seemed to accept the explanation and hurried off to fetch the water.

Jacob lightly pressed the damp cloth on Natalie's forehead and was rewarded with a slight groan. Her eyes stayed closed. He attempted to loosen a button on her shirt with his free hand and fumbled clumsily for a few seconds until it fell away.

"What are you doing?"

He glanced up from the task to find Natalie looking directly at him, dark hazel eyes scrunched in a mixture of confusion and admonitory.

"Loosening your top," Jacob explained quickly, feeling like a peeping tom caught in the act. "Letting you get some air."

"You fainted, mum," the boy said, hustling back into the room with a large glass of water. "Right at the front door."

Jacob nodded quickly, thankful for the corroborating account before stopping. "Wait...Mum?"

"Fainted." Natalie repeated as if suddenly remembering. She sank back into the sofa, her embarrassment clear.

"Sorry, you did say mum?"

In his panic at the front door the word hadn't registered with him. Slowly it dawned on Jacob that he recognised the boy from the pictures on Natalie's social media. He had assumed him to be a younger cousin or brother. Natalie had mentioned a son before but Jacob had assumed a boy of primary school age. This kid was as tall as Jacob, gangly and awkward as only teenage boys could be. Jacob tried to compute his age against Natalie's but the maths didn't quite add up.

"Take this," the boy said, handing her the glass, before helping his mother into a sitting position.

Feeling like an intruder, Jacob quietly stepped out of the room to give them space.

Ten minutes later, he was standing alone in the kitchen. He could hear Natalie and the boy talking in the hallway. She entered alone a few seconds later one hand on her head. "Sorry about all this, Jacob."

"It's fine. You've had a stressful hour or two." He watched as Natalie went to her fridge, lifted two bottles of beer and held one out to him. *Peroni*. "Well, it would be rude to say no."

Natalie removed the caps and passed one to Jacob. She rested the cold bottle against her head while Jacob pushed his against the swelling beside his left eye. She offered a rueful smile. "The state of us." Jacob managed a grunt of amusement. "Thanks for helping me," she said, sheepishly, brushing a lock of hair from her brow.

"Any time." Jacob winced as he removed the bottle from his cheek. "You feeling ok?"

"My pride took a bit of a battering, but I'll survive."

"How's..." Jacob wasn't sure he caught the boy's name and gestured in the vague direction of the hallway.

"Dillon? He's fine. Got a little spooked."

"How old is he?"

"He turned fourteen in May."

"Fourteen," Jacob echoed.

"What?"

"Nothing. I know you mentioned a son before but I didn't figure him to be a teenager. How old are you?"

Natalie crossed her arms. "Are you going to ask how much I weigh next?"

Jacob suddenly felt himself gagging on his shoe leather "No, sorry...It's just, you look so young to have a fourteen-year-old kid."

Her expression took on a wicked grin. "Relax, I'm messing with you. Good save though."

"Thanks," Jacob took another sip of beer to hide his rapidly reddening cheeks.

"Thirty-six."

"Oh, you're-"

"Thirty-six, that's right."

Jacob had guessed Natalie to be around his age, perhaps a bit younger and certainly not four years older. "You had him young."

"I married young. Straight out of Uni. Dillon came along the year after."

"Is Dillon's dad from here too?"

"London."

"Is he still over there now?"

Natalie looked away. "No," she said. "No, Dillon's father passed."

Jacob felt his red cheeks go cold in an instant. "Fuck. Sorry. I shouldn't have..."

"-It's fine," Natalie said quickly, waving away any attempt at a clumsy apology. "I get it a lot. Single mother, still quite young, no ring on the finger. Most people assume divorce." She shrugged her shoulders. "Car accident. Twelve years ago. You accept it, eventually, but you forget where the time goes sometimes."

Jacob nodded and couldn't think of anything of use to say so he kept quiet. They lapsed into a silence mercifully broken when Natalie slapped the marble kitchen island.

"Enough morbidity," she said, the cheeriness a little too forced. "We're onto something now. If the tablet doesn't prove it the creep in your office certainly does."

"We've turned the corner," Jacob agreed, still utterly mortified but thankful for the change of topic. "Problem is, I don't know on what. We find the tablet with the code, next thing we know, you're getting drugged by some guy with his own DIY chemistry set."

Everything had happened so fast he hadn't the time to process any of it. The tablet in the vent was weird. As was the wiped computer. By themselves, strange quirks in a strange investigation. The man spying on them at Hilden Mill and the attack in his office was something altogether more tangible. And dangerous.

Jacob rubbed at his chin. "Before we make too many assumptions, we should maybe consider another possible angle."

"Which is?"

"Stalker? Someone like you, I assume you attract a fair whack of weirdos."

Natalie side eyed him. "Someone like me?"

Jacob was sure Natalie knew perfectly well what he meant. "An attractive woman. Successful, with a decent profile on social media. You're bound to get attention from a few creeps."

"Sure, but you can say that about any woman with a degree of fame."

"Fair.

But you haven't been getting anything inappropriate or concerning?"

"No," Natalie replied after thinking for a few seconds. "Nothing that would suggest jumping me with...whatever that was? Chloroform?"

"Or ether maybe." He shrugged. Jacob's chemistry knowledge was rudimentary at best.

"So, you think the man in your office was the same person Mrs. Jameison was talking to?"

If not, a partner in crime...." He said, before trailing off.

"What?"

"Someone with access to chemicals strong enough to render a person almost unconscious and the knowledge to use them?

"Liam Dunwoody?" She pushed her tongue against her cheek as she considered it. "But why? The tablet?"

"That's the only thing I can think of. Roisin took precautions to hide it so there must be some value to it." Jacob set his beer down on the island and perched himself on one of the tall wooden stools. "Thing is, we have no idea what the code is for."

"Bank account? Some online profile?"

"But why hide it in such an awkward place?" He began to peel the label from the beer bottle. "It's all linked. I just don't know how yet."

Natalie leaned against the island next to Jacob. She

109

was still pale from the effects of whatever had been used on her.

"The attack screams rush job," Jacob continued. "He was listening in on us at Hilden Mill, knew we got something but Mrs. Jameison spooks him before he tries anything." He paused to take another swig of beer. "But why jump you at the office if he knows I'm there too? Why not wait until you're walking back to your car?"

"Because he doesn't know who has the tablet. If he goes after me and I don't have it, you could be anywhere by the time he realises."

Jacob nodded. "That makes sense."

Natalie frowned. "Where is it now?"

"The safe in my office, like I said."

"And it'll be ok there?"

"The office is pretty secure," Jacob replied, knowing he wasn't really answering her question. His grandfather had installed the metal security door and barred the windows with wrought iron when the troubles were in full swing. Jacob had never seen fit to remove either. Holdovers from bad old days, best forgotten but which still served a purpose when needed.

"There's something else bothering you."

"There is," Jacob admitted. "And I don't think you're going to like it." He waited until she motioned for him to continue. "We were followed."

"Yeah, I got that."

"Not from Hilden Mill," said Jacob. "Think about it. How would someone know we were there unless they tailed us?"

"So they followed us from the studio?"

"At least. Could be they followed me there and then saw us jump in your car."

Natalie went to touch the bezel of her watch but caught herself. "Who knows about your investigation?" It was the obvious question.

"Helen, Arthur Dunwoody, Sergeant O'Connor, Peter and Catherine Scanlon, and my mate, Michael."

Jacob saw her brow quirk at the last name. "He's a peeler."

"So you think one of them has talked?"

"Helen or Michael? No way. O'Connor? I don't see it. The Scanlon's have no link to the case..." He stopped, thinking about the strange reaction he had got from the husband and wife after mentioning the Follower's while in their office.

"What?" Natalie asked. So Jacob told her. "That was...ill advised," she offered once he had finished.

"Well, what about Ciaran, or Arjun or Mairead?" Jacob replied, feeling suddenly defensive. "I know you said you like the girl, but discrete she is not. Or word could have got back to the Followers or whoever weeks ago that you were looking into Roisin's death. You said you thought you saw strange men lurking about the street. Maybe it wasn't paranoia."

Natalie's look of alarm caused Jacob an immediate flush of guilt. "Chances are, they were following me," he added quickly. "I'm the professional you've hired, after all. Either way, it's time to get the police involved."

"You think that's wise?"

"Absolutely. This isn't Hardy Boys and Nancy Drew. Someone forcibly drugged you and then tried to beat seven shades of shit out of me. We need to report it."

"Alright. I'll call them tomorrow. Not sure I can face it tonight."

"You can tell them I kept the rag. They'll be looking a statement off me anyway."

As he spoke, Dillon entered the kitchen, glanced briefly in Jacob's direction, and made a beeline for the kitchen cabinets. After the furore of Natalie's fainting on the doorstep had died down, the boy had clammed up, growing a good deal shyer in Jacob's presence.

"None of that," Natalie said sharply as her son reached for the cupboard. "I'm about to cook dinner. Speaking of which," she turned back to Jacob and tapped her watch. "It's getting late. You must be famished."

"Oh, no. I'm grand," Jacob lied as he stood.

"You'll stay for dinner." It was a statement rather than a question and the tone put an end to any protestations. Jacob sat back down.

The food, when it came, was simple but delicious serving of pasta with cherry tomatoes and cloves. Natalie opened a bottle of red and the three of them ate around the kitchen island. Dillon kept his eyes on his food the entire meal and asked to be excused immediately after finishing. He hurried away after sticking his plate and cutlery in the dishwasher.

"Seems like a good kid."

"He is," Natalie smiled. "Not a great conversationalist, as you might have picked up on."

"Making the most of the summer holidays?"

"Not at all. I think he's looking forward to going back to school."

Jacob made a face. "Gross."

"Right?"

They both laughed. Good company and good food. It'd been a while since Jacob had found himself in such a situation and he had missed it dearly. With the dinner finished, he felt that he should make his excuses and go, not wanting overstay his welcome. But another part of him told him to stay, enjoy the companionship of someone who wasn't family, employee, or former colleague.

Natalie topped up his glass, delaying any immediate thoughts about an exit. "And what school did you go to? And if you say the school of hard knocks, you may get out the door right now."

"I only skirt the line of complete walking cliché," Jacob replied as he raised the glass. "I was a Methody boy."

"Ah, I was wondering about that stick up your ass. Explains a lot."

"How about you?"

"St Dominics."

"On the Falls?"

"You know it?"

"Only from driving past when I worked over in the West."

"Right. Your mysterious past as a police officer."

"Not so mysterious. I did a few years response in West Belfast and then moved across to Major Crimes as a Detective and then packed it in."

"Not a lot of police pack it in over here. It's a job for life for most."

"Most but not for me." Natalie studied him for a second as if deciding to accept his answer. "How about Uni?" he asked, jumping in.

"University of London. Goldsmiths. You?"

"I managed a year of Law at Queens before I dropped out to join the police."

She whistled. "A Law degree from Queens is nothing to be sniffed at. Why the change?"

"You mean why switch from a future of nice suits and fancy cars to wrestle around in the gutter with some drugged-up house breaker?" She nodded and he paused to consider the question. "I wasn't doing it for me. The law degree, I mean. Plus, I thought if I joined the cops I could make a bit of a difference. Wanting to do some good, you know?"

"What were you saying about being a walking cliché?"

His mouth quirked with the ghost of a smile. There was a lot more to it, none of which he wanted to cover. "How about you?" he asked instead. "What made you make the change from newspaper reporter to podcaster?"

She pointed a finger at him. "And best-selling author."

"And best-selling author."

She rested her chin on her hand. "After Nick passed, I tried to give it a go in London but both of his parents had predeceased him. My friends over there were still young, no responsibilities, hardly any had children yet. I was lonely, so I made the move back to Northern

113

Ireland. Not an easy choice but I thought it best for me and Dillon."

Jacob motioned around the kitchen probably close to half the size of his whole apartment. "Seemed to work out ok."

Her smile was sad. "It did. I lost some of my passion for my work. I'm not sure when. The change from Fleet Street to Belfast was what I put it down to, but now I'm not so sure. Like you said, it worked out well and the important thing is, Dillon is happy here and we have good family support."

"You're close with your folks then?"

"I am. We're Italian on my father's side, in case the name didn't give it away. Big get-togethers, family dinners at least one Sunday a month, all that. We go out to Florence every couple of years too. That's where my grandparents came from."

"From Florence to Belfast?"

"Nonna and Nonno moved over in the fifties. Before the place went to hell. Nonno got rich by opening a chain of ice cream shops.

"Bold move for a place where the temperature only hits twenty degrees twice a year."

"He was a bold man," she said, her expression wistful. "I miss him. How about you, Jacob? Are you close with your family?"

"Some," he said neutrally.

"Never married?"

He shook his head. "Engaged once but we broke it off. Well, she broke it off."

"What happened?" Natalie asked, before holding up both hands. "Sorry! That was pretty intrusive."

"It's fine," Jacob said. "She was a solicitor. We met at Queens. Stayed friends after I left and started dating a few years after that. She was a rapid climber on the career ladder. Hated that I never went for promotion. She could just about tolerate slumming it with a basic peeler but she was never going to settle with someone with such apparently low prospects as a private eye."

"Well, she can go to hell."

Jacob smirked. "Yeah. She can."

He had come back from his final meeting at PSNI headquarters to find Catherine's bags already packed. Four years later, it was only the loss of his career that he mourned, but the memory of watching the woman who supposedly loved him load suitcases into the boot of her car still left a bitter taste.

"It was all about perception," Jacob said, after taking a long drink. "How people saw her."

"Sounds like you had a narrow escape."

He nodded as he glanced to the bay window that overlooked Natalie's large, and well-maintained back garden. It was the sort of place he'd have once imagined himself in, relaxing after a long day at the office with a gaggle of kids and his better half. Dusk was giving way to night and with it descended a certain melancholy for a past life he had never known.

He decided he could no longer press on Natalie's generous hospitality. His taxi was outside less than ten minutes later.

"I'll call around tomorrow morning, after I speak to the police," Natalie said as she walked him to the door. "We can decide how we're going to attack this."

Jacob agreed, said goodbye to Natalie and then to Dillon who had appeared on the stairs.

As he got into the taxi, Jacob took one last look toward the house. Natalie still stood at the door. As the car pulled away and she remained, silhouetted against the light from the hallway, Jacob wondered whether it was the pleasure of his company that she had hosted him for dinner, or whether she was afraid of what they had stumbled into.

## 11

Jacob arrived at the office early and found Helen already at her desk. He had phoned her immediately after arriving home from Natalie's and told her about the attack.

"Is Natalie alright?" Was the first thing she had asked.

"A little freaked. More than she's letting on," Jacob had replied. "Listen, I think it's best you stay away from the office for a few days."

"And what will you do?"

"Keep working with what I have. Try and find out what I've stepped in and how bad it smells."

"Then so will I. You need someone looking out for you, Jacob Kincaid."

He could have argued the point but King Canute had more joy ordering the ocean back up the beach than Jacob ever would have telling Helen to do something she didn't want to.

Wordlessly, she held out a cup of coffee towards him. Jacob took it and gave her shoulder a quick squeeze in return, a silent thank you for being there.

She had moved Roisin's PC to the floor beside her desk. Jacob scooped it up under his free arm and saluted her with his cup as he went into his office.

Picking up the phone, he dialled 101. He provided the switchboard operator with each reference number he had gleaned from the calling cards in Roisin's apartment and asked that the investigating officers for each be requested to get in touch. He knew the officers were under no obligation to get in contact and definitely had more important things to take up their time. Still, he hoped that with roughly ten separate incidents, at least one would get back to him.

He checked his computer next. The office had a CCTV camera installed at the top of the stairs. It was a premium system with HD video but it was less than useless. The man who'd attacked him and Natalie had arrived masked and left the same way, turning left at the bottom of the stairs and disappearing from view. Black clothing, black mask, average height, skinny build. He'd been careful, taking care that no tattoos, hair style, beard, or any other sort of distinguishing mark were visible.

He rewound the footage. As the figure reached the top, he glanced up at the camera, giving a clear glimpse of the unsettling balaclava and its messy white stitching. Jacob felt someone walk over his grave as he suppressed a shiver and closed the CCTV app and then shut his computer down.

He switched the keyboard and mouse leads from his PC to Roisin's and connected it to his monitor. Turning it on, he saw what he had expected. The PC had been completely wiped back to its factory settings. So much for that slim hope, he thought to himself.

After plugging his own computer back in, he walked over to the kitchen and opened one of the cupboards used to store equipment. Retrieving a zip-lock bag, he returned to his office and opened the safe. The cloying odour from the rag used to incapacitate Natalie reached out from where it had been confined.

"Ooof!" Helen exclaimed from the door. She watched as he lifted the fabric, holding it well away from his face, and dropped it into the bag. "There are easier ways to meet girls, you know."

She moved closer to examine the bag and took it as Jacob held it towards her. She mimed an exaggerated sniff, careful to not actually inhale any of the fumes. "Oh!" she cried, putting the back of her wrist to her head. "My goodness, Mr. Kincaid. With all this excitement, I do feel as though I am getting the vapours!" She fell against Jacob in an Oscar worthy swoon and was only stopped from clattering to the ground by Jacob holding her upright.

"Jesus, Helen! Stop!" he laughed, trying to haul her back to a standing position as she committed herself fully to the bit. A polite cough from the main office drew his attention from the shenanigans and he turned to find two police officers, a man and a woman, watching them. Forgetting himself, Jacob let go of Helen who dropped to the floor with a surprised yelp.

"Uh, morning," Jacob said sheepishly, his focus split between the new arrivals and helping Helen to her feet as she brushed herself off.

"Morning," the female officer replied. She was in her early twenties, with blonde hair tied back smartly. She regarded him from behind a pair of thick, black framed glasses. "We were looking for Jacob Kincaid."

"That'd be me."

"I understand you were a witness to an assault on Miss Natalie Amato last night." Her gaze drifted to the shiner that had bloomed around Jacob's left eye.

Jacob invited the pair into his office and Helen closed the door after they declined her offer of tea or coffee. The female peeler, who introduced herself as Constable Hughes, informed Jacob they had just recorded a statement from Natalie at her house and recapped what she had told them. Jacob confirmed Natalie's recollection as matching his own and briefly recounted the donnybrook between him and balaclava man.

"Are you willing to provide a statement to go along with Miss Amato's?" Hughes asked.

"Sure." Jacob said, already certain the police wouldn't catch the guy. He was masked, gloved and probably smart enough not to get caught on any street facing cameras before he slipped into the summer evening crowds. "You should probably have this too," Jacob said as handed over the zip-lock bag with the rag inside.

"What were they after?" Hughes asked, as she turned the bag over in her hand.

"Beats me."

The look Hughes gave suggested she didn't believe him. Still, she produced a statement page and transcribed Jacob's account of the incident, minus the part about him breaking the tablet over the masked man's head.

When the statement was recorded and signed, Jacob waved them around to his side of the desk to show the footage of the man entering and leaving the office. Hughes retrieved a USB from a pocket in her flak jacket and Jacob copied the video file across to it.

"This will probably go to CID," Hughes said, as Jacob handed her back the USB. "We're dealing with injuries of a common assault level, but I think the drugging aspect is worrying enough that the investigation will fall to them. In the meantime, I'll have your office flagged for passing attention, get some marked cars driving past a few times a day. Hopefully that'll ward off any return visits."

Jacob thanked the officers and was showing them to the door when Natalie walked in. You would be hard pressed to believe she had been attacked in the same spot a little over twelve hours before, Jacob thought. She greeted both officers by name, thanking them for responding to her report so quickly and then promptly following up with Jacob.

Helen watched as the two officers said their goodbye and waited until Jacob had closed the door behind them before asking Natalie how she was.

"Fine, thank you, Helen. Takes more than a little chloroform to keep me down," she replied airily. "So." She turned to Jacob; the façade unfaltering. "What's our play today?"

"Tomas McKinstry," Jacob answered, sticking his hands in his pockets. "He has a history with the Followers, a history with Roisin, and as far as I can tell, is the only other person who has spoken out against them publicly."

"Sounds like a plan," Natalie said. "Will we take my car?"

"I'll drive. You're the one paying me, doesn't feel right I get chauffeured around as well."

"You still want to talk to Luke too, right?" Natalie asked as they descended the staircase.

"I do. To me, if I'm looking at this logically, and I'm treating it as a murder, Luke Fisher has to be worthy of some attention. The phone calls, the slashed tyres, all that stuff, sound like the actions of some loser who couldn't take the rejection."

He sensed Natalie grimace. "Those phone calls and messages she got, a lot of them were warning her off the story," she said.

"The story that Luke had been working on with her? Sounds to me like the calls could have been committed by someone who knew how to play on Roisin's fears."

"And what about what happened in your office last night?"

"That, I'm still trying to figure out," Jacob admitted. "But you were worried enough about Luke's behaviour at the party that you stayed on to make sure he didn't try anything suspect."

"I didn't want him harassing Roisin. I didn't say I thought he was capable of murder."

"You'd be surprised by what people are capable of," Jacob said. He had seen evidence of it all too often. "Either way, I'd be wanting to talk to Luke. I already spoke to everyone else at the party, so why not him, especially as he probably knew Roisin better than anyone else who worked on the podcast?"

Natalie gave a murmur of agreement, appeased, at least for now. As they walked the short distance to Jacob's car, he noticed just how tense she really was. In his office she was protected by privacy and numbers. Out on the street however, her shoulders hunched forward ever so slightly and her eyes darted, watching ahead. With every few steps she would throw a glance behind.

"Not that I mind the company, but like I said last night, you're going to have to start charging yourself a fee," Jacob said, attempting to distract her as they reached his car.

"Do I cramp your style?"

"Not at all, but you don't need to watch me at every step."

"Truthfully, I'm a bit bored," Natalie said as she opened the passenger door to the Clio and paused, finding the seat taken over by polystyrene cups and empty cans of energy drinks. Jacob reached across and quickly scooped the rubbish into the foot well behind his seat. She continued, "I've hit a patch of writer's block on my next book and need to step away from it for a spell."

"What about the podcast?"

"We're on a bit of a wind down over the summer. After the Followers arc we decided to put out a few less intensive episodes, give everyone time to recharge their batteries. More casual chat and recaps about past cases before launching back into the regular schedule come September."

"Most people spend their summer hols sunning themselves on the beach, not driving around in a decrepit Clio visiting halfway houses."

She smiled at that. "I'm a journalist. I might have lost some of the fire when working for the papers, but that doesn't change who I am. A good investigation? A proper scoop? There's nothing like it."

"That we can agree on."

The morning traffic had eased and Jacob quickly made it through town and onto the M2 motorway. It was only a short distance before they exited and turned into the Harbour estate, following the road down into

Sailortown.

Over five thousand people had once lived in the small, cobblestoned streets of red-brick terraced housing, packed tightly together at the edge of the Belfast docks. Urban redevelopment, particularly the construction of the M2 back in the late sixties, had resulted in Sailortown's slow but sure demise. Only two churches, two pubs and a small row of houses remained of the once bustling enclave. The rest had been flattened and replaced by waterfront hotels and modern office buildings.

Jacob turned off the main road, passing a rundown Seafarer's Mission. The gleaming, glass fronted offices at Clarendon Dock may have only been a stone's throw away, but you could almost believe it was a different city in a different time. A shuttered church and derelict looking bar were the main features of the little side street they now found themselves on.

The decrepit surroundings didn't quite tell the whole story, Jacob knew. Sailortown still retained some of its former seedy, hard-boiled undercurrent, although this was now used as part of the local charm harnessed to attract rather than deter any visitors. The dive bar drew a younger crowd, offered a fine selection of craft beer and hosted raucous folk music nights, whilst the church, deconsecrated and without a congregation, was still used for cultural events and Dungeons and Dragons meet-ups.

The Star of the Sea Hostel on the other hand, had held fast against any effort of local regeneration. It was a squat, ugly building, not fit for purpose twenty years ago. The faded brown brick must have looked depressing the day the hostel been built and time had done it no favours.

Peering up, Jacob saw the warm morning sun had been lost behind a bank of dark clouds. An uncomfortable humidity remained in the air but as he stepped out of the car, he felt the first faint patter of rain on his cheek.

A trio of men, all mean-eyed and smoking, stood outside the hostel entrance. They watched as Jacob parked across the street and kept their gaze on him and Natalie as they approached, only moving out of their way at the last moment.

One of the men muttered something that got a laugh from his two mates. Jacob's neck reddened even though he knew the crack wasn't aimed at him. He held the door for Natalie who thanked him before offering a hard glare at the card who made the quip, who met her eye and took another slow drag from his cigarette.

The lobby was small, dark, and smelled of strong disinfectant. The faded lino floor stuck to the bottom of Jacob's shoe with every step. Further access to the hostel was barred by a heavy security door without a handle. To their right was an office, protected from the lobby by a layer of thick glass. A woman dressed in a maroon polo shirt with the Star of the Sea logo over the right breast stood behind the glass a suspicious look clear on her features. Behind her a man, black, maybe in his early forties and wearing the same uniform, sat at a computer.

"Don't worry, we're not the police," Jacob said, knowing exactly where the woman's mind had immediately jumped. "We're looking for Tomas McKinstry."

"Tomas?" The woman asked with a frown. She was young, maybe mid-thirties, but she considered them with a pair of hard and tired eyes. "What do you want with him? I know you're not family."

A couple of raised voices sounded from the floor above. An argument was brewing. The two hostel employees glanced up towards the sound before the man stood. Jacob watched him walk past the security door and disappear up the stairs.

The woman unlocked the door with the press of a button under her desk. "Maybe you should come in." She wanted them out of the way. The residents of the hostel were wary of strangers and many were violent.

Frayed tempers and suspicious minds from men at the bottom of the barrel.

"I'm Natalie Amato," Natalie said as she entered the office. "I'm a journalist. I believe Tomas was previously working on a story that I'm now investigating."

"A journalist?" the woman asked. Jacob could see her name badge read Amanda. "Can I ask what this is about? I'd rather Tomas not be bothered unless it's important."

"Maybe Tomas can make that decision," Jacob said, suddenly impatient. Amanda glared and Natalie shot him a look that told him in no uncertain terms to butt out. "Sorry," he muttered, taking a step back. In Jacob's mind, Tomas was an adult, capable of deciding for himself. It wasn't for Amanda to make his mind up for him about who he could or couldn't see.

"I can't get into the specifics," Natalie replied, her tone soft, placating. "Data protection issues, I'm sure you understand. What I can tell you…" Natalie stopped and looked up.

Jacob had his back to the glass that looked out into the foyer. He turned to see a male coming down the stairs. He was much too thin with a shaved head, hollow cheeks and darting blue eyes. Tomas McKinstry had lost at least forty pounds since the pictures on Roisin's Facebook profile had been taken, but it was unquestionably him.

Amanda stepped up to the glass. "Tomas, these people…."

She didn't get any further. Tomas took one look at Jacob and was off to the races, haring for the front door.

Jacob tore out of the office and into the lobby. The trio of smokers looked up in surprise as he burst through the front door but one still had enough wherewithal to stick out a foot and trip him. He stumbled and only just about managed to keep his footing.

"Jacob!" He heard Natalie call after him. He ignored her. Tomas had opened a twenty-metre gap and was tearing up the road. It was a dead end for vehicles but a pedestrian gate in the tall metal fencing led through to Clarendon docks.

A group of teenagers, using a small civic space to skate and smoke, parted for Tomas as he approached. Jacob followed him through a haze of weed smoke and body odour and saw Tomas was slowing. Not a moment too soon either, as Jacob was practically blowing out of his arse. He gritted his teeth and ignored the creeping stitch in his side as he trailed Tomas along the harbour's edge, past a number of newly constructed waterfront offices.

The gap was closing. Tomas glanced over his shoulder before darting left, disappearing between two of the buildings. Jacob slowed as he rounded the corner, and ran headfirst into him. The other man took a step back, eyes wide with fear. He had run into a dead end. Before Jacob could get a word out or even attempt to catch his breath, Tomas swung a punch. It was weak and slow but Jacob was bushed and had let his guard drop. The blow connected painfully with the top of his nose.

Tomas McKinstry, as surprised as anyone the blow had landed, dropped his fists. Wincing, Jacob punched him hard in the stomach. Tomas sunk to both knees with a pained gulp. "Shit," Jacob said, knowing he had hit the smaller man much too hard. "Sorry."

He turned at the sound of footsteps to find Natalie jogging toward them, cool, collected and without a hair out of place. Jacob, on the other hand, was breathing hard and could feel the sweat stick to the back of his t-shirt. Natalie pushed past him with an annoyed look as she knelt next to the man still on the floor, placing one arm across his shoulder. "Tomas, It's Natalie Amato. Do you remember me?"

"Sure..." Tomas grunted through laboured breaths. "You work over at the Sentinel."

"I did. I left the paper a while ago."

Tomas nodded, grunting again as he did. Jacob rolled his eyes, believing he was perhaps laying it on a bit too thick now. He'd been hit by an out of shape private detective, not Carl Frampton.

"We were hoping to ask you some questions."

"Like, why were you running?" Jacob said.

"Thought you were someone else." Tomas looked up at him. "Maybe wanting to do me in."

Jacob bit his tongue at that, keen to press but keener still to avoid Natalie's ire.

"Tomas, can we talk?" Natalie asked.

"Sure."

Jacob helped the man to his feet and once he had sufficiently recovered, they walked to one of the bars they had passed on their way to the hostel. Despite outside appearances, the interior of the bar was cosy, and more importantly, quiet, its ambience only slightly dented by the M3 overpass running directly overhead. They picked a table in the corner for maximum privacy.

Jacob returned to the table with a beer for himself and an orange juice for Natalie. Tomas had declined a drink. "It's about the Followers, isn't it?" he asked as Jacob sat.

"What makes you say that?" Natalie replied, playing it cool.

Tomas's laugh was humourless. "What else could it be about? Years trying to make it as a writer and that's the only thing that got noticed. Just a shame it got noticed by the wrong people. Just a shame...about Roisin."

"You were close?"

"We met at Uni, up in Coleraine. I dropped out after a year, changed my degree from journalism to creative writing at Queens. Four years we were together."

Natalie glanced across the table to Jacob who gave a faint shake of his head. He hadn't seen anything on Roisin's Facebook to indicate the two were lovers.

Gently, Natalie touched Tomas on the arm and broke his sombre reverie.

"Sorry," he said, snapping back to reality.

"It's fine." She tapped the table with a finger,

picking her words carefully. "Is that how Roisin came to learn about the Followers? Through you?"

"Yeah," he nodded. "She got in touch when I got out of the hospital last time. "It'd been a couple of years since we last spoke. We met up. I didn't tell her the full story, not at first. She was a good person, too good for this city. She knew something had happened but I didn't tell her, didn't want to expose her to it. She wore me down though. She got me talking."

Jacob leaned forward. "Roisin heard what had happened to you and that's why she wanted in. Am I on the right track?"

"Yeah." His voice was thick with regret. "I didn't have the stomach for the fight anymore but I didn't want Roisin involved. It was too dangerous and I told her so. Those people..."

"But Roisin didn't listen," Natalie said.

"I didn't put my foot down. I should have said no but she was insistent the story had to be told. I was too weak to do it so she stepped up."

"I don't think you're weak, Tomas." Natalie gripped his arm lightly.

Tomas bit down on a knuckle as tears welled in his eyes. A choked sob got out, drawing attention from the only other occupied table in the place. Meanwhile. Jacob shifted uncomfortably in his chair and looked into his pint.

They waited for Tomas to compose himself. "I listened to your piece on the Followers," he said to Natalie as he wiped tears with the back of his hand. "It was good."

"Thank you." Natalie said, her smile modest.

"But shallow."

Natalie's polite smile didn't falter. "Uh huh."

"What I mean is, you barely got below the surface. The stuff that I found...it'd blow your socks off."

"Roisin was going to make her own podcast. Did you know that?" Jacob asked.

"Yeah. She took all the notes that I had compiled.

Pages and pages of research." Jacob's mind flashed to an empty safe, easily big enough for a couple of reams of paper. "And then she had her own stuff too," Tomas continued. "She wouldn't tell me what exactly, but the way she talked you would have thought it would have been the biggest story this island has seen."

Jacob stopped himself from rolling his eyes. He had no doubt people had a vested interest in Roisin's story but Ireland, North and South, had a long, bloody, and scandalous history. He kept the opinion to himself, keen to avoid another of Natalie's stern looks.

"We've been to Roisin's apartment," she said. "Any physical notes are long gone."

"I know. I have them."

Jacob and Natalie leaned forward together. "You have them?" Natalie asked, her voice barely a whisper.

"About a week before she died, Roisin came to the hostel. She was afraid. She had brought all my old notes back and said it wasn't safe for her to hold on to them anymore."

"Did she say why?" Jacob asked.

"No. She wouldn't tell me much. Only asked that I keep them safe. That..." he stopped to clear his throat. "That was the last time I saw her."

"Surely she would have needed those notes to work on the podcast," said Natalie.

"She could have transcribed them," Jacob said. "Or scanned them onto her computer."

"Tomas. Can we see them?"

He shifted in his chair. "Roisin trusted me to keep them safe. Even if I'm not going to do anything with them, I know they need to be protected." He stopped, running a hand over his scalp. "They need to find the right person."

Jacob thought a reporter with some fifteen years experience, a familiarity with the story and a podcast reaching a monthly audience of up to one hundred thousand people would be just the right person. Once again, he decided not to voice his opinion.

"Ok," Natalie said, deciding now was not the time to push. She glanced at Jacob. "Anything we haven't covered?"

Jacob thought for a second. "Do you know Roisin's brother?"

"Liam? Not really. We met a few times. I always thought he was a bit of a tosser."

"How so?" Jacob asked.

"Just the way he got on. Looked down at me and Roisin. Total hypocrite. He had a drug problem as heavy as mine. Not to mention he'd borrowed serious money from their da and never paid it back."

"Is there a way we can stay in touch?" Natalie asked Tomas.

"I have a mobile but I don't like talking on it. I'll leave your names on my visitor list at the hostel. I think I'd prefer to talk in person about all this. The walls in there have ears."

Jacob and Natalie shook his hand and promised to be in touch. Jacob slipped him one of his cards which Tomas pocketed before walking back towards the hostel on his own.

"What do you think?" Natalie asked.

Jacob watched Tomas slowly making his way down the road. His hands were shoved deep in his pockets, his head bowed low, even on an empty street, shielding himself from the world. A broken man.

"I don't know," he said. "But I would like to get a look at those notes."

# 12

"At least they didn't vandalise my car," Jacob said as he and Natalie reached the Clio.

"How can you tell?" Her expression had a mischievous edge.

"Touche."

They left Sailortown behind and circled back onto the M2, following the road until it merged with the M5. As they exited the motorway the increasingly bruised sky finally erupted into a violent summer storm. Lashing rain sent the Clio's wipers into overdrive as thunder rolled slowly overhead.

They drove through Whiteabbey, perched on the side of Belfast lough. Across the water, Samson and Golitah, the great cranes of the once proud Haarland and Wolfe shipyard lay dormant but still dominated the dark skyline. The shadowed monoliths kept a silent sentry on the lough as a lone cargo ship trundled out towards open sea.

"Roisin knew something was going to happen," Jacob said, breaking the silence that had descended with the storm. "That's why she gave Tomas his notes back."

Natalie murmured her agreement. "That night at her place she was telling me her story would have big ramifications."

"Tantalisingly mysterious of her, but not exactly helpful. I don't suppose she revealed any details of this massive scoop?"

Natalie's sigh held a note of frustration. "No, she kept pretty schtum on the specifics."

It was less than a minute later when they arrived at Luke Fisher's home in a small development of smart, neatly-ordered townhouses just past the Jordanstown Campus of Ulster University.

"His car's here." Natalie nodded towards a two-seater BMW convertible.

"Knew he was a wanker," Jacob said, eyeing the car as Natalie wrapped the front door.

When Luke Fisher saw Natalie on his door step, his expression turned sour. "What are you doing here?"

Natalie forced a smile that held no warmth. "Luke, this is Jacob Kincaid. He's a private investigator looking into Roisin's death."

"Uh huh." His attention shifted to Jacob. "And what's that got to do with me?"

All in all, Luke Fisher was not a bad looking guy, Jacob had to admit. He was in his late twenties with a sunbed developed tan and a t-shirt at least a size too small, squeezed over a well-developed chest. His dark hair was styled smartly and for reasons unknown to Jacob, he appeared to have purposefully cultivated a chinstrap.

"Nothing," Jacob replied. "But I'd like to ask you a few questions." For a second, he thought Fisher was going to close the door in their faces but instead he opened it slowly and motioned for them to come inside.

"Private investigator, huh? You don't look like one."

"Well, I left my fedora and trenchcoat in the car," Jacob replied.

Fisher eyed Jacob suspiciously as he led them into the living room. His pad was small, but well kept. Jacob and Natalie seated themselves on a leather sofa while Fisher remained standing, his arms folded.

"Mairead told me you weren't letting Roisin's death drop."

"Of course she did," Natalie said quietly.

"Did she tell you anything else?" Jacob asked, filing

away the information Fisher was still in contact with at least one member of Natalie's podcast team. Fisher shrugged; his smug expression accentuated by that ridiculous thing he probably had the gall to call a beard. "I'm led to believe you and Roisin were close," Jacob said, trying a different tact.

"For a spell, yeah."

"What happened?"

"We broke it off."

Jacob nodded, deciding it best to keep up the pretence. Fisher was a liar with a wounded ego but knew he had the advantage of Natalie and Jacob wanting to talk to him.

"When was the last time you saw her?"

"At her apartment the night of the party." He glanced at Natalie. "She was in a state. Absolutely gished." He held Natalie's gaze. "Disgusting."

Jacob felt Natalie tense beside him. "How'd you get home that night?"

"I'm sure Natalie's told you all about it. Led me on, got frigid and then fired me the next morning over it."

"That is not what happened," Natalie said, her voice cold.

Jacob held a hand up to cut in before Fisher could reply. "That's not why I'm here."

"No?"

"No. Like Natalie said, I'm here looking into Roisin's death. If there was foul play, I want to expose it."

"Foul play," Luke laughed and took a step closer. He'd probably once watched a self-help video on YouTube and got the idea that remaining standing while they were seated gave him some sort of psychological advantage.

"You believe it was an accident?" Jacob asked.

"Of course it was a bloody accident!" Luke replied, his voice rising suddenly.

They'd barely been in his company for two minutes but Jacob felt he already had a measure on who Fisher was. The type of man who could flip on a switch. He was manipulative, Natalie herself had said how well he had hidden his true self when they had worked together. He was a bully, but only against those weaker than himself. Unfortunately for Fisher, he had no power beyond their need to talk to him. Natalie was older and much more successful, on a level he no doubt craved, while Jacob was of a similar size and wouldn't be physically intimidated.

"You worked with Roisin and Natalie on the Followers of Eden." Jacob kept his tone conversational, ignoring the outburst as he sank back into the seat and rested one leg over his knee to show Fisher he was at ease. "What do you think?"

"Bunch of weirdos but so what?"

"You don't think they had anything to do with Roisin's death?"

"Jesus! The silly bitch was stocious. Slipped and cracked her head. The end. Finito." Fisher's pride was still hurt from Natalie's rejection and subsequent sacking, and now he was trying to get a rise out of her. She dug her fingers into the leather but didn't give him the satisfaction.

Jacob glanced around the living room. Unlike Roisin's apartment there were plenty of photos on display but most were either of Luke alone or with an older couple, presumably his parents. "What if I told you, I thought differently? That I believe there was a killer and that I was pretty confident I'd have the proof soon enough."

"I'd say you were a loon, mate. Mairead told me all about it. The room was locked, no one else was in there with her."

"Yet on the day she was found, you texted Natalie, asking if Roisin's death was an accident." For the first time since they had met, Fisher's smug front faltered. "After all the stuff the Followers are alleged to have done, you believe it was an accident?"

"That's the word though, isn't it?" Fisher replied,

clawing some of the bravado back. *"Alleged*. Do you have any proof?"

Jacob shrugged. If they had proof, now would have been the time to lay at least a couple of cards on the table. Fisher chuckled. He was an ignorant prick but he wasn't dumb.

"Jesus, you guys are serious, aren't you?" Fisher laughed again, forcing it. "And here I thought you were coming to make me an offer."

"What are you talking about?" Natalie asked, her patience straining.

"Roisin's notes."

Jacob looked at Natalie. Tomas had mentioned he'd left them with somewhere for safekeeping but surely not with this plank.

"You have Rosin's notes?" Jacob asked. "How?"

"She gave them to me."

"Bullshit," Natalie snapped. It was the first time Jacob had heard her swear.

The outburst only increased Fisher's smugness. "Believe what you want but I'll show you." He disappeared up the stairs and returned with his phone in his hand.

"These notes were written on the world's smallest typewriter, I take it." Jacob said.

"Funny," Fisher said flatly, before turning his phone towards the pair. The screen displayed a picture of what looked to Jacob like a small, black plastic box set on a kitchen counter.

"An external hard drive," Natalie said. Fisher nodded in the affirmative and she stabbed a finger towards him. "You stole it."

"What's that pesky little word again? Oh yeah, proof. Don't suppose you have any to back that up?"

"What do you want, Luke?" Natalie demanded.

"Ten," Fisher replied, pocketing the phone.

"Ten?" Jacob asked. "Ten what? Backslaps and attaboys?"

"Thousand." He licked the corner of his lip. "Think

fast, I have one buyer interested already and they've made a generous offer."

"A buyer?" Natalie couldn't hide the derision in her voice. "Who? No one else is talking about the Followers and I don't think a cult in Northern Ireland is going to shift too many column inches across the water."

"It's the Followers themselves," Jacob said. "He's looking to sell Roisin's notes to them."

"Jesus, Luke." Natalie said. "You have no idea who you're getting into bed with."

"That suits me fine."

"How do they know you have the notes?" Jacob asked.

"I contacted them. I waited until the furore over Roisin had died down and then reached out a couple of weeks back. We've been haggling over a fair price ever since."

"These aren't some loony cultists. Sorry, these aren't *just* some loony cultists," Jacob said. "They have reach and they have backing and they're not above getting their hands dirty."

"I'm not an idiot," Fisher sneered. "Calls on prepaid mobiles and VPN's on my laptop to hide my IP location. When I make the exchange it'll be in a public place with plenty of witnesses."

"It's illegal," Natalie said.

"And a lot of trouble for a few grand."

"Yeah? Well, you can blame Natalie for that. I have to make a living."

"Burglary and blackmail isn't much of a living," said Jacob.

"You can debate the ethics between yourselves. I have something, the Followers want it and so do you. Seems like simple supply and demand to me."

Natalie stood up, having heard enough. "Jacob, we're leaving."

"Run along, Jacob," Fisher teased as Natalie stormed out ahead of him.

"People who play stupid games, win stupid prizes,

Fisher. You'll find out."

Fisher shouted something after him but Jacob ignored it, hurrying back to the Clio, head down against the rain. "Jesus," he said as he got back into car. "What a numpty."

Natalie shook her head. "He had a touch of arrogance about him when he worked with us but I never knew he was such a shithead." She rested her head against the seat before turning wearily to Jacob. "What do you think? Is he bluffing?"

"About the notes?" Jacob pondered for a moment. "Maybe. Maybe not. It makes sense for Roisin to have kept them on something a lot more accessible, not to mention more easily hidden, than reams of paper."

"And that's why she gave Tomas his originals back. She didn't need them."

"And for safekeeping. If the digital copy fell into the wrong hands, which it looks like it has, at least they had the physical." He sighed. "Ten grand. A lot of money. Whatever Roisin had on that drive must be worth seeing. We need Tomas to hand over the notes, or at least let us see what's on them."

"I'll work on him," Natalie said. Journalist to journalist. But it'll take time. What about you?"

"For now? Back to the office and then home for a hot bath. Soothe these battered muscles."

Natalie reached up, cupped his chin, and tilted his head so she could get a look at the shiner under his eye. She hadn't mentioned it all day. Her smile was sympathetic and Jacob felt his heart beat faster. "Big tough private eye," she said before the hand fell away.

Jacob cleared his throat. "That's me," he said, starting the engine.

*

Natalie had parked on Upper Arthur Street. Jacob pulled in at the kerb and watched as she got safely into her car. She waved as she pulled away. No other cars moved off and no one seemed to be paying her any attention. Jacob gave it five seconds before he followed.

He was three cars behind Natalie's. Jacob hung back in the centre lane through Dunbar Link onto Great Patrick Street and saw Natalie follow the road towards the M3 and her home in the East of the city.

Satisfied no one was tailing her, Jacob took a left and parked up in the multistory on Edward Street. He returned to his apartment to pick up a coat and then walked back to the office.

Helen looked up as he entered. "All quiet?" He asked, shaking off the soaking coat and hanging it by the door.

"All quiet," she confirmed.

Jacob ran a hand through his wet hair. "Why don't you get out of here?"

"It's a bit early, no?"

"Get a start on your weekend. I assume you have plans, unlike some of us."

"Opera at the Opera House. A novel concept, I know. You?"

"Nothing. Close up. Go home. Waste the weekend."

Once Helen had gone, Jacob checked his emails, made a coffee and threw half of it down the sink. His inbox was empty and the office phone silent. He closed up and walked slowly back towards his empty apartment.

The heat wave of the previous few days was already a distant memory and the storm had brought a chill. Still, the city bustled. Rush hour traffic stood at a standstill and the footpaths were packed as commuters and students rushed home.

No one gave Jacob a second glance as he passed, head low. When he reached Talbot Street, he quickened his step to match the worsening rain. Home was straight ahead. He didn't register the car as it sped around the corner. It was only when it braked sharply, tyres squealing in protest as it came to a stop a few feet in front of him, that he looked up.

The man who jumped out of the driver's seat was a bruiser in an ill-fitting suit. Maybe not quite six foot but built like a brick shithouse. "Here, c'mere!" He pointed a meaty finger at Jacob as he advanced, his other hand clenched into a fist.

Jacob had already been hit twice in less than twenty-four hours. Once he could understand. Twice? Ok, this was Belfast, but a third?

His uncle Harry had been a sports nut. With Jacob's father thoroughly disinterested in anything other than his own work, Harry had taken a young Jacob to Judo and boxing lessons. It was the grappling sport that Jacob always had the affinity for. He'd got his black belt as a teenager that now took up space in the back of a wardrobe, but he had kept at the sport until his mid-twenties until passion lost the battle with lethargy.

On the other hand, he never had much love for boxing or the rough kids from the local estates who used him as a punching bag in their sparring sessions. Still, he had still picked up a rudimentary grasp of the sweet science.

As the man approached, Jacob was already on the balls of his feet. He sprung forward, a right cross whipping out and catching the man flush in the jaw.

The man didn't go down. In fact, he barely staggered. Jacob froze a second before throwing a second punch. This time the man was ready and caught his arm. Before Jacob could even think about falling back on some of his old Judo moves, his world turned upside down and he was kissing the concrete whilst a large, and now thoroughly pissed-off bruiser was doing his level best to wrench Jacob's shoulder out of the socket.

Jacob heard a car door slam, followed by the quick click of high heels walking towards them. "That's enough." Female. Calm but firm. The pressure on his shoulder lifted a fraction.

A manicured hand reached out and helped him to his feet. The woman was slightly taller than Jacob. Her skin was a rich shade of ebony. High cheekbones and a straight nose gave her a regal profile, while large, almond-shaped eyes, spoke to a depth of intelligence that clearly didn't miss much.

"You must be Jacob Kincaid," the woman said. Her English accent was clipped and refined.

"That's the rumour," Jacob replied, stretching his shoulder.

"Cora Adebayo." The woman waited for her companion to open the back door of their car. "We need to have a talk."

# 13

Aside from Adebayo and her companion, the street was empty. His eyes flicked back to the direction he had come from. He could make a break for it, bolt across the junction and onto Writer's Square where there would be at least a few witnesses.

"Relax," Adebayo said, reading his train of thought. "If we'd have wanted to snatch you, you'd already be in the boot of the car."

"Reassuring. What do you want?"

"Like I said, just a friendly chat."

"I'm not going anywhere with you." He left it unsaid that he'd go down screaming if they tried to make him.

"Alright." Adebayo held up a hand. She reached into the car and came back with an unmarked beige folder. "Let's take a walk." She turned to the man who had face planted Jacob on the ground. "I'll see you back in the office."

"You sure?" he asked, not taking his small, dark eyes from Jacob. The man was squat, with broad shoulders, a barrel chest and a broken nose that hadn't been reset. Unlike Adebayo, his accent marked him as a native son of Belfast.

Adebayo looked to Jacob. "Quite sure."

Jacob watched as the man drove away. "Whose he supposed to be? Your HR guy?"

"C'mon," Adebayo said, ignoring the jibe with a nod of her head. Jacob fell into step beside her. His curiosity was piqued and for now, overrid his concerns about who

Adebayo was or who she worked for. "You've had an interesting few days, Mr. Kincaid."

"Well, I'm an interesting man."

"No," she said with a shake of her head. "You're not. Don't get me wrong, by all accounts you're a rather talented investigator but your business deals with, and by no means do I intend to offend when I say this, small fish. Unfaithful spouses, missing people, occasionally some work for one of the local papers."

"And you know this, how?" Jacob asked as they crossed Donegall Street towards Writer's Square. The rain had let up but the space was quiet, occupied by a rabble of teenagers sitting on the steps at one end of the square, and a small group of homeless people from the local shelter at the other.

Adebayo again ignored his question. "But now you're looking into an unsolved murder."

"An accidental death."

"Oh, you still believe that? That's why you're pestering CID and the beat cops in Lisburn? All for an accidental death?"

Adebayo stopped and seated herself on the concrete border of a flowerbed. Jacob sat next to her as she crossed one long leg over the other and turned her attention to the square. Aside from the front entrance of Saint Anne's Cathedral there was little to see, apart from the separate groups of alchies and raucous teens.

"I was hired by a friend of Roisin's to look into her death," Jacob said as the silence stretched, knowing full well what Adebayo was doing.

"And you think the Followers of Eden are involved?"

"I never mentioned the Followers." Jacob shifted in his wet seat and tried to keep his expression neutral.

"Yes. you did. When you spoke to Sergeant O'Connor a couple of days back."

"Who are you?"

"I told you already." Her blue eyes finally shifted back to Jacob. "Cora Adebayo."

"And who do you work for, Cora Adebayo?" Jacob

knew she was prodding him, looking for some kind of reaction.

Adebayo reached for the folder resting on her knee. She selected a few sheets of A4 paper and held them out to Jacob. "Have a look at these."

The first sheet was a glossy print of a crime scene photo. A man lay on his back with one leg draped over an overturned chair. Lifeless eyes stared towards the ceiling. Jacob felt Adebayo watching him. He turned to the next sheet; a photo of an empty light bulb box sitting on a kitchen counter. The next was of a vacant light socket.

The last three photos were from the unfortunate man's post mortem. The first; a full body shot of the naked corpse laid out on the cold metal of a mortuary bench. The second, a close-up of his face and the last showing deep purple bruising to his neck.

"Thoughts?" Adebayo asked as Jacob flipped back to the first sheet.

"Stood on a chair to change the light bulb. Slipped, fell and broke his neck. Why are you showing me this?"

"You don't think it's suspicious? Person slips in the home, takes a freak tumble, cracks his head, and dies? What's so different between the sad demise of one Peter Funston and Roisin Dunwoody?"

"I don't know."

"Well, I can tell you a couple of similarities. Both were the sad victims of accidents in the home. Two of roughly around twelve thousand that happen in the UK every year."

"OK."

"Secondly, Peter Funston was in a similar line of work as yourself. He was employed as an investigator by Bell, Fullam and Price. I'm sure the name is familiar to you."

Bell, Fullam and Price were one of the biggest solicitor firms in Belfast. Jacob had been flummoxed on more occasions than he cared to count by their representatives whilst still on the job. "Bell, Fullam and

Price looking into the Followers?"

"Testing the waters so to speak. They had been approached by a Mrs. Marie McGreavy." Adebayo let the name hang in the air. "You don't listen to Miss Amato's podcast?" She prompted, realising Jacob's blank stare wasn't him trying to play it cool.

"The farmer whose land the Followers were after?" Jacob said once the name finally clicked.

Adebayo nodded. "Seems like the widow McGreavy had suspicions that her husband's death was the result of foul play."

"He fell into a slurry pit. It's unfortunate but hardly unheard of in this part of the world."

"No, but if you care to look close enough, it's rather striking how many people who have crossed the Followers, wind up dead in strange circumstances. Miss Dunwoody, Mr. Funston, Mr. McGreavy." Adebayo paused as she reached into the folder again.

The picture she passed to Jacob was of a man splayed out on the ground. His left leg was broken grotesquely, lying at an impossible angle to the rest of him. Dark red blood had pooled under the ruined body. "Michael Dunnery was a skilled fraudster. He attempted to blackmail a reasonably senior figure in the church. Two years ago, he took a running jump off the top floor of his apartment block."

She riffled through her folder and produced more sheets to hand to Jacob, this time of a man and woman, maybe late thirties, or early forties, lying in bed. If it wasn't for the corpse grey skin you would have believed they were sleeping. Jacob turned to the next image and immediately looked away. A young boy, no more than eight years old, stone dead in his bed, still clutching his teddy bear.

"Joseph Henderson was an estate agent and an elder in the church. For reasons unknown, he was excommunicated. Rumour has it, he was going to turn whistle blower. Unfortunately for Joseph and his wife and son, the gas boiler in their house was faulty. The three of them suffocated in their sleep before Joseph ever got a chance to tell his story. This one actually made the local news but only as a tragic accident in the home. The Followers were never mentioned."

Jacob handed the sheets back to Adebayo. "Are you trying to warn me off? Is that it?"

"Trying to make you see what you're up against. What you do with that information is up to you."

"You seem to have a lot of interest in a bunch of religious nuts."

"It's my job to have an interest in things that threaten the security of this country. Even in the far flung reaches of Northern Ireland." Her tone was a touch scornful.

"A threat to security?" This time it was Jacob who couldn't hide his derision.

"You've heard of Scientology?"

"Of course."

"How many members do you think they have in America? Considering their wealth, their reach and their fame."

Jacob considered it for a second and pulled a number out of his arse. "Half a million?"

"Try twenty-five thousand. In a country of roughly three hundred and thirty million."

Jacob saw where she was going. "And how many do the Followers have here?"

"In Northern Ireland alone, we think somewhere around a thousand. That's not even taking into account their following in the Republic."

"Jesus."

"They're not all fanatics of course, but enough of them are and to label them simply as religious nuts is disingenuous at best. They have a strategy and have timed it perfectly." As she spoke, she leaned forward. "Think about it, Jacob. We live in a time when science and academia are disparaged, doctors maligned and mainstream religion is accused of going soft. The Followers have slowly built up a base of wealthy and influential patrons and now they're going to go all out on their recruitment mission. They'll go for the outliers, common folk who feel marginalised, gullible people looking for a promise of a quick fix. It's an age-old tactic. The difference is, the Followers have the clout to stay. Five of Northern Ireland's richest people are senior members in the church, not to mention at least two assembly members up in Stormont."

"You think someone would stop them," he offered, realising Adebayo had stopped her sermon and was waiting for him.

She sighed. "Yes, you think someone would." She stood and reached into her jacket, producing a card. "Maybe if your investigation uncovers something of interest, you'd consider giving me a call."

Aside from her name and a phone number, the card was blank. No sign of who she really was or who she belonged to.

"That's it?" Jacob asked, holding up the card.

"That's it," Adebayo replied. "Although I'm sure I'll see you around." The ghost of a smile touched her lips as she turned away.

Jacob watched as Adebayo crossed back through Writer's Square. Instead of continuing across the road to Talbot Street, she took a right, heading along Donegall Street. Jacob looked back at the card, considered ripping it up and then pocketed it instead.

He waited until Adebayo was out of sight before he stood and broke into a run, crossing the square and up Talbot Street, taking a right onto the cobbles of Hill Street, already busy with Friday evening revellers. He hurried through as best he could and took another right, down an alleyway where a throng milled outside the Duke of York pub. He made his way through the crowd carefully, mindful of spilling anyone's pint and getting a punch to the back of the head for his troubles.

With the thickest group of drinkers safely navigated, he jogged a few paces and then slowed as he approached the end of the entry that led onto Donegall

Street.

As Jacob peered around the lip of the alley he saw no sign of Adebayo. Thinking he'd lost her already, he walked towards Waring Street, figuring that was the direction she was most likely to take. Fortunately for him, Cora Adebayo was not hard to spot in a Belfast crowd. She was about seventy metres ahead, striding down Bridge Street before disappearing down Joy's Entry.

Jacob followed her path down the entry and through to the pedestrianised part of the city centre. Hanging back but keeping Adebayo in view, Jacob was surprised at how easy she was making this for him. He had expected double backs or changes of direction into some of the old entries or alleyways but she stuck to the main thoroughfare. There were no looks into the wing mirrors of parked cars or shop windows, not even a glance back over her shoulder.

By the time she turned onto Great Victoria Street a few minutes later, Jacob was only twenty metres behind her. He crossed at the junction, keeping tabs on her from the opposite side of the street and watched as she entered one of the buildings.

Waiting for a break in the traffic, Jacob hurried across the street and with his head down, walked past where Adebayo had entered, stealing a glance into the lobby, and catching a split-second glimpse of the woman entering an elevator. He stopped, counted to twenty and turned back, stepping into the building's lobby.

Small, cool, and tiled, the only occupant was a white shirted security guard at the desk. His grey hair and moustache were both smartly trimmed. Jacob nodded to the man as he passed. Faded tattoos on tanned forearms led Jacob to guess the man was ex-military or ex-paramilitary. Or both.

"Help you Sir?" the security guard was now standing, his hands clasped easily behind him.

Quickly, Jacob counted the floors on the elevator

plan and the business listed against them. There were six; two chartered accountants, a business management firm, a homeless charity, a software analyst, and a personal injury lawyer. "Just looking for the DMV," he said. "Theory test for my LGV licence."

"Wrong building I'm afraid, Sir. It's a few down. Clearly signposted."

Jacob slapped his forehead. "Jesus, I'm an eejit!" The security guard made no effort to refute the suggestion as he watched Jacob walk back out onto the street.

Out of sight of the lobby, he crossed the road and looked back at the building. He counted the floors and then counted them again, coming up with seven.

# 14

Jacob tossed through the night. He was exhausted but like every night for the past week, sleep stubbornly refused to take him. Too many questions gnawed their way through to his slumber-addled brain.

Who had been watching him and Natalie at Hilden Mill?

Who had attacked them in his office?

What did Luke Fisher have on that hard drive?

And who the hell was Cora Adebayo?

It was half five and the sun had begun its slow climb. With a groan, Jacob got up and showered. When his phone buzzed a little after eight, he had expected to see Natalie's number and swallowed disappointment when he saw it was from an unrecognised landline. He considered letting it ring out before deciding to answer.

"Kincaid?"

It took Jacob a second to place the voice. "Tomas?"

"One and the same," McKinstry replied.

"What can I do for you?"

"You know the coffee kiosk across from City Hall? Meet me there in half an hour. Do me a favour and dress down, ok?"

Before Jacob could say anything the line went dead. He wasn't sure how much he cared for the thought of McKinstry assuming he didn't have anything going on in his calendar that he could just drop everything and meet him in thirty minutes. It just so happened he didn't, and he could dress down with the best of them.

At such an early hour, the traffic and footfall in the centre of town was light, save for a group of Asian tourists crowded around the gates of City Hall, snapping photos of the old building and its green copper dome.

Jacob arrived at the kiosk a couple of minutes early and found McKinstry already waiting, sheltered under an old raincoat and hood. As Jacob approached, he held out a steaming Styrofoam cup. Good guy this McKinstry, Jacob decided, taking the coffee.

"Let's take a walk," he said, waiting for Jacob to fall in beside him. "Guess I'm not as hard to track down as I thought I was. Still, I'm impressed you managed it."

"Natalie will have to take the credit for that."

"All of it? Even my history with Roisin?"

Jacob shrugged. "It was luck as much as anything."

"What you two were asking yesterday. It's a lot, you know?"

"I know," Jacob said. "If you don't mind me asking, why are you coming to me and not Natalie?"

"She didn't answer her phone."

"Ah."

"Nah, I'm messing with you, mate." His expression didn't change at the joke. "Maybe I'm too old fashioned, but after what happened to Roisin, I don't want another dead girl on my conscience."

"Fair," said Jacob, ignoring the implication that him getting hurt instead wouldn't give Tomas too much concern.

They walked in silence. He remembered reading Tomas's blog and not being overly impressed with his writing. The style he had adopted was exhausting, quick bursts of short, compact sentences. He was trying to sell himself as a writer as much as the story he was telling. That was fine for James Ellroy and the seedy underbelly of 50's LA, but for an exposé in modern day Belfast, it fell flat. Now that he'd spent time in McKinstry's company, he could see it was a personality trait that had bled into his writing. The man was a ball of nervous energy, eyes perpetually jumping around as he walked in small steps, his head on a constant swivel.

Tomas stopped suddenly and stared through Jacob. "Are you going to take the Followers down?"

"Take them down?" Jacob repeated, taken somewhat aback at the man's sudden change of tone.

This wasn't a crusade for Jacob. He wasn't in it for the scoop. And while he wanted to see the notes Tomas possessed, it was to assist him for the job he had been hired for. This was business and Natalie was paying him to investigate Roisin's death, not to bring down a cult. Of course, in the unlikely event a link could be proven between her death and the Followers, then they could very well fall, but none of that was his concern.

"Take them down," Tomas reaffirmed. "If someone can bring their crimes to the public, if someone can expose them, then their whole house of cards will fall."

Jacob ignored the hyperbole. "Beyond what you wrote on your blog there isn't much on them." He thought about what to say next carefully. "Even on your blog..."

"-There's nothing concrete? That's true. I might have blown my load a little early. You know how it is. The thrill of a journalist getting a scoop has to be something similar to a cop getting a break in a case."

Jacob took a sip of his coffee. "I never said I was a peeler."

"You didn't have to."

"Is it a problem for you?"

"I'm from the West. Had a few run-ins with the cops in my teenage years before I wised up. I wouldn't have come to you if it was an issue." He paused as they waited to cross the road. "And you're right. A lot of what I wrote was conjecture and all from anonymous sources. I had the foundations of a story but I had to build the picture. To do that, I had to dive in head first.

"How?"

"There's two ways in to the Followers. They recruit the vulnerable or they recruit the rich. I was never going to pass as rich so I went undercover. Lost weight, shaved my head and started mooching about the known rough sleeper spots, let my face get seen in a few of the shelters. There's one of them, down in the centre of town, the Followers took it over a few years back.

"I remember Roisin and Natalie talking about this in their podcast. The Followers buying and renovating shelters."

Tomas nodded. "It's not charitable. They get some clout, some positive press and some tax exemptions as a recognised religion and a charity."

"Smart."

"More than you know. Recognised religion means tax breaks. The shelters and the soup kitchens mean they get recruits. They go to these places and promise hot food and a warm room in exchange for listening to a few sermons. Hard for people in their situation to say no to that, right? Then they weed out the time wasters, people who are only doing it for the benefits, who might chance their arm and come back two or three times. The others though? The easily led? The mentally unwell?"

"The ones who can be turned," Jacob finished.

"Exactly. From non-believer to disciple. I mean why not? They've been kicked around by society for years. Why wouldn't they revere the organisation that's saving them from the streets. The Followers clothe them, feed them, maybe offer employment. For every one hundred people that they scoop up, maybe only one joins the church. But that one might be the zealot they want."

"What about the rich?" Jacob asked. "Hot food and a warm bed aren't going to turn them."

"Networking. The Followers promise them success. They put them in touch with other influential members of society and they vow to help each other. Contracts, interviews, hiring practises, you name it. Why do you think there's so many of the great and good affiliated with them? It's not that different from the old Free Mason influence. Of course, you scratch my back and I'll scratch yours is framed to suggest the church is the reason for their new good fortune. And if you haven't achieved what you hoped for, it's simply because you're not donating enough scratch. More money in the coffers means success for you, guaranteed."

"It's sorta brilliant," Jacob said.

"My admiration is grudging but it's there."

Jacob thought back to his meeting with Cora Adebayo. "And you think they're capable of murder?"

"Any religion is capable of murder. Anyone from here knows that well enough."

"You said you thought me and Natalie were coming to do you in."

"Figured I was maybe a loose end. But I was stupid to think they'd get to me like that. They'll never do it outright. They won't meet you head on. Hell, they won't even stab you in the back. They'll come at you sideways."

They walked in silence for a spell. "How did they get you?" Jacob asked quietly.

Tomas sighed. "Intimidation. Harassment. They found out about me quickly. I'm sure they must have had someone like yourself check me out. I've had a fair share of demons; addiction and mental health. They pulled me down, further and further. Eventually the pressure got too much, I was clean for years but I relapsed and I spiralled, or I spiralled and relapsed, I don't really remember. They kept the pressure on. I managed to wean myself off the smack but my head was fried. I spent nearly two years up in Gransha."

Jacob nodded. He wasn't sure what to say.

"I thought the same thing was happening to Roisin. The phone calls, the damage to her car..." Tomas said.

"And when she wouldn't cave, they killed her?"

"Right," Tomas replied, his voice hoarse.

"What about your notes?

"I gave them to Roisin before I went in to Gransha. Asked her to keep them safe."

"Where are they now?" He caught Tomas's wary look. "I mean, are they safe?"

"Stashed at the hostel. Old building like that, you could search from here to judgement day and not find all the hidey holes."

"You know myself and Natalie are keen to see them."

"Why? Truthfully, Kincaid."

"Natalie believes Roisin was murdered. If that's the case it was likely to suppress whatever information is in them." He left out their meeting with Luke Fisher and the ten grand he'd requested. Last thing they needed was a second person squeezing them for cash.

"And there's no ulterior motive?"

"No." Jacob replied with a shake of his head. "I'm getting paid to investigate this case and my goal is to present the truth to my client."

"I wasn't talking about your motives."

Jacob frowned. "Who? Natalie?"

Tomas nodded slowly. "If she was able to break this story it would blow the last piece from her little podcast out of the water."

"She had the chance to do that already and declined."

"Declined or not given the opportunity? Roisin wanted to break the story on her own. Natalie didn't like it but she didn't have a choice. The offer of collaboration was made so she could get at least some slice of the pie."

"I dunno..." said Jacob.

"No? Why's that? Because Natalie Amato is all sweetness and light? She's a businesswoman. She saw the value in the notes before and now with a murder added in? I'd say we're talking massive exposure. Not just for her podcast but her books, not to mention tv and film offers."

Jacob didn't reply.

"You thought she was straight up? That she was avenging Roisin's death?"

It all made sense but Jacob still couldn't quite buy it. He fancied himself the cynical sort but had never applied the thinking to Natalie. Kind, good natured and warm hearted. He had never thought to look past that. In truth, he never wanted to. He could have asked himself why, but he already knew, from the moment she had walked into his office.

Tomas patted him on the shoulder. "Dose of reality, eh? C'mon, let me show you something."

He led Jacob to a few streets over, stopping across the road from a homeless shelter. Judging by the glass façade and fresh paint job, this was one of the shelters acquired and renovated by the Followers.

A few centre users hovered near the door, smoking and paying them no mind. "You have the time?"

Jacob checked his phone. "Nine thirty-two."

Tomas sat himself on a bench and Jacob joined him. Five minutes passed before Jacob broke the silence when it was clear Tomas wasn't going to. "What are we doing here?"

"Just wait."

It was just before ten when the minibus arrived. *Followers of Eden* was stencilled on either side of the vehicle in bold yellow font along with their star crest.

"You know what it means," Tomas asked pointing to the star. Jacob shook his head. "Safety," he said, pointing to the anchor symbol before making his way around the logos on each point. "Community, loyalty, endurance, and obedience. Everything required of a good Follower."

Jacob watched as a man and a woman got out of the bus. The woman was in her early twenties with dirty blonde hair plaited neatly. The man was in his forties, clean shaven and grey. They were both dressed identically in crisp, white short-sleeved shirts, white trousers, and white shoes. The pair greeted a couple of the centre users at the door. Judging by the responses they were familiar faces.

"What are we looking at?" Jacob asked as the Followers went inside.

"Weekend recruitment."

A short time passed before the Followers re-emerged, accompanied by five others, clearly shelter users. The male Follower opened the sliding door to allow them into the bus.

"Where do they go?"

"They have a church and cultural centre down off Botanic Avenue. If you're looking to join, that's where you go."

"What about the Tabernacle out in Carrick?"

Tomas shook his head. "Full-fledged members of the church only. And only the right members at that. The ones who pay the fees or those who are devoted enough to be allowed in. Behind closed doors."

As they watched, the female Follower noticed them. She ambled over, her smile wide. "Hi there," she greeted enthusiastically. "Fine morning."

It was grey, overcast, and threatening rain. Jacob nodded his agreement. "Sure is. I've heard about you guys. The Followers of Eden, right?"

"That's right." She stuck out a hand which Jacob took. Her grip was strong. "I'm disciple Annett and we're keen to spread our message to anyone who would like to hear it. We have a centre right here in the middle of Belfast actually. Why don't you drop in sometime, we're open every day, eight in the morning until ten at night. Your friends on the bus are going to enjoy charity and listen to the word from our Emissary. Why don't you join us?"

It belatedly occurred to Jacob that Disciple Annett assumed that he was a shelter resident. Before he could answer, the male Follower appeared from behind the bus.

"June!" It was a snapping call designed to attract her immediate attention. The young woman turned and was given a firm gesture to return to the bus at once.

She offered a sympathetic smile. "Looks like we're going. If you are interested, please come down to the centre anytime."

She returned to her companion who shared some sharp words with his fellow disciple before turning his attention to Jacob and Tomas, watching them with undisguised hostility.

Jacob offered a friendly wave which, as intended, only seemed to annoy the man more. He stalked to the driver's seat, not taking his eyes off them until he was in the vehicle.

"What was his problem?"

Tomas sighed. "I think he recognised me."

"Yeah?"

"I remember him from my investigation. Didn't think the same people would still be doing pick-ups."

"Is it going to be a problem?"

"Na. Fuck 'em."

Jacob laughed. "Fuck 'em."

# 15

Jacob meandered back towards his apartment, no rush to be anywhere else. The streets were quiet, the relatively early hour combined with the mizzly rain kept the crowds at bay. He checked his phone and found no one had been looking for him.

Tomas had promised that he'd at least consider handing his notes over to him or Natalie. There was no point pushing him, he would make his decision in his own time. Jacob would take a step back and let Natalie make her pitch.

He reached Saint Anne's but instead of heading to his apartment he jumped into the Clio. A little over ten minutes later he arrived in the suburbs of Ballyhackamore. He parked on the kerb outside a smart semi-detached house and rang the doorbell.

Harry's face lit up when he saw who was standing on his doorstep. "Jesus, Jacob! Come on in!" He slapped his back before putting an arm over his shoulder. "Let me guess," he said, pointing to the shiner, "I should see the other guy."

Jacob let his uncle guide him into his house and seated himself in the front room as Harry busied himself making coffee. Harry kept a neat and tidy home but the rumpled duvet on the sofa, the drawn blinds and telltale scent of body odour in a lived-in room told Jacob his uncle had been sleeping downstairs again.

"Fight with Noreen?" he asked as Harry handed him a mug of coffee.

Harry grunted. "A big one. Packed her bag near a week ago and went over to her sisters. This is it for us this time. I swear it."

"Sure it is," Jacob said as Harry returned to the kitchen. His Uncle and Noreen had been engaged since before Jacob was a teenager. Every few months they'd have a bust-up and depending on the severity of the falling out, Harry would be banished to the sofa or Noreen would pack her bags and move in with her sister for a few days.

"Want a taste of Irish in your coffee?" Harry asked, peering around the door with a bottle of Bushmills in hand.

The clock on the mantelpiece told Jacob it had just gone half eleven. "No, Harry. Thanks anyway. How come you're sleeping down here? If Noreen's away, I mean."

Harry waved a hand as he topped up his coffee. "Ach, never liked sleeping in a bed alone. Did I ever tell you about that time in Bessbrook? When they mortared the station?"

"Only a few dozen times."

"I'd just turned into my pit after a twenty-hour shift," Harry continued without hearing him. "Next thing I know, I'm flung out of my bed and the whole bastarding station is rocking. Christ..." He shook his head at the memory.

Jacob settled back into his seat. Harry had always been open about his time in the police and in his nephew, had found an avid listener. Unlike Jacob's father, who had climbed the ladder all the way to Superintendent through administrative, office bound positions, Harry had served the majority of his time as a Detective, chasing down the worst of Northern Ireland's criminals whilst the country was in the depraved grip of the Troubles. It wasn't until he was older and a peeler himself that Jacob realised Harry's openness was a coping mechanism, his way of handling all the shit he had seen.

158

"That was really it for me in Bessbrook," Harry went on. "I couldn't have taken it anymore. We'd lost a couple of lads to a shooting just a week or so before. "Thank Christ I got moved up to Belfast a month later."

Harry and George Kincaid had shared a similar experience at the beginning of their Policing careers. Harry, the eldest by a year, had joined the RUC less than twelve months before his brother. Both Kincaid siblings were nineteen and both, as was customary for young, single recruits at the time, were sent to bandit country, South Armagh. Harry had gone to Bessbrook and George to Forkhill, two remote stations in hostile land a few miles from the Irish border.

George Kincaid had never talked about his time as a young Constable in Forkhill. That part of his life was a closed book for everyone. Jacob had never prodded. Harry's stories had told him enough of the reality they had faced on those lonely outposts to realise why.

After serving his time in South Armagh, George transferred to Belfast as a Sergeant, and took care to keep himself well away from front line Policing for the remainder of his career. Harry on the other hand, had made detective after his transfer to Belfast and had regaled a young Jacob with his old stories of hunting down and putting away murderers, terrorists, and armed robbers. He painted himself and his colleagues as hard working and harder drinking men, putting the province to rights, one cleared crime at a time.

His uncle never reached higher than the rank of sergeant but he didn't want to. Harry Kincaid was a peeler's peeler and belonged on the street. Even long retired, people had still asked Jacob when introduced, if he was any relation to DS Harry Kincaid, the man had brought people like Millar Melville, the Romper Room Ripper, to justice. No one ever asked about superintendent George Kincaid, human resources.

It was Harry who Jacob came to for advice. Harry who listened, sympathised and offered counsel. As an investigator he was unmatched. It was everything else

Harry struggled with. Kincaid Investigations had barely survived under Harry's stewardship after taking over from Jacob's elderly and ailing grandfather. Functioning alcohol abuse, his other coping mechanism, was not conductive to a reliable business owner and is what had led to his retirement from the PSNI, who were less tolerant of the old and accepted proclivities of their RUC predecessors.

Harry had packed in the private investigator bit when Jacob was still in the police. It was only through his own professional laxity that the office hadn't been sold before Jacob had taken over.

"How's Victoria?" Jacob asked, nodding to a picture on the mantelpiece of Harry with his step daughter.

"Just made Inspector actually," Harry said, his smile wide. "Moved up to Glasgow with the new girlfriend."

"At least someone with a Kincaid connection is still flying the Policing flag."

Harry nodded, looking at the picture fondly before turning back to Jacob. "So, what's the case?"

"Case?"

"I know you by now. You want to run something by Uncle Harry. You sure as shite didn't come over here on a Saturday morning to play catch up."

That was true but it saddened Jacob how quickly his uncle had seen through him. He and Harry were close, but like most of his relationships over the past few years, Jacob hadn't held up his end. Events missed, calls not returned and texts ignored. It was a familiar pattern and one he needed to rectify before he shut everyone out.

"You got me," Jacob admitted with a rueful smile. "And this one is something."

"A head scratcher?"

"A mindfuck more like."

Harry rubbed his hands together gleefully. "Lay it on me, cub."

So Jacob did. The podcast, the cult, and the dead

girl. The spilled wine and the coffee table. The fourth-floor apartment with the bolted door. The attic and the roof with no access. He told Harry about Tomas McKinstry, Luke Fisher and Liam Dunwoody, and Natalie too. He told him about the tablet in the vent with the strange code, the missing computer and phone, the attack in his office, the paper notes, and the hard drive available to the highest bidder.

Harry didn't interrupt. When Jacob was finished, he gave a low whistle. "Jesus."

"I thought it was all BS at first, but now...." He ran a hand through his hair.

"Harry took a swig of his coffee. "Let's break down what you have."

Jacob talked Harry through the investigation once more and this time his uncle gave his slant. But for every solution he offered, Jacob shut it down. The windows? Barred. The attic? Sealed. A killer hiding after the deed? The apartment searched.

Jacob knew what he was doing. He had gone through the same breakdown with Natalie at the apartment and with Michael at the bar. *What have I missed* was becoming a familiar mantra with this case.

"You know it all points to one conclusion," Harry said, once his ideas had dried up.

"An accident."

Harry nodded.

"Not with the attack in my office. Something is going on here. I just don't know what." He rubbed at his chin, feeling the untidy beard growing ever scruffier. "Another thing. A couple of days ago I was approached by a woman, Cora Adebayo. She said she's been looking into the Followers too."

"Police?"

"I'm thinking government. MI5. Maybe NCA?" He watched as Harry shifted in his seat. "What? You think that's nuts?"

"Not at all. NCA came about well after my time but MI5 have been operating here for years. Wouldn't trust them as far as I could throw them. What did this Adebayo character want?"

"A friendly chat to let me know that these Followers have a fortunate habit of finding their problems turning up dead."

"She told you this?"

"With photographic evidence to boot."

"There is another possibility," Harry said after a few seconds of deliberation.

"What's that?"

"That she's a plant, trying to scare you off."

Jacob shook his head slowly. "She had crime scene photos..."

"Which can be faked or obtained on the internet. I take it you don't know what any of the victims she mentioned to you looked like?"

"No," Jacob admitted. He thought back to how easy his tail of Cora had been. He had thought it a case of carelessness or even a lack of appreciation for his skills. Had he been duped? Was Cora a creation, a scare tactic to warn him off the case? He remembered what Tomas had told him. They would come at you sideways. "What's your gut feeling, Harry? Forgetting all the other shit. If you were treating at it as straight up murder, where would you look?"

"The money," Harry replied after considering the question. "If I had a case like this back in my day, I'd be asking, who benefits from the victim popping their clogs? Her brother. How? Well, that's for you to figure out. Only one of us here is a detective anymore."

Jacob knuckled his eye. "So that's your advice? Keep with it?"

"Of course! That's what a detective does but you know that, so why are you asking?"

Jacob shrugged, feeling suddenly tired. "I don't know."

"I think you do. I think you realised this is a case that matters and it scared you."

The exact thought had been shared by Jacob the

first time he had visited Roisin's flat. Hearing it out loud however was a different matter and he was about to protest when Harry held up a hand to shush him.

"Just hear me out. We know how your career ended. It was a shame and it wasn't right. But you've been wallowing for four years now. You can't move on because you don't want to move on."

Jacob folded his arms. "You're going to talk to me about wallowing, Harry?" His uncle sank back into his chair with a sigh and as a wave of heavy guilt washed over Jacob. "Sorry," he mumbled, not able to look his Harry in the eye.

"It's fine. You're right. "It's not been good these last few months. I'm hiding in a bottle most nights of the week. Thought I'd kicked it but I go back. The thing is, I'm doing better than a lot of the guys and girls I served with. I think that's what hurts." His eyes glazed as lost himself in some past event.

Jacob looked at his uncle. His hero. The functioning alcoholic in an empty house, sleeping alone on his sofa, haunted by ghosts. He wasn't sure why the question came to him but he asked it anyway. "Was it worth it?"

Harry came back to the room and finished the last of his spiked coffee with a grimace. "I'd do it all again."

Jacob promised his uncle a phone call later in the week to update him on how the case was progressing. They'd be fine, Jacob knew. Harry was the forgiving sort and by the afternoon the jab would have been forgotten, or at least never mentioned again. It was the best Jacob could ask for.

He stifled a yawn as he made his way through the traffic on the Newtownards Road. He couldn't remember the last proper night's sleep he had. Exhaustion was slowly gnawing away at him. He was becoming tired, irritable, snapping at people who didn't deserve it and then getting on himself for doing it.

He could have gone home and taken a much-needed nap, but didn't. The guilt of what he had said to Harry needled him, spurring him on to actually do something to try and assuage his conscience.

He managed to find a parking space close to his office. Jacob locked the security door behind him and went upstairs into the stillness of Kincaid Investigations. The odour of the chemical used on Natalie still lingered in the air.

The takeaway flyers came off the pinboard and were stuffed into a desk drawer. He logged on to his computer and brought up Roisin's *Facebook* profile. With a quick scan of the albums he found pictures of Roisin, Tomas and Liam Dunwoody. He used an app on his computer to create head shots for each of them and sent the images to the printer. He found Luke Fisher's *Instagram* account and clipped the first picture he saw and then repeated the process for Arthur Dunwoody on his company's website.

Jacob brought up *Instagram* again and found Natalie's profile in his recent searches. He tapped his mouse as he pondered for a second before screen shotting her most recent upload; a picture of her and Dillon with the beach at Helen's Bay in the background. Jacob cropped out Dillon and printed the picture of Natalie along with the rest.

After attaching the set to the pin board with tacs, he scrawled the names of each person on individual Post-It notes.

He returned to the computer and the folder with the pictures he took in Roisin's apartment. The replacement door, the gouges left by the bolts on the old frame. The vent, the attic and the security door, the coffee table, the stained floor, the windows and the open safe. His printer sounded ready to take off with the deluge of jobs he was sending its way.

Pictures of the smashed tablet and the rag used to incapacitate Natalie followed, along with a screenshot from *Google Maps* of the building Cora Adebayo had disappeared into.

With the printer finally silent, and likely in desperate need of a cigarette, Jacob collected all the images and stuck them to the board. He took three more post-its and wrote *HARD DRIVE*, *PAPER NOTES* and *TABLET* on them.

With the pieces in play, Jacob began to work through what he had.

Roisin Dunwoody; victim. Dead of an apparent slip and fall. Jacob moved the images of the replacement door and the original frame with the gouges left by the bolts underneath Roisin's picture.

He moved the other images of the building across too. The grille and padlock blocking access to the roof and attic. The windows, all locked from the inside. A picture he had taken before leaving, showing Roisin's apartment on the top floor with no way to climb up other than by ladder.

Jacob grabbed another post-it and wrote *FIRE ALARM* on it before attaching it to the board. Mrs. Jameison had said it sounded for around fifteen minutes. A distraction to trick Roisin into opening her door and then covering the sound of her murder?

It could explain the bruising on her chest but Arthur had said there had been no defensive wounds, no other marks, or bruises anywhere else on her body and nothing under her fingernails.

As a theory it still made sense but the thought of the killer staying in Roisin's home after the deed didn't sit right with Jacob. They had no way of knowing how long they would be waiting for someone to check up on Roisin. They would also need to have relied on the door being forced open and then replaced with one that they could unlock from the inside to escape. Not to mention the problem of somehow concealing themselves from the police for a number of hours in a large, but very sparse apartment.

He turned to the involved parties.

Tomas McKinstry. Friend and former lover. Also a man with a long, self-admitted history of mental illness and drug addiction. Failed journalist. One who had suffered a hell of a lot and failed to break the story that

Roisin had eventually managed to.

Luke Fisher. Another former lover, angry and rejected. Attempting to bribe the Followers after somehow finding himself in possession of a hard drive allegedly containing Roisin's research. Could he have killed Roisin in order to silence her or was it the familiar story of a spurned man getting the most final kind of revenge?

Liam Dunwoody. The unknown. Another party with a known drug habit and a sizeable inheritance doubled by his sister's death. With his job and skill set, Liam was the most likely to have the means to commit the murder without ever entering the room.

He moved to the picture beside Liam's. Arthur Dunwoody, an engineer himself and a damn successful one. Described as cold by Natalie. Still, his daughter was dead and Jacob didn't expect the man to be pumping the air in celebration. As a killer? Jacob couldn't see a motive but he also remembered a remarkable lack of surprise when Jacob had turned up at his doorstep offering wild theories that Roisin had actually been murdered.

Jacob pinned the image of the chemical-soaked rag between father and son. Who else would have access to that kind of substance? The question was why would Liam or Arthur want the tablet that has been stashed in Rosin's kitchen vent?

He didn't have the answer for that yet, so he turned to the last image. Natalie Amato. She had hired him to find a killer, when everyone else had already moved on, believing the death to be accidental. Jacob had assumed that tracking the killer down was Natalie's sole intention. That morning's conversation with Tomas McKinstry had sewed the first seeds of doubt that had slowly blossomed over the last few hours.

Natalie had a lot to gain by breaking this story. Was it a case of a cynical business move rather than simply avenging the death of an innocent woman? A woman who by Natalie's own admission she was not close with.

Did Natalie belong on the board? Jacob tried to ask himself honestly, ignoring his juvenile crush as best he could. He was about to tear the picture down but stopped. All angles had to be looked at, whether he liked it or not. He left the picture where it was.

He moved on to his next question. One that he had begun to ponder over the last day or so. What if murder hadn't been the killer's intention, only the end result?

The notes on the Followers were valuable. Luke was confident enough to ask for ten grand for what he had on that hard drive. Tomas had told them Roisin had given him back his original paper copies but they were taking him at his word. Could it have been a case of him seizing them by force when realising how important they really were, killing Roisin in the process and then lying to their faces?

He looked at the picture of the open safe and moved it next to the post-its where he had written *HARD DRIVE, PAPER NOTES* and *TABLET*. What if someone had broken into Roisin's apartment to take the notes and had been discovered? No defensive wounds because the intruder had shoved Roisin away immediately. She slipped, hit her head and the wine she was holding left a convenient explanation for how she had died.

Or had the killer found the notes were no longer in Roisin's possession, decided she was too much trouble to keep around and bashed her head against the coffee table.

He rubbed his eyes as took a step back and perched himself on his desk. His phone vibrated beside him. He picked it up to find an unknown number calling. When he answered it was a female voice who spoke.

"Jacob?"

"Yeah?"

"It's Mairead. From the podcast?"

"Mairead, hi!" Jacob said, standing up suddenly. "What uh, what can I do for you?"

"Well, I was thinking about how you said I could call

you if I remembered anything about your case."

"Yeah?" Jacob looked up at the pin board and marvelled at the serendipitous timing.

"Well, I couldn't think of anything."

"Oh." Jacob felt himself deflate in an instant.

"But then I remembered you said I could call you and maybe arrange for you to buy me a drink."

"Oh yeah?" Jacob tried to hide his surprise by playing it cool. Or at least giving an impression of what he felt playing it cool sounded like.

"So, you free tonight?"

"Absolutely," Jacob replied, deciding playing it cool was not his style.

"Excellent. Um, how about The Garrick? Say, half seven?"

"Yeah, that'd be, that'd be good. Yeah."

He could hear the smile in her voice as she spoke. "Alright. I'll see you then."

Jacob grinned as he put the phone down then picked it back up and checked the call log. Satisfied reality was still in place, he took one last look at the board. Roisin Dunwoody could wait another day.

# 16

As Jacob jostled his way through a group of rowdy students crowded by the front door, he saw that Mairead had beaten him to the pub and managed to claim a table at one of the small booths. She waved as she saw him approach.

"What are you having?" He asked, pointing to the drink in front of her.

"Gin and tonic." Mairead was almost shouting to be heard over the din. She had lost the glasses and was wearing her dark hair loose over one shoulder. The casual work outfit had been replaced with a button-down linen shirt and smart khaki trousers.

Jacob managed to squeeze himself into a free space at the bar and was steadfastly ignored for the next ten minutes. The Garrick had been open for business since the 1800's and along with The Spaniard, was one of Jacob's favourite watering holes in the city. The wood-panelled walls were plastered with vintage mirrors and advertising boards promoting local tipples, many of which were long out of production. The fireplace sat unlit but ancient oil lamps cast a warm glow over a pub enjoying a roaring Saturday night trade.

Eventually, Jacob returned to the booth with Mairead's gin and a pint of a local craft beer for himself. She slid across the padded leather bench freeing up a space so he could sit next to her. "Cheers," she said, holding up her drink.

"Cheers," Jacob replied, clinking his glass against hers. "Have to say this was a bit unexpected."

Mairead smiled demurely. "What can I say? I found you kinda intriguing."

If Jacob had been asked to come up with a word to describe what Mairead had thought about him after their first meeting, intriguing would be somewhere down near the bottom of the list, stuck between dashing and suave.

"Ah, c'mon! Don't try and play it cool." She slapped his arm playfully as he failed to think of something clever to say. "It's not everyday someone turns up at your work investigating a murder!"

Her excited tone caught the attention of the two men at the table closest to them. Jacob wasn't sure if they heard what was said over the commotion of the busy pub but he motioned for Mairead to keep it down.

In Belfast, you could never be sure who was listening and the notion that you might be police could be enough provocation for someone to bring up old grudges. Jacob making the distinction that he was actually a private detective was unlikely to carry much weight. He waited a couple of seconds before leaning forward to keep their conversation private.

"So you do think it's a murder?"

"Well, not at first but Natalie has been so sure, since the beginning. That thing in your office sounded so scary."

"She told you about that?"

Mairead nodded. "She's been keeping us updated ever since she hired you. She's lucky you were there." She pointed to his black eye. "Does it hurt?"

Jacob affected a casual shrug. "I've had worse."

"Really?"

"Na," he admitted. "What else did Natalie tell you?"

"Hmm...about Roisin's ex-boyfriend at the hostel and how Luke was trying to sell Roisin's hard drive." She thought for a moment. "I think that's it really."

Jacob took a long drink of beer. Mairead seemed to

know as much about his case as he did. He wasn't sure how he felt about Natalie divulging so much of what had happened to others who were on the periphery. Then again, she was the boss, so she called the shots. If the investigation were to be compromised by loose talk, it would be on her. Although he was confident he could rely on Michael and Harry's discretion, he wasn't so sure about the Miss Gumshoe team.

He looked up at Mairead as she people watched. Luke Fisher had let slip he had been in contact with her recently and Jacob remembered Natalie's assertion about her being a nice girl, but maybe someone you wouldn't trust with your deepest, darkest secrets.

"Do you know anything about the notes Roisin had?"

"No. I mean, I figured she had some. She must have if she was going to make her own podcast."

"Were you all going to be involved in that?"

"I think so. Roisin and Natalie were still in the early planning stages but I think Natalie wanted to keep us around."

"Why not keep it on Miss Gumshoe?" Jacob asked, playing dumb.

"With all the backlash I think Natalie was content to take a back seat."

"Backlash?"

"The podcast got some pretty threatening e-mails and letters. Legal stuff threatening to take us to Court and some personal stuff too. Natalie didn't tell you?"

"She did not," Jacob lied. "What kind of letters?"

"I'm not sure exactly. Natalie never told us anymore than the basics. But I think she gave it up as a bad job about hosting the show on Miss Gumshoe. Helping Roisin as a producer at least gave her some involvement."

"What about now?"

She frowned. "How do you mean?"

"Roisin's story. Natalie is planning to continue it, right?"

Mairead looked down at her drink. "I'm not really sure we're meant to say anything."

"Fair enough. Forget I mentioned it." Her response had told him enough.

"So." Mairead rested her head in her hand. "What's next?"

"Another beer probably."

She laughed politely. "Funny. I mean in the case, what's your next step? The next clue?"

Jacob sighed; his reluctance clear.

"What?"

"You and Luke Fisher."

"What about me and Luke Fisher?"

"How close are you?"

"You mean how likely am I to go running to Luke when we're finished and blab?"

"Basically."

"Luke's a wanker. He texted me after Roisin died, looking for a shoulder to cry on, or so he said. I fell for it and then quickly came to my senses."

"How much have you told him about my investigation?"

"Nothing! Last I saw him was about the same time Natalie said she was thinking of hiring someone to look into Roisin's death. I'm not sure we've even spoke since then." Jacob nodded slowly, and then felt the slow rub of a foot against his leg. An intimate gesture and a good deal more forward than Jacob would have anticipated. "C'mon. I won't tell a soul. Not even Natalie." She pouted for maximum effect.

"Not a soul," Jacob said, pointing a finger.

"Cross my heart."

Jacob took another drink as he weighed up whether this was a bad idea against the possibility, however scant, of getting his rocks off. "I talked to Roisin's father a few days back," he said, the decision made immediately. "Let him know I had taken on the case. He let it slip that Roisin and her brother were going to be the beneficiaries of a rather sizeable inheritance upon his death."

"Is he old?"

"No and fitter than most guys half his age. Still, Roisin's brother has a job that gives him access to all sorts of chemicals that in theory could be used to kill or incapacitate someone."

Mairead's face lit up. "Which means he didn't have to enter the room."

"Exactly."

She clapped her hands together. "That's so clever."

"And completely unproven. I could be well off the mark but it's the only theory I have that makes sense and I'm using sense in the loosest possible terms."

His phone vibrated. He reached into his pocket to find it was Natalie calling him.

"Jesus." Mairead's tone taking on a mortified edge as she tilted her head to read the caller ID. "Mother checking up on you?"

"Maybe," Jacob said, pocketing the phone and letting it ring out. "But it's Saturday night. I'm off the clock for a few hours."

"The way you were looking at Natalie back at the studio, I'd say you fancy her."

"She's my employer," Jacob said, trying not to sound too defensive and failing. "Besides, I'm not sure I'd have much of a shot."

"Well, Jesus. That's a nice thing to hear with the girl you're actually out with. Yeah, I fancy her but I don't like my chances so here I am."

"Oh, that wasn't…"

Mairead snorted. "Relax! I'm fucking with you."

As his cheeks reddened his phone vibrated again. He tutted in and declined Natalie's call with a swipe of the screen before powering the phone off.

"So, what about the Followers?" Mairead asked with a wry smile as Jacob put his phone away.

"What about them?"

"Natalie was convinced they were behind what happened to Roisin. You don't think that's the case?"

"I'm not sure that angle made much sense. The podcast had already released and there's other ways to stop whatever Roisin was working on."

"Natalie mentioned something about the paper notes being with Roisin's ex. Thomas?"

"Tomas," Jacob corrected. "Lives down in a hostel in Sailortown."

"But you haven't seen them?"

"No. Look, Mairead, can we not talk shop? I'd like to step away from Roisin Dunwoody for an hour or two."

Mairead offered a sympathetic smile. "Sorry, I just find the whole thing fascinating. No more questions about it from here on, I promise."

They sat and talked. Jacob about his policing career, skirting around how it ended and his segue into Private Detective work. He didn't want to talk shop but without his job he wasn't sure what else was there to him.

He avoided Roisin Dunwoody and instead stuck to old cases. Mairead was a keen listener and seemed genuinely interested in his world. She talked about her family, of a single mother raising five children after their father walked out when Mairead was only seven. She talked about growing up in Derry, her interest in media, her move to Belfast and how she came to work with Natalie through her job at Wheelman.

The hours slipped by, the crowd thinned and soon last orders were called.

As the pair stepped outside, Jacob turned his phone back on to find a number of missed calls from Natalie. Mairead laughed, looking over his shoulder. "You sure it's not a school night?"

He scrolled down. The last was only ten minutes ago. He hit the call button and raised the phone to his ear before turning back to Mairead. "What's your plan?"

"Head down to the taxi rank."

"A taxi in Belfast on a Saturday night? Good luck."

"And what would you suggest?"

"My place is down in Saint Annes. Come back with me. Have a nightcap."

She scrunched her nose. "I dunno..."

"C'mon, it'll..."

He was interrupted as Natalie answered her phone. "Jacob? Jesus, where have you been?"

"Out," Jacob said, immediately defensive and not sure why. "What's up?"

"Have you checked the messages I sent you?"

"No. Still trying to work my way through the deluge of missed calls." He glanced at Mairead and was rewarded with a titter of laughter.

"Just look at the link I sent. Don't hang up!"

Jacob did as he was told. Usually cool and collected, Natalie sounded uncharacteristically flustered on the other end of the line.

The link took him to a video. It was dark at first with the sound of someone fumbling with their phone mixed against a male voice, muffled but clearly shouting. The screen turned white for a second as the cover was lifted and then slowly focused to show what appeared to be a church.

The people in frame were looking behind them at the sound of the commotion. The camera turned, shakily to show Tomas McKinstry shouting at the top of his lungs. "Fuckers! I know what youse did! Murderous fucks!"

Behind the camera operator someone laughed nervously. "Oh my God," a female breathed, not wanting to draw attention to themselves.

"Get him out here now! I want to talk to the fucker!"

Mairead moved beside Jacob to watch the video. By now Tomas had been flanked by a group of Followers in their traditional white garb, who were in turn joined by two burly men in smart suits.

"Get your fucking hands off me!" Tomas screamed as one tried to take his arm. It was no good. He was seized roughly and hauled from the church, his feet not touching the ground on the way out.

"Fuck me," Jacob said, putting the phone back to his ear.

"It's already got two thousand odd views on TikTok," Natalie said. "I've no idea what set him off. He phoned me this morning but I was at a family event and missed the call."

"He called me too. I met him in town but he seemed good. In control."

"You didn't say anything that could have set him off?"

"What would I have said?" Jacob snapped, annoyed at the implication, and tired of the attitude he felt he was getting from Natalie.

She ignored the petulance. "I've been trying to call the hostel, in between calling you. The couple of times I got through he wasn't there. They haven't picked up in the last hour. I really think someone should check on him."

"Ok?"

"Jacob, I know it's asking a lot."

"I can't. I've been drinking and I have no hope of getting a taxi. Why can't you go?"

"I can't just leave Dillon home alone, it's almost two in the morning and..."

"...And you don't want to go down to Star of the Sea on your own," Jacob finished. He couldn't blame her for that. The hostel was a rough place in daylight. He rubbed his face. "Look, I'm outside The Garrick. Come pick me up and we'll head down together."

"Alright. Thank you, Jacob. Give me fifteen minutes, ok?"

"You get all that?" He asked Mairead as he pocketed his phone.

She seemed to think for a second. "You think there's a chance she'll give me a lift?"

*

Jacob and Mairead were the only people left on the street when Natalie pulled up at the kerb twenty minutes later. A ruffled and sleep addled Dillon sat grumpily in the front passenger seat.

"Mairead?" Natalie turned in surprise as her sound

editor climbed into the backseat of her car.

"Hi!" Mairead waved brightly as Natalie shot Jacob a look. Annoyance? Maybe a flicker of jealousy? Jacob reminded himself he was pretty drunk and it was probably none of the above.

"So," Natalie said lightly as the car moved off. "What were you two kids up to tonight then?"

"Just a few sociable drinks," Jacob replied quickly.

"Jacob was giving me the inside scoop on the investigation."

Jacob closed his eyes. He was rather taken with Mairead but it was clear she couldn't hold her water even if she was drowning.

"Was he now?"

"Nothing you haven't previously divulged, I'm sure."

The car lapsed into silence for the remainder of the short trip down to Sailortown.

The two streetlights closest to Star of the Sea were out and the desolate street was cloaked in long shadows. If someone was watching, Jacob doubted he would have seen them from spitting distance. He exited the car with Natalie and walked to the front door of the hostel.

Amanda, the young woman who had been there the day before, was manning the desk and buzzed the pair through the front door. "Sorry, residents only after eight PM."

"We're looking for Tomas."

"Haven't seen him since I came on duty."

"When was that?"

Amanda checked a gold Michael Kors watch. "About five hours ago."

"We're worried about him. Have you seen the video that's been going around?"

Amanda shook her head. Natalie retrieved her mobile, found the video and passed the phone under the glass partition. Amanda watched the video in silence but Jacob could see her wince at what she was looking at, "Seems like Tomas is undergoing one of his episodes," she said as she handed the phone back.

"What sort of episodes?" Natalie asked.

Amanda hesitated a second. "He's schizophrenic. And he has addiction issues. For the most part he handles it well but he has his bad days. That might be the worst I've seen though."

"Can we check his room?"

"He's not up there. All residents are required to sign in." She nodded to a guest book next to Natalie's elbow.

"He could have snuck in," said Natalie.

Amanda pointed to the front door. "That's the only entrance."

"There's no other way in?" Jacob asked, dubiously.

"There's a fire exit," Amanda admitted slowly. "But it's meant to stay closed."

"Can we check his room anyway?" Natalie asked, the concern in her tone clear. "Something might have set him off and it would be helpful to know what."

"The rooms are for residents only and they have a right to privacy."

"I understand that," Natalie replied patiently. "But this is Tomas's well-being we're talking about. If something triggered him, it could be in his room."

"Or he might have hurt himself," Jacob added. He'd attended more suicides than he cared to count. Tomas himself said he rarely left the hostel. His stomach fluttered with the apprehension of what they might find and part of him secretly hoped Amanda would stick to her guns.

He was out of luck. Amanda debated for a moment before producing a key from under the desk. She slid it under the partition. "Room 202. Second floor."

Natalie gave the woman a reassuring smile before leading Jacob up the stairs two at a time.

"You don't think this could have waited until the morning?" Jacob asked, trying to keep up.

"I knew Tomas had some vulnerabilities," Natalie replied without looking back. "But for him to go off the radar the day after we meet him? That doesn't concern you?"

Jacob said nothing. Mental health and drug addiction. He had seen this play out more times than enough to know the behaviour was concerning.

There was more to it as well, although it was left unsaid. If Tomas had hurt himself, both of them would have to shoulder some of the guilt. They had tracked him down and brought up history he had tried to bury.

Aside from the sound of a tv further along the dim, narrow corridor, Star of the Sea slept. When Natalie unlocked the door to Tomas's room, they found a small space stinking of stale cigarette smoke but otherwise neat and orderly.

Jacob checked the bathroom. The shower was a much-favoured suicide spot for those looking to shuffle off this mortal coil. Nudging the door open with his toe, he inched himself into the room until he saw it was empty. "He's not here," he said, releasing the breath he hadn't realised he had been holding.

A small wooden desk and rickety chair had been crammed into the corner of the room. The desk was clear but Jacob saw that the two side drawers were both stuffed with loose documents and assorted junk. He started to rifle through the first.

"Just checking if he left behind a note or anything that might give us some clue what set him off," he explained as he caught Natalie watching him. She nodded slowly and turned to an old wardrobe, opening its door to begin her own search.

Jacob began a search of the second drawer. "Usually they leave a note where it can be found. I doubt he's..." Jacob stopped as his fingers brushed against a smooth glass surface, unseen amongst the clutter. He reached in and took hold of a small brown bottle filled with a clear liquid. The bottle was unmarked although a label had clearly been peeled off its surface. He unscrewed the cap and was hit with the same unmistakable odour that was on the rag used to knock Natalie for a loop. Behind him he heard Natalie gasp sharply.

He turned to face her, bottle still in hand. Jacob felt his stomach tighten as he saw what she was holding.

Wordlessly, Natalie held out a black wool balaclava with clumsy white stitching.

# 17

A sudden violent rainfall chased Jacob and Natalie back to her car. "Did you find anything?" Mairead asked as they jumped in, slamming the doors behind them.

"No." They answered in unison.

"So, he wasn't there?"

"Mairead, let's get you home," Natalie said as she started the car. "And get you to bed, Dillon."

"Whatever," Dillon said, stifling an irritated yawn.

Mairead tried to catch Jacob's attention but he only gave her a tired shake of his head. None of it made sense. Tomas calling him to meet that very morning before going bugaloo and storming a Follower service. Strange enough even without finding the mask and the little brown bottle in his room.

 Jacob had to admit that he never made the connection between the similar builds of Tomas and their attacker. The masked man was dangerous, someone who was comfortable with violence. Tomas had been taken out with just one gut punch.

*They'll come at you sideways.*

The words rang in his ears as he felt his anger boiling.

The car braking broke him from his reverie. Mairead thanked Natalie for the lift.

"I'll give you a call," Jacob said as she opened the door, realising he had ignored her for the entirety of the journey, his mind firmly elsewhere.

It sounded rather lame but she reached across and gave his arm a gentle squeeze. He caught Natalie's eyes watching them in the rearview before she quickly looked away.

Ten minutes later, they were back at Natalie's. Jacob hadn't even questioned where they were going. Dillon made a beeline for the stairs and his bed while Jacob followed Natalie into the kitchen. She waited until she heard her son's door closing on the floor above before turning to Jacob. "What. The. Fuck?"

Jacob shrugged. It was the only thing he could think to do.

"I don't get it."

"What is there to get? He conned us and good."

Natalie grumbled, not committing to voicing her opinion just yet. Jacob reached into his pocket and brought the balaclava and little brown bottle as if they were the ultimate and irrefutable proof.

"But why?" she asked, refusing to look at the mask.

"That I don't know," said Jacob. "But think about it. What's the first thing Tomas did when he saw us."

Natalie put her hands on her hips. "He ran."

"Right. That whole thing about someone looking to do him in. It didn't sit right with me from the start but I didn't question it. He ran because he thought the two people he had attacked the day before tracked him down and he was due a shoeing."

"But he seemed so genuine. About Roisin, I mean."

"He was. Genuine in his guilt."

"You mean..."

"Why not? He certainly seemed bitter enough about what happened to him. The Followers hurt him bad. All that shit he went through, only for Roisin to take his work and make something of it. A three-episode podcast with hundreds of thousands of listeners and her own series on the way. Now Roisin is dead and he can take centre stage."

Natalie rubbed her eye. "And the video?"

That stopped Jacob short. "For our benefit," he said

slowly, trying to think it through. Tomas knew we'd see it." He shook his head, thinking about their meeting earlier. How Tomas had focused on the Followers. Trying to get Jacob to see who the bad guys were when it was right in front of his face, buying him coffee. "We need to find him."

Natalie took the phone from her pocket before raising it to her ear "Nothing," she said, after a few seconds.

"Keep trying. Chances are, Amanda won't tell him we were in his room and if he doesn't notice the balaclava and bottle missing, he'll have no idea what we found. We can try to arrange a meeting."

"A meeting?"

"Lean on him. Get some straight answers." Jacob left it unsaid just how hard he intended to lean once he caught up with Tomas.

Natalie tried to call again with the same result as before. Her eyes flicked up from her phone. "How did you and Mairead get on?"

"Why?" Jacob asked, surprised at the question at this particular time. "Is it a problem?"

Natalie raised her eyebrows but concentrated on the phone. "Why would it be? You're both adults. As long as it doesn't impact your work for me, why would I have an issue?"

"Right," Jacob replied as he rubbed at his face. He wasn't sure if he was relieved or a little disheartened, and decided to change the subject. "Tomorrow I'm going to try and talk with Luke Dunwoody."

"The gassed room theory."

"Tomas already let it slip he and Liam have met."

"What's your approach going to be?"

"Direct."

"Is that the smart move?"

He managed a humourless laugh. "The soft touch hasn't gotten me anywhere so far. I have nothing on him other than a half-arsed theory. If I get close enough to the truth, shake him up, he might crack."

"Or he could clam up and you lose your shot."

"Or he could tell me I'm talking nonsense and smack me in the mouth for even suggesting he had anything to do with his sister's death. Choices, choices." Natalie gave an irritated sigh as she lowered her phone once more. "He'll turn up."

She looked at her watch and stifled a yawn. "It's late. I don't think we're going to accomplish much more tonight."

"Right," Jacob said, taking his cue to leave.

"I'll drive you." Natalie grabbed her car keys from the counter.

"No, don't be silly. It's going on three in the morning. I'll get a taxi."

"On a Saturday night in Belfast?"

"I know a guy."

It was an hour after leaving Natalie's that he finally managed to snag a passing black taxi who took him home for an extortionate price. He jolted awake as the it came to a stop behind the Cathedral. Jacob slipped the driver his money, told him to keep the twenty pence in change and got out.

The storm hadn't abated and Jacob stuck his head down against the deluge and crossed the empty piazza towards home.

It wasn't until he was a few feet from the entrance to his building that he realised he wasn't alone. The figure detached itself from the long shadow offered by the awning of a restaurant and stepped towards him. Even above the rain, Jacob could hear the unmistakable rack of a baton extending.

The figure seemed to hesitate before leaping at Jacob, the previously unseen baton now swinging in a high arc above his head. Cold metal glinted in the moonlight.

Jacob stumbled back as the tip of the weapon missed him by the skin on his teeth. Losing his balance, he fell and landed painfully on his rear end. The figure advanced as Jacob scooted backwards before scrambling to his feet.

The stranger swung again but slipped on the rain slick piazza tiles. He dropped to a knee, giving Jacob the time he needed to take off into the wet Belfast night.

Running up Hill Street, he turned into the entryway past the Duke of York, the same route he had used to tail Cora Adebayo the day before. His attacker, recovering quickly, was close behind and gaining. The thought of the baton turning him into the business end of an ice lolly gave Jacob an extra jolt of speed.

Head down and legs pumping as fast as they could possibly carry him, Jacob headed towards the deserted city centre. He passed five bars, all closed. Any other city in the UK and they would still be crammed full of Saturday night revellers. Belfast was a ghost town.

Careening out into Royal Avenue, he heard a yell from behind. Chancing a look, Jacob could see his pursuer had lost his footing and went sliding on his arse straight into a bin.

Acidic bile bit at the back of Jacob's throat as he sucked in a lungful of air. The figure slowly got to his feet and Jacob got the feeling he wasn't the giving up type. He took off again, knowing the masked man wouldn't be far behind.

He had a plan. Half-baked but preferable to collapsing a lung. With a final spurt of effort, he tore up Royal Avenue, into North Street and then an immediate left into Church Street, ducking behind an entry for an underground garage.

Jacob crouched behind a low wall and waited, fighting to control his breathing as sweat and rain stung his eyes.

The footsteps were loud and Jacob could hear them slowing to a jog as the man attempted to trace his quarry. He waited, thinking he had continued up North Street but a long shadow falling across the entryway nixed that brief hope.

He held on until the man was almost on top of him before he let out a bellow, fuelled by fear and adrenaline in equal measure, and leaped out from his cover. His punch was clumsy but caught the masked man on the temple.

As the man stumbled Jacob made a grab for the baton, managing to get a grip around its tip. The masked man panicked, attempting to wrench the weapon away. Feet skidded over the slick road surface as both men jostled desperately for an advantage. Jacob rammed his head into the other man's face and saw a flash of blinding white light. It was far from the perfect Belfast kiss but the man wheeled away, the baton dropping from his hands.

Jacob kicked the weapon into the gutter and grabbed a handful of collar. "Wait-" The figure managed to gasp before Jacob doubled him over with a punch to the gut, followed by a second. He groaned and dropped to his knees. Jacob took a step back and kicked him hard in the ribs. The masked figure grunted and rolled over, covering up to ward off any further blows. Whoever he was, he was no fighter.

Jacob booted him again, more out of principle than anything else. He leaned against the nearest wall, fighting the vomit that rose in his throat. He spat and tried to catch his breath as the man on the ground continued to shield himself.

"Christ," Jacob said between ragged breaths as he reached down. A hand went up but Jacob shoved it away angrily and took a hold of the plain black balaclava, wrenching it free.

It took him a second under the orange glow of the street light to put a name to the face. He recognised him but couldn't remember where from until it suddenly clicked. "Doctor Rourke?"

Dishevelled, bloodied and breathless, but unmistakably him. Jacob counted the days since he had carried out the surveillance job on the good doctor and his adultery. Less than a week but it felt much longer. Defiant eyes now glared back at him.

Before Jacob could say anything, blue light swirled

around the dark street. Jacob hadn't heard the sirens but a second later an unmarked PSNI Skoda pulled up a few feet from where Jacob stood over Rourke.

"Hands! Show me your hands!" The first peeler out of the car bellowed, one hand on the canister of PAVA spray attached to his belt.

Jacob did as instructed and allowed himself to be roughly seized by the officer. Any resistance at this stage with the man so amped up would have Jacob kissing wet concrete. He allowed himself to be pulled away from Rourke as a second cop car screeched to a halt behind the first.

Jacob felt the first cuff go on before the second manacle bashed against the bone on his wrist. You're meant to keep those oiled," Jacob said wincing as the officer tried again with the same painful result.

"What's been going on here then?" The officer asked, fumbling for his handcuff key to open the second manacle as his partner took hold of Jacob's arm. The second pair of peeler's ambled over to where Rourke still lay.

"Defending myself."

"Looked like you were kicking the shit out of your man there," the cop holding on to Jacob helpfully offered.

"Not me. The minimum amount of force required to keep myself safe, nothing more."

"Paddy," one of the second pair called over, holding up the baton he had just found in the gutter.

"He chased me with that," Jacob said quickly. "Waited for me outside my home and chased me over half of bloody Belfast trying to bash my brains in."

Paddy nodded, scribbling in his notebook before he moved over to Rourke. The good Doctor was now standing, roughly helped to his feet by the larger of the second set of officers. Jacob couldn't make out the conversation between Rourke and Officer Paddy but was certain he heard the words "Solicitor," and "No Comment." With an annoyed shake of his head, Paddy walked back towards Jacob.

"Look, my name is Jacob Kincaid. I'm a private investigator. I was recently hired by that man's wife to look into whether he was having an affair. Turned out he was. Now he seems to be holding a grudge." Paddy's look was skeptical. Jacob knew it well; it was the same expression he had worn every day for the eight years he had been on the job. People lied to the police. It was as irrefutable a fact as where the sun rose and set.

"My ID is in my wallet. You can run my name if you want." Jacob gave his date of birth and home address. He seriously doubted he was going to escape a night in the cells but he was determined to be as helpful and open as he could.

Paddy's partner, who still had Jacob by the arm, found his wallet and the ID within. He showed it to Paddy who took it and stepped away, holding his radio close to his mouth. "Uniform, Alpha Tango Seven One. We've located these two men, both currently detained. Can you run a name for me and recap the description from the witness of who was the one seen with the weapon?"

Jacob knew Belfast centre was thick with CCTV. He'd have to be the unluckiest dickhead this side of the Irish Sea if not one camera had picked up their little chase. "Hey!" he called out to the two officers with Rourke. "What does that look like to you? There, down by your left foot." The officer glanced down and scanned the ground before seeing what Jacob was referring to. Kneeling, he picked up the balaclava Jacob had dropped.

"We're waiting to hear back from our camera operators." Paddy said, returning to where Jacob was standing.

Jacob nodded and raised his hands to wipe the rain off his face only for them to be roughly shoved down by the peeler still holding on to him. "Keep your hands down, mate."

He decided not to argue the point. "Busy night?"

Paddy replied with a grimace. "We were on our way back to the station, hoping to get a break when this call came in."

Before Jacob could offer his sympathies a third police car pulled up at the junction of the little street. "Couldn't be that busy. Half of the peelers in Belfast must be here." He watched as Michael Healy stepped out of the passenger seat and couldn't hold his relived smile.

"Alright, Paddy?" Michael said hurrying over.

"Alright, Heals," Paddy replied. "What brings you here?"

"For him, actually" Michael nodded toward Jacob.

"Wanted?"

"No, just a pal. Heard is name on the radio and thought I'd make sure he's ok. Has he been scooped?"

"No, not yet," Paddy replied. It was clear by the tone in his voice that he wasn't sure what Michael was playing at. This wasn't Coalburn's patch and to show up and question the officers on scene, even on behalf of a mate, was bad form. "We're waiting to see what the CCTV guys say."

"I heard the call. Male being chased by another. Possible weapon involved."

Jacob felt Paddy bristle. "I know what the call was. I'm sorting it out."

Michael held up his hands in apology. "No offence meant, Paddy."

Paddy looked like he was about to say something further but stopped and stepped away, hand going to his radio mic. "Send."

Jacob watched but Paddy gave nothing away. He turned to Michael who would be hearing the same transmission and was heartened with a reassuring wink. "Alright," Paddy said, turning back to Jacob. "CCTV seems to confirm your story. Doesn't really explain why you gave the man such a trimming though."

"Self defence." Michael cut in.

Paddy turned to Michael and Jacob wondered if his

friend was going to snatch defeat from the jaws of victory and cost him a night in custody after all.

"Listen mate," Jacob cut in, stepping in front of Michael, forcing Paddy to look at him. "It was self defence. But I know you need to do your bit, fair enough. You have my name and my address. You can follow-up with me in slow time. I'm an ex-peeler, I know the score and I won't mess you about." Paddy didn't look convinced. "What's he saying?" Jacob pressed, nodding towards Rourke. "Nothing, right? So, no counter allegation."

"Are you willing to make a statement?"

"I've drink on board but I'll give an initial account on body worn if you want."

Paddy considered for a moment before Michael tapped him on the shoulder and motioned with his head for them to step away. They called over one of the officer's standing with Rourke and together the trio retreated for a quick conflab.

When finished, Michael approached with another wink and uncuffed him. "Your lucky day," he said. "I told Paddy I'd record your initial account right now while he takes your friend down to custody."

"What's he getting lifted for?" Jacob asked as he watched Paddy give Rourke the good news. "Assault and possession of an offensive weapon?"

"Obstruction too. He's not telling them anything. Not even his name."

"Dickhead." He rolled his wrist as the handcuff came free.

Michael led him to his police car and Jacob sat in the back with a heavy sigh. The adrenaline dump was in full effect. In the front passenger seat, Michael removed the body worn video camera from his flak jacket and pointed it towards Jacob. He pressed the record button and was rewarded with a single *beep*.

"Alright Mr. Kincaid, tell me what happened tonight."

Jacob kept his account concise and brief, including

the details of his work for Patricia Rourke and skipping the part about the headbutt and follow-up kicking he had dished out to her other half.

"Want us to take you home?" Michael asked when the video was finished.

Jacob shook his head. "It's only across the square." In the panic of the chase, he had almost managed to circle through the city centre all the way back to his apartment.

"It's bucketing."

"I'm not going to get any wetter," Jacob said, knowing he looked like a drowned rat.

"Alright," Michael said slowly.

Jacob was half out the car when he remembered. "Michael? I need a favour?"

"Keeping you out of the cells isn't a favour?"

"Another one."

Michael gave an amused grunt. "Go ahead. I'll add it to your list of IOU's."

"I'm looking for someone. We're worried about him and have no idea where he is."

"Has he been reported as a Misper?"

"He will be. He's from West Belfast originally but God knows where he might end up."

"I'll keep an ear out. What's the name?"

"McKinstry. Tomas McKinstry."

"No worries," Michael said with a nod. "You get yourself home."

Jacob thanked Michael and his silent colleague, who had used the time in the idling car to catch up on his sleep, and hurried across a deserted Writer's Square.

He noticed the car as he crossed the road to Talbot Street. It followed him slowly. He considered walking on but instead stopped, letting it pull up alongside him.

"Mr. Kincaid." Cora said, leaning towards the small space in the opened window.

"Miss Adebayo. Should I even ask what you're doing in this part of town at this time of the morning?"

"Working. Nothing exciting until I heard some

rather interesting chatter on one of the radio channels."

"You have access to the police radio net?"

Cora gave him a look which suggested she could neither confirm nor deny such a thing and motioned for him to get in.

"Apologies about leaking over your fine leather seats," Jacob said as he closed the door behind him.

"What happened tonight?"

"An unhappy husband of a recent client. Tried to take my head off with a baton."

"All part of the job, huh?"

"I charge extra for aggrieved spouses looking to settle the score."

"No Follower connection?"

"No. Just a cheating husband. Beside from what you told me, it's not really their style."

"Unless they're trying to scare you."

A fair point and up until Neil Rourke actually had to fight, a solid tactic. But Jacob's research and surveillance on the Doctor hadn't revealed a link between him and any religious group. If he wasn't at work, he was either at the gym or with his bit on the side.

"Have you found anything else?" Cora asked, sensing Jacob had dismissed the idea without actually saying it.

"What? Since our meeting yesterday?" Cora didn't reply, ignoring the childish tone. "No," Jacob said. "I'm going to talk to Liam Dunwoody tomorrow." He wasn't sure why he told her but he did.

"Roisin's brother?"

"You know him?"

"Educated guess. What's your angle there?"

"Inheritance and the means to do it."

"And any Follower link there?"

"No." Jacob shot back testily. Cora nodded slowly. "Sorry," Jacob said.

"It's fine. Just remember what I said. You find anything..."

"Sure." Jacob opened the door and stepped back

into the wet night.

"Bridge Street." Cora called out as he closed the door.

"What?" Jacob ducked his head down to peer through the small opening in the window.

"That's where I made you yesterday. Just in case you were wondering." A faint smile touched her lips. "You're a curious man, Jacob Kincaid."

"That I am," Jacob said to himself as he watched her drive away. "That I am."

He trudged back to his apartment, falling into bed after quickly drying himself off and throwing his soaked clothes in the wash basket. When sleep came it was erratic. Repeatedly he dozed off only to jolt awake a few minutes later.

Black shadows scaled the wall of his apartment building, trying to get to him. They were silent creatures, lithe with long claws on elongated limbs, intent on ripping the flesh from his bones. He had barricaded every door and window but still they came. The shadows diffused, falling away into black wisps that coiled like smoke through the flimsy barriers.

He opened his eyes. The room was in complete darkness but white stitched eyes hovered over him. He screamed and launched himself at the monster before waking up with a start, cocooned in sweat drenched bed sheets.

# 18

Jacob was woken from a dead sleep by his phone vibrating on the bedside cabinet. He answered without looking, his head still buried in his pillow.

"Did I wake you?" Natalie asked.

Jacob raised his head a fraction to read the time on the screen. "It's half eight on a Sunday morning."

"I've been trying Tomas again. Still no answer."

Jacob rolled over onto his back with an exhausted groan. His throat was dry and his stomach rumbled. The sheets had been pulled off and thrown in the corner of his room "Have you spoke to the hostel?"

"Yeah. They've contacted the police. He's going to be classified as a Missing Person."

Jacob bit back a yawn. The police would do their bit; a check of local hospitals, a drive past of some known rough sleeper hangouts, Tomas's details circulated on the internal email system. He also knew it would be cursory at best. The local beat cops were already too overstretched to put any sort of concerted effort into tracking down a transient with a drug habit.

"He'll turn up," Jacob said, repeating what he said the night before without feeling the same level of conviction.

"You'll let me know how you get on with Liam?" Natalie asked, changing the subject.

"Of course."

"Alright. I'll keep you posted if Tomas surfaces."

With the call ended, Jacob forced himself out of bed.

He allowed himself a long soak in the shower before polishing off two bowls of Frosties.

Hopping in the Clio, he made the short drive to Mallusk, on the outskirts of Belfast. Helen had tracked Liam Dunwoody's last known address to a fashionable development of new build houses. As Jacob pulled up outside, he noticed that unlike his neighbours, Dunwoody's garden was unkempt, overgrown and littered with children's toys. One of the glass panels in the front door had a long crack down the middle.

The door was answered by a tired looking woman. The smell of green in the house beyond was strong, even at the front step. Upstairs, a child cried. When Jacob said he was looking to speak to Liam the woman left him standing without a word. She ducked her head into the nearest room, said something he couldn't make out and then headed for the stairs and the fussing kid.

Liam appeared a few seconds later. He was pale and thin, wearing a grotty t-shirt with the famous Nirvana 'Flower Sniffin' motif on the front and old chequered pyjama bottoms. "Yeah?"

"Liam, my name is Jacob Kincaid. I'm a private investigator. I've been hired by a friend of your sister to look into her death."

Dull eyes regarded him. "That was an accident," he said finally.

"Was it? Do you mind if I come in, have a chat?" He took a step into the hallway before Liam, stuck between playing host or telling him to get out of his house, could make up his mind either way.

With the decision made for him, Liam shrugged and led Jacob into a cluttered living room, ripe with a fusion of cigarette smoke, cannabis, and stale body odour. An overflowing ash tray, cartons from the previous night's Chinese and three half-finished mugs of cold tea sat on a stained coffee table.

Liam didn't offer him a seat but Jacob found a space on one of the sofas while Liam sat in a chair and picked up a still lit cigarette. Liam was thin but his frame was lanky, a least half a head taller than Jacob. "I wondered when you'd show up," he said, taking a deep drag of the cigarette.

"You were expecting me?"

Liam coughed. "So you think my sister's death wasn't an accident?"

"I have a lot of pieces," Jacob replied. "Just trying to get them to fit."

"Sounds like you have nothing."

"No? Well, I have a suspect with both the motive and the means to carry out the murder."

"Oh yeah?" Liam asked, taking another long drag.

"Yeah. It's you, Liam."

Liam spluttered on cigarette smoke. "What?" He managed to eke out the word between a spasm of coughing.

"Well, think about it. Suspect? A man with a well-known drug habit and associated debts. Motive? A rather sizeable inheritance. Means? Access to the chemicals needed to carry out the murder."

"Chemicals?"

"You're a fire suppression engineer. Your father owns the company you work for which I'm guessing gives you a lot of leeway as to what you can get your hands on."

"I haven't worked in months. I don't, I couldn't..."

"You're telling me you wouldn't have access to chemicals or gasses? Couldn't source something?" Jacob held up a hand to stop any protestations although Dunwoody seemed too shocked to offer any. "When I took this case I thought it was nonsense. Now too much has happened for me to just write it off. But here's the issue. I still can't get around the fact Roisin died in a locked apartment. No way in or out. Nowhere to hide. No way to do the deed, unless the killer never entered her apartment. Add to the fact that myself and a friend were attacked in my office by a man wielding some pretty potent chemical substance and those of us with a suspicious mind will start asking questions."

Liam's expression went from surprise to full on panic. He glanced to the table. "You're off your rocker, you know that?" he said, attention shifting back to Jacob, his voice taking on a notably shriller edge.

"Convince me otherwise."

"Jesus," Liam stubbed out the cigarette. "No, alright. No, I'm not doing this."

"Why? I told you; I'm trying to get to the bottom of this. Help me out. Tell me why you wouldn't be a suspect."

"It's impossible, that's why." Jacob held out a hand, inviting Liam to educate him. "You've been to Roisin's apartment?"

"Twice."

"Then you've seen how big it is. It'd take a ridiculous amount of agent to fill the place enough to have effect. Not to mention somewhere you could even pump it in from."

"Like the vent."

"Yeah, sure. But Roisin's place was three or four floors up."

"So you use the roof." Jacob said. He knew access to it was blocked but wondered if Liam would trip up and mention he knew this too. "Lower yourself down and pump the room full of whatever."

"Genius. All I needed was a winch to lower the cylinders down, a generator to release the chemical and hope that the coroner missed the signs of poisoning."

"Which are?"

Liam gave an exasperated sigh. It had never seemingly occurred to him to just tell Jacob to get out. Book smart but common-sense stupid, was Jacob's impression of the man. "It depends on the agent. If it were something like Carbon Monoxide you would see cherry red colouring of the skin and organs."

Jacob kept his face neutral. The theory of the gassed room was reliant on the fact the pathologist had missed signs of poisoning. No one, not even the initial attending police officers would have missed such obvious signs on the skin. "What about Carbon Dioxide? I'm no expert but I've done a little reading and I believe it doesn't leave much skin discolouration and is not always the easiest to spot even after blood analysis."

"I suppose," Liam began. "But you're talking a serious amount of the stuff to fill..." He stopped as he caught himself. "I'm not discussing this."

Jacob decided to try a different tact. "You didn't seem that surprised to see me at your front door."

Liam lifted another cigarette from the packet sitting on the arm of his chair. "You called with my father. Figured you might come here. I just didn't think you'd be accusing me of killing my sister."

"So...what did you think I would accuse you of?" Jacob watched the tremor in Liam's hand as he failed to light the cigarette. Hangover? Comedown shakes from coke or pills? Or had he been rattled?"

Liam blew out a lungful of smoke with a shaky breath. "Forget it," he said.

"C'mon. You're already halfway to telling me."

Liam's eyes flitted back to the coffee table once again. He seemed to be on the verge of spilling but instead sighed and sank back into the grimy cushions. "I'm saying nothing else."

Jacob stood up and made a show of wiping his trousers with his hands. "What do you know about the Followers of Eden?" He watched Dunwoody sink further into the chair. "You knew Roisin was looking into them, don't bother denying it. Do you think that's what got her killed?"

"It was an accident," Dunwoody said hoarsely, staring ahead.

"Tomas McKinstry doesn't think so. How well do you know him?"

"Tomas? I haven't seen him in years.

"You wouldn't lie to me Liam, would you?" Dunwoody refused to meet his eye. Jacob favoured with him a final lingering look. "I'll be in touch."

Liam followed him out, stopping to grab a phone

Jacob had not seen through the clutter on the coffee table. The front door was firmly shut and locked the moment Jacob stepped outside.

Returning to his Clio, Jacob drove into the neighbouring street. He turned the car so he had a view of Liam Dunwoody's front door. Five minutes later, Liam exited, hurrying to a clapped-out VW Golf parked in the driveway.

"Jesus, Liam. There's no way you're going to make it this easy for me."

Yet it seemed like he was. Straight into the car, no checks for anyone watching. He drove past Jacob without a second glance, concentrating on the road ahead.

The traffic was light coming out of Mallusk and Jacob took care to hang well back as Liam joined the M2 and headed towards Belfast.

Twenty minutes later they were in the city centre. If Liam had noticed the Clio taking the exact same route as him, he gave no indication. He turned down a small side street close to Queens University, parked the Golf and walked into the nearest building.

"Well, isn't that something," Jacob marvelled as he coasted slowly past and read the sign above the door.

### *Followers of Eden*
### *Cultural and Information Centre.*

"What the hell are you at Liam, me old chum?" Jacob asked himself as he did a lap of the block before parking his car across the street from Liam's.

He reached into his glove box and rummaged around the mess inside until he found what he was looking for, a Sony digital voice recorder. It was a cheaper model he kept it in the car in case of emergencies. He checked the memory, then made sure the sound was recording and quickly pocketed it in his jeans.

When he entered the centre he saw it was more like an office than a church. Open, airy, with a marble tiled floor. Multiple doors led away from the lobby but all were closed.

The receptionist at the front desk was strikingly beautiful. Her buttoned-down blouse was crisp white with the blue Followers logo over her left breast. "Good morning, Sir. Do you have an appointment for an introductory meeting with one of our elders?"

"Uh, no. Afraid not. I'm here for my friend. The eejit left his phone in my car." Jacob fished his own phone from his jeans and showed it to her.

Her smile didn't falter. "I'm sorry, Sir. We've had no one come in for quite some time before you."

"I just left him off at the front door. I watched him walk in here with my own two eyes."

"Again, I apologise Sir but no one..."

They turned as the door on the far left of the lobby opened. Liam Dunwoody looked up and then stopped in his tracks as he saw Jacob at the front desk.

"Isn't it strange how you run into people in the weirdest places."

Liam put his head down and headed for his car. He had the door before Jacob pushed it shut. "I really think we should talk."

"Please," Liam said, eyes darting between Jacob and the building they had just left.

"Please what," Jacob said lowly. "Picture this, a man is asked about a murder. He denies any knowledge. He's asked about the involvement of a certain cult. Again, he denies knowing anything about it. Less than an hour later he's spotted coming out of a building owned by said crazy cult. Conclusions will be drawn, I'm sure you'll appreciate."

Jacob glanced down the street to see the pretty receptionist peek her head out towards them before ducking back inside the building.

"Talk fast, Liam. I'm guessing a few calls are being made."

"I had nothing to do with my sister's murder."

"So it was a murder."

"No! I mean, Jesus, I don't know! I really don't!"

"What were you doing in there?"

"I was told to come."

"Why?"

"I told them about your visit. They told me to come straight here."

"Why?" Jacob prompted again, feeling an uneasy shift in the pit of his stomach. He ignored it. "What's your connection to these loonies?" Liam started to speak but then stopped. Jacob's patience had reached an end. He grabbed the other roughly by his t-shirt. "Tell me!"

"It's Luke!"

"Luke? Luke Fisher. You're telling me Luke Fisher killed...."

"-No! I mean, I don't know! We had a plan...Roisin's list, we could have made a fortune!"

"What list? What are you talking about?"

Jacob turned to see two burly men emerge from the cultural centre. Their appearance made Liam talk double time. "I needed the money. He didn't but I did! I did! I'd met Luke when he and Roisin were going with each other. I took it! I watched her put the combination in the safe and I took it!

Jacob tried to follow the babbling. "You, Luke, and Tomas. The three of you are in cahoots?"

"No! He stiffed me. We met up and he took it. Told me it was for safe keeping. I haven't seen him since. He's cut me out. I don't even know where he lives! I tried to bluff these guys but you can't, they have me by the balls, trying to get that hard drive!"

By now the burly bruisers were joined by a third man in traditional Follower white, with the addition of a red braided cord looping over his left shoulder. "Sir, would you come with us please?"

Jacob heard Liam whimper as he let him go and pushed him towards the trio of cultists. The man with the cord stepped past Liam as if he wasn't there. "If you would come with us, please," he repeated.

"Me? I wish I could but I have prior engagements.

Places to be, people to see. You know how it is."

"I'm afraid I'm going to have to insist. His Eminence isn't a man to be kept waiting."

Jacob glanced past the man to the so-called cultural centre. Huber was inside and he wanted to see Jacob. It reeked of a trap. "I'm going to have to decline."

A shadow fell over him as one of the two pieces of muscle stepped up from behind, looming over his shoulder. Electricity crackled and blue light danced across the metal prongs of the taser he held down by his side.

"Well, I guess I could move some things around."

Liam had melted away so quickly Jacob hadn't even seen him go. For now he had other concerns. The Followers led him around the side of the centre into an alleyway and through a service entrance. The two thugs shadowed either shoulder, preventing any chance for him to run. The fact they had avoided the bright, open and camera heavy lobby was not lost on Jacob.

Rather than being brought to the pulpit or an office with a throne, he was escorted to a small windowless room and shoved inside. The heavy wooden door was pulled closed behind him and locked. White walls, one light, a wooden chair, a wooden table and the 1999 yellow pages. Nothing good happened in this room.

He had been heartened by the fact they hadn't taken his phone until he checked it and saw there was no signal. He tapped each wall in turn. Solid. The room would hold its sound.

The whole thing had been a set up. Not by Liam Dunwoody, the man an unquestionable glipe without an ounce of cunning but someone had told Liam to come here knowing Jacob would dutifully follow. It was a timely reminder that he was nowhere near as smart as he thought he was.

Time dragged and while the churning in his stomach didn't subside, his mind wandered. He thought about what Liam had said when he was babbling outside. *A list. A chance to make a fortune.*

Was Roisin involved? Natalie had been adamant that Luke had stolen the hard drive from her and Jacob had accepted the narrative. Were they both getting lost in the tale of the dead girl and assuming the scheme wasn't her idea.

He knocked the door. Sat on the chair. Sat on the table. Checked his phone. Paced. Back to the chair. Knocked the door again. Paced some more.

The time on his phone told him two hours had passed before the key turned in the heavy lock. One of the bruisers from before stepped in, followed by a much shorter man. Diminutive, even to someone of Jacob's average height, the man's presence in the small room was nonetheless unsettling. Skeletal thin, with sharply pointed features and the bleak eyes of a predator. While the bruiser didn't glance Jacob's way, the smaller man fixed him with an unflinching gaze as they waited.

It was a relief when a third man joined them. Jacob recognised him at once. Everything about Seymour Huber was unnervingly false. His brow was a tad too high. His smile was too wide, the teeth bleached an unnatural white. Taut skin had been pulled tight over the lower face leaving the telltale creases of surgery under his cheeks.

"Mr. Kincaid, I can only assume."

"Seymour Huber."

"Guilty, guilty." His voice was a strange mishmash of an American accent softened considerably by the years spent on Irish shores. "It seems to me you've been asking all sorts of questions about our community. I'm glad to see you've finally come to the source rather than relying on conjecture and innuendo."

"How did you know I was asking questions?" Jacob asked.

Huber waved the words away. "Why don't you have a seat?"

"I'd rather stand."

The thin man who still hadn't taken his eyes off Jacob suddenly sprang forward, kicking the wooden chair towards him. Jacob didn't quite manage to hide a flinch as the chair scraped along the floor before turning over, crashing loudly in the bare room. The echo reverberation faded slowly into a heavy silence.

Huber continued to watch Jacob; the false smile unfaltering. Slowly, Jacob picked up the chair, turned it over and lowered himself on to it. The skinny man moved behind him.

"Better," Huber said. "You'll forgive me my indulgences. I'm used to preaching from a pulpit so I'm most comfortable like this."

"Is that what this is? A sermon?"

Pain shot through his ribs as a lightning-fast fist snapped out before he could brace for it. Jacob gasped and fell off the chair onto his knees.

"Sit him up please, Nathaniel." Huber's tone didn't change. "You'll have to excuse my acolyte. His devotion is unmatched and he takes any slight against the church rather seriously." Bony but strong hands clamped onto his arms and pulled him roughly back onto his chair. "My church has been fighting slander for some time now. Most of it directed by two women. I trust you're not going to pretend you don't know who I'm talking about."

Jacob winced as he shrugged and reflected that between here, the fight in his office, getting chased by Neil Rourke over half of Belfast and being put on the floor by Cora Adebayo 's companion, he'd had better weeks. "I've been hired to investigate the death of Roisin Dunwoody. She was doing a story on your church."

"A hit piece. I believe that's the accepted term in her circles."

It hurt too much to attempt a second shrug. "What do you want?"

"The same thing we've wanted from the start. A clear name. A chance to exercise our right to religious freedom without being dogged by falsehoods."

"So do it. How does this relate to me?"

"Are you a fool, Mr. Kincaid, or are you just very

adept at playing one?"

"To be honest, I'm not really sure."

Huber sucked air through his teeth. The sound conveyed a mixture of disgust, frustration, and impatience. "I'm a pragmatist," he said after a lingering silence. "Money talks. If you can bring me what I want, I'll offer you a rather generous finder's fee. This is a onetime offer, Mr. Kincaid."

Jacob gritted his teeth as he raised his head to look Huber in the eye. "And what is it that you want?"

Huber sighed before looking at the bruiser. The man responded with a bow of his head before leaving the room. Seconds later, another man entered. Like the thin man he wasn't dressed in a suit or traditional follower attire. Instead, he wore dark clothing and steel toe capped boots. He was young and heavy, with baby-like cheeks and fat, unattractive fish lips. His dark blonde hair was limply plastered to his head.

"I can see this is only going to go one way," Huber said. "You're a stubborn man, Mr. Kincaid and I will not lower myself to haggling with the likes of you." He moved to the door and waited for the thin man to open it for him. "My two security officer's will escort you out."

Jacob had no doubt the escort would be preceded by a rather severe trimming in the sound proof room. "In the interest of openness, you should probably know I've been recording the whole time." He did his best to project a confident smile as Huber turned back towards him. "Left pocket."

Thin Man reached down and pulled out the voice recorder. He held it out to Huber who snatched the device, turned it over once and threw it to the floor. He ground the device under the heel of his polished shoe. "Clumsy me."

"It's the twenty first century, Huber. Those things broadcast in real-time. My partner is listening in as we speak."

Huber's face gave nothing away. He leaned down to whisper something in the thin man's ear who gave a curt nod in reply.

"Goodbye, Mr. Kincaid. I trust we won't be seeing you around here again."

Fish Lips seized Jacob by the arm and led him into the corridor, through the back of the old building and into the back alleyway. Without breaking stride, he spun Jacob around and rattled him with a punch to the side of his skull.

He stumbled backwards into a wall, only just able to keep himself standing.

"Not the face," Thin Man said, stepping forward and firing off a fast one-two combination to his midsection.

Jacob fell to the ground and retched. Fish lips followed up with kicks. Jacob covered his head and balled himself up as best he could. Fish Lips continued to kick him savagely around the back. When he grabbed him by his jacket and hauled him to his feet, Jacob didn't fight back. He allowed himself to be dragged along the alley and back onto the street where he had parked. Fish Lips shoved him to the pavement and left him lying.

Jacob sucked in lungfuls of air as two women dressed in their Sunday best, crossed the street to avoid him.

The bluff about the recording had probably saved him from a lot worse.

# 19

"Jesus, Jacob! Are you ok?" Natalie asked as Jacob finished filling her in on what had just happened.

"Oh, absolutely not." Jacob winced as he took stock of himself in the rearview mirror. To his credit, Fish Lips had followed the direction to avoid hitting him in the face to the letter. He'd done a cracking number on the rest of him though. "Huber seemed to think I knew more than I was letting on. He danced around the issue without actually saying what he wanted."

"The hard drive?"

"Has to be."

"And you played dumb?"

"What can I say, it comes naturally." Natalie didn't laugh so Jacob pressed on. "By the sounds of it, Liam Dunwoody is in deep with the Followers. Him, Luke, and I guess Tomas, had a scheme to extort money through some sort of list. At some point Luke Fisher got possession of the hard drive and fucked up their plans royally." As he spoke, he saw Thin Man and Fish Lips exit from the alleyway they had beaten him up in less than twenty minutes before. "Gotta go."

"Hang on a sec-"

He ignored Natalie's protest as he ended the call. He didn't have his Nikon with him, so had to make do with the camera app on his phone, snapping a few blurry pictures of the pair as they climbed into a gleaming silver Range Rover. Jacob let them get to the end of the road and waited until they turned left before following.

He had a hunch he knew where they were going and by the time they were on the M2, he was certain.

As he cruised past Liam Dunwoody's house he could see Thin Man pounding on the front door while Fish Lips went around the back. He kept low in his seat but neither of the thugs looked his way. With no one answering the door and apparently no way in around the back of the house, the two men gave it up as a bad job and returned to their car. They didn't drive away.

You're in for a long wait, lads, Jacob thought to himself. Liam had almost definitely taken the time afforded to him by Jacob having seven shades knocked out of him to get home, get packed and get lost.

Jacob turned his Clio and followed the road back out of the development. The row of houses where Liam lived backed onto weed choked waste ground. Retrieving a handful of loose hairpins and a pair of pliers from the glove box, he climbed over the wire fencing that corralled the waste ground. He jumped across the bank of a dirty stream and then over the back fence to Dunwoody's property.

He kept low, hoping no neighbours had seen him and tested the patio door. As he had expected, it was locked. He took one of the hairpins and bent it until both ends were ninety degrees apart. Removing the plastic pieces from the tips, he inserted one end into the lock. He took the free tip and folded it back over itself to serve as a handle. Fetching a second pin from his pocket, he used the pliers to bend it into a makeshift lever.

He inserted the lever gently into the keyhole, waiting for the telltale catch. Keeping the pressure on the barrel, Jacob slid the first pin into the lock, just above the lever. He eased the pick in, feeling around for the seized pin. It was a few seconds before he heard the first *click* of the pin giving way. He quickly worked the rest of the pins in the same manner until the lock was picked.

Jacob closed the door behind him softly as he

stepped into the kitchen. Like the living room, the rest of Dunwoody's house was a tip. He kept low as he searched, not wanting Fish Lips or Thin Man to catch a glimpse of a moving shadow at a window and come looking.

Medication boxes had spilled from an open cupboard onto the kitchen counter. Almost all were empty and few had a prescription label. Jacob filed through them quickly and found opiates, buds, and benzos, but no Prepentaline.

A dog-eared diary sat on the kitchen counter. Liam had plenty of appointments with his GP but not much else of note. Jacob flicked through the book quickly, stopping at the back page where Liam had scribbled *LF* next to a mobile phone number. Luke Fisher, almost certainly. Jacob took the number down in his own phone. He flicked through the diary again but couldn't see a number for Tomas.

He threw the diary back on to the counter and dropped to a crouch as he moved through the living room and then up the stairs. Drawers and wardrobes lay open in the master bedroom. No suitcases. As he'd thought, the Dunwoody's had cleared out in a hurry. Probably the first smart move Liam had made in a while. Jacob was keen to talk to him after getting baited into his little meeting with Huber, and the two thugs outside didn't look like they were paying a social call.

Jacob continued his search for a few more minutes but it was clear the house was a bust for any evidence tying Liam to having anything to do with Jacob's case. He crept back down the stairs and exited by the patio, gently closing the door behind him. He was about to hop back over the fence onto the waste ground when his eyes drifted to the garage at the side of the house.

He tried the handle of the wooden side door but found it locked. The path separating the house and the garage looked out onto the street but he was concealed from Fish Lips and Thin Man's view by where they had parked.

Not wanting to risk being seen as he tried to jimmy the lock, Jacob put his shoulder against the door and felt it give with only a slight bit of force. Taking one step back, he barged into the door with his full weight and was rewarded as the lock gave way with a noisy *crunch*. He crouched down in the dark garage and held his breath to see if the sound had carried.

After a few moments, he stood slowly. The garage was tidier than the house, which admittedly wasn't saying much. Any hopes of finding anything to support his gassed room theory were quickly quashed by a cursory check of the place. There were no gas canisters, no tubing or hose. Just a lot of junk and forgotten mementos in damp cardboard boxes.

At its far end was a row of cabinets. Jacob went through them quickly, out of a sense of completeness rather than a belief he would find anything. As he rifled the last cupboard, he pushed one closed box aside and heard the *clink* of glass. He reached in and lifted the box out. Opening it, he found it full of small brown bottles, just like the one he and Natalie had found in Tomas's room. As before, none of the bottles were marked and all had their original labels peeled off.

He lifted two of the bottles and stuffed one into his jacket pocket. "Well now, Liam. How are you explaining this?" he asked himself, turning the second bottle over in his hand as he walked to the door and bumped straight into Fish Lips.

The thug, one hand on his zipper after having a sneaky pish down the side of Dunwoody's house, looked at Jacob in surprise before turning towards where he and Thin Man had parked.

Before he could shout for help, Jacob brought the bottle he was holding down on top of his head. The glass didn't smash but did produce an extremely satisfying *Thonk* as it clattered off Fish Lips's skull and bounced out of Jacob's grasp, smashing on the concrete path.

He went down and tried to grab at Jacob's leg. He shook away the clawing hand and channelling his inner

David Healy, kicked Fish Lips straight between the legs with all the strength he could muster. The man gave a wordless grunt as he slumped over.

Jacob didn't look back as he took the garden fence at a running jump, bounded over the little stream and had the Clio's tyres squealing as he headed back towards Belfast, making sure nothing was in his mirror.

He parked well away from his office. With the security door locked firmly behind him, he printed the best of the blurry bunch of pictures he had snapped of Thin Man and Fish Lips and added them to the pin board underneath the *FOLLOWERS* post-it. He then took the post-it with *HARD DRIVE* scrawled on it, and the picture of Liam Dunwoody and moved them next to the image of the two men. He regarded his work as he phoned Michael.

"You have any idea what time it is?" his friend asked by way of greeting, his voice raspy with sleep.

"It's going on three." Jacob replied.

"That's right." Michael said, curtly. "And if you'll recall less than twelve hours ago, I was keeping your arse out of a custody cell. You got to go home after that. I didn't. I didn't get to bed until after nine this morning because I had to arrest some drunk wanker driving on the wrong side of the road at half six." Jacob didn't say anything, which seemed to take some fire out of Michael's anger. "He actually told me it was ok because he was driving with only one eye open so he wasn't seeing double. You believe that?"

Jacob waited until he was sure his friend had finished. "I need a favour."

"Jesus! Jacob!"

"It's important," he cut in quickly. "I'm sending a picture of two guys. Can you show it around. See if anyone on the job knows them?"

"Who are they?"

"Probably no one."

Michael sighed deeply. "Alright, Jacob. Let me see what I can do."

"Cheers, Michael. I owe you one"

"A damn sight more than one, mate. Oh, and Jacob? That other fella, McKinstry? He was officially reported missing this morning. Saw it on the screen before I finished. If I hear anything more I'll let you know."

Jacob thanked him, hung up the phone and turned his attention back to the pin board and to the picture of Arthur Dunwoody. He wasn't sure what had initially prompted him to add Roisin's father to the muddled mess on the board. Did he think he was involved in Roisin's death?

His initial assertion had been no and it still was now.

But he thought back to what Liam had said. His father had told him Jacob might be coming. Why? Jacob hadn't given any indication about his immediate suspicions regarding Liam. Did Arthur Dunwoody know more than he was letting on?

Jacob locked the office and stepped out onto the street slowly. He took the long route back to his car, ducking down side streets and alleyways, doubling back several times until he was content no one was tailing him.

Less than half an hour later he was back at Arthur Dunwoody's estate on the Loughbeg Road. As he made the turn into the long driveway, a man in a suit appeared from behind one of the gate pillars and held out a hand, motioning for Jacob to stop and lower his window.

"What's your business here?"

"Tell Mr. Dunwoody that Jacob Kincaid is here to see him."

The man stepped back and raised a radio to his mouth. Whatever he said was brief but a few seconds later he waved Jacob through. There were no cars in the driveway but Jacob caught the twitch of a curtain in the guest cottage as he got out of his Clio.

He rang the bell of the main house and waited. It was Arthur who answered the door, not the severe Mrs. Hamill. Dressed in a designer polo shirt and smart chinos, if he was surprised to see Jacob again, he gave no hint. "Come in, Mr. Kincaid. Liam wasn't sure you'd show up but I had every confidence you would, providing you were able to get yourself away from those loons." He led Jacob into the kitchen. "Drink?"

"Sure." Jacob had no idea what Dunwoody's game was, but was content to play along.

The older man went to an ornate drinks cabinet, selected a bottle of whiskey and brought it over to the kitchen counter "Well then. Tell me what you have found." He lifted two tumblers from a nearby cupboard.

Jacob reached into his pocket and brought out one of the small brown bottles he had found in Liam's garage. Dunwoody's cool grey eyes regarded it dispassionately. "Your son is in deep with the Followers. Best I can figure, he tried to bribe them with whatever information Roisin had stored on a hard drive. The hard drive is now in the possession of Luke Fisher and Liam is being squeezed to obtain it."

It was an educated guess. Liam didn't seem like the zealot type but he certainly seemed stupid enough to get himself mixed up in games he didn't understand. Intimidated by the more powerful and played by those more conniving.

Arthur Dunwoody set one of the tumblers down in front of Jacob. "Did he tell you what's on this hard drive?"

"A list of some sort. At first I thought it was a record of their transgressions but now I'm thinking something more salacious." He was spit-balling and Dunwoody had a fearsome poker face. "Money." Jacob let the word hang in the air but Arthur didn't flinch. "It always comes down to money. Soup kitchens and homeless shelters being used to launder money. Enough money that certain people would be keen to make sure that hard drive never sees the light of day."

Dunwoody gave nothing away. "Drink up, Mr. Kincaid. I hate to see good scotch go to waste."

Jacob shared a similar sentiment and reached for

the tumbler before stopping. He took the glass Dunwoody was holding and slid the one he had been poured across the marble counter to rest in front of the older man. Dunwoody's smile was grudging. "You're not a trusting man, Mr. Kincaid."

"Not recently."

Dunwoody allowed himself a mirthless chuckle before he knocked the drink back in one. He sauntered back across to the counter and poured another.

"Blackmail then," Jacob said.

"I know it's cliché to say such a thing, but I find blackmail such an ugly word. Like you said, it always comes down to money. That hard drive is a commodity people would pay money for. A lot of money."

"And when they refused? A name could be leaked, or a story about some alleged transgression published."

"Perfectly simple and simply perfect."

Jacob scratched his beard. "Why not mention this the first time I was here?"

"Why would I? Up until you showed up at my front door, I had accepted Roisin's death to be an accident. It got me thinking I accepted that narrative a little too quickly."

"Was it Roisin's idea? The blackmail?"

"God, no. Nothing could overcome that journalistic integrity. Roisin was on a crusade. It was all Liam."

Jacob found it to believe an empty head like Liam could plan breakfast, never mind extortion. He kept the thought to himself. "But Liam cocked it up. He needed the money, got impatient and when Roisin refused to play ball, he stole the hard drive from the safe in Roisin's apartment."

Dunwoody swirled the scotch in his glass. "And without Roisin's cooperation he had nothing, just names and fairy tales."

Jacob nodded. "He needed her as the conduit. The person who could leak the stories when required either through her job at the Sentinel or on the podcast she was creating."

"And I'm sure you can put the rest together."

"Luke said all the right things and somehow talked himself into getting the hard drive. As soon as he did, he cut Liam out and is now trying to extort the Followers."

"Whilst the Followers put pressure on Liam to retrieve it." Dunwoody took the small brown bottle and turned it over. "Should I even ask?"

"Found it in Liam's garage. Something similar was used to attack Natalie Amato a few nights ago." He watched Dunwoody give the slightest shake of his head but Jacob doubted it was concern over Natalie's wellbeing. "She's fine and it wasn't Liam who attacked her, although I've no doubt he sourced it for the man who did."

"My son, the patsy." Dunwoody spoke as if tasting something unpleasant.

"How did the Followers get to him?"

"He tried to bluff that he still had possession of the hard drive. Attempted to pass off a fake as the real deal. By the time he realised his ruse had been rumbled they already knew everything about him. I'd been doing my damnedest to get Liam to bring his family to the estate. At least that way I know my grandson would be safe. Whatever happened today was enough to finally convince him."

Jacob felt like Dunwoody was waiting for him to say something. Instead, he took a belt of his whiskey.

"I don't know Luke Fisher," Arthur continued. "But he's small fry. If he still has the hard drive, it's only because the Followers have deemed him as a problem not worth sorting. Yet. When they do, they'll take it back and what is on the drive will be lost forever."

Jacob nodded again.

Dunwoody set his glass on the counter. "Let me spell it out for you, Mr. Kincaid." His voice had taken an impatient edge. "Find Luke Fisher, find the hard drive and bring it to me. I'll pay handsomely. A damn sight better than Miss Amato."

Jacob took another drink of the whiskey. "Last time

I was here, you were offering a reward to find your daughter's killer."

"And that still stands. Find me the killer and find me that hard drive. This isn't about money, Mr. Kincaid, not anymore. It's about revenge. I want them to bleed and that hard drive is the way I'll do it."

"Not anymore?"

Dunwoody looked back down at his glass without answering.

Jacob rubbed tired eyes. "Jesus. It was your idea." He couldn't believe it had never occurred to him until that moment. "Liam came to you with a story about what Roisin was working on. She wouldn't play ball with your little plot so you roped your idiot son in to steal the hard drive. Then you could leak what was on it to some connection you no doubt have in the media. Stop me when I start telling lies here, Dunwoody."

He watched the older man's brow narrow. There was the cold man Natalie had told him about. "Does it change anything?" Dunwoody asked tersely. "My idea or my son's, I'm still offering you a payday bigger than what you make in a year."

"I'm working on sole retainer, Dunwoody."

"You're a damn fool, Kincaid." Dunwoody's voice was more cutting than a winter wind sweeping over Belfast lough. He finished his scotch with a grimace. "Get out of my house and out of my sight."

# 20

By the time Jacob made it outside, the security man who had greeted him had moved to the front of the guest cottage, joined by a similarly attired colleague. Neither said a word but they didn't have to. The message was clear. He wouldn't be talking to Liam Dunwoody any time soon.

He mulled over what Arthur had said on the drive back to Belfast. Whatever was on that hard drive was explosive. Enough for Liam and Luke to have grand plans of blackmail. Enough to rope Tomas McKinstry into their little scheme. Enough for Arthur Dunwoody to see the ruination of people he held responsible for his daughter's death.

Jacob didn't care what was on the drive or who had it. His interest was solely on his case but as far as he could tell, the hard drive might be the only thing that could give him a break.

Luke Fisher wasn't any sort of fighter. Jacob knew he himself was far from a tough guy, but he could take the hard drive by force, if necessary. But Luke wasn't stupid. He wouldn't keep the drive in his house. He needed somewhere secure. Somewhere only he had access to. If he was going to get the drive, Jacob needed to find out where that somewhere was.

He stole a look at himself in the mirror and suddenly questioned where his mind was going. He was an investigator, a decent one, when the mood took him. He might not be happy in his work but he had always held himself to a particular standard. An obligation to the client that hired him that they would get the best version of himself. It was his own code and he realised, with more than a heapful of pity, one of the few things that actually still mattered to him.

It was early evening by the time he made it home and his plans didn't stretch past soaking in the bath and maybe daring to contemplate a proper nights sleep. He checked his phone as he locked the door to his apartment behind him and smiled as he saw Mairead had texted. It was a short message, asking how his day was going. His phone rang as he typed up a reply.

"Still no sign of Tomas," Natalie said by way of greeting.

Jacob sighed and knuckled an eye. Tomas, the third man in Liam Dunwoody's half-assed scheme. He decided the bath could wait a couple more hours. "I'll head out. Check some usual haunts, see if I can get a lead on him."

"Alright, let me know if he turns up. I'll keep bothering the hostel."

Turning on his heel, Jacob fetched his car and drove the short distance to Writer's Square. He made a quick loop of the rough sleeper spots from the Square to the bars along Hill and Skipper Street, and then the shuttered department stores of Royal Avenue. Of down and outs there were plenty, but no Tomas.

He walked back to the Clio and increased the search area towards City Hall and Great Victoria Street. He showed Tomas's picture to anyone who would meet his gaze. At a Drop-in Centre on Amelia Street, the picture was recognised by one of the volunteers. She was a kindly older woman and while she couldn't put a name to the face, she was able to recall that he had said that he was a writer. Unfortunately, it had been years since she had last seen him.

Jacob kept going, racking his brain for any homeless hot spots he might have missed. He drove down Botanic Avenue, the roads around Queens University and the small park at Crescent Gardens overlooked by a once grand row of regency style terraced housing, now almost all derelict. Everywhere he stopped, hollow-eyed people regarded him, gaunt and defeated. Some were aggressive, others scared and all were mistrusting. Jacob looked away when some asked for spare change that he hadn't thought to bring.

With the search list exhausted, Jacob walked slowly back his car, It was all a waste of time, most likely. Tomas still had his room in the hostel. It was the place he was most likely going to turn up. Still, Jacob reminded himself, Tomas wasn't a well man and trying to predict what he'd do in his current mindset was a fool's game.

The time on his phone told him that it had just gone eleven when he rang Natalie. "Still no sign?" he asked.

"No." Her voice was irritable. "The hostel has blocked my number."

Jacob couldn't help but laugh. "Really?"

"Yes, bloody really! About half an hour ago. Doesn't even ring anymore."

"Let me try. Maybe he's wandered back."

He hung up and found the number for the hostel. When he tried it, the call didn't connect. The line was dead. The thought of the phone being ripped from the wall as the only solution to Natalie's harassment cheered him. It was barely a ten-minute drive to Star of the Sea, so he headed towards Sailortown.

When he arrived, he found the front door to the hostel open but there was no one behind the glass partition. The light in the office was dimmed but a television cast an eerie glow over the clutter inside. Jacob tried the security door that led into the rest of the building but as expected, found it locked tight.

He knocked on the glass and then the door, figuring the night staff were catching some sneaky Z's in one of the back rooms. He knocked again after waiting close to a minute. As he stepped back, a thick, cloying odour reached his nostrils. It reminded him of the soldering irons in his old technology and design classes back in school. He scrunched his nose but it took him a second to realise what the smell actually was.

Jacob pressed himself against the door, trying to peer through the glass beyond. His heart skipped as he saw thick smoke coiling slowly down the poorly lit corridor beyond.

"Fire! Fire!" He smashed the flat of his hand against the security door for all he was worth but knew the sound wouldn't carry.

It was only when he pressed himself up against the door again that he saw a pair of legs splayed out in the corridor to the right.

Jacob threw his shoulder into the door but it didn't budge. He took a step back and launched a hard kick and then another but the door held firm. Frantically, he searched for an alarm point but there wasn't one to be seen in the small lobby.

Swearing with desperation, Jacob ran back out onto the street. The smell of smoke was already clinging to him. Through a downstairs window he could see the deep orange outline as the fire began to spread out from a room on the ground floor, roughly behind where the reception was located.

He remembered there was supposed to be a fire exit at the back of the building. He dialled 999 as he ran. When the operator picked up, Jacob shouted at them to send the Fire Service to Star of the Sea Hostel. That there were people trapped inside. He could hear the operator ask for more details but he didn't have time. At least one person was hurt and everyone else was unaware of the fire spreading below them.

He found the piss-stench narrow alleyway that ran behind the hostel and followed it until he came to the hostel's emergency exit, mercifully unlocked. He opened it and stopped.

The corridor beyond was already thick with billowing smoke. Jacob's sense of self-preservation was incredibly strong, but he couldn't walk away without at least finding a fire alarm and trying his best to get to the person on the ground.

"Fire!" Fire!" He ran down the corridor, pounding every door he passed, although most looked like offices or store rooms rather than accommodation. "Fire!"

He was almost back at the security door when he finally spotted a red alarm point on the wall to his left. He broke the safety glass, pressed the button and was met with only silence. He hit it again and again. "Shit!"

He pushed on, futilely trying to wave away the thickening plume. When he reached the lobby, he saw who the feet belonged to. Amanda, the young woman who had been on duty on his two previous visits. She lay on her back, her eyes closed. Beside her an overturned mop bucket had spilled water over the old tiles.

At the far end of the corridor fire licked along the wall and reached for the ceiling. It was terrifying in its overpowering roar and speed of consumption. Jacob tried to shut out the ravenous monster and crouched next to Amanda. A firm shake of her shoulders got no response. He grabbed her under the arms and heaved her up, slipping on the slick tiles.

"What's happening?" a thickly accented voice asked.

Jacob turned to find the man who had been in the reception the first time Jacob had been at the hostel, watching him from one of the doors he just had passed. The man's eyes were bleary and his hair dishevelled. He had just woken up but Jacob had thought his desperate shouts and smoke would have been a hint. "Help me! he shouted as he dragged the unconscious woman along the corridor.

The man's jaw slackened as he finally twigged what was going on. Even so, he ran towards Jacob and grabbed Amanda under the legs. Together they ran for the exit, spilling out onto the street.

The man tried to set her down in the alley. "No!" Jacob shouted, before breaking down into a spluttering cough. "Further!" He just about managed to get the words out. "Get her in fresh air and clear of the building."

By the time they made it across the road and a safe enough distance away to set Amanda down, the fire was licking at most windows on the ground floor. Jacob knew it would soon begin to travel up.

Star of the Sea slept.

Jacob pointed to the man; lost as he took in the scene. "Call the fire service. Make sure they're on their way." The man called after him but he was already running back towards the hostel. "Oh Jacob, the fuck are you doing?" he said to himself as the heat of the building reached out. The fire was warning him, trying to force him back towards cool, clean air. Jacob kept his head down and pressed on.

He shut his eyes as he forced his way back inside. By now the smoke was deadly black. Running at a crouch, he stayed as low as he could until he reached the nearest staircase. Reaching the landing of the floor above, he pounded on each door along the corridor. For those residents who heard him, the message was clear. No one waited for a second warning. They tumbled out into the corridor, half dressed, eyes set with abject terror.

The heat grew and Jacob knew the fire was pursuing him. Sweat and smoke stung his eyes. Only a few doors on the first floor remained closed. Jacob hoped their rooms were empty or the residents not home. He couldn't wait to find out.

He forced himself up the next staircase. Stunned faces, woken by his frenetic shouts met him in the corridor. Jacob recognised the man who had tripped him on his first visit to the hostel barge past. Rather than take the stairs to safety, he ran up towards the top floor.

Jacob could swear he heard the old building groan as the inferno ate her from the inside. From the upper floor, people began spilling down, all in some form of undress. Jacob didn't see the man who had gone up to raise the alarm and knew he couldn't go after him. If the blaze spread any further he would be trapped.

His feet barely touched the steps as he came back down. He allowed himself one last look at the first floor, content that no one remained on the landing before taking the stairs down to the ground floor in two jumps.

The fire that had started at the far end of the ground floor had spread, devouring its way down the length of the corridor. Jacob shielded his face and stumbled towards the exit, enveloped in the deadly embrace of black smoke. Blinded, he willed one foot in front of the other. If he stopped he was a dead man.

Suddenly he was free of the unyielding grip of the smoke and felt himself tumbling forward. His hands instinctively went up and broke his fall, skinning themselves on the rough alley floor.

Strong hands grabbed at his shoulders and pulled him away. Jacob forced his eyes open as water was poured on his face. He coughed, spluttered then retched, and retched again. He spat away nothing.

A firefighter pushed an oxygen mask over his face and he sucked on it greedily. "Easy, easy," she cautioned, leading him towards a row of waiting ambulances. Blue strobe lights cast the dank little street in an otherworldly glow.

A police officer in a luminous high viz coat was setting up a cordon, fastening blue and white scene tape between two lampposts at the far end of the street, sealing it off.

Jacob waved away assistance as a paramedic approached. The firefighter who had helped him towards the cordon edge had already disappeared. He slumped against a wall next to the police cordon. The two cops who were manning the point looked at him briefly before turning their attention back to the fire.

Firefighters braved the inferno and returned with three people. One of them screamed as he was loaded into a waiting ambulance. The fire had seared most of his skin and melted whatever clothing he had been wearing, fusing the material against his chest and legs.

Jacob closed his eyes, trying and failing to block out the helpless squeals and the unrelenting wail of the ambulance siren as it carried the doomed man away.

Prostrate against the bricks, Jacob watched the old hostel die. By the time the fire was under control a couple of hours later, some of the building had already collapsed in on itself. It wouldn't be saved. Bulldozers would knock it down. Apartments would take its place and a golden plaque would mark the spot where people had died horribly, forgotten to history, like so many Belfast tragedies before.

The first shards of morning sun touched the blackened corpse of Star of the Sea and the Firefighters carried out the first body.

## 21

Few people lived in Sailortown, which meant onlookers were thankfully low. Press photographers had been and gone but two local news vans remained, ready to beam the devastation across the country for breakfast television.

Jacob waited as the police officer on the cordon point radioed through to get the ok for him to be let through to get his car. The old hostel was a charred shell but the firefighters seemed content enough that what remained of the structure wasn't in danger of collapse.

The officer finished his transmission and nodded to Jacob. "Just stay this side of the street," he said, holding the tape up for him to duck underneath.

Jacob wasn't sure what had kept him there, watching the hostel burn. Shock. Numbness at the devastation. Sheer relief at his own escape. He had watched fire fighters carry out three bodies out under sheets. He was certain there would be more.

He had managed to catch the one who had pulled him clear as she took a break near the cordon and asked her if they had any idea what had caused had caused it.

"Initial guess is electrical," she said after finishing a bottle of water in one go. "Old building like this, probably had the same wiring in it since the sixties."

Jacob had looked past her to the hostel. Star of the Sea was a dump. A tipping place for the unwanted. He would have bought an electrical fire any other week of the year except this one.

A new wave of tiredness seized him the moment he eased himself into the Clio. Home was less than five minutes away.   He was bone tired, the surge of adrenaline that had taken him into the burning building had long since dissipated but he knew he wouldn't sleep. He also knew he couldn't go home. The empty apartment was more than he could face.

When Natalie answered her door he felt a gut punch of guilt as she sagged in relief. She had lit up his phone for most of the night. Jacob hadn't replied and the messages and calls had only stopped once his phone battery had died.

Even at seven am and dressed in an old hoody and leggings she was lovely. Jacob felt his heart ache. He was lonely and hurt and had no idea why he was standing on her door step and felt all the more annoyed at himself because of it.

Her nose wrinkled a fraction. It was the first time Jacob even noticed the smell. He stank. The smoke, the fumes, the melted wood, and plastic, clung to him.

"What happened?" she asked, taking him by the shoulder and leading him inside.

He told her, as best he could remember. How he discovered the fire. How he had got Amanda out. How he had tried to warn everyone else. How he failed. How he stood and watched the hostel burn with people still inside.

"Tomas?"

"I don't know."

"Jacob. What you did..."

He turned away. He didn't want to hear it.

She patted his hand lightly, understanding. "Can I get you anything?"

"Coffee."

"You're out on your feet. Coffee is the last thing you need. Hold on and I'll get you a glass of water."

Jacob mumbled a thank you as she left the room. He closed his eyes for a second and when he opened them, found he was lying down on the sofa, a blanket draped over him. He fumbled for his phone to check the time, forgetting it was dead.

Pushing the blanket away he stood and made his way into the hall. Music drifted from the kitchen. He followed the sound to find Natalie at the kitchen island, her laptop open in front of her.

She looked up as he entered. "I came back in and you were dead to the world. Figured you needed to sleep it off for a spell."

"How long was I out of it?"

"Nearly five hours," she said, looking at her watch. She stood and grabbed some neatly folded clothes and a towel that had been placed on a nearby counter. "Fresh threads," she said, handing the pile over. "Bathroom is upstairs, third on the left."

Jacob ran the shower until it was almost scalding. The pungent smell of the fire stuck to him. He scrubbed himself close to raw trying to get rid of it.

He regarded himself in the mirror after he had finished. The water had turned his pale skin pink, at least in the areas not covered by blue and purple bruises, but he was clean.

When he returned to the kitchen Natalie had a mug of coffee waiting. "Godsend," Jacob said as she handed it over. He pulled at the neck of the t-shirt. "Dillon's?"

"Ex-boyfriend. From many moons ago. Thought I had donated all his stuff to charity but a couple of things slipped the net." She waited while he sat next to her. "How are you feeling?"

"I'll survive."

She nodded and didn't push him for anything further.

"Seems like we have a lot to catch up on. It can wait though."

"No time like the present."

Natalie let him talk and waited until he had finished. "If I've got my timeline right, Luke or Liam already had the hard drive. So why would anyone kill Roisin?"

"Maybe the killer was unaware that Roisin no longer

had it. A burglary gone wrong. Or maybe they killed her anyway to keep her quiet." He rubbed his face with both hands. "The Followers. Or Luke Fisher, getting rid of an obstacle. Or Liam Dunwoody, furious at her for putting the kibosh on his little scheme. Or Tomas McKinsty for who knows what reason." He stopped. As always with this case, it all came back to the locked room problem. Plenty of suspects and absolutely no plausible method. Frustration welled in him suddenly. "Don't worry, no matter who did it, you have a story."

Natalie frowned. "What's that supposed to mean?"

He sighed, already regretting where this was going. "Forget it."

"No, I won't forget it." She levelled a finger at him. "If you have something to say, say it."

The smart thing, Jacob knew, would be to keep his mouth shut. Instead, he said, "All of this, for a girl you admit you weren't close to?" He framed the question to give her a chance to speak, to help him out of this deep hole. When she didn't say anything, he dived in with both feet. "I mean, you have an angle in this too. It can't just be about justice for Roisin."

"Is that what you think?" Her expression had turned cold but the note of hurt in her voice was clear.

"Am I wrong?"

Natalie opened her mouth to speak but was cut off by Jacob's phone buzzing. He had left it to charge on the pop-up socket in the middle of the island while he showered. "Hello?"

"Good morning. This is Constable Warnock from Lisburn Police Station," the voice on the other end replied. "I was looking to speak to Jacob Kincaid."

"Speaking." Jacob put the phone on loudspeaker, set it back on the island and tried to ignore Natalie's glare.

"Hi, Mr. Kincaid. I apologise for taking so long in returning your call, I was on leave over the weekend and only back on duty this morning. I understand you were looking to speak to someone who was dealing with

Roisin Dunwoody?"

"That's right. I was hired by Roisin's family to investigate the circumstances of her death." He had told the lie so often it now came easily. "I know in the weeks prior to her passing, she had reported a series of incidents to police. I had tried to contact the IO for each of them but so far, you're the first one to get back to me."

"I'm probably the only one likely to get back to you," Warnock replied, her tone apologetic. "I happened to be the Investigating Officer for the first two incidents. As they continued, my bosses thought it would be easier to have one point of contact rather than stretch it over multiple officer's and sections."

A rather nice little stroke of luck, Jacob thought. "I guess I'm just looking to get your take, Constable. Was there anything to what Roisin was reporting?"

"Oh, very much so. She had some form of evidence for most of the reports she made. Damage to her car, call logs, screenshots of the emails."

"I don't suppose you can tell me any specific details?"

Warnock hesitated, wary of treading on data protection issues. "It depends on what you want to know."

"Were you able to trace any of the calls or emails?"

"Unfortunately not. We were able to identify that the calls and texts were sent from pre-paid mobiles but we couldn't obtain any buyer information or the locations from where they were purchased."

"How about the e-mails?"

Warnock paused again. "They were one of the last things Miss Dunwoody reported. The forms hadn't been completed before her death and the incident was filed away after…"

Jacob nodded as Warnock trailed off. He knew from experience that the paperwork to apply for such information was a ball ache, with several stringent criteria that had to be met to ensure nothing was breached in terms of the right to a private life. For the completing officer the application was a persnickety nightmare that usually required several reworks before the receiving unit would accept it. She wouldn't admit it but Warnock was probably relieved about dodging that particular piece of admin.

"What about CCTV?"

"No, nothing. Whoever damaged Miss Dunwoody's car was smart enough not to get caught on camera."

"What about the time she thought she saw someone lingering about near her apartment?"

"Same result. Local response crews called out but didn't see anyone matching the description."

"And no doubt there were no witnesses to any of these incidents."

"I'm afraid not, no."

Jacob asked a few more questions but Warnock couldn't provide much. Thanking her for the call he hung up on another dead end.

"I should go," he said, taking his phone out of the charging point, not meeting Natalie's eye.

She nodded stiffly. "What are you going to do next?"

"Go home, change. Try to find out if Tomas was in the hostel last night."

He turned to go, lifting his clothes, heavy with the stench of smoke and made it as far as the kitchen door.

"Jacob." Natalie waited for him to turn around. "I am the client. You are under my employ. I don't expect my motivations to be questioned. Are we clear going forward?"

Jacob got caught between nodding his acceptance and uttering an apology before he turned on his heel and left. It had been a mistake to come. To blur the line between professional and personal.

When he got home his soiled clothes went straight into the washing machine. Once changed into a fresh set of his own, he made a pot of coffee accompanied by several rounds of toast lathered in butter.

He began to ring around the local hospitals. The Royal Victoria, the Mater and the City had no one with the name of Tomas McKinstry in their care. The victims of the hostel fire, living and dead, had all been brought to the Royal and all had been identified by hostel staff. He asked about unnamed patients, unconnected to the fire. The Royal and the City had none, the Mater one, but she was fifty years old and been in a coma for the past week.

He yawned as he set the phone down. He was reasonably confident Tomas had not been in the hostel when it went up in flames but he doubted he could say the same for his notes. Either way, he wouldn't know until Tomas resurfaced.

Kicking off his shoes, Jacob swung his feet around so he could lie across the sofa. A wave of exhaustion hit him suddenly and within seconds he could feel himself drifting off.

Through the haze, his mind lazily wandered back to the night before. How he had found Amanda and the overturned mop bucket. The fire was too much of a coincidence for him to buy, yet the firefighters seemed to believe it to be accidental. Amanda had discovered the blaze and attempted to put it out before presumably being overcome by the fumes or smoke.

With what felt like every sinew of his body protesting, Jacob pushed himself up from the sofa, put his shoes back on and walked to the Clio. He made the short drive up the traffic clogged Westlink to the Royal Victoria, arriving in time to catch the end of the afternoon visiting hour.

The reception was busy and he waited in line for several minutes until he reached the front of the queue. He explained to the receptionist that he was a brother of a woman brought in from last night's hostel fire.

"Ok, no worries," she said brightly. "What's your sister's name?"

"Amanda."

"And her surname?"

"Ah…Good question."

He beat a hasty retreat from the incredulous

receptionist who unsurprisingly didn't buy the story that he couldn't remember his own sister's last name.

As he hurried past a group of smokers outside the main entrance, he stopped, recognising the man who had helped him carry Amanda out from the fire.

"Hey," Jacob said, sliding up to him.

The man studied Jacob warily from behind a pall of blue smoke before recognition set in. When it did, the man shook his hand heartily and asked how he was doing.

"Pretty good," Jacob lied. The smell of the man's cigarette was enough to make him queasy. "How about you? You alright?"

"I'm good," he said, in a heavy French accent. "I travelled here in the ambulance with Amanda. I was hanging around and the Doctor asked for my help in identifying one of the...." His voice trailed away and he took a deep drag from his cigarette.

"How is she? Amanda?"

"Good, considering. Think they're keeping her in for the day. To monitor her, you know? I was waiting around to go and visit but her mother and sister are up there. Didn't want to intrude." He finished his smoke and ground it out on top of the bin he was standing beside. "So what are you doing here?"

"I was hoping to see her actually." Jacob watched as the man frowned. "I'm looking for a friend, Tomas McKinstry. That's why I was at the hostel last night. Were you there when he left?"

"No. But I know he stormed out the day before."

"Oh yeah?"

"Yeah. Not sure what set him off. The early shift said he had a letter waiting for him in reception. No idea who from. He takes it, goes up to his room, five minutes later he leaves. Very angry apparently."

"A letter? What about?"

The man laughed. "How would I know?"

"Right," Jacob said as he rubbed his face. "Tomas storming off. Is that unusual behaviour?"

"Eh...Not so unusual. A lot of our guys can be volatile. Tomas usually keeps to himself though. We were told about it, just so we could keep an eye on him when he came back."

"But he didn't?"

"Not as far as I know."

"Amanda was manning the desk. Maybe he arrived back when you were napping."

"Maybe." His tone was guilty.

"Look...."

"Francis."

"Francis. I don't want to bother Amanda. I just need a couple of minutes of her time and then I'll get out of here." He watched the other man sigh. "I'm looking out for Tomas. Nothing else."

"Alright," Francis said slowly. "She's up in ward twenty-eight."

Jacob shook his hand again and hurried away, knowing he didn't have much time before visiting hours finished. Using the rear entrance off the Falls Road to avoid the circumspect receptionist, he rode the elevator up to Amanda's floor.

He spotted her, propped up on two pillows, talking to the mother and sister Francis had mentioned. He hung back. The other two women looked as if they were saying their goodbyes.

He waited a beat after they had passed him on their way out before he approached. By the time he reached Amanda, her eyes were closed and he had to cough softly to get her attention. She blinked and Jacob thought he saw the hint of recognition when she finally managed to focus on him.

"Hi," he said quietly, his voice barely above a whisper. "I was at the hostel last night..."

Amanda managed a tired smile. "Francis told me. How you helped him carry me out." Her voice was hoarse. "He didn't come back last night. Tomas."

Jacob nodded. "How are you feeling?" he asked, ignoring the gnaw of guilt at using her to answer his questions.

"Thankful," she replied. "Aside from the big bump on my head, I'm alright. Francis told me what you did. Running back into the building to try and warn everyone. That was brave."

"Do you remember what happened?" Jacob had no wish to dwell on the previous night.

"Not really. I remember smelling it. I was watching a show on my phone in our front office. I went out to the corridor, saw the smoke and an orange glow coming from the storeroom. I ran back and started hitting the fire alarm but nothing happened. Next thing I know, I'm waking up out on the street with Francis over me."

"I tried one of the alarm points too. The whole system must have been down. Is that common?"

"I'm a support worker, I wouldn't deal with any maintenance issues but the hostel is very run down. I'm sure you could see that yourself."

Jacob nodded. "Well, it was lucky you didn't throw that bucket of water over an electrical fire."

Her features creased. "Bucket?"

"That's how I found you. Out cold with an overturned mop bucket beside you. I figured maybe you passed out but I guess you could have slipped and hit your head. You don't remember?"

Her laugh was weak. "I remember thinking I needed to get the fuck out of there."

Jacob offered a half smile as he rubbed his chin. "You really don't remember getting the bucket?"

Amanda looked to the ceiling before she shook her head. "No. Sorry."

"Or going towards the fire?"

Another shake of the head.

"Alright, Amanda.  Look, I'll let you rest. Take care."

"What's your name?" she asked just as he turned to go.

"Jacob. Jacob Kincaid.

"Thank you, Jacob."

He mumbled a quick goodbye and took himself out

234

of the ward. Francis was gone when he walked back past the smoking area. He had just made it back to his car when his phone vibrated. It was Michael.

"Alright, mate," Jacob answered. "What's happening?"

"Nothing much. Back in work."

"You're a whore for the OT," Jacob said, climbing into the driver's seat. "You know that, right?"

"Yeah..."

Jacob heard the tone and braced himself. "What is it?"

Michael's sigh was heavy. "I was just having a gander at the call screen. "Looks like a floater washed up down near the harbour this morning."

Jacob closed his eyes and leaned back into his seat. Michael had stopped and Jacob prompted him to continue with a short, "Yeah."

"The guy still had his wallet. No photo ID but he had his national insurance card. Name of Tomas McKinstry. Description the crew on scene gives is slim build, short, maybe thirty to thirty-five years old. Sound like your guy?"

"Yeah," Jacob replied. "Yeah, that's him." He ran a hand through his hair. "Was there any word on injuries. I mean, does it look..."

"-No. Not on the call log at least. But there is a linked serial from last night. Anonymous report of someone taking a header off the M3 overpass into the Lagan. Looks like Lagan Search and Rescue had a look but they didn't find anything. Lucky the current only washed him up a little bit down the shore a bit and didn't carry him out to sea."

"Yeah," Jacob agreed. "Lucky."

## 22

Jacob punched the steering wheel once and then again. The horn blared with the second shot, startling a woman walking in front of the car. She gave a stern glare, his upheld hand of apology ignored as she stalked off.

"Fuck," he said to himself. Experience told him he really shouldn't be shocked. Drug abuse and mental health problems were a dangerous combination, even without the trouble Jacob and Natalie had brought to his door.

He sank back. Tomas chucking himself into the dark waters of the Lagan the same night the hostel burned down and his notes were lost. He had read once that *coincidence* was the word used when you couldn't see the levers and pulleys.

Conspiracies began to take shape. Tomas storming out of the hostel. Amanda not remembering trying to fight the fire. He stopped himself. Did he really believe someone would burn down a building full of people just to get rid of Tomas's notes?

He thought about his first meeting with Cora Adebayo and the story she had painted. A dead child clutching his teddy. Peter Funston and the overturned chair. The broken body of a con man splattered on the concrete. People who crossed the Followers and met a tragic end. Would a group capable of those crimes be above treating some down and outs as collateral?

His weariness gave way to a slow boil anger. Roisin

Dunwoody was dead. Tomas McKinstry was dead. Jacob and Natalie had been attacked. People had suffered and one smug dickhead was trying to make a profit. He started the Clio.

When he arrived at Fisher's house, he marched for the door but stopped as he reached for the handle. A deep breath extinguished some of the fire in his belly. Be hard but don't step over, he told himself. The work of a private investigator sometimes skirted a fine line of legality and he often played fast and loose with the strictest definition of some laws. The questionable morality of the job he could stomach, but his own integrity was something he wouldn't compromise.

He took another steadying breath, preparing the front to face Fisher with. Ready, he slapped the wood loudly. He took a step back and waited. Nothing. He did it again, his hand stinging with the effort.

Looking up, Jacob couldn't see any movement in the first-floor windows. He moved to the living room and pressed his face against the glass. The room was dark behind the partially closed blinds, but there was no sign of Fisher.

Taking his phone from his pocket, he tried the number he had found in Liam Dunwoody's diary. He thought he could hear the faint sound of a ringtone coming from the house. Luke was home.

Walking back to the front door, Jacob was about to knock again when he stopped. His exhausted brain took a moment to process what it was seeing beyond the thin pane.

"Fuck!"

Holding on to the guard rail for balance, he launched a hard kick directly below the door handle. The crunch of wood was loud but the door stayed upright. He hit the same spot again and was rewarded with a *crack* as the wood gave way. The door buckled with a third kick and Jacob paused, panting with the effort.

A neighbour, two doors down, was brought to his

front door by the commotion. "I'm calling the police!" he shouted.

"Call an ambulance!" Jacob yelled back as he rammed his shoulder into the door. It gave way fully and Jacob went sprawling into the little hallway.

The body of Luke Fisher dangled above him.

Jacob's shoulders sagged. The ambulance wouldn't do Luke any good. He was stone dead. His skin was death white and rigor had already stiffened the body. Unseeing eyes looked down dully towards the floor.

Jacob stood. Fisher had secured a rolled-up bed sheet around the newel post on the landing above and stepped off a chair that now sat overturned next to where Jacob had landed.

He retreated outside, taking in a lungful of air. The neighbour had disappeared. The cops would be on their way, responding to a report of a man trying to force his way into a house.

Dialling 999, Jacob asked for police. Once connected, he told the call handler that he had just arrived at his friend's house and had found him deceased as a result of hanging. He also advised that he had forced the door, and that they probably had a call on screen to the same address regarding someone trying to break in. The police would still come of course, as they would for any unexplained death, but they wouldn't break their necks getting there. It's not like the dead man was going anywhere fast.

It also gave Jacob time.

Luke had not shown them the hard drive, only an image on his phone, but Jacob remembered that the drive had looked like it had been placed on a kitchen counter.

Jacob went back into the house and began his search. Luke had kept a tidy home and for every drawer Jacob rummaged through, he made sure to put everything back. If the police turned up and found a dead body and half the place pulled apart, they might start asking the wrong questions.

He worked quickly but carefully, moving his way around the living room, finishing at the same point he had started from before moving on to the kitchen. He searched through drawers and cupboards, checked tubs of protein powder for false bottoms and cans of beans to see if any had been hollowed out but came up empty.

As he finished looking under the sink he stopped, noticing for the first time two glasses in the basin. Both still had the residue of red wine. Trying to ignore the dangling body, Jacob hurried up the stairs. A quick check of the master bedroom, the bathroom and the study revealed Fisher was thankfully alone.

He recommenced the search in the kitchen before heading back upstairs. Thirty minutes later, it was obvious the hard drive was not in the house. Hearing the slam of a car door, Jacob moved to the nearest window and saw a liveried police vehicle parked behind Fisher's BMW. Two peelers were walking towards the house.

Jacob met the officers, both male, at the front door. The first was a tad overweight, the paunch on his belly stretching the green fabric of his short-sleeved shirt. The other officer was younger, clean shaven and clearly nervous. His first sudden death, Jacob guessed.

He gave them a few details then went out to his car, letting the officers work without crowding them. They'd check for anything suspicious; a suicide note, pills, the usual. A paramedic would have to pronounce life extinct and their Sergeant would need to attend too. Not to mention the photography branch, body recovery, and finally, the undertaker.

A few minutes later, the younger officer appeared, somewhat paler than when he had went in. Jacob didn't blame him. His first sudden death had been a hanging too and he'd spent most of the time fighting the urge to either vomit or faint. It got easier with time.

"Mind if I grab a few details?" he asked, lifting his notebook from the front pocket of his flak jacket.

"Sure."

He took Jacob's name, date of birth, address, and phone number. When asked about his relationship with Fisher, Jacob kept it vague.

"Because you found the, uh, deceased, a statement might be required. Are you happy enough to do that now?"

Jacob agreed and the officer led him around the back of the house and into the kitchen, tactfully avoiding the dangling body. He sat himself at the table and took a couple of statement pages from his folder. Jacob remained standing. The statement was brief; detailing what time Jacob arrived, what he saw, how he gained entry, and what he did upon finding the body.

As the officer read the statement back to him, Jacob noticed a diary tucked into a small space between the fridge and microwave. He had missed it in his initial search. Keeping his eye on the young peeler, he shuffled over to where it sat and pocketed it, just as the older officer entered.

"All good?" he asked.

"Finishing up," his colleague answered. "Just need a few signatures."

The senior man looked at Jacob with sympathy. "Bad business."

Jacob didn't reply. He took the offered pen from the younger peeler and signed the statement pages. Once finished, he declined the offer of a lift home and left the house by the kitchen.

Once in his car, he opened the diary. Hair appointments, sunbed sessions and a few lunch dates. Nothing that stood out. He found the page with the date Roisin died. The party at her apartment was there. Writing sessions at the Wheelman studio that had been planned for the weeks after were scratched out in angry pen strokes.

Flicking forward, he stopped as he spotted Mairead's name alongside the name of a restaurant down by the Loughshore at Whiteabbey. The date was around two weeks after Roisin's death. It was well before Jacob had met Mairead and he was surprised by the sudden pang of jealousy. He knew it was immature in the extreme but it was there all the same.

Mairead had been adamant she hadn't seen Fisher recently and a quick check through the remaining weeks seemed to confirm her story.

He leafed through the remainder of the diary but found it blank from the end of August onwards. It was only when he reached the last page that he found a card tucked into the plastic divider on the back cover.

B*ig Box Storage Facility.* Someone had scribbled *1172* in black ink at the top. Tapping the card against the steering wheel, Jacob's eyes drifted back towards Fisher's house. He got out of the Clio and closed the door quietly.

The police had left the front door as they had found it and Jacob could hear them talking in the kitchen. There were no keys in the door or in the cabinet beside it.

Stepping over the chair, he inched himself up the stairs, cautious of any creak that would give him away. From the kitchen, he could hear the younger peeler laugh, some of his sense of humour returning. The trepidation of his first sudden death was now firmly behind him and by the time he made it back to the station he'd probably be able to crack a joke about how Fisher was just hanging around.

Jacob made it to the landing and edged along the hallway until he reached the main bedroom. From the doorway he spotted a set of keys on the bedside table. He lifted them. The first key, attached to a BMW lanyard, was clearly for Fisher's car. The next two appeared to be house keys.

The final key, however, was a good deal smaller, most likely for a padlock. He slipped it off the ring and pocketed it.

Setting the rest down where he had found them, he had made it halfway down the landing when someone called out, "Hello?"

Jacob froze and came up blank as he scrambled for an explanation as to why he had snuck back into a dead man's house.

"Alright, buddy, how's it going?" It was the older peeler who spoke, and Jacob realised he was talking to someone who had just arrived. A paramedic most likely.

He hurried back into the bedroom, his escape route cut off. He had two choices; wait for the scene to be closed, which could take hours, if he wasn't discovered beforehand, or find another way out.

As he deliberated, the decision was made for him. "Where's the pisser in this place?" The new voice asked.

"Upstairs," the older officer replied.

Jacob allowed himself a single silent curse before he opened the bedroom window. He eased himself out, one leg following the over the lip before lowering himself down with both hands holding onto the sill.

It was still a decent sized drop, and he took a moment to decide this was a silly idea before letting go anyway. He landed, hissing as an electric jolt shot up his leg.

He leaned against the wall and let the pain die down. Once ready, he kept low, moving at a crouch past the kitchen window, around the side of the house and to the safety of his car.

Pulling in at the park on the Loughshore, he saw the crowds had not been put off by the cool, overcast day. Red jacketed brass musicians were setting up in the band stand as a mammoth cruise ship bringing in a fresh batch of tourists lumbered through the grey water of the lough towards Belfast. He phoned Natalie.

"Yeah?"

Jacob ignored the gruff greeting. "I have a lot to catch you up on."

"You only left here like two hours ago," she replied, her tone shifting slightly. Annoyed or not, her interest was piqued.

"I know," Jacob said, "And it's not all good news." He waited for Natalie to speak but when she didn't, he continued. "Tomas and Luke Fisher are dead."  Blunt but that was the point. He didn't want any ambiguity.

He heard her gasp. "Dead? How?"

"Suicide. At least that's how it looks."

"Suicide! I..." She scrambled for the words. "Wait, Tomas or Luke?"

"Both."

Stunned into silence, he took the opportunity to fill Natalie in on Tomas apparently taking the leap of the motorway overpass, and how he had just found Fisher, hanging in his home.

"Jesus," she said, when he had finished. "That can't be coincidence..."

"-There's more," Jacob cut in, "I couldn't find the hard drive in Luke's house but I did find a key. I think it's for a storage facility. Big Box. It's on West Bank Road in the harbour estate. I'm heading over now."

"I'll meet you there."

# 23

Belfast Harbour handled around a quarter of the maritime trade for the whole of Ireland. The sprawling estate could also boast that it had been the birthplace of the world's most famous ship, which was still floating when she'd left Belfast, the former production base for one of the world's most iconic TV shows, although Jacob much preferred the books; and the home of an airport, an ice hockey team and its own police force.

None of this was on Jacob's mind as he made the journey to the harbour from Fisher's house. He played amber gambler as he shot through a set of traffic lights and kept the pedal to the floor as he overtook a line of three, slow moving lorries before nipping back in front of the lead vehicle to make the sharp turn onto West Bank Road.

The card he had found at Fisher's didn't give an exact location of where Big Box Storage was on West Bank and Jacob passed warehouses, factories, parcel couriers, and even an MMA gym before he found it.

The car park was empty, save for an ancient Vauxhall Cavalier parked beside a portacabin serving as a reception and office. A man, presumably the Cavalier's owner, and obviously a firm believer in the self-reliance of self-storage, slept soundly at the sole desk inside, not stirring as Jacob walked past.

Access to the main building where the units were housed was up a rusted metal ramp and through a loading bay. Empty trolleys, cardboard boxes and stacks of wooden pallets were strewn about. A faded plaque by the entrance told anyone who cared to read it that the building had once been a cold storage facility.

The cooled interior was cavernous. Mercifully for Jacob, the units were neatly ordered and clearly numbered. The largest, roughly the size of a single car garage, were next to the door Jacob had entered through.

As he walked further into the facility, the units got smaller and more numerous. He made it to the back wall and then followed the last row as the numbers ascended as far *750*. Jacob checked the card again: *1172*. He backtracked but couldn't find anything higher.

It was only when he was halfway back to the entrance that he noticed what he had initially taken for an open and empty unit was actually an old freight elevator. He went inside, pulled the heavy door across and locked it in place. Then he pushed the only button on the wall panel and waited as the ancient gears lumbered the elevator up to the next floor.

He quickly found unit *1172*. Jacob smiled as the key he swiped from Fisher's fitted perfectly into the lock.

Fisher had packed the small unit tight. Most of the space was taken up by stacks of cardboard boxes. An old desk and leather sofa were propped against the back wall and an office chair with ripped padding sat to the right.

The hard drive was in plain view, sitting on the old chair. "You wouldn't believe the trouble you've caused," Jacob said as he lifted it. A long power cable and a shorter USB adapter were wrapped around the drive. Turning the device over, he saw it had a keypad.

He reached for his phone to call Natalie but saw there was no signal. Putting the phone back in his pocket, he glanced to the boxes. Curious, he peered inside the top box to find a pile of books. He brought one out.

*The Tale of Latora* by Luke Fisher. The title font was

jarring, flat and in no way integrated with the books cover image. Fantasy was far from Jacob's favourite genre but he guessed by the pointed ears, that the man and woman, who stared back with badly photoshopped glowing purple eyes, were meant to be elves. A floating amulet hovered between the hands of the lady elf. Even by amateur standards the design was the drizzling shits.

Jacob flipped the book over and quickly read the blurb. It had been described by an unnamed critic, almost certainly Fisher himself, as his magnum opus. Judging by the overflowing boxes, Jacob guessed that not everyone held the work in such high esteem.

The quality of the cover suggested the books were self-published. Not a cheap proposition for an unknown author. With his work obviously not selling and with losses no doubt incurred, it was perhaps little wonder why Fisher had turned his hand to blackmail.

As Jacob wondered if the book he was holding might be worth something with the untimely death of its author, the old elevator rumbled into life.

He put the hard drive in his coat pocket and slid the shutter down before securing the padlock back in place. A rational mind would tell him that it could be anyone coming up to use one of the several hundred storage units. Gumption and the experiences of the past week told him he should be so lucky. Head down, he walked quickly into the row behind *1172* and waited.

The sound of the elevator door echoed loudly. Heavy footsteps clipped a brisk pace on the concrete as they made their way in his direction. There was nowhere to hide in the perfectly ordered aisles. Jacob waited as the steps grew louder before stopping and then restarting. He listened, judging the other person to be a row or two ahead, moving parallel to where he was standing. Jacob crept forward, moving on the balls of his feet. Peering around the corner, he saw the coast to the elevator was clear.

He took off running and heard a voice shout as he barrelled towards the elevator. He slid to a halt and jumped in. As he tried to haul the metal door across, an arm shot into the narrowing gap. Fish Lips, an ugly bruise on the top of his head, braced himself against the wall and tried to force the it back open.

There was less than a foot between them and Jacob couldn't miss. He drew his right arm back and launched *The Tale of Latora* with all the strength he could muster. The spine caught Fish Lips on the bridge of the nose and he wheeled away, giving Jacob the time he needed to lock the door in place.

The trip to the ground floor was ponderously slow. Once there, Jacob left the lift open, trapping Fish Lips on the upper level and giving him time to reflect on the drawback of being a henchman.

Jacob made it as far as the loading bay when it hit him. He could only give a strangled gasp at the sudden, sharp pain that shot through his body. His muscles turned to jelly as he flopped to the ground. A baseball bat was Jacob's first thought. This was Belfast after all, and you couldn't argue with the classics.

He tried to move but his body wouldn't comply. A pair of feet stepped into his view and Jacob was just about able to turn his eyes up to see Thin Man hovering over him, an ugly smile on his pinched face. The stun gun clicked menacingly as electricity crackled between the two metal prongs on its tip.

"Stay put," Thin Man said. "I know a guy who is eager to talk with you."

Jacob had no intention of staying put but as Thin Man walked back into the main building, he could only just manage to roll over into a front crawl, dragging himself towards the metal ramp.

From inside the building he could hear the low rumbling of the freight elevator. Not good. Fish Lips had seemed to rather enjoy kicking lumps out of him behind the Follower's centre. And that was before Jacob had dinged a bottle off his face and punted him in the goolies.

Teeth gritted, he pulled himself onto his knees and

tried to stand, stumbling onto the ramp. He made it halfway down before his equilibrium failed him and he went head over arse, coming to a sudden stop on the wet uneven concrete.

"There he goes," he heard Fish Lips call from behind him. Jacob turned to see Fish Lips descend the ramp as Thin Man hung back. "I've still got the blow torch in the car. Go and grab it."

The mention of the blow torch was like a lightning bolt up his back passage. He hauled himself to his feet and started to run but his legs gave out with only a few steps. He collapsed onto his back as he fell, scooting away as Fish Lips advanced; his glee barely contained at Jacob trying to delay the inevitable.

Jacob didn't hear the screech of brakes. Neither had Fish Lips apparently, only looking up a half second before the Audi SUV hit him, throwing him onto the bonnet and tumbling out of sight.

The Audi's passenger door was shoved open and Jacob leaped for it with his last remaining strength.

"Go!"

Natalie didn't need a second invitation. She slammed the gear stick into reverse and careened out onto Westbank Road, narrowly missing a lorry. A low, angry horn blared loudly as the Audi's tyres squealed, struggling for traction as it sped away.

"Jesus, your timing is outstanding!"

Natalie's eyes were wide. "I just ran a man over."

"Yeah," Jacob agreed, sinking back into his seat. "Fuck him." He had seen Fish Lips get to his feet as they took off. Unfortunately, Natalie hadn't seen fit to reverse back over him.

Instead of heading for the motorway and potentially getting stuck in traffic, she took a left, heading deeper into the harbour estate, along a quiet road with factories to their right and a damp but empty riverbed on their left.

Jacob saw a silver Range Rover in the rear mirror and watched it grow larger. "Natalie..."

She glanced up and stepped on the accelerator without further prompting.

The Range Rover closed the gap and didn't slow. Jacob bit back a curse as its bumper rammed the back of Natalie's Audi, jolting them both forward in their seats. Natalie's knuckles were white as she gripped the steering wheel, only about managing to keep her car from fishtailing.

They were trapped between fenced-off factory yards and the riverbed. The Range Rover moved into the right lane, pulling level with Natalie's Audi. Metal screeched against metal as the two cars came together, pushing the Audi into the kerb hard enough that Jacob thought the rear wheel had come off.

Ahead, the road curved sharply. The Range Rover moved across to ram them again. As they reached the apex of the corner, Natalie aimed for an unmarked entryway in the corrugated steel fencing.

The manoeuvre took the Range Rover by surprise, and it could only follow the road parallel as the Audi steamed through a private wharf, past an ancient warehouse and three land-moored boats at the water's edge.

The gate at the far end of the wharf was closing, its yellow light flashing a warning. Natalie didn't take her foot off the accelerator. Jacob grabbed the Jesus handle and braced himself as they hurtled back out onto the road and straight over the top of a mini-roundabout that bounced the Audi through the air. They landed hard and Jacob wasn't sure how much more punishment the car could take.

A complex of decaying warehouses stood on their left. Thin Man and Fish Lips were pushing to make up the ground lost and were inches from Natalie's back bumper. At the last second, she swung toward the entrance. Jacob's heart caught in his throat as the wall of the nearest building rushed to meet them. Natalie made the turn by inches, yanking the wheel hard and somehow keeping the Audi under control.

In the mirror, Jacob saw the unexpected turn had been too sharp for the Range Rover. It had slammed on its brakes and was now manoeuvring itself to follow.

The warehouses were fenced off from the road and split up the middle by the edge of Belfast Lough. They were playing a dangerous game, Jacob knew. All it would take was for Thin Man and Fish Lips to catch up and give them the slightest kiss to nudge them into the water.

They were gaining again as Natalie circled around the water. Whether the appearance of an exit gate was down to Natalie's local knowledge or blind luck, Jacob had no idea and had no intention of questioning. Tyres squealed as Natalie rejoined the road, righting her vehicle as she headed towards the border of the harbour estate and the edge of Sailortown.

A horn blasted as they bounced across another roundabout. This time their pursuers didn't hit the brakes, careering after them without slowing.

In the road ahead, two lanes of traffic had formed, slowly moving off from a set of traffic lights towards the city centre. Jacob bit back a curse as the light changed to red just as the last car passed it. He glanced at Natalie and was rewarded with another spurt of acceleration.

"No!" Jacob choked on the word as he realised what she was doing. "Ffffuuuuccck!"

She swerved into the empty left lane and hurtled across the junction. A car coming from their right was forced to slam on its brakes to avoid crashing into them.

Thin Man and Fish Lips tried to follow, only to narrowly miss another car coming from their right. The Range Rover spun on the road, coming to a halt facing in the opposite direction.

Natalie let out an exhilarated whoop, banging the steering wheel in triumph.

"Nice driving," Jacob said.

She flashed a smile, her pretty features flushed with adrenaline. "Thanks," she replied breathlessly. Jacob could see her hands trembling but the glint in her eye was unmissable. "Are you ok?"

"Never better. Now, if you'll excuse me while I pass out."

"The hard drive!" she said as if suddenly remembering. "Did you find it?"

Natalie bit her bottom lip as Jacob held the device up. He directed her into a side street and then to a multistory car park a little further along. The location would keep them hidden and out of sight until he could be confident their trail was cold.

Parking up, Natalie killed the engine and took a deep breath. "That was something."

"It's been a day," Jacob agreed.

Natalie took the hard drive from him and turned it over. "And we're only getting started." she said before her face fell suddenly. "Tomas and Luke..."

Jacob nodded but said nothing

"I'm not alone in what I'm thinking, right? That it can't be so coincidental."

"Levers and pulleys," Jacob murmured.

"But it seems so out there," Natalie continued, not hearing him. "We're talking about someone staging their murders to look like suicides."

Jacob cleared his throat. "There's something I should tell you about. Or someone, rather. She uh, kinda slipped my mind."

To her credit, Natalie listened without interruption as Jacob told his story about Cora Adebayo. How he had been approached, the images she had shown him, her mutual interest in the Followers.

"When was this?" she asked when he finished, clearly debating on what to say first and picking a neutral option.

Jacob thought for a moment. The last few days had blurred together. "Three days ago, give or take."

"And you didn't tell me?"

"I didn't think-"

"-What? Didn't think it was important?" Natalie shot back. "The Followers have a history of opponents turning up dead in convenient circumstances and you didn't think it was related to what happened to Roisin. The job I hired you for."

"It doesn't change anything." He ignored the sharp look Natalie threw. "It doesn't! Either way, we still have to find a suspect and how they did it." He tapped the hard drive. "This is the key, right here. We find out what's on this, we break the whole case open."

# 24

They took a roundabout route to Helen's house, cutting through side streets and into estates, doubling back to ensure they weren't followed. The Range Rover would have been conspicuous as a tail, but Jacob couldn't be certain that Fish Lips and Thin Man didn't have another vehicle at their disposal.

"This is the place?" Natalie asked, bringing her car to a stop.

Two stone pillars sat either side of a secluded driveway. A gold plaque on the left pillar read; *Andilet House.*

"This is it."

Andilet House was a rendered neo-classical villa, at least that's what Helen told Jacob the first time he had been there. "The neo-classical style is characterised by the shallow hipped roof, raised quoins and the fine detailing to parapet and eaves." Jacob had listened and nodded politely as Helen had given him the tour, not wishing to offend his first potential client by appearing ignorant and asking what the hell quoins were.

Built in the boom of Belfast's industrial expansion, and passing through the ownership of various members of the city's elite, Jacob had never pried into how Helen had come to own Andilet House and like almost everything else about her life, she had never offered.

She was waiting for them by the front porch and brought the pair through to the kitchen. Patio doors led to a garden with a lawn so pristine it that would put centre court at Wimbledon to shame. High green hedges kept the back of the property completely private. Between here, his visits to Natalie's house and the Dunwoody estate, Jacob was beginning to feel rather inadequate in the domicile department.

"Tea?" Helen asked.

"Coffee, please," Jacob said. "Black."

"For me too please, Helen."

"Two coffees," she said before turning back to Jacob. "You look like hell."

"You don't know the half of it." Jacob set the hard drive on the table and quickly brought her up to speed.

"This is getting serious," Helen said, once he had finished. She had brewed a pot of coffee as Jacob had talked and now served it.

"Serious is what happened to Natalie back in the office," Jacob said. "This is something else entirely. You think you could grab your laptop? Let us have a gander on what the hell is on this thing."

"Of course." She placed the mugs in front of them before leaving the room.

"I hope she's kept it handy. If it's on the other side of the house it'll take the best part of the day to make the trip on foot."

Natalie managed a polite smile and Jacob took a drink of the coffee before stretching his legs out under the table. Tiredness coursed through every part of him. The lack of sleep, numerous adrenaline highs followed by the equally severe dumps and the various kickings he had endured over the past few days were catching up hard.

"I'm sorry," he said.

"Hmmm?" Natalie asked, turning to look at him. She had been lost in the details of the intricate coving between the ceiling and kitchen walls.

"I said, I'm sorry. About earlier at your place. You're

right. I'm the employee. It's not my place to question your motivations."

"I should apologise too." She stopped to fiddle with the bezel of her Breitling. "I'm a journalist at heart. Always will be, no matter what hat I wear. You were right; if there's a story here I want to break it. And if gets more eyes on my work or more opportunities to grow my business, I'll take them."

Jacob nodded. She was a pragmatist and he couldn't hold it against her.

"But I meant what I said back in your office the first time we met. I came to you because I believe Roisin was murdered and I believe someone needs to answer."

And there was the rub. In truth, he was no closer to finding who had killed Roisin Dunwoody. The job he had been hired to do. With Tomas and Luke dead, and Liam holed up on his father's estate, the three people he believed could have shed some light were now out of reach.

His phone vibrated before he could reply. He checked it to find a message from Mairead.

**Drinks tonight? How about your place?**

Replying with a single thumb-up emoji, he dropped the phone on the table. He could sort out the details later when he had less on his mind.

"Anybody interesting?" Natalie asked, watching from over the lip of her mug.

"No," Jacob replied a little too quickly.

"Got it," Helen announced as she returned to the kitchen with her laptop in hand. She set it on the long table and connected the computer to the hard drive before swinging the screen around to face them.

Natalie glanced at him but Jacob indicated for her to go ahead. She pushed her seat forward and adjusted the laptop slightly. When she tried to access the hard drive, she was met with a password request screen. She took out her phone and found the picture she had snapped of the code on the tablet found in Roisin's kitchen vent.

Jacob found himself holding his breath as he watched her carefully input the code. For a second it looked like they were out of luck as the loading icon froze in place before the drive finally granted them access.

"Jesus," Jacob said he took it in.

Dozens of folders were neatly ordered in alphabetical rows. Natalie scrolled down and found one labelled, *Tomas*. Opening it, they found it contained PDF's of scanned handwritten notes.

"You know what that is?" Jacob asked.

Natalie smiled. "Tomas's notes. Roisin already had them backed-up." She continued exploring the files. Roisin had taken the time to not only scan but transcribe Tomas's notes, typing out what seemed to be verbatim copies of the originals. "Christ, there's a lot here," she said, scrolling through the pages.

"This must have taken weeks to copy across," Jacob agreed.

Natalie exited back into the main folder and continued scrolling, stopping on a folder titled, *Interviews*. When she opened it, she found a list of audio files. One was of an interview of Tomas, clocking in at close to two hours. Another was with the widow McGreavy.

"We reached out to her for the podcast but she declined," Natalie said, as opened the audio clip and fast forwarded with a rueful shake of her head. The woman had a broad rural accent and spoke with a bluntness evident even in the snippets Natalie lingered on.

"Seems like Roisin was able to convince her," said Helen.

"Not just her." Natalie motioned to the other audio files. Most were titled with just single names. "I wonder who they are?"

"One way to find out," Jacob said.

"All in good time." Natalie replied happily. "All in good time."

She backtracked back to the main folder once more.

After a few seconds, the mouse came to a stop over a lone PDF. It had no name, labelled only as \*\*\*. Natalie clicked on it.

It took Jacob a second to realise what he was looking at.

The jackpot.

A list of names in one column, an amount in the column next to it.

Money. A lot of money.

Natalie scrolled down. The descending rows went to almost two hundred deep. "Jesus," she said. "Some of these names."

Jacob and Helen leaned in either side. Even a brief gander at the list was a revelation. Jacob saw a high court judge, several solicitors, a well-known tv personality, a former footballer who had squandered his talent on booze and women, and two members of the assembly, one Sinn Fein, the other DUP, political differences forgotten for a new type of fanaticism.

Natalie sorted the rows into a descending order of amounts donated. At the top row were Ivan and Margaret Gould and two other names; Adam and Catherine, presumably the Gould's children. The Gould's alone had put well over a million into the church coffers. The next few donors weren't lagging far behind in their tributes.

"It wasn't just the money," Jacob said. "It was the names. If this got out, along with Roisin's podcast, it would have damaged too many people. They'd sever ties, all these donations would be lost and no church is going to stand for losing money. If Roisin was killed by the Followers, this is what they killed her for."

Neither Natalie nor Helen replied. A thick air of nervousness had descended on the room. They had finally broken what was behind the whole investigation and now reality was setting in. They were no longer dealing in what-ifs and half-truths but cold hard facts.

Natalie reached the end of the list, scrolled to the top and then began again.

Jacob rubbed his chin. "Can you search for a few names?"

"Shoot." Natalie's voice was quiet.

"Peter Scanlon."

Natalie typed the name into the search bar. "No, nothing."

"Any Scanlon's at all?" His mind wandered back to the office on the Castlereagh Road and the brief moment Scanlon's wife wouldn't meet his eye.

"None."

"What about an O'Connor?"

"Nope."

There were no McKinstry's, Fisher's or Dunwoody's. Jacob racked his brain thinking of other names, people he had come across while working the case. They tried Armstrong, Jameison and McGinn and came back with nothing.

"Sweeny?"

"Nada."

"How about Rourke?"

"The guy who attacked you?"

"The man himself."

Natalie typed it in. "Hmm. What was his first name?"

"Neil."

She tutted. "Sorry. There's a Rourke here but it's a Pat Rourke."

Jacob leaned closer. "Pat?"

"Yeah, Pat. As in Patrick."

"Patrick," Jacob said. "Right..."

# 25

It had taken a concerted effort from Jacob to convince Natalie to keep the hard drive at Helen's for now. The content was a treasure trove for any journalist worth their salt and she was desperate to dive in with both feet, but had eventually relented to stashing it in a place Jacob was reasonably sure no one would think to look.

With a meeting with the Miss Gumshoe team scheduled for early in the morning and a promise to take Dillon out for pizza that night, Natalie had said her goodbyes and vowed to be in touch the next day to decide on their next move. "Wait by your phone," she said, as she left and Jacob knew she was only half joking.

Helen saw her out before hurrying back, finally able to drop the straight face routine. "Pat Rourke?"

Jacob leaned back with both hands on his head. He hadn't let on to Natalie that the name had meant anything to him. "The angle never even occurred to me," he admitted, with a rueful shake of his head. "The Followers hear about the marital woes of one of their members. They approach her other half with a chance to even the score with the fella that exposed him and hope it scares me off the case."

"And if you find out who it was, you naturally assume it's just him looking to get even."

Jacob finished the dregs of his cold coffee with a grimace. "Can you give me a lift?"

He kept low in his seat as they drove past Big Box. With the coast appearing to be clear, Helen dropped him off street a short distance from the entrance. If his car was being watched, Jacob wanted to minimise the chance of Helen being seen with him. He hurried to the Clio and drove back into Belfast, parking a couple of streets away from the Grand Central Hotel.

Jacob spun a quick yarn to the young receptionist at the front desk about how he'd just arrived in town after living in England for five years and wanted to surprise his best mate. She bought the hoodwink, and while she didn't go as far to provide a key card, she had been helpful enough to give him Rourke's room number.

He took the lift to the tenth floor and waited until the corridor was clear before knocking. He could hear movement within and placed his thumb over the peep hole, waiting until the handle went down before shoving his shoulder into the door. Rourke was knocked backwards, sprawling onto the carpeted floor as Jacob closed the door behind him.

It was one thing to surprise a man with a baton on a dark night. It was another when the same man was standing over you, with what you could only fairly assume was revenge on his mind. Jacob had been of the opinion that Rourke wasn't much of a fighter, and he was certainly in no hurry to jump up and defend himself.

"Doctor," Jacob said.

"What do you want?" Rourke asked, not able to hide the tremble as he spoke.

Jacob pointed to a chair by the window. "Have a seat." He waited until Rourke complied before continuing. "I've been thinking, in between bouts of getting beaten up and finding dead bodies, that your little stunt the other night didn't make a lot of sense." Rourke shifted in his seat. Jacob reached into his pocket, and set an audio recorder on the table. "I've got a proposal."

"A proposal?" Rourke's voice was heavy with

derision.

"That's right. I'll take a sad song and make it sound a lot sweeter."

"How do you mean?"

"I mean, no statement to police about the assault on me. I can't help with the offensive weapon, but I'm sure your record is as clean as a nun's knickers. You'll get away with a caution at worst."

His hand hovered over the record button. Rourke nodded once and Jacob pushed the button down. "I thought it was all about revenge at first. After all, that makes the most sense. But a doctor chasing a man through the streets. It's unseemly. A man of your stature and good standing would never stoop to the level of a common thug. Unless you were put up to it."

Rourke reached for a jug of water. Jacob took a step back on the off chance the doctor decided to launch it at his head. "I mean, they probably couldn't believe their luck when they found out the private investigator your wife hired was the same one looking into their crimes."

"Their crimes?"

"Not the time to be coy, Doctor," Jacob said, his tone taking an impatient edge. "What do they have over you?"

The Doctor's brow creased, as if not understanding the question. "Debts," he eventually replied. "Gambling."

"Must be serious money if a cardiologist can't square his losses."

"My wife took control of our finances. I've got some money stashed away but not enough. Not with a divorce looming. Patricia made it clear that's where we're heading." His gaze turned hard. "Thanks to you."

"Thank yourself. I wasn't the man fucking about." Rourke put his head in his hands. Jacob ignored the contriteness. "Was it one of these men who approached you?" He held out his phone and showed Rourke the picture of Fish Lips and Thin Man he had snapped outside the cultural centre.

"No," Rourke said with the briefest of glances.

"You didn't look."

"I don't have to. I've known Peter for years."

Jacob's heart skipped a beat. "Peter?"

"Yeah, Peter. That's who you're talking about, right?" Rourke faltered slightly. "Peter Scanlon?"

"You're saying Peter Scanlon paid you to attack me?"

Rourke's face captured his shame. "He told me I only had to scare you."

Jacob shook his head, unable to grasp the connection. "Why?"

"He didn't say."

"And you didn't think to ask?"

"I needed the money." Rourke said quietly. Jacob motioned around the plush hotel room. "Patricia," Rourke replied. "She was good enough to leave some money aside for me to stay somewhere comfortable until I get something more permanent."

"How much?"

"How much did Patricia set aside?"

"No, you fuckin' eejit! How much did Peter Scanlon offer?"

"Five grand."

Jacob shook his head; none of it made any sense. "How do you know him?"

"Our wives have been friends since uni."

"Your wife and Catherine Scanlon?"

"She was Catherine Gould back then but yes."

Jacob closed his eyes.

Catherine Scanlon, née Gould. The daughter of the biggest financial backer of the Followers of Eden, and the wife of the man who runs the management company of Hilden Mill. The unseen connection was in laser sharp focus.

Jacob ran to his car. Hitting rush hour traffic, the journey to Scanlon Property Management was painfully slow. He had given Rourke a stern warning to keep his mouth shut but was worried the Scanlon's would have closed shop by the time he got there. Parking the Clio on double yellows, he reached the door just as someone was locking it. Jacob shoved it open.

"Oi! What are you playing at?"

The man's protestation was loud enough to draw Peter Scanlon from his office.

"Mr. Kincaid..." His eyes darted nervously. "What can I do for you?"

Jacob held out the audio recorder. "I've just had the most interesting conversation with Doctor Neil Rourke."

Scanlon paled and took a step back as Jacob moved towards him. "Mr. Kincaid, I can explain. Just not here. Please."

"Should I call the police?" asked the man who had been locking the door.

"No! No, that won't be necessary." He motioned Jacob towards his office. "Please."

Catherine Scanlon stood as her husband ushered Jacob in. She was surprised, but kept her composure a good deal better than her spouse. "What is this?" she demanded.

"I'd say it's exactly what you think it is. What else would I be here for?"

Her eyes bore into Jacob as her husband licked his lips and looked away. Jacob set the audio recorder on the desk, hit play and then skipped forward.

*"...You hardly looked."*

*"I didn't have to. I've known Peter for years..."*

Jacob let the recording go on. Peter Scanlon looked increasingly sick while his wife listened with her head bowed.

*No, you fuckin' eejit! How much did Peter Scanlon offer?*

*Five grand.*

*"How do you-"*

Jacob pressed pause. "There's more but I think you get the gist," he said, lifting the recorder. As he slipped it back in his pocket he pushed the time skip button and then hit record.

Catherine Scanlon would not look up so Jacob slapped the desk hard enough to startle her. "Your father is the biggest financial backer of the Followers of Eden by some distance," Jacob said, once he had her attention. "I come to you, looking for information about a possible murder at a property you manage. A murder I believe has at least some link to the Followers of Eden. A few days later, someone you paid to attack me, tries to take my head off with a baton. His wife is a fully paid member of the church, just like you."

Peter Scanlon shook his head. "It's not....it isn't-"

"-It's not what you think," Catherine Scanlon cut in.

"No? Your father-"

"-It's my mother." Catherine interrupted sharply.

"Your mother?" Jacob made no effort to hide his derision. "From what I've heard, she's a new age Lord Lucan."

He watched Catherine Scanlon's lip tremble and didn't feel the least bit guilty. "My father," she said, shakily. "He had his head turned by Huber years ago. My parents are conservative, traditional. That includes family. Everything my father did, my mother supported."

"What does that have to do with anything?"

"Just, let me finish, Mr. Kincaid, please." She waited until Jacob motioned for her to continue. "I wasn't even a teenager when my father first took us to hear Huber speak. I don't even really remember it happening, the slow infestation into our lives. When my father wasn't working, he was at Huber's side. At meetings, at study groups, at charity events. We were there too. My mother, my brother and me. Thank God, I got out when I did. I got into uni across the water. Managed to expand my horizons. When I came back home after graduation I was fully aware of who and what the Followers were."

"My parents though." She shook her head sadly. "By then, my father was indoctrinated fully and my brother, dutiful as he is, went the same way. My mother however…On the outside she was still the faithful wife. The family pillar. But she had doubts. My father had given so much to the church but Mummy had enough. She was talking about leaving my father. I don't know if my father suspected something was up, or got wind of it somehow…. He moved them both into the Follower compound five years ago. I haven't seen her since."

"We've completed a number of missing people reports with the police," Peter Scanlon added quietly. "They go to the compound and speak to Margaret."

"Or someone claiming to be Mummy," Catherine said.

Peter shrugged. "As far as the police are concerned, if she's at the compound then she's not missing."

"Why not report her as a concern for safety?"

"We've tried that too. Same result," Catherine replied. "She tells them she's looking to live a private life in the compound and doesn't want contact with anyone from outside the church."

"A real tale of woe," Jacob said flatly. "But you may start giving me a straight answer. How does any of that relate to my case?"

"A few weeks ago, my father rang Peter. A strange enough occurrence. Neither of us have spoken to him in years. He said that he needed a favour. Access to the attic space at Hilden Mill."

"Did you ask why?"

"Of course we did and when he wouldn't tell us, we said no."

"We were visited the next day by a man," Peter said. "He mentioned Catherine's mother by name and said it would be in her best interests if we cooperated."

Jacob brought his phone out. "Was it one of these men?" He showed them the blurry image of Thin Man and Fish Lips.

"Him," Peter said, picking out Thin Man immediately. Catherine nodded.

"Was it the same man who approached you to make the offer to Rourke?"

265

Husband and wife shared a look. "Yes," Catherine answered.

"Didn't it strike you as strange when a woman died in one of your apartments shortly after he was prodding about in her attic?"

"Well, no." Peter Scanlon actually managed a nervous titter.

Jacob's patience snapped. He grabbed Scanlon by the lapels of his suit and shoved him against the nearest wall.

"Get off him!" Catherine tried to pull Jacob away from her husband but Jacob held firm.

"We didn't think anything of it until you showed up, I swear!"

"You expect me to believe you're that stupid?"

"Cecil!" Scanlon's voice was shrill. "Cecil Armstrong!"

Jacob loosened his grip. "The site supervisor?"

"Yes!" Scanlon took the opportunity to pull his lapels free and stumbled back. "He was there when I turned up with those two men. Didn't like the look of them. I told him it was none of his business but he's a hardheaded sort. After they were finished, he took the key from me and said if anyone wanted back up into the loft, they'd have to come to him directly."

"As far as we were concerned, Miss Dunwoody's death was an accident." Catherine Scanlon eased herself between Jacob and her husband. "The police said as much and we know the apartment. There was no way in, except for maybe the attic but we knew Cecil had the only key. This was at least a week or two before Miss Dunwoody passed. If she was killed, it wasn't anything to do with us letting those men into the loft."

Jacob thought for a moment. "Maybe Armstrong was bribed to open up the attic."

Catherine Scanlon snorted. "I don't think you know Cecil Armstrong."

"No," Jacob said. "But maybe I should find out."

\*

"You again," Cecil Armstrong said by way of greeting after opening his front door to find Jacob.

"Me again," Jacob agreed. "Mr. Armstrong, I wasn't honest with you the first time we met. I'm not Roisin Dunwoody's cousin."

"No shit."

"My name is Jacob Kincaid. I'm a private investigator. I've been hired to look into Roisin's death." He took a card from his wallet and handed it to Armstrong, who regarded it but said nothing. "I strongly suspect it was a murder and not an accident." Jacob brought out his phone and showed Armstrong the picture of Thin Man and Fish Lips. "Do you recognise either of these men?"

"The two fellas who came with Scanlon to get into the loft."

"What did you think of them?"

"Suspicious as hell. They didn't look like workmen; didn't have any tools and they had no reason to be up there. When I asked Scanlon what was going on, he told me to shut up and give him the key to the padlock for the security door. He's lucky I didn't lamp him right there."

"But you gave him the key anyway."

"Aye," Armstrong replied, "But I didn't like it."

"What happened?"

"I followed them up but they told me and Scanlon to wait at the bottom of the loft staircase. They came back down five minutes later. Scanlon was twitchy the whole time. I didn't know what to make of it all but then the wee lassie came to me."

"Roisin?"

"Told me she had heard them moving about in the attic. I told her it was nothing to worry about but she was scared."

"Did she tell you why?" Jacob asked.

"I asked but she wouldn't say."

"Did you check the attic?"

"Course I did."

"And?"

"And? And nothing. There was nothing there. Nothing out of place."

"What about the attic doors?"

"Checked them too. All were still nailed down."

"You sure?" Jacob pressed.

"Don't patronise me. I'm not daft. I know what a nailed down door looks like."

Jacob rubbed at his chin. "You and the Scanlon's both told me the old floor is rotting. How-"

"-Tape." Armstrong said impatiently. "The builders used yellow tape as a guide on the floor to let them know which parts were safe."

"Have you seen the two men since?"

Armstrong puffed out his cheeks. "Maybe a week later. Came back on their own and asked for the key. I told them to get lost. They said they'd ring Scanlon. I told them they could ring Jesus Christ himself, they weren't getting it. They left and Scanlon rang me about five minutes later in a blind panic. I told him he could tell me what was going on, or he could fuck off. He fucked off."

Jacob half-smiled. He was a cranky old bastard, but he rather liked Cecil Armstong. "So, when Roisin died, it didn't strike you as weird?"

"Sad, yes. Weird?" He considered the question and then shook his head. "Just an accident."

"Even with those two fellas snooping in the attic?"

"Like I said, they were up there for maybe five minutes tops. The attic door was still in place. I take it that's where you're getting at with that talk about a murder?"

Jacob nodded. "I'd like to take a look. Satisfy my own curiosity if nothing else." Armstrong shuffled and glanced away. Jacob felt a familiar sinking feeling. "What?"

"The key's gone."

"Gone? Stolen?"

"Uh, no," Amstrong said, suddenly bashful. "Gone.

As in, it's at the bottom of the Lagan." He saw the look Jacob threw him and turned defensive. "Listen, those two men and Scanlon, I didn't trust them an inch. Without the key they had no way up there."

Jacob closed his eyes, not quite believing what he was hearing. "And if someone needs to get up to the loft for an actual, genuine reason?"

"Five and a bit years this complex has been here and no one's never needed up before."

Jacob spotted a key card sitting on Armstrong's desk and snatched it. "Hey!" He ignored Armstrong as he left the office, striding across the courtyard towards Roisin's apartment complex. "I'm telling you, there's nothing to see," Armstrong called, quickening his step to catch up.

They took the elevator to the top floor. "Just go quiet," Armstrong warned. "Auld Mrs. Jameison in 4E could talk the hind legs of a donkey."

Everything at the grille was as Jacob remembered. The door was firmly shut, the large padlock was still secured in place, the scorch mark where the kids had been messing about still stained the wall.

Jacob pulled at the metal grille and shook it, frustration welling. He thought he had cracked it. The crooked developer with the familial link to the Followers. It had all fallen into place. Perfectly set until suddenly it wasn't.

"Told ya," Armstong said.

Jacob ignored him and stalked back to the elevator.

# 26

Jacob parked the Clio and trudged back to his apartment. With the key to the loft apparently missing, there was no way into the attic or onto the roof, which ruled out the last avenue of theory Jacob had for the locked room murder.

Unless he had been tricked. Could the Scanlon's whole story have been a ruse? A red herring to buy some breathing room while Jacob took himself off to Hilden Mill? As for Armstrong, was the man actually as disgruntled an employee as he let on, or was he covering for his bosses with a fairy tale about the thrown away key?

He decided those questions could wait for another day. He was dog tired. It hardly seemed possible the fire at the hostel had been that morning. All he wanted to do was order a pizza, jump into a steaming bath and then crawl into bed and sleep for a week.

When he saw Mairead waiting by his apartment door, he knew the night had other plans. Despite the grey day, she was clothed in a fetching red summer dress, split at the thigh showing off a pair of strong, tanned legs. She looked up from her phone as Jacob rounded the corner at the far end of the corridor.

"What are you doing here?" he asked, the words coming out more bluntly than intended.

"You didn't text me back," she answered brightly. Two shopping bags rested by her feet.

Jacob remembered her message from earlier.

"Shit." He pinched the bridge of his nose. If there was any sign that he needed to sort himself out, this was it. A beautiful young woman had not only sought him out for a date, but had done her best to keep up the contact. As usual, Jacob hadn't held up his end in any way, shape, or form. "Sorry, Mairead."

"Don't worry about it," she replied, waving the apology away as Jacob unlocked his front door. "You had a lot going on by the sounds of things." She noticed Jacob's frown as he picked up one of the bags. "I was with Natalie at the studio when you called her."

"She tell you what it was about?" Jacob asked, leading her across to the small kitchen and setting the bag on the counter.

"Just the basics. She rushed out pretty much as soon as she hung up with you. But that's Natalie for you."

Jacob gave a quick smile. "I never heard you badmouth her before."

Mairead shrugged as she began to lift the contents from a bag. "She's my boss. Besides, the first time we met she was probably hovering by the door, listening in, and the second time I was enjoying our date too much."

"So, it was a date?"

"Well, yeah. Or did I pick up the situation wrong?"

"Not at all," Jacob said quickly. In truth, he had been in two minds as to whether Mairead had a genuine physical interest in him or just drawn to the weirdness of his job. "I had fun."

"Me too," she replied as she took in the apartment. "Have to say, this is not what I expected."

"No? More books and less dirty dishes with tragic bachelor vibe?"

"Something like that." She held up a packet of pasta. "Hope you like spaghetti."

Jacob's stomach rumbled at the mere suggestion of a proper meal. He hadn't had one since Natalie had cooked for him a few nights before, subsisting on coffee and cereal since. "Love it."

"Good. There's wine in that other bag. Get pouring."

While Mairead worked on dinner prep, Jacob took a bottle of Pinot Noir and poured two glasses. "You doing alright?"

Mairead looked up from the onions on the chopping board. "How do you mean?"

"I know you said Natalie rushed out, but she told you..." he trailed off, realising he might be about to let his mouth run away from him once again. "Uh, about Luke."

"Oh," Mairead said, faltering. "Yeah, she told us. Like, super briefly. What can you do?" She asked with a shrug.

Jacob was surprised at the casualness which she affected. A coping mechanism perhaps. She kept her eyes on the chopping board and Jacob thought it best to let the matter drop.

He watched as she dropped chopped onion, carrots, and garlic in with the bacon and mince already sizzling in the pan. "I hope you don't find this too presumptuous," she said, grabbing the bottle of wine and filling Jacob's still half-full glass. "Showing up on your doorstep, I mean."

"I've had worse surprises," Jacob replied. "Did Natalie say anything about it?"

"About what?"

"When you asked her for my address. I assume that's how you got it, unless you started knocking on random doors and worked your way up from the ground floor."

"Oh, right," she chuckled. "I texted her but she didn't say much. Other things on her mind, I guess. Why? Looking to make her jealous?"

"Just curious is all," he replied, stifling a yawn.

Mairead flicked the bottom of his jaw playfully. "We might have a fader here." She took the Pinot and poured the remainder into Jacob's glass, filling it almost to the rim.

He decided to let her work and took his glass over to the balconette. He opened the doors, taking in the view of the piazza below. Rain was falling steadily and the few people who were out and about hurried to their destinations with heads bowed or hidden under umbrellas.

When he returned to the counter a few minutes later it was with an empty glass. By now, Mairead had added tomatoes, purée, stock and a generous heaping of wine to the pan. With the first bottle already polished off, mostly thanks to Jacob, she selected a fresh one from the rack on the kitchen counter. He couldn't help but notice how much more generous she was with his servings compared to her own. Still, it was good wine and easily drunk.

When dinner came, it was delicious. Conversation was at a premium as Jacob devoured the meal Mairead had put in front of him and apologised as he set the knife and fork on his plate.

"No worries," she replied happily. "I take it as a compliment."

They cleared the dishes before Jacob excused himself to use the bathroom. When he returned, he found Mairead hovering over his glass. She turned, a new wine bottle in her hand. "You snuck up on me."

"Trick of the trade," he said, managing a tired smile. The alcohol and hearty meal were doing little to alleviate his already exhausted state. When Mairead handed him the refill he hesitated in taking it. "I have an early start tomorrow."

"You're kicking me out already? After I cooked you dinner?"

He acquiesced with a shrug and took the offered glass. Mairead walked back to her seat at the kitchen counter while Jacob remained standing. Absently, he turned to one of the potted plants he kept. The leaves were turning brown and in need of water. He crouched to give it a closer inspection. "Any plans for tomorrow?" he asked with his back still to Mairead.

"Meeting the podcast team again. After the one today ended so abruptly."

Jacob nodded as he moved to the tall fiddle fig by the balconette doors. Like its counterpart, it was also suffering from Jacob's neglect. "Anything interesting?"

"Planning out the new season. Throwing out ideas...What are you doing?" She asked with a laugh, watching as he sauntered, apparently aimlessly, around his apartment.

"Sorry," he chuckled. "Checking up on the kids. Been so busy this past week I haven't given them any attention." He felt the vibration of his phone in his pocket. The call was from a withheld number. "Jacob Kincaid."

"It's Peter Scanlon." The voice on the other end came back as a tense whisper.

Jacob held up a hand of apology and took the phone into the bedroom. "Mr. Scanlon, this is a surprise."

He could almost feel the other man licking his lips. "Cecil told me what happened."

"Yeah?"

"Mr. Kincaid, what we told you was the truth. I can't account for what Cecil did with the key." Scanlon's tone was desperate. Jacob inched to the bedroom door and opened it a fraction. Mairead didn't notice him watching her. "What will it take, to stop you going to the police."

Jacob didn't answer. Mairead moved over to the open Balconette. The red summer dress hugged her lithe figure.

"Money?" Scanlon prompted.

The question broke Jacob from his reverie." "Money?"

"Yes, money," Scanlon hissed. "We can pay-"

Jacob killed the call. Scanlon and Rourke were a problem for another day. He approached quietly. Mairead turned once he was beside her.

"Work?"

Jacob gave a solemn nod. "Always work." He yawned again. "Sorry," he said, hiding his mouth behind his hand and somewhat unsteadily, walked towards the sofa. It appeared as if the wine had suddenly caught up with him.

He sat down heavily and closed his eyes. A second later, he felt Mairead sit beside him. Close. Her breath like a warm kiss on his cheek.

"I think I'm done for the night." His words were slurred, clumsy.

He heard Mairead sigh. "Okay."

"Sorry," said Jacob, adopting the tone of a man who knew he'd blown it. "I guess I'm not the drinker I used to be. Let me make it up to you. Let's get dinner later this week."

"No, that's alright." Her tone suggested there wouldn't be a third date. Jacob supposed he should be thankful she wasn't telling him they could be friends at least.

"Oh come on," he said, his voice getting deeper, his eyes heavier.

"Don't worry about it," she said. "Look, let me help you."

Jacob let her manoeuvre his legs onto the sofa. She fetched the throw quilt from over the rear cushion and placed it over him. "Sleep tight, okay?"

He didn't reply but could hear her soft footsteps crossing the kitchen. On her way out she was good enough to turn out the light, casting the apartment in long, dark shadows as night fell over Belfast. She seemed to hesitate before closing the door gently behind her.

Jacob wasn't sure how much time had passed before the handle gave the softest of creaks and the door eased open. The figure, silhouetted by the glow from the corridor, took in the still apartment before creeping over the threshold. They moved quietly but with purpose, making a direct line for the sofa.

Jacob waited until the quilt was pulled away before he hit the light switch.

Fish Lips looked up in surprise, the quilt still in his hand. The pillows Jacob had hidden under it wouldn't have stood up to close scrutiny, but had done their job in the darkness.

"I wondered which of you it would be."

To his credit, Fish Lips still managed a somewhat menacing smile. "How did you know?"

"Call it intuition." He could see the man had a backpack slung over one shoulder. "How were you going to do it?"

"Honestly? I hadn't decided yet."

"Dealer's choice, eh?"

"Something like that." He dropped the blanket on the floor and pointed to the cushions with grudging admiration. "It doesn't change anything you know. You have to go. Just might get a bit messier than I'd have liked."

Jacob could feel the blood pounding in his ears, his pulse quickening. He blocked out the part of his mind telling him to run. He'd already made the decision. "You think you're the man to do it?"

"I'm the one they sent."

"Who's they?"

Fish Lips laughed darkly. He wasn't falling for such an obvious trap.

"Well, whoever they are, I think maybe they should have sent someone a little more impressive."

The other man's eyes narrowed. The jab had found its mark. "Let's see."

Fish Lips swung the bag from his shoulder. Taser, rope, and a myriad of other unpleasantness were likely inside and within his reach.

Jacob bounded across the small space and threw himself forward, catching the other man around the knees, heaving him upwards with all the strength he could muster.

They flew back, their fall broken by the coffee table. Wood shattered as the table collapsed and Fish Lips, who had taken the brunt, wheezed as Jacob jumped on him. His first punch connected with the man's flabby face, the second missed as Fish Lips turned his body and

Jacob's fist hit splintered wood.

He'd feel the pain later. Fish Lips pushed up against Jacob's chin and managed to land a hard shot to his ribs. Jacob grunted, moved his head, and bit down on the hand pushing against him.

Fish Lips squealed. His free hand shot up, fingers extended, looking to catch Jacob in the eye. One of the digits found its mark and Jacob hissed as his vision blurred. The sudden, intense pain was unbearable, even in the ferocity of their struggle. Jacob pulled his head back, giving Fish Lips the space to kick Jacob away.

Jacob rolled but Fish Lips got to his feet first, shoving him back to the floor. He knew if he stayed on the ground he was dead. He took a boot to his spine as he twisted his body away. He tried to stand and took a blow to the side of the temple. Stunned, he fell back to one knee and only managed to get his feet under him through sheer instinct.

Fish Lips charged, knowing Jacob was dazed. A wild punch missed and they came together, groping for any sort of advantage in their frantic struggle.

Jacob groaned as a short punch caught him on the ribs. He lowered his head and pushed against Fish Lips's jaw, using the leverage to clasp his hands in a body lock around the other man's midriff. He tried to force Fish Lips off balance with his leg but as he did, he stepped on the dropped quilt and lost his balance as his foot slid across the floor.

Both men went sprawling but as they fell, Fish Lips twisted and landed on Jacob, driving the air from his body at the same time the back of his head struck the hard wooden floor. Jacob groaned, seeing stars. He expected more blows to come but instead heard footsteps. He rolled, seeing Fish Lips reaching for the backpack. He heard the crackle of the taser before he saw it.

Bloody-mouthed and wild-eyed, Fish Lips charged. Jacob felt the jolt of electricity as the weapon grazed against his side. He pushed the pain away as his hand gripped Fish Lip's wrist while ramming his free forearm into the man's throat, driving him into the nearest wall. Straining with effort, Fish Lips tried to bring the tip of the weapon against Jacob who struggled to keep the arm pinned to the wall.

He heard the hocking of the throat but didn't have time to avoid the thick phlegm as Fish Lips spat, catching Jacob square in the eye. It was enough of an opening for Fish Lips to jab forward with the taser.

Jacob sidestepped and threw a desperate punch. There was no technique or finesse, just sheer fear mixed with spiking adrenaline. The shot arced through the air and took Fish Lips square on the jaw. His legs wobbled and the taser clattered to the ground.

Shouting some unintelligible insult, Jacob threw another shot, using the last remnants of whatever energy he had left. Bone smacked against bone and Fish Lips stumbled, losing his footing, crashing into the steel guardrail on the balconette.

Jacob saw the man's eyes go wide as one side of the rail came out of its foundations, knocked loose by the sudden weight. Fish Lips grabbed at nothing as screws, plaster, and concrete fell away into the open night air.

Steel scraped against concrete as the rail dragged along the balconette's lip. Fish Lips tumbled into the void but somehow managed to grab part of the rail dangling over the edge.

"Help!" Terror strangled the plea in his throat as he tried to pull himself up. "I'll tell you-"

The *crack* was deafening in the sudden stillness. A chunk of the wall rail fell away and took Fish Lips and the rail with it.

Time seemed to stretch until the sound of the body hitting the ground four storeys below echoed in the empty piazza.

Jacob didn't look. He knew what he would see.

He crossed the room, found his phone, and with shaking hands, rang a number.

"I need your help."

# 27

He had done what he could for Fish Lips as he waited. Which was to say, not much. Against all reasonable odds, he found the man was still breathing. Glassy eyes stared up at the night sky as the blood pooling under his body swirled and mixed with dirty puddles of rain water.

Paramedics and the police turned up within minutes but it was Cora who arrived first. She had listened to Jacob's shaky account on the phone without interruption and told him what to do next.

Jacob had said little when the police showed up and had been placed in handcuffs before Cora intervened. There had been some confusion until an officer with inspector epaulettes arrived, flanked by two sergeants. No one said anything to Jacob but the cuffs came off.

As people much more important than him discussed their next step, Jacob sat on a windowsill of one of the restaurants and wondered just how many times in the past week his name had appeared on police systems.

Night slowly gave way to the first purple hues of dawn. With his apartment being held as a scene until CID, CSI and photography had done their bit, he decided he might as well get comfortable. At some point he drifted off and awoke to the sound of approaching footsteps. He blinked away the grit behind his eyes to see Cora looking down at him. The hulking figure of her colleague who Jacob had met a few days before was at her shoulder. This time Cora introduced him as Colin Ambrose.

"It's all sorted, for now," she said. "You'll have to make a statement to the police in the next couple of days."

"The way the past week has gone, they might as well set me up with my own interview room." He looked up at Ambrose. "You get it all?"

Ambrose nodded. Jacob had left a recording of his confrontation with Fish Lips on a USB in his apartment. He had hoped to goad the man into some sort of confession but the plan; stupid, reckless, and ill-advised, had went south faster than he had anticipated. Adebayo and Ambrose could use it and the conversations with Rourke and the Scanlons as they saw fit.

"We got word from the hospital," Ambrose said. "He's still critical. Touch and go, most likely go. We have a name for him too. Reece Donnelly."

Jacob shrugged. The name meant nothing to him.

"Quite a healthy juvenile record," Ambrose continued. "Was in the foster system for years. Had a few assaults and burglaries as well as more troubling stuff. Voyeurism, harassment of a teacher, even got lifted on suspicion of rape when he was sixteen, although those charges were dropped. These kids, go in the system, twists a lot of them up."

"A perfect candidate for Follower recruitment," Cora added quietly.

"Fuck him." Jacob was relieved not to have the man's death on his conscience, for now at least, but that was as far as his sympathy extended. He flexed his right hand where a dull, throbbing pain had set in as the night wore on. "You know he tried to take a blow torch to me?"

"In the apartment?" Ambrose asked.

"No, earlier today." Cora and Ambrose didn't reply. "He shook his head. Who carries a blow torch around?" As Jacob asked the question, he touched his head against the window and sighed deeply. "Fuck me."

"What?" Cora asked.

"What time is it?"

She checked her watch. "A little after seven."

"I'm free to go?"

"You are."

"Feel like indulging me just a little bit longer?"

She quirked an eyebrow but nodded slowly. "Alright."

"Take me to Hilden Mill."

They found Cecil Armstrong already in his office. He looked up as Jacob entered but his attention immediately shifted to the tall woman trailing behind him.

"Mr. Armstrong," Jacob said. "Would you be so kind and let us into Roisin Dunwoody's apartment block."

Armstrong shook his head wearily but still climbed to his feet. "You expecting to see something different from twelve hours ago?" He fetched a key card from his desk and handed it to Jacob.

"I really hope not."

Jacob led Cora and Armstrong over to the old mill building. They took the stairs to the fourth floor, walked past Roisin's apartment and through to the doorway that led to the attic staircase. The grille was secured with the padlock like it had always been.

For Cora's benefit, Jacob tugged both the lock and the grille but neither budged. He unslung the black backpack he was wearing over his shoulder and placed it on the ground.

"You won't be able to pick a lock like that," Armstrong said, watching from behind Cora as Jacob rooted around in the bag. "Not in a month of Sundays."

"No," Jacob agreed, "I won't."

It didn't take long. A few minutes later, Jacob was picking his way across the massive, dusty mill loft, using the fading yellow tape on the floor as a guide until he reached the trap door to Roisin's apartment.

It was the end of the mystery.

*

Jacob found the four members of the Miss Gumshoe podcast team in Studio A, seated around a circular table in the recording booth. He entered without knocking.

"Jacob," Natalie said, turning in her seat.

"Surprised to see me?"

"Well, yes," Natalie replied, now half standing. She was defensive, taken aback at the unexpected intrusion.

"Oh, sorry, Natalie. I was actually talking to Mairead." He waited until all eyes in the room turned to the younger woman. Her pale skin had turned ashen. "Let me guess, I look well for dead?"

Natalie held up a hand, clearly irked. "Alright. Just what's going on here?"

"Someone tried to kill me last night." Jacob watched Natalie's expression turn slack. "One of Seymour Huber's thugs. One of the men who chased us through the harbour. Broke into my apartment with the intention of doing me in. He appeared to know where to find me and seemed rather surprised that I was standing upright rather than the unconscious body he'd been expecting."

Natalie's gaze followed Jacob's to rest on Mairead. "I don't..."

"She set me up. She set all of us up. Me, Luke Fisher, and Roisin Dunwoody."

Tears were already welling in Mairead's eyes. Natalie took hold of the table edge, steadying herself before sitting slowly back in her seat. Jacob kept his gaze firmly on Mairead. "No denial. Funny how you got my address from Natalie when she's never been to my place. A small slip, but it's hard to shake that seed of doubt once it's been planted."

"What the fuck," Arjun whispered.

"I had a hell of a time getting rid of the wine down the sink, or in the nearest flowerpot, or over the balcony. The glasses have already been taken away by the police. I'm confident the lab will show at least some Prepentaline residue. The same drug used on Luke Fisher to knock him out so his suicide could be staged. The same drug you used to try and sedate Roisin the night of the party. The same drug we found empty cartons of in Roisin's apartment to add to the ruse of a tragic accident."

It felt as if no one around the table was daring to breathe. He allowed himself a glance to Natalie. He wasn't sure what he had expected to see. Validation? Horror? Relief? Instead, her expression was like stone, unreadable. Her shoulders were high and tense, her chin jutted.

"I struggled for a while, trying to marry up the facts of what we knew against the murder theory. It all seemed so implausible. We knew Roisin was drunk but still sensible enough to lock her door after everyone had left, meaning her killer had to get in through a different means. The attic was the obvious solution, except access was blocked by a padlock that couldn't be picked or broken by bolt cutters. Even if you got past the padlock, the attic door itself was nailed shut."

"It was brilliantly simple. I saw the fire damage myself and put it down to some of the kids playing stupid games. All it took was a blow torch and a chisel. A few minutes and the lock was gone. I did it myself not even an hour ago. As for the nails in the attic door?" He looked back to Natalie. "Easy enough to work free, but noisy."

"The fire alarm," she said quietly.

Jacob nodded. Loud enough to mask the sound. Once the nails were out, the killer had his access to do the job and has his escape route once it was done."

"As for Roisin, the drugs should have fully kicked in. She should have been dead to the world an hour or so after the last of the doses you'd slipped into her drink. Except it didn't go quite to plan. Arjun, you told me that the last drink you had at the party finished you off completely."

It took Arjun a second to realise he was being prompted. "Um, yeah," he said quietly.

"I'm guessing you took Roisin's drink by accident. Meaning Roisin didn't get her full intended dose. The fire alarm was enough to rouse her. Maybe not fully compos mentis, but enough to have her up and about, drugged out of her tree. Enough to spook the intruder who sends her flying into the edge of the coffee table with one push. They mocked up the wine spill and got out of there. Judging by the gouges in one of rafters, I'm guessing they used a rope to get in and out. They replaced the broken lock with a duplicate and no one was the wiser. Seeing was believing."

Jacob walked slowly around the table until he was standing in front of Mairead. "Tell me I'm wrong."

She shook her head.

"Jesus," Natalie breathed.

"What'd they offer you?" It was Ciaran who asked the question.

Mairead's lip trembled. Her voice came out in a whimper. "My brother. He's in debt to the paramilitaries back in Derry. They approached me and said they'd get him into their rehab program. Get him out of the city. Even get him a job."

"And all you had to do was set someone up to be killed," said Jacob.

"I didn't think they would...They told me they were trying to get something back that belonged to them."

"The hard drive. Of course, unknown to them, Liam Dunwoody had already stolen it." Jacob turned to Ciaran. "What was it you told me you saw? Angry whispering and finger pointing? Most of it from Roisin? It was so unlike her. I'm guessing the night of the party was when Luke decided to make his pitch to either buy it back or go along with his blackmail plan. Which meant the Followers had more problems. Not only did they not have the hard drive, it was now in possession of someone who wanted money for its return. Someone who thought he could put the squeeze on." He walked slowly towards Mairead. "What about Luke? Did you think you were only setting him up to be robbed too?"

"They said it would be the last time."

Jacob stood over her, gripped both arms of her chair and leaned in close. "What about me?"

Mairead closed her eyes. The tears ran freely, staining her freckled cheeks.

Jacob moved across to the studio door and opened it. "You get all that?"

"Every word," Cora said, as she entered, still holding the recording device Jacob had given her in the car. She was flanked by two uniformed police officers.

Mairead made it until the handcuffs clicked before she broke down into sobbing hysterics. None of her three co-workers looked in her direction as she was led screaming from the studio. Jacob watched her the whole way. Cora nodded to him, the faintest smile on her features before following the arrested woman out and closing the door of Studio A behind her.

Jacob sat heavily on the now free chair, utterly exhausted. In the distance, the crying faded slowly.

"So, I take it the rest of the meeting is cancelled?" Arjun asked, breaking the thick silence.

With an arm across either shoulder, Natalie walked her two remaining employees out. Twenty minutes passed before she returned alone and flopped into the chair next to Jacob. "My God."

Jacob couldn't think of anything to say.

Her hand reached out and took his. "Are you ok?"

He was drained. Beaten. Exhausted. There wasn't one part of his body that didn't hurt. He held on to her hand. "I'm fine. How about you?"

"Shocked." Her gaze was distant. "Shocked," she repeated.

"I should have seen it sooner."

"How?"

"Think about it. The man listening in at Hilden Mill and the chase from Big Box. What did those two incidents have in common?"

Natalie thought and then closed her eyes. "Mairead," she said quietly before lashing out and slapping the table. "I was with Mairead beforehand."

"Don't beat yourself up. I didn't catch on either. Sweet, naïve Mairead." He thought about their night in

The Garrick, her questions about Tomas and his notes. How the Followers had manipulated the info she'd passed on. The initial realisation that he had been wrong, that Tomas had only ever been an innocent man, was like a gut punch as he sat on the windowsill of the restaurant a few hours before. He cleared his throat, not wanting to dwell on that well of guilt. "A lot to take in."

Natalie scoffed. "Talk about an understatement." She looked to the door as if expecting Mairead to come back in laughing about the elaborate prank they had just pulled. She gave herself a shake. "What happens now?"

Jacob assumed she meant Mairead. "Interviewed. Charged. Remanded."

"And the Followers?"

"Who knows? I doubt Mairead will stand up to any sort of interrogation. The police might offer her a deal. With what she was mixed up in, not to mention what you have on that hard drive...."

Natalie nodded slowly and then laughed.

"What?" Jacob asked.

"I had been thinking last night, after I left Helen's. about the stuff that's on the hard drive. There's so much information to collate and verify."

"Yeah?"

"I'll need an investigator..."

"Are you offering me another job?"

"Well, it's not how I envisioned making the pitch, but yeah, I suppose I am."

"I'm flattered but maybe we can talk about it another day."

Natalie smiled and patted his hand. "Sure."

"You have any plans for tonight?"

"Well, at some point I imagine I'll wake up and find out this was all a horrible dream."

"I phoned Helen on the way back from Hilden Mill. Told her the case was cracked. We're having a little celebration. Me, her, my mate Michael. You're more than welcome and I'd daresay you could use a drink."

Her mouth quirked into a smile. "Just one?"

# 28

A grey drizzly rain was waiting for Jacob as he left Wheelman. Cora and Mairead were long gone. Natalie had remained in the studio, alone with her thoughts. Jacob doubted she had ever imagined that the case would have ended up here when she'd first walked through the door of Kincaid Investigations.

 But here they were. She had proposed the locked room murder and he had provided the solution, if not the killer. More than a little ambiguity remained on that score. Whoever killed Roisin had to rely on a decent amount of athleticism to descend, and then scale either a rope or a makeshift ladder in and out of the apartment. Jacob had a hard time envisioning Fish Lips making such a climb. His partner on the other hand, was a more than viable candidate.

Not that Jacob could prove it and by now, Thin Man would be in deep hiding. Cora Adebayo and her people were keen to speak to him but Jacob knew that he wouldn't surface any time soon, if ever.

Mairead and Fish Lips, if he survived, would be made amenable for their part in Roisin and Luke's murders. That someone would be held accountable was probably the best Jacob would hope for.

He had no doubt the Followers propagandists were already in full damage control mode. Huber and his flock would distance themselves from the scandal as best they could, but whatever Mairead was willing to give up could be damning, potentially implicating the church in at least two murders. Combined with whatever Natalie had on the hard drive, the damage could be irreparable, just like Tomas had hoped.

None of which was Jacob's concern. Justice was someone else's job. He had done his.

With a sigh, he drove home. The scene had been closed and his apartment was once again his own. Finding the key where the police had left it under the welcome mat, he locked the door behind him and climbed straight into his bed. For the first time in eight days, Jacob slept peacefully.

When he awoke, it was late in the afternoon. He showered, lingering under the hot water as he washed the remnants of the last week and a bit away. A locked room mystery brought to life. A victim who would see some measure of justice. A money grabbing racket damaged and maybe, just maybe, starting to crumble. He had made the case. He had shown his worth as a detective. A case that mattered.

Closed.

Today had been the case of a lifetime. Tomorrow, it was Tuesday.

Tomorrow it was back to cheats, swindlers, and tearful spouses. The summer of Roisin Dunwoody was over, and Jacob was back to where he was before Natalie Amato had walked into his office.

But still, there was a glimmer. A job offer. A chance to delve deeper into the misdeeds of the church. A chance to follow a trail he cared about.

All that was for tomorrow, he told himself. One way or another, the next job would come. For now, he vowed to enjoy the moment, to savour validation that for so long he had been lacking.

Once dried and changed into some fresh threads, he selected a bottle of wine from the rack and drove over to Helen's.

She greeted him with a wide smile and an expensive bottle of bubbly. "Hell of a case," she said, leading him into the kitchen.

"Hell of a case." Jacob agreed, taking the bottle as Helen held it out to him.

He peeled the coiffe and Helen whooped as Jacob popped the cork. Filling two flutes, he handed one to her.

"To Kincaid Investigations," Helen said by way of toast.

"Kincaid investigations." Jacob clinked his glass against hers.

Michael arrived a short while later. He kissed Helen on the cheek and slapped Jacob on the back. "Well," he said, shrugging off his coat. "Tell me everything."

It was a long story but Jacob had an enraptured audience of one. Michael knew little aside from what they had discussed in The Spaniard, almost a week before. Helen listened as she prepared a dinner of duck and dauphinoise potatoes, already up to speed.

"Jesus," Michael said, once Jacob had finally finished.

"Right?" Jacob replied, polishing off the last of his champagne. He felt good. The warm sense of satisfaction hadn't faded and didn't feel like it was going anywhere fast.

"Just so I understand...." Michael began.

"Who set the fire at the hostel?" Jacob guessed.

"No." Michael waved the question away as if Jacob was a simpleton. "It's obvious one of those thugs hit the girl from behind and made it look like she'd slipped when trying to fight the fire."

"Why kill Fisher?"

Michael shook his head. "What I want to know is, you finally manage to bag a date, with an actual woman, but it turns out she's only seeing you so she can pump you for info and then set you up to be offed?"

"That's the gist of it, yeah."

"Better luck next time, eh?"

Jacob saluted his friend with his glass.

"What about this Natalie then?" Michael asked. "I thought you said she was coming."

"She is. Guess she's trying to be fashionably late."

"She waits much longer she's just going to be actually late," Helen put in.

Jacob checked his phone, dreading finding the waiting message to say that she couldn't make it, the polite apology followed by an excuse that something had come up. When he saw he had no missed texts or calls, he took it as a positive sign.

He wanted to see her. To be around her and enjoy her company. This was her moment of triumph as much as his. More so, if he was being honest. Something had struck her as wrong from the moment Roisin had died, and only she had had the conviction to question it. Even Jacob, more often than he cared to count, had tried to write the girl's demise off as an accident.

Now Natalie had her answer, her validation, and so much more. What would follow could make her career. Jacob was happy he was able to play his part.

It was a few minutes later when he felt the vibration of the phone in his pocket. He set his glass down and pulled it out, deflating when he saw the message was from an unknown number. He'd had a lot of unknown numbers calling him over the past week and he struggled to remember if any had led to anything other than trouble.

He was going to ignore it until he noticed a video was attached. Curiosity piqued, he opened the message and hit play.

His guts turned to water.

Natalie's kitchen. He could hear muffled movement off camera. The video remained steady. The camera wasn't being held. By its position, Jacob guessed it had been placed on the windowsill and left to record.

Helen, carrying plates to the table, stopped to watch over his shoulder. "What are we-"

Jacob silenced her with an angry shush, his heart racing. Cold sweat was clamming on the back of his hands. Wordlessly Michael crowded his other shoulder.

The kitchen door opened. Natalie walked into

frame. She was dressed for a night with friends, in a patterned short sleeve blouse and white trousers.

Jacob's chest constricted. He couldn't breathe.

The video continued as Natalie busied around the kitchen, tidying away a couple of dishes. She checked her watch and then glanced directly at the camera, her eyes meeting Jacob's for a fraction of a second, before she looked away.

Natalie took a step and then stopped. Slowly, her head turned back to look at them. Jacob wanted to shout. To scream. To tell her to get out of there. Instead, he watched as her brow furrowed before her eyes went wide.

She knew.

Across the kitchen, the door to the pantry shot open. Natalie flinched, twisting towards the sound. The figure who burst into the kitchen was a blur, dressed all in black, hidden behind a balaclava.

Natalie's feet were planted to the ground as he ran at her. At the last second, she moved, trying to make a break for the hallway door but she was too late.

The masked man caught her wrist and yanked her back towards him. She screamed but  was silenced by the thick white cloth shoved over her nose and mouth, muffling her shouts to frantic, terrified protests.

She fought desperately to break free but her attacker pulled her close, wrapping an arm around her chest. Natalie hit, clawed and kicked but the masked man took it. Her left hand reached up to try and pry the hand away from her face, pulling with everything she had, but it held firm.

With crushing inevitability, her struggling became weaker. Her protests, quieter. Her left arm flopped down to her side and swung limply. Jacob watched her deep brown eyes roll back and then close. She took a deep shuddering breath as her head lolled and knees buckled.

Her attacker kept the cloth in place, making sure she was out before shifting his face towards the camera.

The clumsy white stitching over the nose and mouth inspired no fear this time. Only hate. Jacob knew with a burning certainty that he'd get this man.

Eventually, he took his hand away from Natalie's face and left the cloth drop, but they didn't move. He kept one arm around the small of her back, keeping her upright so they stood facing the camera.

"The fuck is he doing?" Michael asked, his voice strained.

"He's taunting me," Jacob said.

The man in black let Natalie's unconscious body fall against him. He scooped her up into a cradle carry. He lingered there, like an ugly imitation of a fifties b-movie monster and the fainted damsel. Seconds crawled while he remained in the same grotesque pose. Finally satisfied, he walked out of frame with Natalie dangling in his arms.

The video cut off on its own. It had been edited and then sent to him.

Jacob rewound, trying and failing to ignore Natalie's fear and her frantic struggles, her cries of alarm. There was no wall clock, in the kitchen and he couldn't make out the time on Natalie's oven or on her watch.

The phone vibrated again. He took a breath, steadying himself. It was a picture of Natalie. She was unconscious, lying on her right side on top of a plastic sheet in what looked like the boot of a car. Her eyes were closed. Her wrists had been bound with rope to her front, with more looped around her thighs and ankles.

"Oh Jesus," Helen breathed.

Jacob zoomed in on the picture and caught the time on Natalie's watch. Ten to seven. He glanced at the clock on his phone. It was just about to go eight.

"More than an hour ago," Michael said, reading his train of thought. "What do we do?"

Jacob didn't answer. Instead, he set the phone down and waited. Seconds stretched. Blood pounded at his temples. His mouth was dry. He tried to control his breathing as he fought the urge to be sick.

He answered his phone on the first ring.

"Yeah." The word struggled out of Jacob's throat.

"You know what I want." The voice was distorted. Disguised.

"Yeah."

Corrion's factory. Carrickfergus. One hour. I don't think I need to tell you what happens if you don't show."

"If you hurt her, I'll..."

"-You'll do nothing." The anger twisted the voice until it was almost unintelligible. "You're no hero so don't be getting any idea otherwise. Corrion's. One hour. You come alone. You tell no one. If I get a whiff of cop or anyone apart from you, she dies. If you don't make it within the hour, she dies."

The line went dead.

# 29

"Please, Jacob. It's a set up!" Helen's voice was frenetic in a way he had never heard. She had fetched the hard drive as he'd told her to, but was now refusing to hand it over.

"Of course, it's a set up!" Jacob shouted, aware every second here was one wasted. "But what choice do I have?"

"Call the police," Helen pleaded, taking a step back. "Show them the video." She looked to Michael, desperate for support.

"By the time they make a decision it'll be too late," Michael said quietly. "But it is a trap, Jacob. You're giving him two for one."

Jacob didn't disagree. "If I don't show with the hard drive, Natalie is dead."

He left it unsaid what he knew Michael was thinking. Natalie was already dead. This was nothing more than a lure to reel Jacob in and get rid of him too. He pushed the thought from his mind. He had to believe she was still alive. That there was still a chance.

"What are you going to do?" Michael asked, his voice flat. He knew Jacob's mind was already made up.

"Give him what he wants." The person holding Natalie, almost certainly Thin Man, had all the cards. The best Jacob could do was hand over the hard drive and hope it would be enough for him and Natalie to get out alive.

He was angry. Angry at the Thin Man. Angrier at himself for getting so careless. He'd been certain that Thin Man would have gone to ground. He had been so set on enjoying a rare win, that he hadn't thought of the last hand they could play. Of course, they knew where Natalie lived. Mairead had been to her house. Jacob hadn't even considered it and now Natalie's life was in danger.

Helen sagged as Jacob took the hard drive from her but made no attempt to stop him.

They followed him to the front door. Helen pulled him close, hugging him fiercely. "I'll wait for your call," she said.

Jacob nodded, clasped Michael's hand, and then hurried to his car.

Evening traffic was light and Jacob pushed the Clio to her limit as he hammered it down the motorway and out of Belfast. He drove through Whiteabbey, the water of Belfast Lough shimmering a dark purple as night fell. He kept his foot to the floor past Jordanstown, and the road where Luke Fisher had lived and died, ran a red light at the roundabout on the edge of Greenisland and sped on to Carrickfergus.

Corrion's factory was located on a twenty-five-acre site on the outskirts of the town. Once employing well over a thousand people, the factory was now a wasteland, a sprawling collection of crumbling, derelict buildings, and rusting machine parts.

A large wooden sign for Gould construction, complete with a picture of Ivan Gould and his hard hat, proclaimed the place had been purchased for development of cheap residential housing.

High metal fences ringed the grounds but as Jacob pulled off the road, he could see the old gates had been pushed open. His invitation.

The factory was impossibly big and Thin Man hadn't given Jacob specific directions on where to meet. He still had twenty minutes to spare but panic gripped him as he wondered if this was a game, a race against the clock to find Natalie in this warren of crumbling concrete.

He turned the Clio and parked it facing towards the gates, possibly buying a few vital seconds if things went south and he needed a quick getaway.

As he approached the main body of buildings, his footsteps scrunched loudly over loose gravel. It was the end of summer and the days were growing shorter. Twilight cast long shadows in the desolate waste ground. A light breeze ruffled the long weeds but the factory was still until a sharp whistle pierced the air.

He turned toward the sound and saw the figure, almost obscured in the dark doorway of the furthers building. When he was sure Jacob had seen him, the figure walked inside. Jacob took a breath and followed.

Aside from a row of workbenches, the space gave no clue to what it's former use had been. Electricity still flowed, powering a row of uncovered bulbs dangling from the ceiling the length of the expansive interior.

Jacob couldn't hide his sigh of relief when he saw Natalie. She was alive and appeared to be unhurt. The Thin Man had tied her up in an old wooden chair. Rope curled around her upper chest and torso, pinning her against the backrest, while her wrists were bound to the arms.

She nodded to him. Her eyes were wide but steady. There were no tear streaks or smudged mascara. She was afraid but hadn't given her kidnapper the satisfaction of showing it.

Thin Man stood behind her. Natalie flinched as he put his hands on her shoulders. "Looks like I lost the bet. I didn't think you'd come. She said you would."

"And here I am."

"And here you are. The hard drive?"

Jacob held the device out and Thin Man pointed to one of the old workbenches. Jacob walked over and set it on the peeling countertop. "Now what?"

The Thin Man lifted his jacket to reveal a hip holster. Opening the thumb guard, he brought a pistol out and looked at Jacob with what could almost have been considered sympathy. "You had to know how this would go."

Jacob watched Natalie clench her jaw, fingers digging into the arm rests. He licked his lips. "It was you, wasn't it?" he asked, unable to mask the tremor in his voice.

"What?"

"All of it. I thought it was your mate after he showed up to my apartment, but he was only the lackey."

"My protégé. It should have been me, but he insisted. He had a score to settle." His sigh was wistful. "He had a talent for this kind of work."

"Not that talented considering he splattered on the ground a few hours ago."

Thin Man's look turned cold. "You should have been dead to the world by the time Reece got to you."

"You know we know how you did it? How you killed Roisin Dunwoody. The police already have a witness. Hell, by now I'd say they already have her confession, signed, sealed, and delivered."

"Mairead?" Thin Man laughed. "She'll never see the inside of a court room. The prisons over here have an alarming rate of inmate suicide. I'd guess her conscience gets the better of her before she ever sets foot in front of a judge."

Jacob bit his lip. "That night in my apartment. You somehow managed to scale the wall."

His mouth curled in a faint smile. "I had a different life before I found the light. Call it a recon job. Just to see if I could. Much like the first time I visited Natalie's a couple of months ago." He ran the back of his hand down the side of her neck and smiled as she tried to pull away. "You never did get that window latch in the utility room fixed."

"Why not just do me in then?"

"You weren't a threat. Just some snoop, sticking his nose in. We only take extreme measures in extreme circumstances."

"We?" Jacob motioned around the old workroom. "Is this a Followers of Eden sanctioned hit? You expect me to believe Seymour Huber authorises people to be killed?"

"Emissary Huber knows what needs to be done"

"Like Tomas McKinstry and Luke Fisher?"

"We were willing to pay Fisher a fair price for what he had. When it became clear he was trying to put the squeeze on, it made the decision for us. As for McKinstry, he should have been dealt with a long time before. You know, when the time came, he didn't even fight it. Let us carry him from the car and throw him off the overpass without even a whimper."

Jacob took a breath. The gun was still pointed down. Thin Man was enjoying this. He took a perverse pride in what he did, like a craftsman enjoying his handiwork when the project was done. "Why a locked room?"

"Because of your friend here. With Natalie Amato on the case, we knew she would have run anything with a sniff of foul play into the ground."

The ghost of a smile touched Jacob's lips. "Yet she still found you out."

"And look where it got her."

"That's it then, another two bodies? What's your plan?"

He laughed as he realised what Jacob was doing. "You've seen too many movies."

"So I've been told." Jacob's shrug was of a defeated man. "There's no one coming. Indulge me. I'm dead anyway." He knew he was playing for time and it was running down fast. He was slipping towards oblivion and had no way out.

"You disappear," Thin Man said. "I know a few likely places. Natalie will be found in the boot of your car in a couple of days on some remote lane way. Strangled, most likely. They'll find the drugs who used to knock her out in the glove compartment to go along with the rag I left in her kitchen. A sad tale of unrequited love turned deadly."

A lump rose in Jacob's throat. One last insult after he was gone. The work would be forgotten. Not just for this case but the years he'd put in as a police Officer. All for nothing. He'd be remembered as a murderer. It was cold, well beyond a simple act of revenge for what had happened in his apartment. "Dealer's choice," he said quietly, echoing what he had said to Fish Lips.

This time Thin Man didn't reply. Slowly, inexorably, he raised the gun.

Jacob looked straight at the barrel. He watched the slow depression of the finger on the trigger.

Inevitable. Inescapable. Irrevocable.

Natalie screamed.

The shot was deafening in the vast emptiness of the derelict building. Jacob didn't offer a witty retort or try any last second heroics. He cringed, made a stupid face and hoped it would be quick.

As his body sensors, preempting their permanent shut down, slowly eked back into life, Jacob realised he wasn't dead.

He opened his eyes a crack. Thin Man lay on his back, a bloody hole dead centre of his forehead.

In the doorway, Cora Adebayo was frozen, her Glock pistol still on aim.

Vomit rose in his throat. Jacob choked it back as his legs wobbled. "Fuck!" The word came out as almost a scream. Pure, unfiltered relief that he was somehow still on this mortal coil. He fought to control himself. Emotions danced through him, overwhelming his senses. "Fuck," he said again, quieter this time.

Cora didn't respond. For once, the ice cool demeanour had vanished. She looked at Jacob, the Glock still raised to where Thin Man had just been standing. Jacob crossed the room quickly, put his hand on top of the pistol and guided it gently towards the ground.

"He's dead?" Her question was a whisper.

"Well, he's certainly not resting his eyes," said Jacob.

"I had to."

Jacob wasn't about to argue. "Yeah, you did."

He patted her shoulder and hurried over to Natalie. She hadn't said a word. Rigid against the chair, it looked like she had been struck mute by what had just happened.

"You alright?" Jacob asked, worried she might be slipping into shock.

She managed a nod but nothing more. Jacob took his pocket knife from his jeans and began to cut at her binds, freeing her wrists and then the rope looped around her body.

As the last cord fell away, she jumped against him, hugging him fiercely. Jacob returned it with equal force. He needed it as much as she did. Two people who had just escaped death seeking the most basic form of comfort.

"I thought..."

"Yeah." It didn't need to be said.

Natalie let go as Cora approached but stayed close. "Help is on the way," Cora said. Her gun had been holstered and she now held a phone in her hand. "Police, ambulance, my guys."

Jacob nodded. He handed her the audio recorder he'd activated while still in his Clio. "Should make for some more interesting listening."

# 30

The collapse was spectacular in its speed and reach.

When the sun rose above the Follower compound the next morning, it brought police and search warrants. Seymour Huber was marched out of his kingdom in handcuffs. The recording of the Thin Man was enough to implicate the Emissary and his church into three ongoing murder investigations.

The PSNI, co-operating with an unnamed government agency, hit several Follower centres and churches, including the tabernacle in Carrickfergus and the cultural centre on Botanic Avenue, later the same day.

After calling a hasty press conference at PSNI headquarters, Deputy Chief Constable Will Bennett announced that the Major Crimes Team were opening an investigation into what he called an insidious and dangerous cult. The top priority of said investigation was the reopening of several incidents where people involved with the Followers of Eden had met an untimely end, including local journalist, Roisin Dunwoody.

In the weeks that followed, almost a dozen church Elders followed Huber to Maghaberry prison. Leadership of the church fell to its second in command, William Murty, who circled the wagons and proclaimed that they would weather the storm. Few believed him.

Mairead Donaghy was moved directly from police

custody to solitary confinement at Hydebank Wood woman's prison. She saw no one except the same six officers detailed solely to her care. A deal would be offered for what she could shed on the Followers but she would still serve time for the part played in the murders of Roisin Dunwoody and Luke Fisher.

Natalie paid out of her own pocket for a plot at Milltown Cemetery for Tomas McKinstry's funeral. No family member claimed the body, and none turned up for his burial on a cold, wet September morning. Aside from the priest, only Jacob, Natalie, Francis, and Amanda watched as he was put to his final rest.

Despite her ordeal, Natalie coped well. Determined not to let what had happened impact her in any negative fashion, she threw herself into her work. She returned to the Belfast Sentinel temporarily, helping to produce a front-page exposé, listing the top donors to the Followers of Eden. She declined any credit and kept her name away from the article, determined to give the shine to Roisin Dunwoody and Tomas McKinstry, the brave journalists who had died so the story could be told, and whose pictures adorned the front page next to their byline.

Jacob laminated it and along with Natalie, returned to Tomas's plot and left it next to the temporary wooden cross that would serve until his headstone could be placed. Tomas had played his part in bringing the Followers down and people would know his story.

The same would not be said for the Thin Man. Not one Follower attended the pauper's funeral for the last survivor of Huber's original flock, or claimed his ashes following the cremation. It had taken considerable digging by Cora to come up with who he was. Nathaniel Lynch, the youngest child of a scrabble-poor circus family from the south coast of Ireland. They had been Huber's first converts and in Nathaniel he had found a particularly devoted disciple amongst the large and secluded brood. The unwavering devoutness had been used and manipulated by the man he had worshipped.

Arthur Dunwoody contacted Jacob two days after the incident at Corrion's. He was less than happy with the loss of the hard drive but as he said to Jacob, a man's word was still a man's word. He had promised a substantial reward for finding who was responsible for his daughter's death and Jacob had followed through. The fifty grand was his.

Jacob told him to shove the money up his hole. He had nothing to link Arthur to anything criminal that he could give to Cora. It seemed to be the familiar story of the rich man getting away with his misdeeds once again but he thought back to the lonely figure at the paddock fence. Roisin's death was on him and something he would have to live with for the rest of his life. In Jacob's mind that was a harder sentence than any court could ever hand out.

Ivan Gould was forced out as CEO of the company bearing his name shortly after the exposé in the Sentinel. Rumour had it, His Majesty's Revenue and Customs were looking into financial irregularities between Gould Construction and firms with Follower connections and were keen to talk to the man responsible. Gould never gave them a chance. He was found dead in his garage, having fed a hosepipe connected to the exhaust of his still running car through the driver's window.

Catherine Scanlon did not attend her father's funeral. Nor did his wife. A check by police revealed Margaret Gould was alive and well, but had no wish to have contact with anyone outside the Follower compound. The attending police officers had no concern for her safety and noted she did not appear to be under any duress, although the presence of the burly man who Margaret identified as her butler and who lingered throughout their short time in Mrs. Gould's house struck them as odd. But then, what religious type isn't a little bit strange?

Cora left it up to Jacob what he wanted to do with the evidence he had against Neil Rourke and the

Scanlon's. Jacob decided to let it drop. They had been manipulated into their actions, and while he wouldn't forgive, he was content to forget.

*Miss Gumshoe* continued production. A new writer was hired, along with a new sound editor. A new position was created too; Lead Investigator. It seemed the show's creator knew someone who fit the bill. It wasn't full-time work, but it was a nice little earner for Jacob to run down leads as he and Natalie probed into what was on the hard drive, and it gave him a break from the standard private detective fare.

Aided by the piece in The Sentinel, *Miss Gumshoe* saw an upsurge in new listeners. The upcoming season was hotly anticipated with the Roisin Dunwoody mystery the planned centrepiece of Miss Gumshoe's launch onto YouTube.

"I have an idea," Natalie said to Jacob as they sat at a café close to the Wheelman. "For our new season. But it's out there."

"More out there than proposing a murder in a locked room?" Jacob asked, stirring sugar into his coffee.

"I'll let you decide."

Jacob had listened, agreed that it was crazy and told her he wanted no part of it. Within minutes she had worn him down and by the time they were paying for lunch he had given her his tacit approval.

It was a week later when Jacob walked through the front door of Wheelman and towards Studio A. He thanked Ciaran as he held the door open and Natalie smiled as he approached

He saw Arjun and the new crew members watching from behind the studio glass. Jacob waved awkwardly and then sat down. There were two cameras on the table, one facing him and the other, Natalie.

Natalie looked at him. "Ready?"

He nodded and swallowed.

She gave a thumbs up to the booth. The warped notes of a piano began to play. Natalie clutched a mug of coffee as the haunting tune built to its crescendo. When the notes faded, she leaned towards her mic.

"Murder and mystery, crime, and passion, the gruesome and the unexplained. You'll find it all when you sit down with Miss Gumshoe. My guest today, and for the entirety of this ten-part series, is private investigator, Jacob Kincaid."

He leaned forward and mumbled something that sounded vaguely like hello.

"Jacob saved my life over the summer," Natalie said, turning to look at him. "How we got there is a long story. A story of murder, subterfuge, lies, deceit, and betrayal. A story that begins with the loss of a friend and colleague and ends with the same. Listeners, I present to you, Blood on the Broadcast."

# *Glossary*

If you're not native to Irish shores, you've likely come across some unfamiliar words and sayings during your journey with Blood On The Broadcast. I've put together this brief glossary to assist you through the lush pastures of a few Northern Irish colloquialisms and slang:

| | |
|---|---|
| Auld | Old |
| Dandered | Walked |
| Eejit | Idiot |
| Glipe | A different type of idiot |
| Grand | Fine |
| Headcase | Crazy |
| Hoak | Rummage |
| Lifted | Arrested |
| Peeler | Police Officer |
| Scunnered | Fed Up |
| Skedaddle | To Depart Quickly |
| Stocious | Drunk (very) |
| Wee | Small |
| Yarn | Talk |

# Authors Note

Once again, I want to offer my deepest thanks dear reader, not just for taking a chance on a debut novel by an indie author, but for sticking with me and finishing the story. I sincerely hope you enjoyed *Blood On The Broadcast* and are enticed by the promise that Jacob and Natalie will return in future investigations.

If you'd like to keep up to date with what's in store for Jacob and Natalie, or any of my upcoming works, you can sign up to the mailing list on my website at sdwhamilton.com

When I started writing this book, I always had it mind to give Belfast an authentic and honest feel, as if the city were as much a character as anyone else in the story. With that being said, certain liberties were taken. Star of the Sea, Coalburn police station and Corrion's factory are completely fictional, existing only in my head, as do the Followers of Eden and the PSNI's Major Crime Team. Hilden Mill is a real location but as of writing, the derelict linen mill is just that.

Writing a book is a labour of love, one that is repaid when sitting down and typing up a note like this, knowing that you made it to the finish line, albeit with a lot of help from a lot of wonderful people. I want to sign off by thanking them, and you, one final time. I sincerely hope you will join me for the next one.

- Shannon
  Belfast, Northern Ireland, 12th November 2023

Printed in Great Britain
by Amazon

33834006R00180